Therese Beharrie has always been thrilled by romance. Her love of reading established this, and now she gets to write happy-ever-afters for a living, and about all things romance in her blog at www.theresebeharrie.com. She married a man who constantly exceeds her romantic expectations and is an infinite source of inspiration for her romantic heroes. She lives in Cape Town, South Africa, and is still amazed that her dream of being a romance author is a reality.

Rachel Lee was hooked on writing by the age of twelve and practiced her craft ~~to place~~ all over the United S~~tates~~ *Times* best-selling author now re~~~~ the joy of writing full-time.

FALLING FOR
HIS CONVENIENT
QUEEN

THERESE BEHARRIE

A SOLDIER IN
CONARD COUNTY

RACHEL LEE

MILLS & BOON

First Published in Great Britain 2018
by Mills & Boon, an imprint of HarperCollinsPublishers,
1 London Bridge Street, London, SE1 9GF

Falling for His Convenient Queen © 2018 Therese Beharrie
A Soldier in Conard County © 2018 Susan Civil Brown

ISBN: 978-0-263-26471-5

38-0218

MIX
Paper from
responsible sources
FSC™ C007454

FSC
www.fsc.org

This book is produced from independently certified FSC™ paper to ensure responsible forest management.

For more information visit: www.harpercollins.co.uk/green

Printed and bound in Spain
by CPI, Barcelona

FALLING FOR HIS CONVENIENT QUEEN

THERESE BEHARRIE

For my husband, who so graciously told me I could dedicate my books to other people sometimes, too. You're my best friend, babe. This is your life now.

And for my father.
Thank you for all you've done to get me here.

I love you both.

CHAPTER ONE

THIS WASN'T A MISTAKE. This wasn't a mistake.

Princess Nalini of Mattan repeated the words to herself as she watched the castle she'd called home for the last twenty-six years fade into the distance. With a sick feeling in her stomach, she forced herself to look ahead.

The place that would become her new home—the castle of Kirtida—grew clearer as the boat she was on drew nearer. It was a large ominous-looking building that had her heart jumping and her mind replaying those reassuring words again.

'We're almost there,' Zacchaeus's voice sounded in her ear, and she shivered. It was as much because of the brisk sea air as it was the proximity of the man she was engaged to.

King Zacchaeus of Kirtida.

Mattan had been in an alliance with Kirtida and a third kingdom, Aidara, for centuries. It was called the Alliance of the Three Isles, and up until Zacchaeus had overthrown his father a few months ago, the three islands along the coast of South Africa had been united and strong.

Though there'd been a general concern about Zacchaeus's actions, it had only grown alarming when Zacchaeus had refused communication with Mattan and Aidara after the coup. And then he hadn't attended the State Banquet meant to affirm the alliance between the isles, and that alarm had spurred Nalini's brother, King Xavier of Mattan, and the Queen of Aidara, Leyna, into action. They'd announced their engagement and a day later Zacchaeus had made contact.

Which was the reason *she* was currently on her way to a new home.

She angled towards him, and felt guilt hit her almost as hard as the attraction did.

His hair was dark, complementing the caramel of his skin and the slight stubble on his jaw. The lines of his face were serious, intense, and strikingly carved. If she hadn't been intimidated by the clothing he'd chosen to wear—all black, and a clear show of power—she *definitely* would have been intimidated by his looks. Or, worse still, by the *pull* to that power. By the pull to those looks.

But she couldn't ignore the guilt.

She couldn't be attracted to this man. It couldn't matter that his shirtsleeves were rolled up muscular arms, or that his trousers were perfectly moulded to powerful legs. Not when Zacchaeus had demanded that Nalini marry him before he would sign the papers affirming Kirtida's place in the alliance.

And until those papers were signed her kingdom would be in danger.

'I've had a meal prepared for us,' Zacchaeus said as they arrived at Kirtida. He jumped off the boat and offered her a hand. She hesitated but took it, her lungs tightening at the unease that crept up her arm at the contact.

Because it *was* unease. The dull throb that had started when he'd touched her. The flash of heat. It *was* unease, she told herself again, but couldn't bring herself to look at him.

'I assume you're hungry?'

'You wouldn't have to assume if you'd asked,' she replied lightly, shaking off her discomfort. She'd made the choice to come to Kirtida. She'd chosen to save her kingdom by marrying Zacchaeus. The time to choose was over and, because of that, she needed to be civil with him. 'But I'd love to eat something, thank you.'

Zacchaeus nodded and, after instructing that Nalini's things be taken to the room she'd be staying in while they planned their wedding, told her to follow him. Goose-bumps shot out on her skin as she entered the castle, but she straightened her shoulders.

The interior was a beautiful combination of old and new, its stone pillars rich with history and its wooden floors in a modern style.

He stopped in front of a room with a large dining table and, wordlessly, stepped aside for her to pass. As she did, the staff scattered to accommodate her at the table and, before she knew it, she was seated next to Zacchaeus. She waited a moment and then asked, 'Is anyone else join-ing us?'

A shadow crossed over his face. 'No.'

She nodded and then forced herself to ask her next ques-tion. 'Your parents…are they… Do they still live here?'

The shadow darkened, and Nalini braced for him to tell her to mind her own business. But a few seconds later his face settled into a blank expression, and his brown eyes—a combination of honey and cinnamon that contrasted with the dark features of his face—met hers.

'They're still here, yes. I haven't banished them, if that's what you're thinking.'

'I'm not quite sure what to think, to be honest. I'm not familiar with what happens after a coup.'

Something flickered in his eyes and her stomach dipped. She shouldn't have said it, she thought, but if she didn't… Well, she didn't want to spend the rest of her life biting her tongue. Or falling in line just because she'd been told to. Coming to Kirtida had been a way to escape that life. She wasn't simply going to settle for another version of it.

'They live on the royal property,' Zacchaeus said, interrupting her thoughts. 'Not in the castle.'

'Will I see them?'

'I'm not sure,' he said impassively. 'There might not be enough time before the wedding.'

'Planning this wedding is going to take some time.'

'I'm sure it will.' He paused. 'But let's not pretend that you only want that time to plan a wedding.'

'What do you mean?'

He lifted an eyebrow. 'I know that you're also here because you—or, more specifically, your family—want to know whether I really intend on signing the papers to confirm Kirtida's place in the alliance.'

She told herself not to gape. Forced herself not to ask how he knew. Instead, she went for honesty. 'You're right. Except it's *me* who wants to know. *I'm* the one marrying you to ensure that you sign.'

'You have my word,' he said, and she heard the sincerity in his tone. 'Once Xavier, Leyna and I come to an agreement about the Protection of the Alliance of the Three Isles clause, you and I will marry and I'll sign those papers.'

'And if I don't believe you?' she asked softly, compelled by the voice in her head that warned her against trusting so easily. The voice that she'd ignored when she'd been younger.

'That's why you're here, isn't it?' he replied. 'To figure out whether you can?' She nodded mutely. 'Do that, then.'

The food began to arrive as he said the words, and she was relieved that she wouldn't have to come up with a reply she didn't have. But the servers did their work quickly and, before she knew it, she and Zacchaeus were alone again.

'Your family,' he said, reaching for the glass that held his wine. 'They didn't have anything to say about your plan? To organise the wedding from Kirtida and figure out whether you could trust me?'

She almost told him the truth. But that would have entailed admitting the displeasure of her mother and grandmother at her decision. It would have meant telling him about how they thought that she was being reckless—a description they'd used for her for the past nine years, despite her efforts to change that perception. How even her brother had thought that, and how she'd expected more of him.

No, the truth included a myriad of things that she didn't want to think about, let alone tell *him*.

'It made sense,' she said instead. 'Since, as we discussed over the phone, the wedding will be here, planning it on Kirtida was the logical decision.'

'And you always make logical decisions?'

'Does marrying a man I barely know sound logical?'

He smiled a slow, crooked smile that made him look even more dangerous. 'Reasonable, then.'

'It's not reasonable either. Not for a normal person, anyway. But we're not normal and so, in that sense, this is *both* logical and reasonable.' She paused. 'I also know your people have responded positively to the news of our engagement. So, if I'm here and they see their future Queen plan a wedding with their King, it could strengthen their support of this marriage.'

There was an uneasy silence after her words, and she frowned. 'You don't agree with me?'

'So you told your family this and they agreed to let you come here?' he asked, not answering her question.

The uneasiness began to swirl in her chest.

'You're wondering whether my brother sent me,' she replied, ignoring the feeling. 'He didn't. He wasn't entirely happy with this decision.'

'Because he worried that I would find out why you were really here?'

Because he still sees me as an irresponsible teenager.

'Why would he worry that you'd find out I wanted to

know if we could trust you? There's a reason you figured it out so quickly, Zacchaeus. It wasn't meant to be some great secret.'

'Why didn't he want you to come then?'

'Probably because he wouldn't be able to protect me.' She nearly rolled her eyes.

'He thought you needed to be protected? From me?' Unhappiness flashed across his face.

'Do you blame him? You forced him to choose between protecting his baby sister and protecting his kingdom.'

'But he chose his kingdom.'

'No, *I* chose *our* kingdom.' She watched him carefully, and wondered at the emotion she couldn't quite read on his face. 'Xavier didn't want me to do this. Not as a king, but as a brother. He didn't want to have his sister marry a man he wasn't sure he could trust. So when I told him I would come here, plan the wedding and see whether we *could* trust you, he didn't like it, but he understood.' And because it seemed as if he needed to hear it, she repeated, 'This was *my* choice, Zacchaeus.'

'Why? Why would you choose to marry a man you barely know?'

She frowned at the rush of answers that came to mind, none of which was appropriate to tell him. 'You didn't *really* give us a choice. Your actions over the past few months have shown us exactly what you're capable of. So when I said I chose this, I just meant that it wasn't Xavier who did. There is no real choice when it comes to protecting our kingdoms, is there?'

She watched a stony expression settle on his face and felt her frown deepen. He looked so unhappy at everything she'd just said. As though it was news to him. As though *he* wasn't the one who'd started—*forced*—it all.

'You're right, there isn't,' he answered her quietly. 'Which is why we're in this situation in the first place.'

'Because Macoa threatened Kirtida with sanctions?'

He nodded. She waited for an explanation to follow—any explanation, really, as to why an ally of Kirtida and the alliance had suddenly made threats after years of working together peacefully.

'Why?' she asked when he didn't continue. 'I mean, I know that's why you want the alliance's Protection clause updated before we get married. Before you sign to reaffirm the alliance between our kingdoms. You want protection against international allies like Macoa to be included in the agreement too. But *why* do you need that protection? Since—' she hesitated, and then forced herself to say it '—since I'm going to be your wife, I'd like to know.'

'It's complicated,' he said simply. Darkly.

'I'm going to be Queen to your people, Zacchaeus. Don't you think that's enough to share details about complicated matters with me?'

'You're not Queen yet,' he replied. 'And when you are I'll tell you what you need to know.'

'What you *think* I need to know, maybe.' She clenched her jaw and then forced herself to relax. 'The least you could do is tell me why I'm here.'

'You know why you're here, Nalini.' His eyes were sombre. 'Without our marriage, there's no guarantee that Kirtida's place in the alliance won't be undermined by Leyna and Xavier's marriage. By the bond that that will create between Mattan and Aidara.'

'I'd like to know the *real* reason. The one that had you calling us after you found out Kirtida might not be protected as well as Mattan and Aidara were if Leyna and Xavier married.'

Again, silence followed her words. This time she couldn't help the muscles that tightened in her shoulders.

'There's still no guarantee, you know,' she reminded

him. 'There won't be until you sign the papers affirming Kirtida's place in the alliance.'

'And you know my conditions for doing that. After the negotiations to protect our kingdoms. After our marriage.' He tilted his head. 'Are you hoping I'd tell you I'd sign before either are in place?'

'Of course not.' But there *had* been a part of her that had hoped for exactly that.

'So you're not looking for a loophole? You haven't realised that you've made a mistake after this conversation with me?' He leaned forward, making her briefly notice the food they'd otherwise forgotten. 'You don't want to return to the safety of Mattan?'

'I'm safe here,' she said, her eyes darting towards the door where her Mattanian guards—who would continue protecting her as Queen of Kirtida—stood.

'That wasn't what I meant.'

'I know.' She fell silent. 'I think this will work best if you just say what you mean, Zacchaeus, and don't expect me to guess.'

He nodded and met her gaze. 'I'm not going to change my mind, Nalini. You're going to marry me.'

She didn't look away. Though the trembling that had gone through her heart at his words made her want to, she didn't. This was her life now. And this life had been *her* choice.

She thought of the teenage girl who had once been so filled with hope. Who'd thought that taking a chance on a boy would finally bring her the freedom she'd craved. She thought about the girl who'd had that hope dashed so quickly—so heartbreakingly—that she hadn't wanted to make another decision for herself since.

Until now.

Nalini reminded herself of that. She wasn't the girl who hoped for love or sought freedom any more. Who rebelled and made stupid mistakes. But that was still how her family saw her. The mistake she'd made when she was a teen had completely changed their view of her. More importantly, it had changed *her* view of herself.

When she'd told Xavier she would marry Zacchaeus, she'd seen it as a chance to make up for that mistake. To prove to herself and to her family that she was *more*.

Considering their reactions to her decision, she knew she hadn't succeeded in making them believe that yet. But if she stayed—if she went through with this marriage— she would be saving her kingdom. Her family would have no choice *but* to see her as responsible.

And she could finally, *finally* stop trying to convince them that she was.

'In that case, I suppose this time is even more important for us, isn't it?'

CHAPTER TWO

'WHAT DO YOU MEAN?' Zacchaeus asked his fiancée, watching her closely. 'I thought this was already important.'

'That's why I said *even more* important,' she answered brightly. 'Since we're going to be married, we should use this time to build a foundation for this marriage. Preferably one of mutual respect.'

He didn't answer. It was the second time she'd said something about the two of them spending time together. Getting to know one another. But, just as he had the first time, he brushed it off. There would be none of that.

Even if he *was* fascinated by her.

She'd covered it up quickly, but Zacchaeus knew that there was something more to what she'd just said. Something that proved his suspicions that she wasn't just marrying him to protect her kingdom. Which would make complete sense. She *was* sacrificing her entire future for Mattan. Would she really do that without having some other motive?

And yet, since that was exactly what *he* was doing, why couldn't she?

'Do you agree?' she asked, her eyes steady on his.

He got caught in them for a moment, and almost found himself telling her that he did. But he stopped himself. Forced himself to focus. Reminded himself that just because those blue-grey eyes, those full pink lips, those dark curls with its light streaks, painted a picture he couldn't bring himself to stop looking at—had never been able to—didn't mean he should forget why she was there.

He'd already told her too much. Like the fact that his parents—or rather his father—still lived on royal property. He'd panicked when she'd asked about seeing them, though he was sure he'd answered her without letting her know how much her question had alarmed him.

Because when she'd asked he'd pictured her seeing his father and realising the former King of Kirtida was ill. He'd pictured her asking about his mother and finding out that the Queen had left over two months ago. That somehow she'd learn about how the coup had been staged because of his father's ill health and that the threat against his kingdom was his mother's fault.

No, he couldn't afford to be distracted by how beautiful she was or by the bright light she carried within her. So he would remind them both of why she was there—and it wasn't to get to know one another.

'I agree that our marriage is important.' He paused so that his next words would have the impact he needed for her to understand. 'For the sake of our kingdoms.'

'But not for our relationship?'

'We don't have to have a relationship to be married.'

His parents had proved that to him, hadn't they?

But the silence that followed his words told him that she wasn't happy with his answer. And the longer he waited for one from her, the more the tension grew between them. He remembered for the first time then that they were supposed to be eating. But he couldn't even distract himself by doing that since he knew that their food had gone cold.

'What will the next few weeks look like for us then?' she asked eventually, breaking the silence.

'Well, you're here under the pretence of planning our wedding, so you should probably do that.'

'Alone?'

'Yes.'

'And what will you be doing?'

'Negotiating the Protection clause with your brother and future sister-in-law.'

There was a pause. And then she asked, 'So you expect me to spend all my time planning a wedding?'

'I've already given you my word that I'll sign the documents when the time comes, Nalini. The other reason you're here isn't really necessary.'

'And I'm just supposed to believe you?'

'Yes.'

'Why can't you do the same then? Believe that I'll marry you after the papers are signed, I mean.'

'Because there's more on the line for me. This is my entire kingdom.' And what was left of his family, he thought, his throat tightening. 'I can't just take your word on it.'

She stared at him. 'Do you hear yourself? Do you hear the hypocrisy in what you're saying?'

He shrugged as though her words didn't affect him. '*You* agreed to the terms of *this* situation, Nalini. We haven't discussed the one you're proposing now, and I haven't agreed to it.'

Her eyes flashed, making them more grey than blue, and he felt a dangerous—and unwanted—tug of attraction. 'So not only do you expect me to accept that you'll do as you say, but you also won't even give me a chance to figure out whether I can trust that you will?'

'What would change if you realised you couldn't trust me? Would you return to Mattan?'

Something flickered in her eyes. 'It would change things.'

'Would it? So you'd tell Xavier and Leyna that you can't go through with the wedding and put the entire alliance at risk?'

'It's interesting how you've turned this around. How you've made risking the alliance sound like it isn't something *you've* been doing from the moment you refused to see Xavier and Leyna after you became King.' She leaned forward. 'Like you aren't holding us hostage now and *still* doing it.'

She was right. But he couldn't afford to think of it that way. If he did, he'd have to pay heed to the emotions circling inside him like sharks around prey. He couldn't allow them to attack. Not when the threat of them had been propelling him forward, helping him to focus on what Kirtida needed.

He'd been telling the truth when he'd told her he had more on the line than she did. He'd somehow managed to convince Xavier and Leyna that they needed him just as much as he needed them. But that wasn't true. Zacchaeus needed them *more*.

If Macoa acted on the threat of economic sanctions, it would cripple Kirtida's economy. Worse still, his people would no longer have the wheat so many depended on for their livelihood. Without Mattan and Aidara adding weight to any retaliation, Kirtida would be forced to give in to Macoa's demands.

And giving in would kill his father.

It wasn't an option.

'It might not change what I'd do,' she continued now, her voice no longer heated with the passion she'd just spoken with. 'But it would make me feel better about marrying you. So, I'll ask one more time. Will you spend time with me?'

'I'm a king. I don't have time—'

'*Make* time,' she insisted. 'Make time to get to know the woman who's going to be beside you while you rule your kingdom.'

He so badly wanted to say yes. Not only because something about her made him want to give her exactly what she asked for, but also because saying yes would mean that he wouldn't have the much harder task of avoiding her. Of pretending that he didn't have secrets to keep from her. Like his father's illness, his mother's fleeing—and the mess his mother's actions had left for him to clean up.

But he couldn't say yes. Not when spending time with her would put all those secrets at risk. He ignored the reasons he felt that way—ignored the beseeching expression on Nalini's face that had just as much of an effect on his chest as her beauty did. No, he thought. He couldn't spend time with her.

'I'm sorry, Nalini. I can't agree to that.'

'You can't agree to spend time with me?'

Nalini's heart thumped in her chest as she said the words, a sick feeling settling in her stomach. She'd thought that when Zacchaeus had told her he knew she was on Kirtida to get to know him as well as to plan the wedding, it had meant that he'd been willing to play along.

Asking him to spend time with her had felt too much like begging, and now his refusal of her... It felt intensely personal. As if he *could* make time but wouldn't because he didn't *want* to spend it with her.

'And you really think I'm going to spend all my time planning a wedding?'

'I'll have my secretary draw up a list of things you can do on Kirtida. You'll be so busy you won't even notice that you're alone.'

She gave a short bark of laughter. 'Has that ever worked for you?'

His eyes narrowed. 'I'm not sure what you mean.'

'You're alone here, aren't you? Your parents don't live in the castle and whatever relationship you had with them must have been spoilt the moment you became King. I can't imagine you have any friends, and you're holding your allies hostage. So tell me, Zacchaeus, whether you've ever been so *busy* that you haven't noticed you're alone?'

The expression on his face twisted with an emotion she couldn't identify, and then went blank so quickly she doubted her eyes. But when he spoke the coldness in his voice told her she hadn't imagined it.

'If I agree to spend time with you, Nalini… What happens then?' His brows lifted. 'You've already told me you'll marry me, and you're implying that you trust me to act as we agreed by doing that. So what happens if you get to know me and it *doesn't* make you feel better?'

'It…it would—'

'It might not,' he interrupted mildly. 'You already have all the proof you need to show you that I'm not a good man. I've overthrown my father to become King, so you know I'm power-hungry. My parents don't live in the castle any more, so you know I'm cruel.' He pushed away his plate and leaned his forearms on the table, angling himself so that she had no choice but to look into the arresting lines of his face. 'I demanded that you marry me without even asking you how you felt about it, so you know I only care about what I want. Do you really want to get to know a man like that?'

'You *want* me to see that man,' she said, fighting to keep the panic she felt from her voice. 'For some reason, *you* think it's easier.'

'No, Nalini. *You're* the one who thinks this situation is easier than it is.' He sat back now. 'You're hoping that I'm not that man, and that's why you want to get to know me. But I'm sorry, I don't have time to quell your fears. You told me *you* made this choice. And the thing about making choices is that you have to deal with their consequences.'

She suddenly wanted to scream at him, to tell him that she *knew* everything about choices and their consequences.

She could still feel the girls pulling at her jewellery and clothes that night on the beach. She could still hear the boys laughing at her panic. Worst of all, she could still see Josh's face as he laughed with them, the person who'd told her he'd keep her safe gone, leaving only the sick realisation that he'd never existed.

And then there was the way her family had reacted after...

The fact that she was on Kirtida, having this conversation with him, *was* her dealing with the consequences of her actions.

But, of course, she could voice none of that.

'Fine,' she said quietly. 'I won't waste my time trying to find some redeeming quality in you.'

She saw the surprise but it faded quickly. 'Good. Because you won't.' With those words, he walked out of the room.

She sat there for a moment, not entirely sure what to do, and then stood. It took her another few minutes to figure out that she didn't know where her room was, and was about to ask when a young woman came up to her.

'Your Royal Highness, His Majesty King Zacchaeus has asked me to show you to your room.'

Nalini's chest loosened in relief. 'Thank you.'

She followed the woman—Sylvia—as her thoughts swirled around what had just happened. She had been so sure that Zacchaeus had wanted to say yes to her. That he would have said yes to her, but that he'd stopped himself.

Or had that just been in her mind?

She hated the uncertainty, that special kind of doubt that she hadn't felt in nine years. Or perhaps the kind of doubt she'd felt every day for those nine years. But it felt more acute now, though that was probably normal. Nalini hadn't made a decision of her own—not really—in that amount of time. She shouldn't be surprised now, after she had, that she was being reminded of the fears that had stemmed from that fateful night.

She reminded herself that this decision had been nothing like the one nine years ago. Nalini had gone into *this* one with her eyes open. And yes, perhaps she'd hoped that Zacchaeus would be on the same page as her. That she could find some common ground between them so that marrying him wouldn't be so completely terrifying. But now that she knew where she stood, she had to accept it.

She *would* accept it.

She murmured her thanks to Sylvia when they got to the room, and waited to be alone before she looked around. Like the rest of the castle, the room was a mixture of old and new. It was spacious, the walls and beige carpet no doubt old, but modernised by a king-size bed covered in white that matched the chiffon curtains. Large windows stood above a chaise longue and Nalini immediately opened them, breathing in the fresh sea air.

The day had changed, she noted. The sun had been eclipsed by clouds, the sky a grey colour that felt ominous. The water thrashed against the pier that was visible from her window, and when she leaned forward she could see the faint outline of the castle of Mattan.

The longing for home pulsed in her veins but she knew she couldn't go back. Perhaps that was why the longing felt so desperate. If she went back she would be returning to a life she'd never thought she'd have. A life where she did everything that was expected of her just so that she could prove she'd learnt from her mistakes.

But she'd seen how her sister, Alika, and Xavier's lives had turned out because they'd followed all the expectations of them. It had made them incredibly unhappy, and she'd dreaded that future for herself. But she'd been afraid to do anything about it. Because once, a long time ago, she *had* done something about it and it had broken her heart—and her dreams—in one night.

But when Xavier had announced his engagement with Leyna she'd been given a glimpse of a life she could have. And when she'd last spoken with Alika she had realised her two options.

On the one hand, she could choose to disobey her mother and grandmother to protect her kingdom. They might not be happy with her decision, but for the sake of Mattan they would accept it and acknowledge that it was a responsible choice.

At least that was what she hoped.

It was an added benefit that being on Kirtida would give her the freedom of making her own decisions. She could regain that excitement for life she'd lost so long ago. She could have her independence.

On the other hand, she could listen to them and stay. She could keep on living the life she'd been living. She'd marry a man her mother and grandmother had chosen, just like Alika had, and be unhappy. Just like Alika was.

Alika would never say it aloud, but Nalini knew her older sister. And though Nalini no longer expected love or happiness, she'd hoped for contentment at the very least. Alika had always accepted her fate without complaining. And sometimes Nalini wished she could be like that too. But she wasn't. She knew that if she wanted her chance at contentment she couldn't just accept, or do, what was expected. And Zaccaeus's proposal—*if* it could be called that—had come at exactly the right time for her to act on her realisation.

So she'd gone for the first option. Which had brought her here. To an island where she knew no one except the man who had demanded that she marry him. Who was refusing to spend any time with her, leaving her completely alone.

But she couldn't go back home.

A knock on the door roused her from her thoughts and she opened it to see Sylvia again.

'Your Royal Highness, I'm sorry to interrupt. His Majesty King Zacchaeus has requested to see you in an hour.'

Nalini frowned. 'Why?'

'I'm not sure, ma'am. All he said was that he had a proposition for you. Shall I tell him you'll be there?'

A proposition, she mused. From the man who'd turned down her own barely an hour ago.

Interesting.

'Please do.'

CHAPTER THREE

'YOU WANTED TO see me?'

Nalini's voice pulled him from his work and Zacchaeus looked up to see her standing in the doorway of his library. She had changed from earlier and was now wearing black trousers and a white shirt. The shirt was loose, cut into a V at her neck, and gave him only the barest glimpse of bronze skin. It was in no way inappropriate and yet, by the way his body reacted, he could have sworn that she was hardly wearing anything.

'Yes. Did you settle in well?' he asked in a gruff voice.

'Fine, thank you,' she answered, her tone perfectly polite—cool, even—and so very different to the passionate tone she'd used earlier.

That was his fault, and he was helpless to change it. He'd acted exactly like the man he was trying to convince her he was. Power-hungry, cruel, selfish. And though he might not entirely be *that* man, he wasn't who she wanted him to be either. In fact, he was probably closer to the man he'd told her he was than the man she wanted him to be.

Or did he just believe that because of how his parents had treated him?

'Can I get you something to drink?' he asked to distract himself.

'No, thank you.' She paused. 'Why am I here?'

Right to the point then. Not that he could blame her. He

gestured for her to sit and, after hesitating, she took the seat opposite him.

'I was hoping I could talk to you about something my advisors brought to my attention.'

'I'm listening.'

'Well, they seem to think your suggestion that we spend time together... They think it's a good idea.'

Her eyebrows rose. 'Really?'

'Yes.'

'But...'

'Publicly.'

'Why?'

'So that your soon-to-be people will get to know their future Queen, as you said.' He swallowed, and wondered why he suddenly felt nervous. 'They'll get to see us together. The couple who will rule them. And it'll help them become more comfortable with the idea.'

'You had to have your advisors tell you that it would be a good idea?'

'They had a good point.'

'You just didn't want to hear that point from me?'

He kept his mouth shut. Because he couldn't tell her the truth. That he *had* thought she'd made a good point, but was worried that it wouldn't turn out as positive as she'd made it seem. His kingdom had been...*tense* since Zacchaeus had become King and though they had seemed relieved that he was marrying Nalini, preserving the alliance between the isles, he didn't want to tempt fate. Not until he had the chance to speak to his advisors.

'So what would this entail?'

'It would be a business agreement,' he answered. 'We'd make appointments to arrange things for the wedding. Together. Publicly.'

The time she took to respond had him holding his breath.

'I had a conversation with Sylvia when you sent her to ask me here this evening. The woman who showed me to my room?'

'Yes, I know.'

'Just making sure,' she said easily. Her expression gave nothing away. Unless, of course, it did, and he just couldn't read it because he didn't know her. 'She was telling me how…*challenging* it's been for the kingdom to accept their new King.'

He clenched his teeth. So much for not telling her about that. 'You must have misheard.'

'No, I don't think I did.' Her eyes darkened. 'Clearly your advisors are trying to help you regain the trust of your people after the coup. And how better than a wedding? To remind them of the traditions of the royal family. Make them believe in fairy tales. Weddings are the start of something beautiful, hopeful, and seeing the King who ended the reign of their well-loved ruler—his father—at a new beginning might just make them more open to *his* new beginning. As King.'

'You're right. But I needed to check with them to make sure that what you were suggesting would work.'

He saw the surprise, but she only nodded. 'That's fair, I suppose.'

'So you agree?'

'I don't exactly have a choice, do I?' She clasped her hands together on her lap and he found himself saying words he knew he shouldn't be saying.

'You have a choice, Nalini. You'll always have a choice here.'

Emotion filled her eyes before it was replaced by cool indifference. 'Of course I will. I only meant that it wasn't like I could return to Mattan.' She blinked and quickly added, 'Because it would put them in danger.'

'That's not what you meant.'

'What else could I possibly mean?'

'That's what I'm asking.' He studied her, noting that she was avoiding looking at him and knew his gut feeling had been right. 'There's more to why you're here, Nalini, isn't there?'

'You didn't exactly propose this arrangement as a question.'

'Yes, but you've already told me *you* chose to do this. Tell me why.'

'I have,' she replied stubbornly. 'I'm here for Mattan.'

'And yet the more I get to know you, the more I think that isn't the only reason.'

'But since this is a business arrangement, as *you* said, I don't have to tell you anything other than what I want to.'

Her face lit with the challenge, but there was a dullness in her eyes that…that *bothered* him. He couldn't place a finger on why—wasn't sure he wanted to—and instead he asked, 'So, you agree then?'

'Yes.'

'Great. We'll make appointments to plan the wedding. I'll have my secretary arrange a schedule for us and I'll send it to you for approval.'

She nodded. 'Is that all?'

'No, actually there's one more thing.' But he couldn't bring himself to say the words.

'You have something planned already, don't you?' Her mouth relaxed into what he thought was the beginning of a smile. His body tightened.

'*I* don't have anything planned. But there is…a plan. An appointment for us, really.'

'What is it?'

'An…engagement shoot. Tomorrow.' Damn it, he felt foolish even *saying* it.

'An engagement shoot,' she repeated, and laughed. It

was a soft, happy sound that made him think of a music box. 'You must hate the thought of that so much.'

'It has to be done.'

'Of course,' she responded in a grave tone that echoed his, but her eyes sparkled with laughter.

His lips twitched. 'So, you're fine with this?'

'My schedule happens to be open,' she said wryly. 'Why not?'

'Good.' He frowned. 'I didn't expect it to be that easy.'

'I'm here to serve at your pleasure, Your Majesty.'

It took some time for her to realise that she'd said something provocative, and when she did her eyes widened and colour flooded her skin.

'I didn't mean—'

He couldn't help the smile now, even though his attempts at dimming his body's reaction to her unintended suggestion had proved futile. 'I know.'

'It's because you make me nervous.'

'Why?'

'I'm not entirely sure.' She gave him a chagrined smile, but there was emotion on her face that paralysed him and he couldn't look away. 'Maybe it's because today was the first time you and I have really spoken. The events we've seen each other at…' Her voice faded and he quickly figured out why.

He'd kept himself apart from the Mattanian and Aidaraen royal families at those events. Oh, he'd greeted, had done his duty, but the ease that had always been between the two families hadn't included him. Of his own accord, he knew, and realised that Nalini was referring to that one-sidedness he'd embraced. But he'd known what was at risk if he'd become one of them. His family's most well-kept secret.

His mother's affair.

'Or it could just be because you're a little scary, King Zacchaeus.'

Despite what he'd been thinking of, that drew a smile from him. 'You're not the first person to say that.'

'No, I don't imagine I am,' she replied softly, and her mouth curved up in the smallest of smiles.

For the first time, Zacchaeus realised he was in trouble. No, he corrected, taking in what that smile did to the already lovely features of her face—*and* what it did to his heart rate. He'd known he was in trouble the moment he'd come up with the hare-brained plan to marry Nalini.

He'd convinced himself, just as he had Xavier, Leyna and Nalini, that it had been for the sake of the alliance. And, up until that moment, he'd believed that that was the only reason. Except now he remembered how often his eyes had strayed to Nalini at every event. How her smile, polite as it had been, had made it the tiniest bit harder to breathe.

He thought about how he'd felt after he'd left the discussion with Leyna and Xavier the day he'd told them of his plan—the anger at their responses, the fear that it would put Kirtida at risk—and how it had changed when he'd seen Nalini in the castle passage. He'd felt longing. Hope.

And he'd wished with all his might that his hare-brained plan would work just so that he could have that feeling for the rest of his life.

'Does it bother you?' she asked, studying him. For one irrational moment he thought she was asking about his feelings for her. 'That people think you're scary, I mean,' she clarified, and he told himself to get a grip.

'I don't care what people think of me,' he said in a cool tone, hoping it would have the same effect on his emotions. 'What I care about is that they do what they're supposed to do. What I ask them to.'

'I'm afraid you might not entirely succeed in that with me.'

'Yes,' he answered wryly. 'I didn't think I would.'

'Now *you're* not the first person to say that about me.'

He rested his forearms on his thighs and leaned forward. 'Do you mean Princess Nalini of Mattan was a problem child?'

'Depends on who you ask,' she said lightly, but all trace of humour disappeared from her face. 'What should I wear for the shoot?'

The change in subject happened so quickly, so smoothly, that he had to take a moment to adjust. And, though he didn't press, it intrigued him.

'I've arranged for a few dresses to be sent to your room. You can choose whichever one you'd feel most comfortable in.'

She nodded. 'Are we done?'

'For now.'

'Then I'll see you tomorrow.' She stood and smoothed the fabric of her trousers.

'I'll see you tomorrow,' he repeated and got up with her. They stood like that as the seconds passed and then she finally walked to the door, but turned back before going through it.

'One meal.' When he lifted his eyebrows, she continued. 'We'll share one meal a day. You can choose whichever one you'd like.'

He wanted to smile at the brazen request—at the *nerve*—but all he gave her was a grudging, 'Fine.' She walked out then, and Zacchaeus's eyes stayed on the door until he realised he had no reason to keep staring at it.

He walked to his desk and, leaning back in his chair, took in the view through the glass doors leading to his balcony. The night was clear, seemingly unaffected by the misery of the afternoon. And, as he had so many times before, he silently thanked the designer who'd made sure the furniture arrangement would give him an unobstructed view of the sea.

The stretch of water always gave him a sense of purpose

and, right now, he had to accept that that purpose was to protect his kingdom. And protecting his kingdom meant focusing on the negotiations he was having with Leyna and Xavier and getting to his wedding day so that he would finally be able to sign the papers that would ensure it.

He couldn't afford to be enthralled by his fiancée. He couldn't even afford to *like* her—*if* he listened to his father. Jaydon had warned him against trusting Nalini, though Zacchaeus knew Jaydon's warning had come from his own experience with Zacchaeus's mother.

The woman who'd caused the drama he was currently dealing with.

Zacchaeus couldn't even be glad that she wasn't in Kirtida any more. Not when her departure had made his father's already weak heart worsen. Not when her leaving was the reason that Zacchaeus had been forced into being King before he'd been ready. Not when she was the reason his kingdom was being threatened by sanctions—perhaps even by war—because Kirtida couldn't give in to Macoa's demands.

Not if Zacchaeus wanted to keep his father alive.

Perhaps not liking Nalini *was* the best route to go. If only he could figure out how…

CHAPTER FOUR

'THIS IS ABSOLUTELY RIDICULOUS,' Zacchaeus grumbled under his breath, and Nalini grinned. It was impossible not to smile at his grumpiness, especially when she was quite enjoying herself.

'Oh, stop frowning,' she said. 'Or people will think that you don't really want to marry me.'

'Or they'll think I really hate pictures. Especially fluffy ones.'

'Fluffy pictures?' she repeated. 'Are there cute, fluffy animals around that I haven't seen yet?'

'You know what I mean.'

'Zacchaeus,' she said, and took his hand as they walked down to the castle's gardens where they would be taking the so-called fluffy pictures.

As soon as she realised what she'd done, she snatched her hand back—how had that felt so *natural*?—and gestured for the photographer to continue. She waited until the two of them were alone. 'I know you don't like this, but we have to make it believable.'

'I thought I was doing a pretty good job.'

'You were. But the pictures we just took were official ones, in the confines of the castle. Now we're out here—' she lifted her arms '—in the gorgeous garden of the castle, with the gorgeous trees and colours around us. You have to make more of an effort.'

He narrowed his eyes. 'Are you always this…optimistic?'

Her lips twitched at the disgust in his tone. 'The quickest answer to that is yes.'

'Even though they're taking fake photographs to celebrate our fake engagement?'

'It may not be the traditional way people choose to marry, but it isn't fake.' Nalini fought to keep her voice light, though he was dampening her enjoyment. 'In fact, this is probably as real as it's ever going to be for us.'

'*That* doesn't sound optimistic.'

'Sometimes realism slips in before I get to shine it with positivity.' But she sighed, and felt her mood turn to match his. 'Look, the simplest way for us to get through this is to make it look genuine. No one would question our commitment if they look at the pictures and any onlookers will feel as though they've seen something worth looking at.'

She paused when they reached the path, and decided to tell him what she really thought. 'That means you probably shouldn't touch me like I'm some wounded animal you'd like to save but are disgusted by because you found it on the street.'

His lips curved. 'That's quite the vivid image.'

'Yes, well.' She sniffed. 'I've always had a talent with words.'

'So I'm beginning to see.' He stared at her for a beat longer than she was comfortable with, and then nodded. 'Fine. I'll stop complaining.' He pulled at the neck of the uniform he looked so dashing in with the words, 'And I'll pretend to be in love with you. Or, at the bare minimum, in lust.'

'You just have to look as though you're interested in me,' she said quickly, not wanting to dwell on the way her heart skipped at the thought of either of those options. 'So stop frowning, for heaven's sake, and focus on the fact that it *is* a beautiful day. And that your kingdom will probably respond positively to your efforts.'

She hurried after the photographer then, afraid his teasing would turn into something else. She wasn't worried that that something else would be physical. She had no interest in exploring that, no matter how attractive she found him. Or how he felt about her, she thought, remembering the heat in his eyes when he'd seen her in the blush knee-length dress she'd chosen for the engagement photos.

No, she was more worried about how he got her to reveal things about herself that she didn't want anyone to know. Like the fact that she'd never told anyone that she felt like a problem child. Not even Xavier or Alika. Though she was sure that if she told them they wouldn't be surprised.

They all knew about *that day*—as her mother liked to call it—which had really been the only time in Nalini's life that she'd outright disobeyed her parents. But the consequences had been so far-reaching that it had tainted the years since. For her family *and* herself.

It was the reason she was on Kirtida, marrying a man she didn't know for the sake of her kingdom. It was the reason she was trying so damn hard to make things work between them. She wanted to prove to herself—to her family—that it hadn't been a mistake. That her hopes of changing their perspective of her, of her actions, would pan out. That she wasn't just giving them another reason to think that she was reckless.

Not for the first time, Nalini thought of how much easier her life would have been if she'd been more like Alika. Willing to accept and obey. But she also knew that *easy* meant different things to different people. Yes, it meant less conflict and more safety. She knew because she *had* been more like Alika since *that day*. But it had also kept her living in a little box, so confined, so *afraid* that she'd felt as if the real her—the excited, happy her—had been whittled away slowly until she was only that way with her siblings.

And not because she wanted to be. Because she thought *they* needed it.

Even though it hadn't been there before that afternoon, Nalini twisted the engagement ring on her finger as though the nervous habit had accompanied her all her life. She'd been surprised when Zacchaeus had offered it to her, but he'd done it so unceremoniously that she hadn't had the chance to feel emotional about it.

Not that she *would* have felt emotional, she told herself. She didn't expect love or romance any more—wishing for such things was foolish. She'd learnt her lesson with Josh, hadn't she? Besides, she only had to look at her siblings to confirm it. Sure, Xavier's life was a lot happier now that he'd found love with his one-time best friend, but he'd gone through plenty of heartache before he'd got there.

No, Nalini wasn't interested in love or romance any more. What she *was* interested in was making sure her family knew that she'd changed. She also wanted autonomy in her life, and love wasn't going to give her that. An arranged marriage, on the other hand…

She stopped when she found the photographer, and watched as he squinted against the late afternoon sun. The man had insisted that they take the outdoor photos then, though now Nalini wasn't entirely sure he was confident in that decision. He cursed as he worked, taking practice shots of the stream that led down to a large pond.

'Is it just me, or does it feel like we're interrupting something?' Zacchaeus's voice sounded in her ear just as it had the day before, on the boat. Now, though, Nalini didn't have the sea breeze to blame for the shiver that went up her spine.

But you're not interested in acting on it, a voice in her head told her in a mocking tone that she didn't appreciate.

'Artists,' she replied. 'Temperamental creatures.'

'That's a broad statement.'

'And not one I thought you'd call me on,' she said with a smile. 'I don't think all artists are temperamental. I do think this one is, which is why we'd better get into that frame before it's night and we have to do this again tomorrow.'

'You're right,' Zacchaeus said and took her hand, dragging her to the stream. 'Are we okay here, Stefan?'

'Yes, sir, that's perfect,' Stefan answered, but took at least a dozen more shots before getting to them. 'Could you please move closer together?'

'I told you,' Nalini murmured and took a step forward to close the distance between her and Zacchaeus. Her heart immediately thumped louder, harder, in her chest and she stopped before she touched him.

'Why does it feel like you're the one treating *me* like a disgusting wounded animal now?' he asked, and placed a hand at the bottom of her spine. With little effort he pressed her against him, and her heart rocketed—out of her chest and, she was pretty sure, out of her body.

It hadn't been like this before. Their official photos had been close, yes, but there she'd been at his side. There she'd held his hand, which wasn't as bad as she'd thought it would be. But being face to face like this, their bodies aligned...

It made that attraction a lot harder to ignore. Especially since her mind chose to pay attention to the hard muscles of his body right at that moment.

'Your Royal Highness, could you move closer?' Stefan called from behind his camera.

'Yes, Your Royal Highness,' Zacchaeus teased. 'Move closer.'

'I think I'm close enough,' she answered, but pressed her body a fraction closer to his.

'Now smile,' Stefan called again, and now *Nalini* felt as though the entire thing was ridiculous.

But she had to acknowledge that it was only ridiculous because she had to focus on making sure Zacchaeus didn't think he was making her nervous while remembering to smile *and* to relax her body.

'Turn your heads to face one another,' Stefan asked after a few minutes, and Nalini held her breath as she turned back to face Zacchaeus. Without prompting, Zacchaeus slid his arms around her waist. Her breath caught, and Nalini wondered—illogically, she knew—what it would feel like if the action hadn't been forced for the sake of the photos.

If it had been more…intimate.

The thought sent a wave of heat to her face and she ducked her head, hoping that Zacchaeus wouldn't notice it. He banished that hope by moving his mouth to her ear and whispering, 'What's wrong?'

'Nothing.'

'You're lying.'

'I'm not,' she said, her voice sharper than she intended. 'Nalini.'

The tone of his voice had her looking up again.

And the moment she did she realised she'd made a mistake.

She hadn't noticed before that his eyes held specks of light around the irises. It made his face less intimidating, she thought, and wanted to reach up to smooth the creases between his eyebrows to make it even less so.

'That's *perfect*!' Stefan shouted, shocking her hands into immobility. 'Now kiss!'

Her entire body froze as Zacchaeus's eyes instantly changed from amused to something darker. To something more intense. Electricity crackled from them, hitting her with a voltage that woke all her nerves. It startled her, the intense response of her body to his.

And suddenly she became aware of how taut his muscles had become, how hers had responded. If she kissed him, if she just *touched* her lips to his, maybe that tension would ease…

Before Nalini fully knew what had happened, pain stunned the breath from her as she found herself on her butt. The bottom half of her body was completely wet from the water of the stream she now sat in. It took a moment for her brain to realise what had happened, but she didn't fully have the time to contemplate it before she heard a splash of water.

'Nalini, are you okay?' Zacchaeus asked, crouching beside her.

'I'm fine.' She was pretty sure that she was, at least. 'You shouldn't be in here though. You'll spoil your uniform.'

'It'll survive,' he said wryly and offered her a hand. 'Will you accept my help or are you going to ignore it to avoid touching me?'

'Don't be silly,' she answered, though she hesitated before she took his hand. When she was standing, she looked down at her dress, no longer falling in an A-line around her hips but flattened to her sides. 'I've spoilt this dress.' She looked up at him. 'You shouldn't have come in and spoilt your uniform too.'

'The uniform doesn't matter, Nalini. Neither does your dress. But you do.' His eyes searched her face. 'Are you sure you're okay?'

'Of course I am,' she replied, straightening her spine. Trying to maintain what little dignity she had left. 'Besides my pride, I'm perfectly fine.'

'I have to agree on that one.'

'You do? Why?'

'My pride's tingling a bit too. After all, you *did* just fall into a stream to get away from me.'

'That's *not* what happened,' she retorted, and then

frowned. Was that really the reason she'd fallen into the stream? To get away from Zacchaeus? Now that the fogginess of the stun had cleared, she could remember taking a step back, away from him—*no*, she corrected. Away from *kissing* him. She hadn't meant to make it obvious. She'd just wanted space to think, and to get away from the way her body felt when she touched him.

To get away from how her body had reacted to the prospect of *kissing* him.

Of course her attempt at subtlety had landed her on her butt in a stream.

At that moment her eyes took in their spectators, clamouring against the fence surrounding the garden, their faces a mixture of surprise and concern. The faces of those she could see, that was, considering the number of phones she saw capturing everything that was happening.

Stefan had a horrified expression on his face, although she had noted while Zacchaeus had been helping her that he'd still been taking photos. And then there was Zacchaeus's face, wrought with concern and annoyance.

All of it should have embarrassed Nalini. And, she supposed, she would feel that way later, when she'd had time to process it all. But right then the only logical response she could manage started low in her belly, bubbling up her throat until she couldn't control the giggles any more.

'How are you laughing at this?' Zacchaeus asked, his eyes wide.

'Because...' She told herself to stop laughing, to answer him, but the more she tried, the more she kept laughing. 'It's just...so...*ridiculous*!' she managed between fits of laughter. 'I'm sorry, Zacchaeus,' she said, wiping a tear from her eyes. 'I know this must seem like a terribly inappropriate response, but I landed on my butt trying to get away—'

She broke off at the deep sound that came from the man

in front of her. He was *laughing*. Time ticked by, and still he laughed. The shock of seeing Zacchaeus laugh lasted only a few more seconds before she found herself joining him. She wasn't sure how long they laughed together— she didn't even care that there were witnesses to their momentary insanity. And when the laughter faded there was a sparkle in his eyes that had never been there before.

It made those light flecks in his eyes that she'd only just noticed even more visible. Again, she wondered how she'd missed it, and felt unsettled, like a speck of dust that had been blown away.

'It's no wonder you don't laugh very often,' she murmured softly. 'You'd have the entire female population falling at your feet.'

CHAPTER FIVE

ZACCHAEUS TILTED HIS HEAD, acknowledging—but refusing to dwell on—the warmth that went through his body at her words. 'Is that so?'

Though her cheeks pinked, she nodded. 'I think so.'

'Because my laughter is so charming?'

'Because it makes you look…like a man,' she said. 'Not like a king.'

Caught by the picture she was painting, even though he *knew* it would only start trouble, he asked, 'Does no one notice the man when he's a king?'

'No,' she said softly, her eyes following the hand he didn't seem able to control as it swept a piece of her hair from her face. 'People look at the deeds of a king. That's how they notice his heart.'

'Which means people think I have no heart,' he said before he could stop himself.

He paused and gave himself a moment to stuff the emotions he was feeling back into the box he'd created in his mind especially for them. It was harder than it generally was, and he ignored the inner voice telling him it was because of the woman in front of him.

No, he told himself. His feelings were just becoming harder to cope with because there had been so many of them over the last months. Feelings about his mother's affair, about her leaving. About the demands she and her lover in Macoa were making of Kirtida. About his father's illness, and the fact that he'd forced Zacchaeus to pretend to overthrow him…

There had been no time to deal with them—no time to even *think* of them. But a part of him warned that he would have to face them at some stage. And that if that time didn't come soon, they might just bubble over, forcing him to deal with them.

Though it left a sick feeling in his stomach, it helped him remember he couldn't think of himself as a man— however tempting it was, he thought, looking at the woman who drew him in unlike any other. He *was* a king. Which was why he had to ignore the betrayal, the sadness, the hurt swirling around inside him because of his parents.

Which was why he had to refuse the attraction he felt towards the woman in front of him. He *had* to focus on his kingdom. He had no other choice because *he was King*.

And a king shouldn't be standing in a stream with his fiancée, laughing at something that could be misconstrued.

'We should probably get out of here,' he said, keeping his voice devoid of emotion. And keeping his heart devoid of it too, when it wanted to react to the way her face fell.

'You're right,' she said after a few moments and aimed unsettlingly cool eyes at Stefan. 'Can you make do with what you have, Stefan? I'd prefer not to repeat this process.'

It was a jab at him, he thought. And it hit its mark.

'Yes, ma'am.' Stefan rushed forward now and helped Nalini out of the stream. 'I will edit these pictures immediately and have them sent to the castle for approval.'

'Thank you,' Nalini answered as she stepped onto the grass. Water ran down her legs—long and shapely in the heels she wore—and Zacchaeus had to force his eyes away from them to look for someone who could assist them.

He strode to the nearest staff member he saw and requested that towels be brought to them as soon as possible. When he returned to Nalini and Stefan, Nalini was thanking the photographer again in a voice significantly warmer than the one he'd heard her use before he'd left.

'I'm sure the pictures will come out beautifully,' she said before turning to him. Her eyes went cool again, and something chilled inside him as well.

He told himself that it had nothing to do with the fact that she was filled with light and happiness. That her laughing at something that she could have found embarrassing had been so authentic that he thought it was the first time he'd seen a glimpse of the real Nalini.

Which had him wondering why she thought that she needed to hide the real her.

He shook his head, grateful for the distraction of being brought the towels he'd asked for. He took them and handed one to Nalini.

'You should dry off.'

'I'd prefer to have a shower,' she answered, but took the towel and rubbed it over her legs. She slipped out of her heels and dried her feet and, though he was tempted to keep watching her—what *was* it about her legs that was so captivating?—it reminded him that his feet were wet too.

Like her, he wanted a shower. *And* dry clothes and shoes. Since he'd angled his body so that she would have some privacy from the onlookers, he couldn't dry himself off as she was doing. Yet he was hesitant to leave.

That burst of light he'd seen from her had been so refreshing—and so completely different from the perpetual darkness he'd felt shroud him since the night of the State Banquet. Since before then, he knew, thinking about his mother.

He didn't want to return to that darkness—not yet, anyway. The only way he could see that not happening was if he continued to spend time with her. Because even though he'd managed to dim the light somewhat, he didn't think she'd let it be dimmed for long.

'We'll have dinner in half an hour,' he told her.

'Fine.'

'You're okay with that?'

'Of course I am. I was the one who asked that we share a meal. Dinner is the only meal left today.' She handed the towel back to the woman who'd brought it and picked up her shoes, dangling them from two fingers. 'I hope you feel better once you get out of those clothes.'

'I feel fine.'

She smiled now, an almost feline look that sent a stab of desire through him. 'I was trying to be nice. I meant that I hope your attitude changes. Away from the King and into the man. I like him.'

She didn't wait for a reply and left him speechless. But he was beginning to realise that that was just the effect she had on him. He released a breath, and then forced his feet to make their way back to his room. Stefan immediately fell into step beside him, offering an apology for the way things had turned out, which Zacchaeus waved away.

But he supposed he couldn't blame the people who worked for him for walking on eggshells. Before his father had stepped down, things hadn't been going particularly well in the castle.

Jaydon had lived with his heart disease for years, but it had taken its toll on him. Especially in recent years. He had been determined to keep his illness to himself, only telling Zacchaeus because he'd wanted 'the future King of Kirtida to be prepared'. And when the whispers about him being ill had started, Jaydon had tightened the reins of his rule with those around him, hoping to dispel any rumours of weakness.

But his illness, combined with the weight of the secret he'd been keeping and the fact that things had been getting worse with Zacchaeus's mother, had made Jaydon miserable. His misery had made him unbearable. And since no one—including Zacchaeus's mother—knew why, his mood seemed uncalled for, and so unlike the King many of the staff loved and respected.

It had got worse when Zacchaeus's mother had left. Michelle had claimed that Jaydon's moods weren't what she'd signed on for but, considering the rocky state of their marriage for the last thirty years, Zacchaeus had known she'd merely been looking for an excuse to leave.

That, and the fact that she'd left in the middle of the night with only a brief note explaining her absence.

Now that his kingdom was being threatened, Zacchaeus knew exactly why she'd left. Michelle had known that she would never have got away if they'd got wind of her plans. But after she'd left, and they'd heard she'd arrived in Macoa, his father had taken a turn for the worse.

Zacchaeus had barely had the chance to process it all before his father had asked him to stage the coup. Jaydon hadn't wanted anyone—especially his estranged wife and her lover—to know he was stepping down because he was ill. Two months later, Zacchaeus was still too consumed— now with trying to protect Kirtida—to think about it and the complications his father had created by asking him to do something he really hadn't wanted to.

He shook off the thoughts and nearly rolled his eyes when his staff hurriedly cleared the way for him when he entered the castle. They were so afraid of him, he thought with a frown. Not only because of the nervousness his father had instilled in them, but because they saw Zacchaeus as the man who'd overthrown his own father because of his desire for power. It didn't seem to matter that many of them had witnessed him growing up and knew that he hadn't always been the man they saw him as now.

So he brushed it all off and pretended that none of it

bothered him. But he knew it did, and it was only having Nalini there to remind him of more than just the darkness that gave him some reprieve.

He thought of how he'd felt when he'd seen her in that beautiful pale pink dress. When he'd seen the way her skin had looked almost gold against it. When he'd noticed her shapely legs, and had longed to touch the curls that framed her face.

He hadn't anticipated the way his heart would race when he was close to her. Or the way his body would tighten. He hadn't expected honesty from her, even when it was clear that it embarrassed her. It was almost as though she couldn't help herself.

And it was all so refreshing that Zacchaeus constantly wanted to be around her—despite his warnings to himself.

But since he knew he couldn't afford to dwell on it all, he got ready quickly, forcing himself to ignore how he felt when he saw Nalini already waiting for him when he was done. She stood when he entered the dining hall, and the air in his lungs thickened when he saw that she'd changed into another dress.

This one was floral, flared slightly at the hips, just like the dress she'd worn for the photo shoot. It suited her body, he thought. And then told himself that thinking about her body would only get him into trouble when it became even harder to breathe.

'Am I late?'

'I only got here a few minutes ago, so you're okay.' After he'd helped her into her seat, he took his own. 'Feeling better now?' she asked once he had.

He couldn't help the smile that crept onto his lips. 'I think so.'

'Wonderful,' she said easily, giving him a slight nod. 'It might have been awkward otherwise.'

He laughed softly. 'Do you always say what you're thinking?'

'No,' she replied indignantly. 'I'm a princess. I *have* to think before I speak.'

'So everything you say to me is well thought-out?'

'No,' she said again. 'For some reason it doesn't seem to work with you.' There was a pause, and then she laughed a little breathlessly. 'See?'

He stared at her, and then slowly shook his head. 'I can't quite figure you out, Nalini.'

'It doesn't seem like you *have* to figure me out.' She lifted her shoulders. 'I'm more honest with you than I'd like to be, after all.'

'Oh, I don't think *that's* true.'

'But I'm agreeing with what you just said.'

'I know, and I believe that you can't help but be honest with me. *Sometimes*,' he said, and told himself to tread carefully. 'You shut me out yesterday when I asked if you were a problem child.'

He could almost feel her recoil, just as she had the day before. 'No, I answered you.'

'But you pulled away. Just like you're doing now.'

She tilted her head. 'Isn't this strange?'

The tone of her voice put his back up. 'What?'

'This.' She waved between them. 'The fact that you think *I'm* pulling away from you when you didn't even want to give me a chance to get to know *you* at first.'

'I told you why.'

'No, you told me why you didn't want to plan our wedding together. But even now that we are planning it together, or will be, you've called it a *business arrangement*. Which, by definition, means you don't want to talk about anything personal.'

'That's not...' He trailed off, struggling to find the words to explain himself. 'It's not the same thing.'

'Of course you won't see it that way.' She fell silent when the starters arrived and the wine was poured, and only continued when they were alone again. 'Would you like to prove me wrong? Tell me something about yourself.'

'I already have, Nalini,' he said, annoyance masking the faint panic.

'Like what?' She picked up her knife and fork, and then lifted her brows when he didn't answer. 'See? You haven't shared anything personal with me.'

'Oh, I have,' he answered, picking up his utensils too. 'I remember because it was something I shouldn't have told you.' He froze as soon as he realised what he'd said, wondering how he'd fallen into the trap of saying too much. Again.

Silence followed his words, and Zacchaeus felt the tension slowly make its way up his back and across his shoulders. And then she asked, 'What's your favourite colour?'

'What?'

'Your favourite colour,' she repeated. 'I'm giving you an easy out here. Take it.'

It took a few seconds for him to process and then he said, 'Green.'

'Favourite book?'

'I don't have one.' He shrugged. 'I prefer movies.'

'I'm not sure I can give you an out on that one.' She shook her head. 'In fact, I don't think I've ever been more disappointed in you.'

He laughed, and wondered how she'd managed to defuse the tension. 'I'm sure that's not true.'

'It is if we start counting from the start of this dinner. Which I am.'

'Okay.' The smile he gave her came more naturally now. 'What's your favourite colour?'

'Pink.' She widened her eyes. 'A massive surprise, I know. A princess liking pink.'

'It suits you.'

The surprise on her face was genuine now. 'How would you know?'

'Your dress today. You looked…nice in it.' Which was the understatement of the year, he thought.

'That was blush.'

'It was pink.'

'Ah, yes, the male colour spectrum,' she answered and sipped her wine. 'Where all colours that kind of look the same *are* the same.'

'Exactly.' He grinned. 'What was your favourite thing to do on Mattan?'

Her smile wavered and he cursed himself for bringing up the home he was responsible for taking her away from. He tried to think of another question—one that would bring back the ease that had somehow settled between them—but she answered him before he could.

'Painting.' Her voice was soft. 'I love putting colour on a canvas. Making something that started out as nothing into something.'

'You paint?'

'Not very well, but yes, I do.'

'I don't believe you.'

'Well, you'll have to,' she answered. 'You have no proof that I paint well.'

'I will,' he vowed. 'Soon too.'

'Really? How do you intend to find out? It's not like you can call anyone on Mattan to ask.' Her eyes widened immediately. 'Oh, I'm so sorry, Zacchaeus.'

CHAPTER SIX

'FOR WHAT?' ZACCHAEUS answered easily. 'Reminding me of the reality of this relationship?'

He meant to make light of her slip-up, Nalini thought, but he hadn't *quite* got it right. Which was her own fault, she supposed, for bringing it up. But then she reminded herself that *she* hadn't really been the one to bring it up. *He'd* mentioned Mattan, and her heart had sagged with heaviness at the thought of her home.

Of the home she'd *chosen* to leave and couldn't go back to.

'I've upset you,' Nalini said softly. 'I didn't mean to.'

'You haven't upset me, Nalini.'

She studied his face and then nodded. 'So we're back to this then.'

'I'm not sure what you're talking about.'

'No?' she asked. 'You haven't just stepped back into being King Zacchaeus, and away from getting to know me?'

'You need to stop this,' he snapped, and set down his knife and fork. 'There is no distinction between me as a man and me as a king. They're one and the same. The only reason you've claimed they aren't is because you're hoping—again—for someone who doesn't exist.'

He'd surprised her a number of times since she'd arrived at Kirtida. With his compassion, his perceptiveness. And maybe that had lured her into the fantasy that they could at least be friends. But there would be no friendship with Zacchaeus, she told herself. She needed to remember that when the compassion came out, the perceptiveness. Because she couldn't keep feeling the disappointment tinged ever so slightly with hurt when they disappeared.

'You're right,' she answered. 'It won't happen again.'

Emotion flitted across his eyes, but it was gone too quickly for her to identify what it meant. 'Good. You're finally getting the message.'

She wanted to reply, to put him in his place, but she reined it in. It was pointless, she thought, to try and make him see sense. To try and make him realise that he didn't have to be the jerk she was sitting next to. That he *could* be the man she'd thought he was.

But trying to get him to share anything with her was exhausting, and she'd only been doing it for two days. And yes, maybe that exhaustion seemed so much worse mingled with how homesick she'd suddenly become, but she didn't have to try if he didn't.

And so she wouldn't.

It meant that the rest of their meal was eaten in complete silence. It wasn't something she was used to, the silence, and it made her throat itch to say something—*anything*—to breach it. But that would have meant that she would be trying again, and she refused to.

So each time she wanted to open her mouth to say something, she'd reach for her wine instead. Before she knew it, her glass had been refilled twice and she was feeling the slightest bit tipsy. She was glad when the dessert came and, though the chocolate mousse looked delicious, she barely tasted it in her rush to leave.

'Please excuse me,' she said as soon as her plate was empty, and ignored the frown Zacchaeus sent her.

'No post-supper coffee?'

'So that we could spend another thirty minutes in si-lence?' she scoffed. 'I don't think that's going to help me stay sober.'

She frowned. Why had she just said that?

'You're trying to stay sober?' he asked, and she thought she saw his lips spasm.

'If you must know, yes, I am.' She lifted her chin. 'I don't like tense situations, and it seems like tonight has made me drink a bit too much.'

'Are you…drunk, Princess?'

'Of course not! But,' she allowed, 'I might be closer to it than to being sober.'

'I see,' he answered measuredly. 'Would you like me to escort you to your room?'

'Definitely not.' She took a step back, barely hearing the scrape of the chair as she did. 'You're the reason I feel this way. You're not going to swoop in and play the dash-ing gentleman. It'll only make me imagine you're someone you're not even more. And you don't want that.'

She looked at him and he gave her a nod, though some-thing in his eyes made her feel that maybe he did.

'I will escort myself to my room then. Goodnight.'

Nalini turned with the words and found that her chair was still behind her, so she couldn't stalk off as she'd in-tended to. And now she had to decide which direction to go. If she chose the left, where the rest of the dining chairs were, she wasn't entirely sure she would be able to navigate her way past them without making herself look foolish.

If she chose the right, she would have to face Zacchaeus and…well, she was afraid that she would be drawn in by that deliciously manly smell of his. She'd got a good whiff of it when they'd been posing for the photos, and she knew that it was the kind of smell that made women swoon. And since she was a woman she had swooned too, and she didn't think she'd be able to resist it again.

Especially now, since she wasn't…feeling herself.

'Do you need help?' Zacchaeus said smoothly, only the slightest lilt of amusement in his voice.

'No, I'm fine,' she answered primly, but still she stood, unable to make the decision.

'Are you sure?'

'Would you mind getting out of the way?'

'Of course,' he answered and moved so that he was no longer to her right, but rather in front of her. It didn't help her dilemma, but she knew she couldn't delay for any longer so she walked around her chair and held her breath as she walked past him.

But she misjudged and took a breath before she was far enough away from him.

The scent hit her, and desire crawled deep in her belly. She kept her back to him, ignoring the steps she heard following her. She didn't want to turn around and test the control she had over her desire for him. Not when her mind was offering her a picture of how she'd look in his arms, her mouth on his, tasting the secrets those perfect lips had to offer.

'Are you okay?'

'I'm fine,' she answered, and found that she was. That knock of lust had somehow cleared her mind and the only thing she wanted now was to get away from him. To breathe in air that didn't tempt her but gave her comfort. 'Goodnight, Zacchaeus,' she told him again, still without looking, and walked towards the door.

In a few quick steps she made it out to the hallway and traced her way back to the garden where their pictures had been taken that afternoon. She saw a movement in the shadows and turned only to confirm that her body-guard had joined her.

She smiled at him and then took a deep breath, hoping that somehow the air would reach all the places in her body that felt suffocated. She followed the path back to the stream she'd fallen into, and took a seat on the embankment.

She almost missed the slight tipsiness she'd felt earlier. Because now, with the fresh air clearing her brain, she felt like a failure. As if she'd made a decision and she'd failed at it yet again.

It reminded her of how Xavier had reacted when she'd decided to come to Kirtida. How he'd warned her not to be careless but to take it seriously. It reminded her of how disapproving her mother had been when she'd told them she would be marrying Zacchaeus. How it had been nothing in comparison to the way her grandmother had reacted.

Paulina had flat-out refused that Nalini agree to Zacchaeus's demands. *'His eyes are dark, Nalini,'* Paulina had said. *'You won't be able to change that darkness until you find out what caused it, and he won't let you.'*

Suddenly she realised how much of what she'd been doing on Kirtida had been devoted to proving her family—her grandmother—wrong. Paulina's last words to her had somehow become a symbol of her disapproval, a symbol of Nalini's entire family's disapproval of her decision.

A symbol that haunted her.

Much like the 'I told you so' they had given her when she'd returned from the beach that night so long ago, shaking with fear and disappointment, her teenage heart broken and her dreams shattered.

Nalini saw now that if she'd been able to convince Zacchaeus to tell her about that darkness it would have been a victory for her. It would have been proof that she *had* been responsible in coming to Kirtida. And proof would have given her hope. Hope that saving her kingdom would redefine her. Perhaps it would have even been an opportunity for *her* to tell her family 'I told you so'.

But she'd been wrong. And now she had to face the reality of it.

She needed to start accepting that her family would always see her as irresponsible. That they would always see her as the daughter who'd put herself and the Crown at risk. Once she'd accepted that she could face that perhaps she just wasn't cut out for the life she'd wanted. Perhaps freedom and contentment were for people other than herself. Maybe the only life she had to look forward to was the one she'd seen Alika live. The one Xavier had lived before he'd reconciled with Leyna. A life of obedience and disappointment. Of unhappiness.

She hadn't wanted to be unhappy, but she was beginning to realise that that hope was unrealistic. Unhappiness seemed to be the fate of a royal life. Unless there'd been luck involved—as it had been with Xavier and Leyna— she couldn't think of one other royal who'd found contentment in their relationship.

Her parents and grandparents had fallen into routine, sure, but what they'd had hadn't been anything close to what she'd wanted. So she'd made the crazy decision to marry Zacchaeus, but it hadn't brought her any closer to the life she wanted.

Yes, maybe it *was* time to accept that what she wanted just wasn't going to happen.

'Can I join you?'

Her heart thumped when she recognised Zacchaeus's voice. 'Sure.'

She found herself holding her breath again when he sat down beside her. And then she thought that she could hardly hold her breath the entire time Zacchaeus was there, and exhaled. But when she inhaled she inevitably got that masculine smell of his again. She steeled herself against it and found it easier to do now with a clear head.

At least that was what she told herself.

'It's a lovely evening,' he said, staring out over the stream.

'It is,' she replied, forcing herself not to look at him. But when the silence extended she asked, 'Did you just come out to tell me that?'

'No,' he said, and she waited. 'I wanted to apologise.'

Surprise had her eyebrows raising. 'Why?'

'Because I was a complete ass to you at supper and you didn't deserve it.'

She nodded. 'Thank you.' She bit her lip, contemplating whether she should say what was on her mind. Before she could stop herself, she did. 'Maybe you're right, Zacchaeus.'

'About what?'

'My expectations when I decided to come here.' She took a deep breath. Exhaled shakily. 'I think I made a mistake.'

'No, you didn't.' He angled towards her now, and she frowned. 'You made exactly the decision I would have made. In fact you've made the decision all of us would have made.'

'And that somehow makes it right?'

'For our kingdoms, yes.'

'And that's the most important thing, isn't it?'

'That's what we were taught.'

He shrugged, and something about the movement made her think he didn't like what they had been taught. She turned towards him and took his hand, ignoring the heat that went through her body.

'Tell me.' He turned his head and she felt something inside her quiver at what she saw there. 'Tell me what you can't tell anyone else. I promise it'll stay between us.'

She made the promise despite the voice in her head that told her she shouldn't. If what he told her would help Mattan and Aidara, she should tell Xavier and Leyna about it. But she knew she wouldn't.

Her free hand lifted to cup his face and she found herself moving closer. 'You aren't alone any more, Zacchaeus,' she whispered. 'Don't choose to be.'

Before she could stop herself, she leaned forward and kissed him.

Heat immediately seared her lips, and then softened to a sizzle that sent frissons of warmth through her body. Though he hadn't moved at first—and her heart had raced at the prospect of making such a terrible mistake—he leaned into the kiss now, nudging her lips open with his tongue so that they could taste each other.

She moaned as her tongue joined his and found herself lost in sensations she'd never felt. She'd kissed men before. Her first had been an innocent curiosity that hadn't made her feel as if she'd missed anything. Her next had been with Josh, the boy she'd thought she would one day marry and who'd broken her heart. But even with him the kiss had never felt so…so *right*.

In fact, she felt cheated. Had she known kissing could feel so good she might have done it more. But then she thought that maybe it wasn't the act but the person she was doing it *with*.

And then she stopped thinking so that she could enjoy the way Zacchaeus kissed her as though she were the only woman alive.

She savoured the way her body had gone all tight and achy. The way it felt pleasure lined with a pain that didn't hurt but only served to tell her it wanted *more*.

And then there was the fact that she could finally enjoy the smell of him. The thought had her moving the hand that still held his to behind his neck, pulling him in closer so that she could go deeper.

But she felt a hand rest on the one she'd just moved, gently removing its grip as Zacchaeus pulled back.

'Nalini,' he said, his voice gruff. 'We shouldn't be doing this.'

She blinked. 'Why not?'

'Because…because…' She waited as he tried to find an excuse. And then she realised *why* he was trying to find an excuse and felt her body go cold.

'It's fine, Zacchaeus—you don't have to make something up. I get it.' She shifted away from him and then stood and brushed the skirt of her dress.

'You get what?' he asked, standing up with her.

She fought against the sudden burn of tears in her eyes. Was he going to make her say it? The prospect of the humiliation had her standing a bit taller, and helped her ignore the tears.

'That you *want* to be alone,' she said, refusing to say the truth. That he hadn't wanted her as much as she'd wanted him. That perhaps he hadn't wanted her at all. And that she'd made yet another mistake when it had come to trusting a man.

'It's not that,' he replied, taking a step towards her. But he stopped when she shook her head.

'So you're saying that you're actually going to talk to me? That you're finally going to be honest?'

'I…' It was all he said and she shut her eyes briefly before speaking again.

'You're going to do this alone, aren't you?'

'I don't have a choice.'

'There's always a choice,' she replied, and realised she was speaking to herself just as much as she was to him. 'It's lonely ruling by yourself, Zacchaeus. Not only because you'll be doing it alone, but because it's hard work. It's *important* work. Having someone at your side, supporting you, helping you… It makes things a hell of a lot easier.'

'And what if you choose the wrong person?' he asked, his voice low and uncertain, a tone she'd never heard from him. 'That's worse, isn't it? Having someone at your side who's supposed to support and help you, but doesn't.'

'Are you worried that I would be like that?'

'I don't know you, Nalini. You could be.'

It stung but she merely told him, 'I'm not hiding who I am.'

'You're hiding something though. The real reason you're here.'

She opened her mouth to reply, but emotion had her clamping it closed again. Eventually, she said, 'I guess we're both not telling each other the whole truth then.'

But he wouldn't let it go. 'Is it because of your family?'

'Yes,' she replied, hoping that telling him that would be enough for them to move on.

'What about them?'

'They didn't want me here, and I chose to come. What does that say about what I left behind?' Because he looked as though he was going to push for more, she sighed. 'It's not rocket science. They don't think highly of you because of all that's happened. They didn't want me to marry you. So in coming here I've disobeyed them.' *Again.* 'Does that make more sense?'

He nodded. 'And you? What do you think about me?'

'Honestly?' she asked, and took the slight movement of his head as a yes. 'I don't know. There are parts of you that I really like, and then there are others…' She trailed off, but saw that he understood.

'It's all a bit of a mess, isn't it?' He gave her a soft smile that had her heart beating against her chest like an insistent houseguest at the front door.

'Yes,' she agreed, and his smile got wider. For a moment. And then it slipped from his face, making her wish she could say something to bring it back.

'You're not wrong, you know. Things are a mess here. They have been for some time. And I'm a mess too, because of it.' He paused. 'You don't have to clean up this mess, Nalini.'

'I don't intend to,' she answered, though her heart told her she very much wanted to.

'So we'll keep this strictly—'

'Professional? In line with our business arrangement?' She didn't wait for his answer. 'That's fine.'

There was an awkward silence before she forced her legs to move. He fell into step beside her as they made their way back to the castle.

'Your mother and grandmother,' he said into the quiet. 'They didn't come to see you off because you'd disobeyed them?'

Nalini thought back to when Zacchaeus had arrived at Mattan to take her to Kirtida. It had only been the day before, but the fogginess of the memory made it seem like months.

'Yes. Though, to be fair, they didn't really want to see you either.'

He laughed softly. 'That *is* fair.'

'Based on what they think they know about you, maybe so.' She regretted saying it before the last word left her mouth.

'But now you think differently?'

'I think that I can't go home,' she replied. 'But I can't keep doing this either.' She stopped walking and turned to face him. 'I want to make this work for both our kingdoms' sake—for *our* sake—but not if you're going to keep treating me the way you have been.'

'You're right.'

She hid her surprise. 'No more hot and cold, Zacchaeus.'

'I agree.'

'We respect each other.'

'Yes.' He paused. 'I'm sorry if I gave you the impression that I don't respect you. I do.'

'Thank you.'

They began to walk again.

'I mean it,' he said. 'And I know that—' he nodded his head to where they'd just kissed, and then rubbed the back of his neck '—complicated things.'

'It didn't,' she said brightly. 'We'll pretend it never happened.'

He looked unconvinced but nodded. 'So we'll keep doing our wedding appointments.'

'Yes.'

'And I'll behave at the next meal. We'll have a civil conversation, and you won't have to get drunk to survive it.'

'I wasn't—' She broke off when she saw the grin and felt her lips curve even as the butterflies fluttered from her chest down to her belly. 'A princess never gets drunk, Zacchaeus.'

'Of course not,' he said sombrely and stopped in front of the castle doors. 'And it's Zac.'

'What?'

'Call me Zac,' he repeated. 'I don't really go by Zacchaeus outside of my official duties.'

Inexplicably touched, she nodded. 'Zac it is.'

He smiled. 'Thanks. Rest well tonight.'

'You too,' she replied and returned to her room slightly dazed.

And was completely flabbergasted when she was greeted by an easel, paint and a stack of empty canvases against the wall.

CHAPTER SEVEN

'I'M SORRY, I didn't think to ask whether you'd be here.'

Zacchaeus had planned it that way. He would *just happen* to be having his breakfast in the place he knew Nalini would be having hers. So he'd had time to prepare his response—something along the lines of *Oh, it's fine* and *let's share breakfast anyway*. But the moment his gaze rested on her, there was no hope of reciting anything he'd prepared.

Not when he was desperately trying to keep his expression blank. Because if Nalini knew what he was thinking as he took in the striped shirt she'd paired with a green pencil skirt, she would run far, far away from him.

He swallowed, trying to soothe the sudden dryness in his throat. But the moment he did, he found his eyes travelling down the length of her—pausing at her hips to appreciate how her skirt highlighted the curves of them, and then on her legs which, paired with the heels she wore, looked pretty fantastic too—and his mouth would dry all over again.

When he dragged his eyes away from her body and settled them on her face he realised that it too had that effect on him. Her hair was tied in a bun at the top of her head with a few curls spiralling next to each temple, leaving her face perfectly clear of obstruction. Combined with her clothes, she looked like every sexy librarian fantasy he'd never known he'd had.

And would now never forget, he thought, and forced his thoughts out of the gutter.

'You don't have to apologise,' he said stiffly. 'I decided to come out here this morning.'

'In the name of civility, or because of the meal we're supposed to be sharing today?'

'Civility.'

Her eyes widened and she brought a hand to her chest. 'Are you saying you *want* to have more than one meal with me?'

The scandalised tone had his lips curving up. 'This *is* for civility, so perhaps in future we'll share more than one meal. But today…' He paused and wondered if he should tell her the truth. And then decided she would find out anyway. 'Today I'll be heading to Mattan to continue the negotiations with your brother and Leyna.'

'Oh,' she replied, and the glimmer in her eyes faded.

'Do you want to come with me?' he offered, unsure of why he'd said it except for the fact that he really wanted to bring that light back. But she shook her head and the curls next to her face bounced with the movement.

'No, thank you.'

'Are you sure? You could see your—'

'No,' she interrupted sharply, the meekness in the tone she'd used to deny him the first time gone. There was a beat of silence and then she sighed. 'I just think that going home would… I think it would make things worse.'

'Things with your mother and grandmother or things here?'

'Likely both.' She gave him a small smile. 'It would probably be best for me to stay here and let things settle at home—on Mattan, I mean,' she said very deliberately. 'I'll use the time to explore the castle. To get to know my new home. And you being away should give me the chance to get to know the staff too, without them worrying too much about you.'

She said the last part cheekily but he didn't mind. It was fascinating watching her talk herself back into the happy mood she'd greeted him with. Again, he found himself admiring that optimism, though a part of him wondered how he would ever be able to match that in their marriage.

And then he had to remind himself that he wouldn't have to, since their marriage would be one of convenience only.

'It's so pretty out here,' Nalini said, interrupting his thoughts.

He followed her gaze and settled back in his chair to enjoy the view. He'd had the table set outside under a gazebo in the garden when she'd told him she would be coming to Kirtida. It had been an attempt to make her feel more comfortable, since he knew the way the sun spread across the castle garden in the morning could quieten all kinds of anxieties.

Now that he was sitting here though, watching the way the yellow and orange light claimed the trees and flowers, he wondered why he hadn't done it sooner. For himself. Perhaps because he hadn't been thinking about ways to quiet anxieties before Nalini.

'The pictures will look good,' she said, and he forced himself not to frown at his unsettling thoughts. 'Unless Stefan uses the ones he took slyly when I fell into the stream.'

'He did that?'

'Unfortunately.' She sighed, but gave him a wink. 'Do you think a drenched Princess will still garner enough respect to become Queen?'

'If that Princess is you,' he heard himself say, but quickly continued before either of them could dwell on it. 'He's given us all the pictures though.' Zacchaeus pushed the unopened envelope that held the prints towards her. 'And he's put the ones he suggested we release at the front.'

She picked up the envelope but didn't open it. 'Was he really able to do it so quickly?'

'Apparently.' She nodded, but still her hands didn't move. 'Aren't you going to open it?'

Her eyes met his. 'Why didn't you?'

He struggled to find an answer, and frowned. He'd told himself he'd wanted her to see them first. He'd wanted her opinion before he formed his own. So why couldn't he just tell her that?

'I think that's the reason I can't open it either,' she said, studying him. 'Ridiculous, isn't it?'

'That we don't know the reason we can't open an envelope?'

'That we both know the reason but neither of us want to say it aloud,' she corrected him quietly. And then, as though in defiance, she tore open the flap of the envelope and drew the pictures out, holding them gingerly in her hands as she set the envelope aside.

He kept his gaze on her face as she looked through them. He wasn't entirely sure why, when she'd made a neat stack of the ones she was done with on his side of the table. He could have easily picked them up, looked through them himself. But he couldn't bring himself to when her expression was so much more riveting to look at.

She was trying to keep it blank. And it worked, for the most part. Except he could clearly see she was at battle with herself, trying to hide her emotions from him just as she was feeling them. Then there were her eyes. He thought he'd be able to tell what those emotions were if he could read them. They were screaming, but somehow it felt as if they were doing so in another language.

His heart thudded when he realised how badly he wanted to be fluent in that language.

And then suddenly her face changed into an expression that had him holding his breath. She was staring at one of the pictures—had lifted it closer and he could see the way her hand shook. Her eyes met his and then quickly looked away, and instead of setting the picture down on the pile next to him she set it on the other side of her.

'You're not happy with them?' he asked, desperately wanting to know what she thought. And what had put that look on her face.

'No, no,' she said. 'They're beautiful. Official, a little romantic. Hopeful. I agree with the ones he's suggested we use.'

'But one of them has upset you.'

She shook her head but didn't look at him. 'It was just the picture of us in the stream. It's…it's a little embarrassing.'

'Can I see it?'

She wanted to say no, he could see. But he knew—they both did—that saying no would undermine what she'd just told him. She picked up the photo again, her eyes flitting over it before she handed it to him. His heart hammered as he took it from her, though for the life of him he couldn't figure out why he was nervous about looking at a picture.

But as soon as he saw it he realised why.

It captured the moment they'd been laughing at her fall. They were both standing in the stream, Nalini's dress drenched, as predicted, with the stream only up to his shins. But neither of those facts was important. Their faces were. Or, more accurately, the expression on their faces—on *his* face. An expression he'd never seen before. He looked… He looked *happy*.

There was more too. A freedom, a lightness, that he now remembered the extent of. He'd never felt that way before, and now that he had evidence of it he couldn't keep ignoring that he had. He also couldn't ignore that he'd felt that way because of Nalini. Because of the freedom, the light, the happiness clear on *her* face in that picture too.

It reminded him of the way he'd felt when they'd kissed the night before. The way he was desperately trying to ignore the feelings that kiss had stirred. Or how he was pretending that those feelings weren't the reason he'd hoped to spend time with her that morning.

'We should send these to Mattan,' he said, placing the picture on the stack next to him. Keeping his face blank of the carnage that picture had left inside him.

'That's a wonderful idea.' She'd abandoned the pictures and was now pouring herself some coffee. She smiled at him from behind her cup before she drank, but it didn't shine through her eyes like her smiles usually did. 'The people of Mattan were really happy about the prospect of our marriage. These photos will make things more official.'

'I hope so,' he replied softly, struggling for more words when he was fighting against the voice screaming in his head to bring back the glimmer in her eyes.

'It will.' She placed her hand over his—to comfort him, he realised, though not for the reason she thought—but snatched it away almost immediately. 'I also wanted to say thank you for the painting things you had sent to my room last night. It was very…thoughtful of you.'

'You're welcome.' He paused. 'Will you paint something for me?'

She laughed nervously. 'Oh, I don't think you want that. I'm not very good, remember?'

'So you say, except I'm not looking for a masterpiece. I'd just like something from you.'

Her face flushed. 'Don't say I didn't warn you once you get it.'

'I won't.'

She bit her lip and then smiled at him. 'So, tell me what

I should be looking for during my exploration of my new home.'

He grinned and told her about the secrets of the centuries-old castle. She listened as attentively as he imagined she would to an important political matter. She made comments he knew meant she was listening, and asked questions whenever he paused. And, though he knew he wasn't the world's best storyteller, the look on Nalini's face almost convinced him that he was.

They were wonderful qualities to have as a queen, he thought. She'd make her people feel well loved, listened to, appreciated. It was so different to how his mother had dealt with her people—her *subjects*, he reminded himself of what she'd called them—that he couldn't help but compare the two women.

And then he worried that he was projecting what he *wanted* to see in Nalini onto her, instead of seeing who she really was. Much like he imagined his father had done when he had first married Zacchaeus's mother.

'Do you believe that your ancestor threw himself out of the tower's window to stop his love from leaving Kirtida?' Her voice was low, every feature of her face captured by the legend Zacchaeus had just told her.

'So the story goes,' he said mildly, telling himself to enjoy it—her—rather than think about his mother. Or his father. Or what their marriage had done to him. Or what their choices had left him to deal with now. 'But honestly, if it *is* true, I'm not sure I'd respect the man.'

'Why not?'

He shrugged. 'He killed himself for no reason.'

'No reason?' she repeated, shock claiming the lines of her face. 'It was out of *desperation*. He'd tried everything to show his love he cared about her, but still she didn't believe him. Not when her family had told her he was trouble. That he only wanted to marry her because of her family's wealth.'

He lifted his brows. 'Sounds familiar, doesn't it?'

'Some of it, perhaps,' she replied dryly. 'But we're not in love. They were.'

'And the way to show your love for someone is hurling yourself out of a tower and plunging to your death?'

'Oh, stop being so pessimistic!' she exclaimed. 'He wasn't jumping out of despair. He was jumping out of hope. Her boat was just below the tower's window. If he'd made it—'

'He would have broken every bone in his body.'

'But he could have survived.' She grinned. 'And she would have nursed him back to health and they'd have lived happily ever after.'

He shook his head. 'She'd left him, Nalini. She wouldn't have done that if she hadn't had her reasons.' But when he realised he was no longer talking about the legend he continued quickly. 'You're awfully hopeful, aren't you?'

'Positive, hopeful—' she lifted her shoulders '—they're pretty much the same thing.'

'Maybe,' he allowed. 'But yesterday you weren't hopeful. Yesterday you were being positive. Today? With this story? You're hopeful. I think it might be because you're a romantic.'

'Nonsense.' Her voice sounded forced.

'You don't think you're a romantic?'

'Don't you have to leave soon?'

'I…' His gaze caught his secretary's at the entrance of the castle right at that moment and Zacchaeus gave the man a slight nod. 'Yes, I do,' he told Nalini, but frowned when he thought she looked as though she'd shrunk into herself. 'Are you okay?'

'Oh, yes,' she said cheerfully. Again, it was forced and his frown deepened.

'Did I upset you somehow? I didn't—'

'I'm fine, Zac,' she replied, and for a moment he was distracted by the way his name—the one only his family used—sounded on her lips. 'Go, negotiate. Send my love to Xavier and Leyna.'

He studied her and realised he wouldn't get anything more from her than that. At least not now. So he said goodbye and left for Mattan, making a mental note to ask her about it later.

CHAPTER EIGHT

NALINI SPENT THE rest of the day wandering around the castle, talking to the staff and pretending that morning hadn't happened.

She should have got a clue about how things were going to go the moment she'd seen Zacchaeus—*Zac*—sitting at that table. She should have got a clue when her stomach had flipped at how gorgeous he'd looked in his blue shirt and black trousers. At how her mind had chosen that moment to remind her how hot his kiss had been, or how she'd woken up in a sweat, her chest heaving and her body flushed at the dream she'd had where things hadn't *quite* ended the way they had the night before.

There were countless signs that things were getting slightly too personal between her and her future husband. Like the way she'd felt when she'd taken the envelope from him, knowing that neither of them had wanted to open it out of fear. Fear that those pictures would spark with the attraction they clearly felt for one another. That the images would reveal the emotional connection they shared. That it would be evidence of everything, really, that they were hoping to ignore.

And, of course, it had been exactly that.

It didn't take a master in body language to tell her that there was something going on between them. Not when the pictures had captured moments when she'd been looking at him when he hadn't been looking at her, and vice versa. And in all those pictures it was clear that their marriage wasn't going to be simple. It wasn't going to be convenient. In fact, Nalini worried that what those pictures told her—what that feeling in her chest told her—was that their marriage was going to be very *inconvenient*.

The picture of them both in the stream confirmed it. Though it was completely unflattering in the traditional sense, it had an appeal she'd felt drawn to. Their guards were down, they were happy, comfortable, and all of it seemed to be *because* they were together. She'd seen Zacchaeus realise it when he'd held that picture in his hands too. And so she had immediately changed the subject so that they could get back to boring old breakfast instead of talking about it.

But breakfast hadn't been boring. She'd loved hearing stories about the castle and its legends. It was only when Zacchaeus had told her that she'd sounded hopeful—that she was a romantic—that she'd no longer wanted to have that conversation.

Those characteristics sounded too much like the Nalini who'd got herself into trouble. Who'd been such a believer in romance—who'd been so *hopeful*—that she'd followed her heart so that she could have an adventure in love. That she'd trusted a man—though now, when she looked back, she saw merely a boy—she shouldn't have trusted. She'd had her adventure turn into a nightmare, the consequences of which still motivated her decisions. Still had her wanting to prove that she'd learnt from her mistakes. To prove that she wasn't the old Nalini any more.

An *adventure* that clouded every decision she'd made since with doubt.

The uncertainty of it lurked in the recesses of her mind, waiting for her to let her guard down. And she was afraid—terribly afraid—that her guard was down now, with Zacchaeus.

Fortunately, Zacchaeus hadn't pushed her about why she'd denied being hopeful. And she'd had the rest of the day to herself to build her guard back up. Talking to the castle's staff had been enlightening. Though they hadn't been willing to share much about their King—new or previous—they were open about their lives there. Tentative still, she sensed, about what Zacchaeus's rule would mean for them, but optimistic. She'd got the idea that things hadn't been entirely amazing under King Jaydon's rule, though none of them would confirm it when she asked.

Perhaps she would ask Zacchaeus when he returned, she considered, tilting her head as she studied the painting she was busy with. While she'd been exploring the castle, she'd come across the tower room from which Zacchaeus's ancestor had apparently thrown himself. Though the story of it alone inspired her, the windows, with their one-hundred-and-eighty-degree view of the sea, offered so much atmosphere and light that it was the perfect place to paint.

Shortly after she'd found it she'd changed into casual clothes, set up her canvas and started painting the man who'd supposedly given his life for love.

Which was why it made no sense that the picture she was currently looking at bore a striking resemblance to the man she was about to marry.

'They told me I'd find you here.' Zacchaeus's voice sounded from behind her and she swirled around, angling her body in front of the painting.

'You're back already?'

'Yes,' he replied, narrowing his eyes. 'It's evening, Nalini. How have you not noticed?'

She frowned and looked out of the window to see that he wasn't lying. Somehow, she must have switched on the light in the room because it shone brightly over her painting. Which, unfortunately, made it a lot harder to hide from the man currently staring at her as if she'd lost her mind.

'I must have lost track of time,' she said brightly. 'Were the negotiations productive?'

'We're onto the details now, which should mean we'll be able to wrap things up soon.' He took a step closer. 'Why are you trying to hide your painting from me?'

It took her a moment to find words to respond, but then she said, 'Because it's not done. And you know how us artists are.'

She turned the easel around quickly and then stepped back in front of it when he took another step towards her.

'I think you're lying.'

'I'm not,' she replied, and wondered if he heard the hysteria in her voice. 'It's not done.'

'Oh, I believe that part, but I don't think that's the reason you don't want to show it to me.'

She stepped in front of him when he took yet another step forward, and set a hand on his chest to keep him in place. When he looked down at her, those enthralling eyes almost made her forget why she was stopping him. And when the temperature in them rose she suddenly remembered that she was only wearing leggings and a spaghetti-strap top, having abandoned her oversized shirt in an attempt to stay cool hours ago.

'I…er…perhaps we should get ready for dinner,' she said hoarsely.

'Or,' he replied in a voice that rasped with sexiness, 'you could show me that painting.'

'No, I don't think—'

'Come on, Nalini,' he said, a slow, dangerous smile spreading across his face. 'I just want a peek. I promise I won't distract from your creative process.'

She blinked. Tried to form words. But, for the life of her,

the only thing she could do was swallow, and she wasn't even doing *that* well.

'Please,' he whispered, and she thought she felt the words on her skin when it broke out in goosebumps. He lifted a hand, brushed his thumb over her lips, and her knees nearly buckled, causing her to lean against him. With that teasing smile still on his face, he wrapped an arm around her, steadying her while bringing her body closer against his.

'This…this isn't fair,' she managed to say.

'Not sure what you're talking about,' he replied, but the smile turned cocky.

Damn it, why did that make him even more irresistible?

'It's not going to work.'

'No?'

His arm tightened around her waist and the smile slipped from his face. She felt his heart thud against hers, and realised that he was no longer teasing. She told herself to move, but she was paralysed. Caught in his eyes, in his stare, in his smell.

She *wanted* to be, she realised, as the voice in her head shouted warnings at her. Reminding her what had happened the last time she'd felt something even remotely close to what she did now.

And realising that—realising that whatever was happening between her and Zacchaeus now couldn't be compared to what she'd felt with Josh—had her stepping back.

'Fine, you've got your way.' She fought to keep her tone light but it only highlighted the way her voice shook.

'Are you sure?' he asked, reserved now, the emotion and tension of the seconds before gone.

'Yes, please.'

She gestured to the painting and in that moment was sure she would have given him a kidney if he'd asked for it. Anything to save herself from the intensity of his gaze.

She stepped back as he turned the easel around, and now felt her heart hammer for completely different reasons. Perhaps if what had happened between them *hadn't* just happened she would have been able to pretend that she was really just afraid that her painting wasn't good.

But now she knew better. She knew that that painting would tell him more than anything she would actually say to him ever could.

As did his face, she realised, when he saw the painting.

She was by no means an artist, but as she looked at that painting she realised *it* was art. Because beyond the physical look of him—the striking, intimidating, handsome features of his face—the brush strokes had somehow captured the emotion she didn't think anyone else but her saw.

Including *him*, she thought, looking at the expression on his face.

'You can have it,' she heard her voice say. When he turned to look at her, she blushed furiously. 'I mean, if you want it, you can have it.'

'I'd love it,' he said quietly. 'You're very talented.'

'Oh, I—'

'Just say thank you,' he told her with a small smile, and then turned back to the painting, studying it for a moment longer. 'I've never seen myself this way. Is this how you see me?'

'It *is* you,' she said awkwardly.

'But it's not, too. I feel like this is…like it's a better version of me.'

'I wasn't trying to paint it that way, if that's what you're implying. In fact, I wasn't trying to paint you at all. It kind of just happened.'

His smile had widened when he turned back to her. 'What do you think that means?'

'That subconsciously I was thinking about your request for a painting and painted one of you? Or—' she consid-

ered, trying hard not to make this seem like a big deal
'—you look a lot like your ancestor in my imagination.
That's who I thought I was painting when I came here.
With the legend fresh in my mind and the room being as
beautiful as it is.'

'You were painting a dead man?'

'If you keep pushing me, then yes,' she said cheekily,
sensing that he was coming out of the strange mood.

'I take the fact that you didn't notice the time of day
means you haven't eaten yet?'

'You'd be right.'

She grabbed her shirt from the floor and quickly put
it back on. When she turned back to him, she felt herself
flush again at the look on his face. But she straightened
her shoulders, determined not to feel embarrassed. Again.
The number of times she'd felt that way in this room was
beginning to make her feel self-conscious, and she was
not a self-conscious person.

'So, do you want to have dinner together?' he asked.

'You mean…eat together? Again?'

He tilted his head, his lips curving. 'How long are you
going to keep making that joke?'

'Well, since you actually agreed to have only *one* meal
with me per day, I'm going to have to say a long, long
time,' she teased. 'Maybe in thirty minutes? I need to
take a shower.'

'See you in thirty minutes.'

She walked out of the room and turned back to see him
looking at the picture again. It sent warmth through her.
Not because she'd painted it—though there *was* that—but
because she knew it had given him a new perspective on
himself. Perhaps even the one he'd so vehemently denied
the first time they'd spoken.

That happy glow stuck with her, but chilled slightly
when she saw the wrapped gift on her bed. Its size told

her that it was a picture of some sort, and with shaky fingers she tore the wrapping off.

And felt that glow disappear so quickly, so completely, she wasn't entirely sure it had ever existed.

CHAPTER NINE

ZACCHAEUS BANGED ON Nalini's door, feeling just as thunderous as the sound of his banging. And then she opened it and he felt all his anger and annoyance snap away.

Her face was pale, and the sunny demeanour she always carried with her gone. She was still in the leggings that had driven him crazy an hour ago, but the shirt she'd worn was now unbuttoned, hanging loosely from her shoulders.

'What happened?' she asked dully, and his stomach churned.

'I could ask you the same thing.' He made sure his tone held none of the alarm he felt. 'We were supposed to be having dinner.'

'I…' Awareness shone in her eyes. 'Did I miss it?'

He thought about the extra thirty minutes he'd waited for her, just in case she'd got caught up with something. And then he'd realised she had no intention of coming down and felt his mood turn so quickly that he hadn't given much thought to how striding to her door and hammering on it might have seemed.

Considering it now, he didn't even know what he would have told her *had* she been standing him up. All he knew was that he didn't want the progress they'd made that day to disappear, and he wasn't going to let her spoil it either.

But that didn't seem to be her intention at all.

'Yes, you missed it. Can I come in?'

She nodded wordlessly and he walked into her room, ignoring the strange intimacy of doing so. He looked around quickly, hoping for some clue as to her behaviour. But he only saw her things, and the painting he'd been asked to give her.

'I see they put the painting in your room. I was considering giving it to you when you came down for dinner, but I wasn't sure you'd agree to dinner at all.'

'Who gave it to you?'

'The painting?' He frowned. 'Xavier did. Though he said something about it being from your grandmother.'

'Of course,' she muttered, and shook her head.

'You don't like it?' He walked towards it, his eyes taking in the beach scene. He wasn't entirely sure why it would upset her, especially since the style suggested she'd been the one who'd painted it.

'It's not one of my favourites, no.'

'But…you painted it?'

'Yes. A long time ago.'

'And your grandmother wanted to…remind you of the beach? Does she know we have beaches here?' It was a lame attempt at a joke but he was beginning to feel a little desperate.

'She wanted to remind me about how wonderful my decisions have turned out in the past,' she said sourly. 'And how she'll—*they'll*—never see me in any other way. But I can't believe she actually did this.'

'Did what? I'm sorry—clearly I'm missing something.'

She looked at him now, and some of the misery cleared in her eyes. 'I'm sorry for missing dinner. We can go down now if you like?'

'I'd like to know what kept you from coming down in the first place.'

'Just this reminder of what being home entailed. I was

missing home this morning, but clearly I was romanticising what it was like to actually be there.'

He stared at her. 'Are you going to tell me what this whole thing is about?'

'No,' she replied coolly. He took a moment to process the surprise, and then he clenched his jaw.

'So, our civility is only coming from my side then?'

'Civility being your willingness to have more than one meal with me?'

'I thought I was being civil the entire day.'

'Of which you'd spent what—two hours—with me?' She shook her head. 'You don't get to act righteous because you were willing to be decent for a few hours.'

'Are you being serious?'

'I think you should leave, Zacchaeus.' She walked to the door and pulled it open. Waited beside it.

He couldn't find the words to respond. Hell, he couldn't even process what was happening. Not really. Not since the woman who had the sweetest personality he knew was kicking him out of her room. Not when she was picking a fight with him.

The thought of it had him walking through the door, straight to his bedroom. It had been a rough day, but by the end of the negotiations that evening he'd felt positive. As if finally, things were going right for him.

He and Nalini were getting along well. Though there was still residual tension between them from their kiss, he figured they could live with it. And when he'd been teasing her in the tower room he'd thought that perhaps they could even have a little fun with it.

She'd completely taken the wind out of his sails with that painting. And though the emotions it had created in him had been difficult to identify—similar to what he'd felt that morning when he'd looked at the picture of the two of them—he'd recognised that most of them were positive.

That it had felt *good* to see himself that way. In a way he hadn't thought existed.

It had him thinking about what it meant that Nalini thought about him that way. He'd ignored the warmth that had spread through him at that perspective and had instead settled on having dinner with her. And then this entire mess had happened, and now he was wondering whether he'd misinterpreted what had happened between them.

Between them?

What was he thinking? Perhaps *that* was the problem—thinking that there *could* be something between them. Thinking that there *was* something between them. So, instead of being disappointed about what had just happened, he should be grateful. Because though things were going well between them now, that could change. It probably would.

Hadn't his father warned him that it would? He'd told his father little of his plan to protect Kirtida, knowing what it would do to him if he knew the kingdom was in danger. But Zacchaeus *had* told Jaydon about his planned marriage to Nalini. And had given strengthening Kirtida's ties to the alliance as a reason.

His father had told him then that a marriage of convenience might not work out. That if he chose the wrong person it might turn out to have exactly the opposite effect of what he'd desired. That he might not be able to trust his convenient wife. Zacchaeus had known Jaydon's warning had come from his own experience. And he'd ignored it because of how different Nalini and Michelle had seemed.

Was he doubting that now? he suddenly asked himself. Did he now think they were similar because of Nalini's behaviour? His mother had always been selfish. And her last actions on Kirtida had proved that selfishness yet again.

Michelle had been having an affair with the vice-president of Macoa for as long as Zacchaeus could remember. His childhood had been filled with tension because of it, and he'd grown up with his only example of love a broken marriage held together flimsily by the tape of royalty.

For the life of him, he couldn't figure out why she had chosen to cut that tape *now*. Why had she asked his father for a divorce? Why the urgency? Why the threats?

Zacchaeus knew there was no way his father would survive if his mother asked for a divorce a second time. So he'd intercepted all Jaydon's communications, making sure that *if*—when?—his mother asked again, his father would never find out. He'd positioned his ships at Kirtida's shores in case that request came with an act of violence, and let Leyna and Xavier think that he'd done it to strongarm them into agreeing to his terms.

So did he think that Nalini was selfish like his mother? Or did he just think that his father was right and he needed to be careful around her?

No, she wasn't selfish. She wouldn't be marrying him for the sake of her kingdom if she was. But she *was* hiding something. He'd known that since the day she'd arrived on Kirtida. Her behaviour this evening, over a *painting*, had proved it. Then there was the way she'd reacted when he'd called her a problem child, and again that morning when he'd called her a romantic…

She was hiding something, he thought again. And told himself that that was enough reason not to trust her. She might not be selfish like his mother, but whatever she was hiding… It might be something that made her more like his mother than he wanted to believe.

And if that were the case he couldn't afford to have feelings for her—of any kind. It would no doubt lead to more pain for him—and hadn't he already had enough pain to last a lifetime?

He wouldn't trust her, he told himself. Because if he did, and it turned out badly, where would that leave him?

* * *

But the next day Zacchaeus was *still* trying to convince himself of his conviction not to trust Nalini.

He'd spent most of his morning doing that. His discussions on Mattan had told him that he and Nalini were going to have to speed up their wedding planning efforts. The way things were going, he suspected the negotiations would end that week. And then the only thing he needed to do to protect his kingdom was marry Nalini.

He'd thought about it during a visit with his father. His heart had ached—just as it always did—to see his father's pale complexion. To hear his weak voice. And, like always, he ignored the feelings that pulsed just beneath that ache that had nothing to do with his father's illness and everything to do with the way his father had treated him.

But still he'd realised that it was unfair to compare his mother to Nalini. Even when his father warned him—again—that he shouldn't trust her, he didn't buy that the secret Nalini was keeping would reveal that she was manipulative or selfish like his mother.

Afterwards, he'd spoken to his secretary, asking him for an idea of all that still needed to be done before the wedding. He knew that he and Nalini had an appointment to select the wine and flowers from local providers that afternoon, but he wasn't entirely sure where that would put them progress-wise.

What his secretary had told him then confirmed what he'd been thinking that morning. That there was no way someone who had taken it upon herself to view the venue and church, who had decided on the décor for both, *and* who'd impressed all those she'd come across, could be like his mother.

And then, of course, there were the engagement photos that had been splashed across every newspaper in the kingdom. Including the one they'd both been so taken with the day before, of them in the stream. The photo that, according to his secretary, had set social media alight with comments about how human their King had looked.

By the time Zacchaeus went down to meet Nalini for their wedding appointment he knew that whatever she was hiding wasn't something that made her untrustworthy. But it *was* something that had affected her badly, and he was determined to find out what it was.

CHAPTER TEN

SHE SHOULD APOLOGISE. She'd wanted to, almost immediately after she'd kicked him out, but then she'd remembered *why* she'd kicked him out and had kept her mouth shut.

But now that they were in a car together, ignoring the urge to apologise was a lot harder.

'You had a busy day today.' Zacchaeus broke the silence that had been between them since they'd greeted each other before heading for the wedding planning appointment.

'I wanted to get a head start.'

'Good idea, since we're almost done with the negotiations.'

She waited for the panic to take over, but it was nowhere near as intense as she'd expected. 'Things are moving a lot quicker than I thought they would.'

'Nervous?'

'No. You?' He gave her a look, and she nodded. 'Of course not. You're the one who wanted to get married in the first place. Why would you be nervous?'

It sounded a lot like babbling to her. But then she *was* nervous, though it wasn't about the wedding. At least, not entirely about that. The tension—caused by her actions, she knew—was making her anxious. And the longer it extended, the more she wanted to blurt out why she'd been so awful to him the night before, and the more she wanted to apologise.

But somehow neither of those two things seemed like the right thing to do. No, now she just wanted to get through this damn appointment and return to the safety of the castle. Where she could lock her door and pretend she hadn't let her grandmother spoil yet another thing for her.

And that it hadn't completely destroyed the hope she'd somehow *still* had of her family seeing her differently.

She was distracted when the car slowed down in front of a long row of shops. They had clearly been preparing for the King's visit—Kirtida's national flag hung from every lamppost on the street, and posters of Zacchaeus's coronation plastered in the windows. A small crowd had gathered once the car had stopped, and it took Nalini a moment to realise that the group was mostly female. And that the females were wearing T-shirts that had Zacchaeus's face printed on them...

'I think I've been misinformed about the way your people see you,' she said, and felt her smile grow as she watched one woman grip her friend's hand and do a jump.

He followed her gaze and winced. 'I'm not sure how they always know where I am.'

'Always?' she repeated. 'They?'

Now he grimaced. 'My...fan club, I suppose you could call them.'

Her mouth dropped. 'That's an actual thing?'

'Apparently.' He gave an impatient shrug. 'It's not like I created the group. Or approve of them. They just...kind of... *appear* where I am. Wearing—' he gestured towards them '—*that.*'

'So, if I understand you correctly,' she said in a mock serious tone, 'Kirtida's dark and mysterious King has a fan club of women who wear his face on their chests?'

'Oh, come on, don't say it like that.'

'Like what?'

'Like…like me being dark and mysterious is a thing. Or like my face is actually on their chests.'

She didn't reply, only lifted her eyebrows and nodded to where the group of women were proving his protests wrong.

'Yes, okay, fine. They like me. But it's just a thing that some women do.' Her eyebrows went higher and she had the pleasure of seeing her dark and broody future husband blush. It was charming. 'I don't mean it like that. I just—'

'I know what you meant,' she replied, and ran her tongue over her teeth. 'Do you have shares in the company that provides your face on clothing? Because I think it could look quite lovely on a veil if it's done in the right way.'

'Nalini, you know— Oh, you were joking.' He frowned. 'Is this going to be a thing now? You, teasing me about this?'

'Oh, definitely,' she replied and smiled at him. He returned the gesture and for a moment she forgot about what had happened the night before.

For a moment she allowed herself to be lost in his magnetic eyes. The ones that, the longer she looked into them, told her the darkness her grandmother had once warned her about had been caused by something incredibly difficult for him.

And, heaven help her, because she wanted to find out what it was. She *wanted* to fix him—the *mess* of him, as he'd called it—even though she knew she shouldn't.

The thought had her asking whether they should get out of the car, and immediately the spell was broken. When she joined him outside, she saw that the line of shops wasn't where they would view the flowers or taste the wine.

No, that place had somehow been obscured by the group of now screaming women.

She couldn't stop the giggle when she saw the horror on Zacchaeus's face, but took his hand as they walked through the throng of people to an amateur street festival set up for their benefit. Now that she saw it, she didn't know how she'd missed it.

Her eyes fluttered to the woman next to her—and to her T-shirt—and told herself *that* was why. Because those T-shirts *were* distracting. Just like the face on them was.

She shook it off and sighed in relief when they reached the first stalls. *This* she could do. This was what she'd been trained for. So she said the right things as she looked at the flowers, and drank from the wines carefully, being sure not to swallow anything lest she lose her head again. She greeted children and smiled as the crowd grew larger and a group of musicians—heaven only knew where they'd got their instruments from at such short notice—began to play.

The amateur street festival was becoming a lot more professional, she thought, and found herself enjoying the happy atmosphere. But she also had to acknowledge that a part of that was because she was finally getting to see Zacchaeus as King.

Of course she'd witnessed that already. She'd been dealing with the King from the moment she'd arrived. But it was different to watch him interact with his people. Not because he changed from who he was—he remained the careful, intent man she'd got to know. No, it was more because that deliberate seriousness was surprisingly charming.

It meant that each person felt as though they were the centre of Zacchaeus's attention. As if their concerns were the only ones he had to deal with. As if the flowers he was looking at, or the wine he was tasting, were the best he'd ever seen, ever tasted.

It reminded Nalini of how she'd felt during their kiss. As if she'd been the only woman he'd ever wanted to kiss. As if somehow she was the centre of his universe.

The memory of it sent a flush through her and she grabbed a cold bottle of water from an ice bucket close by and pressed it to her cheek. She felt a tug on her hand then, and looked down into the biggest, bluest eyes she'd ever seen. Her heart already melting, she crouched down so that she could be level with the little girl who had taken her hand, and gave a smile to her mother before aiming it at the girl.

'Hi,' came a soft voice.

'Hello,' Nalini replied. 'Are you here with your mum?'

The girl nodded, but gave no other response.

'Are you here…to see the King?' Nalini tried again and this time the girl's eyes widened and a pretty pink covered her cheeks. Nalini's smile broadened as she realised what she'd been singled out of the crowd for. 'I'll see what I can do.'

She winked at the girl, nodded at the 'thank you' her mother mouthed and followed the path her guards created so that she could find her way back to Zacchaeus.

'I'm sorry to interrupt,' Nalini said when she reached his side, and she saw a spark of gratitude in his eyes when he turned away from yet another young woman.

'No, don't worry. We were just ending the conversation.' He smiled at the woman—whose crestfallen expression immediately brightened—and gestured for Nalini to start walking. 'What can I do for you?'

'Oh, it really isn't what you can do for me, but more about what you can do for one of your fans.'

'I don't think I have it in me to do another thing for one of my fans.'

'No, you do,' she corrected. 'At least you will for this one.'

She stopped in front of the young girl and her mother—both of whom looked suitably impressed that she'd been able to get Zacchaeus there. She didn't ponder why—did they not think she'd be able to get the man she was about to marry to talk to them?—and instead focused on the way Zaccheus had done the same thing she had earlier, and was now crouched in front of the girl.

'Hi, there,' Zaccheus said.

Shy, the girl slipped behind her mother's leg, and the woman immediately went red and started to apologise.

'There's no need,' Zaccheus said. 'It's hard for me to talk to people too, sometimes.' He directed his next words to the girl. 'It's scary, isn't it?' She nodded and angled her body slightly more towards him. 'But sometimes people aren't as scary as they look.' He whispered something in the girl's ear and she giggled.

Watching it sent a punch through Nalini's heart and she nearly staggered backwards. Instead, she smiled at the girl and her mother and slowly moved away from them, feigning interest in the flowers at a stall she'd already seen to make her disappearance less obvious. She kept moving then, through the people, offering smiles, shaking hands.

But, determinedly, she made it back to the car and thanked the heavens that her bodyguards would make sure she had privacy.

She wasn't sure why it had shaken her so much. No, that was a lie. She *did* know. And perhaps knowing had shaken her even more. Because she could see a future with a little girl in it. With little boys too, and maybe even some pets. And in that future she and Zaccheus were those children's parents, and those pets' carers.

She didn't want to be thinking of their future together. But she was and that meant that she was slipping back again. Back into the girl who made plans for her future. Stupid, romantic plans that would never, ever come true. Plans that were idealistic, and only proved that she was naïve. And that she wasn't someone who made good choices.

She knew better than to do that again. She knew better than to blindly trust a man, and make plans for a future together. It didn't matter that she felt as if she knew him better than she'd ever known Josh. Or that the inner voice that had warned her about Josh—that she'd only realised she'd ignored *after* the beach incident—was seemingly quiet about Zacchaeus.

Nalini had sworn she wouldn't go back to being that girl. And she'd chosen to obey her family to prevent that. But after her grandmother had sent her that painting, Nalini could see where she stood with them now. In their eyes, she'd disobeyed them again. And she was finally beginning to realise that, no matter what she did, it wouldn't change the way they thought of her.

So she couldn't go back to Mattan. She had to stay here with Zacchaeus and face the decision she'd made. She tried to focus on the fact that that decision hadn't only been made to prove her family wrong. She'd wanted to save her kingdom too—she *was* saving her kingdom. Because if she didn't focus on that she would have to face the doubt she felt about her decision.

A decision she sensed would do more damage than the one she'd made with Josh...

Damn it, she *hated* this uncertainty. Hated it that the painting hadn't only shown her that her family's perception of her wouldn't change, but that it had actually done what her grandmother had intended. She couldn't deny that it had. Not when that painting had really been a reminder *from* herself *for* herself. A reminder that she should be careful. That she should make sure she could really trust someone before she did anything.

She didn't know if she could trust Zacchaeus. Not with certainty. And she only had to remember the last time she'd taken a chance to know that she *needed* certainty.

She only had to remember how she'd trusted the man who had led her down to the beach that day. Who had kissed her as they'd walked down the path from the castle, and giggled with her as they'd tried to avoid the castle guards.

The man who'd then mocked her when she'd called out for his help as his friends pulled at her clothing, her jewels.

She shut her eyes tight, hoping it would stop the memories. But then told herself to embrace the memories. To let them fortify the part of her that had softened watching Zacchaeus today. She'd known that kind man had existed inside him. And though he'd tried to deny it—to hide it—he couldn't keep that from her any more.

But that didn't mean the King beneath that kind man didn't exist. Until she was completely sure of it, she couldn't trust him. She needed to protect herself. And protecting herself meant that she couldn't trust her own judgement either.

'Nalini?'

She opened her eyes just in time to see Zacchaeus settle inside the car.

'Done?'

'So it seems,' he said evenly. 'Which tends to happen when my fiancée disappears from our wedding appointment.'

'The wedding appointment was long over, Zacchaeus,' she replied in the same tone. 'We saw all the flowers, tasted all the wine in the first two hours. The last few were really just for the sake of your image. To memorialise the people out and about with their King. I saw the photographers,' she said when his forehead creased.

'I didn't know anything about that.'

'I know,' she said, softening her tone. 'It was probably some scheme from your advisors. Hence the fact that this simple appointment turned into a full-on parade.'

'Is that why you left?'

'No, it's not.' But she had no intention of telling him why she had. 'Perhaps we should head back to the castle now?'

CHAPTER ELEVEN

ZACCHAEUS WASN'T SURE his plan would work.

Especially after that afternoon, when things had shifted between ease and tension, closeness and distance with him and Nalini. But still he'd told himself to give his plan a chance.

Which was why he was standing at the edge of the beach that stretched out in front of the castle, waiting for Nalini.

'I think I'm in the wrong place,' came her voice from behind him, and when he turned Zacchaeus heard the soft intake of his own breath.

What was it about the way she wore a dress that had him feeling this way? He knew she didn't intend to do it to him. Not when it was a simple Grecian-style dress that fell to her ankles from a high neckline. She'd let her hair down this evening, but her face was clear of make-up, and he wondered why he thought that she was trying but not trying at the same time.

It was more than likely the latter, he thought. Especially after he'd had to remind her about their deal—the one *she'd* insisted on—to share one meal per day. After *he'd* had to insist when she'd brushed it off, claiming that she was tired. Even if he did believe her, he wouldn't have agreed anyway. He wanted to know why she'd left him during their appointment that afternoon. And why she'd kicked him out the day before.

Was it so wrong that he'd ensured the intimacy, the privacy, of dinner to do so?

'You're not in the wrong place,' he told her. 'This is where we're having dinner tonight.'

'Are you sure? Because I don't see a table anywhere. And the candles—' she gestured to the pathway that was lined with candles '—seem a lot more appropriate for a date than a forced dinner.'

'Aren't they the same thing?' he asked easily. 'I've seen plenty of movies where dates look a lot less comfortable than what we share.'

'Which movies are you watching?' She shook her head in disgust and he took her hand, hiding his smile at the fact that he'd successfully distracted her. 'You've been on dates before. Surely you know that our dinners—or meals—aren't comparable to real dates?'

'I'm not sure that I do. I've never really been on a date before.'

'That can't be true.'

He heard the surprise but it didn't bother him. He was quite enjoying their walk down the beach path that would eventually take them to where they'd be having dinner.

'But it is.'

'Even though the "I love Zacchaeus fan club" exists?'

He chuckled. 'Probably *especially* because it exists.' He paused, considering her question more carefully. 'I think you're mistaking the fact that I haven't gone on a date with the fact that I haven't dated. I *have* dated. Women have come to the castle—appropriate women from appropriate families—and we've spent time together.'

She stopped next to him. 'You think that's dating?'

'For us, yes.'

'Maybe that's true,' she said, and started walking again. 'But it sounds terrible.'

He let out a surprised laugh. 'So you're saying things weren't like that for you?'

'No,' came the sombre reply, and he could sense the shift in her mood again. But then she said, 'I haven't really dated either. The real kind or the kind you're talking about.'

'So I was your first kiss?' he teased, and frowned when she didn't respond immediately. Her soft reply had his heart racing uncomfortably in his chest.

'Yes, you were.' She bit her lip. 'Is that really how it's supposed to be? I mean is it…is it always that…that *wet*?'

She blinked innocently at him and he felt his eyes widen. And then her face transformed and she burst out laughing. It took him a moment to realise that she'd been pulling his leg, and another to see the humour in it.

And then he found himself smiling too. Before long, his laughter joined hers and for the second time in as many days Zacchaeus found himself wiping tears from his eyes at a joke.

'You are *so* naïve,' she said, her finger brushing a tear from her cheek. 'And so *proper*. It's adorable that you think kissing should only happen if you're dating.'

'That's not—' He broke off at her smile and before he could help it he was smiling back. 'I'll get you back for that.'

'I'd be disappointed if you didn't,' she said, her eyes twinkling.

And suddenly he was thinking that things felt like before between them. Like the day they'd almost been friends, and not whatever they were now. He stopped walking when he realised they'd made it, and turned to her.

'We're here,' he said softly, and watched the surprise on her face as her gaze shifted to behind him. Some might have said he'd overdone it—*he'd* told himself as much when he'd been planning it. But the look on her face made it worth it.

She was surprised, sure, but there was more on the beautiful features of her face. She was impressed, a little touched, and the slightest bit overwhelmed. And though he was getting better at reading her, he knew there was more still. He wished he could read it all. All the secrets those features held.

But when her eyes met his again he realised that though he couldn't identify every emotion on her face, he *felt* them. Because his heart had immediately pulsed when she'd looked at him. The awareness he always felt around her had hummed louder in his body. And now his fingers itched—to brush away the hair the slight breeze had brought across her forehead. To brush those full pink lips and see them part for him.

Under the moonlight, he felt utterly captivated by her. As if she'd put a spell on him, and that spell demanded he kiss her. That he taste the sweetness of her mouth again, and perhaps get a touch of that fire of her tongue too.

'It's lovely,' she said, breaking the spell as she took a step back.

He nodded and cleared his throat. 'I thought we could do something nice for a change.'

'Well, it certainly is nice. Shall we?'

She didn't look at him as they walked to the large rock he'd arranged for their dinner to be served on. It was on the other side of the beach, surrounded by smaller rocks, and high enough that the waves merely crashed against it, not engulfing it like it did the others. He hoisted himself up and ignored the hand she gave him. Instead, he put his hands on her waist and lifted, biting back the smile when he saw her eyes widen as he set her down.

'Was that your way of showing me how manly you are?'

'Only if it worked,' he said mildly. He waited a few seconds and then asked, 'Did it?'

He loved the way her eyes crinkled as she laughed at him, and his chest filled with an emotion he didn't recognise. 'Yes, it did. But I'll never admit it aloud again.'

'Once is enough,' he replied cheekily, and winked when she shot him a look. 'I wanted us to have some privacy, so there won't be anyone serving us dinner.' He gestured to the basket next to them. 'But we have enough food in here to feed an army, and wine. Just in case you need it,' he said with a smile.

She gave him a small one back, but it sobered quickly. 'Why do we need privacy?'

'Because I was hoping we could talk.'

He saw her stiffen. 'About?'

'About what's been happening between us the last few days. I'm sorry but... I've missed something, and I'd really love to know what.'

'You haven't missed anything.' Her hands fiddled with the napkin in front of her. 'I've just been...reminded of why I'm here.'

'By your grandmother?'

'No, by myself.'

'Because you painted that picture.'

'Yes.'

'Why? When?'

'Why did you overthrow your father, Zacchaeus?' she shot back suddenly. When he didn't answer her, she threw her hands up. 'See? There are things neither of us want to talk about. So, since we don't need privacy because we're not going to be having this conversation, we can—'

'He's ill, Nalini,' he interrupted quietly, knowing that if he wanted her to trust him—if he wanted to trust *her*—he had to give them both a reason. 'He couldn't rule any more, so we came up with this...this *plan* to say that I'd overthrown him.' He fell silent. 'It was his idea. He didn't want people to think that he was weak.' *One person in particular*, he thought, but didn't say it.

A stunned silence stretched over them and eventually she said, 'So the rumours were true.'

'I didn't realise they'd reached Mattan.'

'They were whispers, really. And so ridiculous that we didn't pay them much heed.' She paused. 'Why would you need to hide that he's ill? Illness isn't weakness.'

'To my father it is.'

'But being overthrown isn't?'

'He thought that if I was the one who was overthrowing him, it wouldn't be so bad. It would make me seem powerful, more ruthless, and he would merely look like the father who had given in.'

'Based on what?' she asked. 'There was no military involvement. My understanding of it was that you forced him off the throne through guerrilla methods. Getting the support of the powerful in the kingdom. Ousting him, essentially.'

'Yes.' He shrugged. 'That's what we told people.'

'And they believed you?' She frowned. 'How could they? Wouldn't you have needed actual support? Wouldn't your inner circle have to know? Do they?'

'We did have actual support. When we came up with this plan, my advisors—who were also my father's advisors—started laying the foundation for the coup. They started whispers of rash decision-making, decisions that weren't entirely in the interest of the kingdom. There was more, of course. But…it wasn't that hard, really.'

He shifted when he saw how she was looking at him, but she merely said, 'So your advisors know he's ill?'

'They know he wanted to step down. And because they're the most loyal people I know, they did exactly as they were asked without much questioning.' He tilted his head and then nodded. 'But I think they know.'

She pursed her lips and reached for the bottle of water in front of her. After she'd taken a sip, she set it down again and settled back in her seat. 'Why did you go along with it?'

'Why…' He trailed off. 'What do you mean?'

'You knew how this would make you look. And *you* didn't want to be ruthless and powerful. That's not how you wanted to be seen as King. So why would you go along with it?'

His mouth dried completely. He took a drink of his own water and cleared his throat, but neither of those things worked. He wasn't sure he could voice an answer. And even if he could find his voice, he wouldn't have the words to answer anyway.

How had she seen through everything he'd just told her? How had she seen through it to *him*? Why did she even care? No one had asked for his opinion. His father had just *told* him what would happen, and had left him to fall in line. There had been no discussion regarding his feelings, and perhaps that had been part of the reason he'd been ignoring them.

Until now.

Until *Nalini* was asking him about it.

'I was…helpless not to,' he said in a hoarse voice, surprising himself. 'It wasn't a suggestion. It was a command.'

'Much like the reason I'm here?' she asked lightly, and the left side of his mouth lifted.

'I suppose.'

She nodded. 'Which means you still had a choice, though you felt like you didn't. You still had that choice. *You* chose to go along. Why?'

'Why did you choose to come here?'

Annoyance flashed in her eyes, but he saw that it covered hurt. He clenched his fist to keep from reaching out to her.

'I came here for my kingdom.'

'Nalini—'

But she lifted a hand, silencing him. 'I came here for my kingdom, but for myself too. I couldn't keep living on Mattan. Not when the life I was living there was destroying every good thing about me.'

CHAPTER TWELVE

'DRAMATIC, AREN'T I?' Nalini said, trying to poke fun at herself. No, she thought. She was trying to make telling him the real reason she'd agreed to marry him seem less severe in her mind.

'Considering what I know about your family, it doesn't really sound that dramatic at all.'

'They're not terrible people,' she said immediately and closed her eyes, wondering why she always felt the need to defend her grandmother and mother's behaviour.

'I'm sure that's true,' Zacchaeus said when she opened her eyes again, his own eyes filled with compassion. 'But families are complicated. Royal families more so. And sometimes what they do…' A shadow, dark and haunting, crossed his face. 'Sometimes what they do *is* terrible. And sometimes *they* can be terrible too.'

'You're not talking about my family now, though, are you?'

'No,' he replied. 'But I would like to know what they did to make you feel this way.'

Should she tell him? He already knew more than she'd ever intended to let him know. But somehow telling him about Josh didn't feel right.

Her gaze met his, and once again she was hit with the compassion in his eyes. She wondered why it was so captivating. Was it because it was so unexpected? Or perhaps because it took away that dark look always lurking in his eyes?

Caught off guard, she spoke before even realising it. 'When I was seventeen, I did something a little…irresponsible.'

She thought about the details, about how she'd got to the beach that day, and couldn't find any words that wouldn't make her seem like some stupid, naïve teenager. She ignored the voice in her head telling her that she had been.

'I was always more rebellious than Xavier and Alika,' she continued, settling on telling him about everything but *that day*. 'And after that thing happened it cemented the way my parents saw me. They used it to make sure I knew my place.'

'Which was firmly under their thumb?'

'Yes. And I… I'd learnt my lesson, so I had no interest in venturing out again. I did everything they'd ask—everything to try and prove to them I wasn't the person they thought I was. Not any more.'

'Like choosing to marry a man you don't know to save your kingdom?'

Instead of being shocked at how much he saw, she nodded. 'But it's pointless. They'll never see me as someone other than the irresponsible person they think I am. Of course, I've only just realised it. With that painting.' She gave him a moment to put the pieces together, and then continued. 'But I also chose to come here because the more time I spent doing exactly what my parents wanted—and then, when my father died, doing what my mother and grandmother wanted—the more the person I was disappeared.'

'The person who snuck homeless kittens under her jacket to take back home to the castle?'

Her lips curved. 'I'd forgotten about that.'

'How could you?' he asked with a smile of his own. 'Don't you still have the scars?'

Now she laughed, even as her hand fluttered up to her chest. 'Fortunately, all evidence of scratches disappeared a few months after that.' She tilted her head. 'How did you know? I was pretty stealthy, even if I do say so myself.'

'You were,' he agreed. 'But since I'd pretty much had the same idea, I'd been watching the kittens, waiting for the right moment to get them. Considering it was the New Year's Day parade on Mattan, and we were there as a part of our "royal duties"—' he lifted his fingers for air quotes '—I couldn't just run from my father's side as I wanted to.'

'We were children,' she replied, rolling her eyes. 'We should have been able to save the damn kittens if we wanted to.' She bit her lip. 'I'm sorry, that wasn't very princess-like of me.'

A sexy smile widened his mouth, and she felt the same butterflies in her stomach as when they'd been caught in each other's gazes earlier. 'Let's make a deal. You never have to be princess-like around me.'

'Are you sure?' she replied in a low voice, vaguely wondering where this flirtatiousness was coming from considering they'd just spilled their deepest secrets to one another. 'Because I can be *pretty* unroyal.'

'Really?' Interest sparked in his eyes. 'Tell me more?'

'Well, once, after I'd been dancing with this guy all night at a royal ball—' she lowered her voice even more, leaned forward '—I asked if he wanted to go back to—' she was almost purring now '—the kitchen with me to get some of the dessert we'd missed.'

He blinked, and then a deep rumble of laughter spilled out from his throat. 'What did he say?'

'After the disgusted look he gave me, he said no.' She lifted her shoulders. 'So I went alone. And really, it was his loss. The tiramisu was delicious.'

'You're really something else, aren't you?'

'I can unequivocally say yes to that. Is it going to be a problem?'

His eyes turned serious so quickly her heart stalled. 'Not for me, no.'

Now her heart twisted. 'Good.'

They smiled at each other, and she ignored all of the thoughts in her mind. The ones wondering at how easy things could be between them at times. How tense at others. How there was always this attraction—that pull—she felt for him.

If she thought about it, she would be tempted to wonder what it meant. Or why she always, always found herself wanting more of him, regardless of where they'd left things.

'What happened to those kittens, by the way?'

'They all went to loving homes in the kingdom.'

'You didn't get to keep one?'

'"A castle is not the place for a *pet*",' she said in the same tone of voice her mother had used on her years ago.

'Wow.' He shook his head. 'That's almost exactly the same thing my mother told me when I asked her whether I could take the kittens.'

'*That's* why you didn't get them?'

He nodded. 'Though I probably would have taken them anyway. Except when I got there they were gone and all I could see was you in a wildly moving jacket.'

She chuckled. 'You believe castles can have pets, don't you?'

'Of course.'

'Great. But, to be honest, I doubt your opinion would have mattered much to me. I would have just let the kids get them anyway.'

She froze immediately, the apology on the tip of her tongue. But she couldn't say it because that would entail her admitting that she'd said something inappropriate. For all she knew, he might not have picked up that she'd—

No, she thought as she saw his face. He'd definitely heard her slip.

'Sorry,' she said, wincing. 'That was a bit strange, wasn't it?'

'A little,' he admitted. 'But not untrue.'

Her cheeks grew hot. 'I suppose.'

'Are you embarrassed that we're going to have a child together? Excuse me,' he added slyly, '*children*.'

'I'm *not* embarrassed. It's just…strange.'

'Not *that* strange though,' he said, and she could hear that teasing lilt to his voice. 'I mean, we *are* going to be married. And we're royal, so we need to provide Kirtida with an heir.'

'Don't get cocky with me,' she warned. 'I know what this marriage entails.'

'Oh, I don't think that you do.'

She bit her tongue, knowing what he was trying to do. And then realised that she could play at his game too.

'Maybe you're right,' she said softly. 'What does marriage entail? Is it…is it like that kiss we shared? You know, my *first* kiss.'

Appreciation lit his face and he gave her a lazy smile. 'It's a lot like that, but a little…more.'

She almost laughed, but found that her breath was strangled.

'It's okay,' he added. 'You don't have to be scared.'

Now she did laugh—and heard it as a gasp for air. 'I'm not *scared*.'

'Are you sure? Because you're acting like you are.'

'I'm not scared,' she said, and for the life of her she didn't know what prompted her to get up, saunter over to Zacchaeus and sit down on his lap. She saw the way his eyes widened, but didn't give herself a chance to see it as a warning. Instead, she lowered her head to his and repeated, 'I'm not scared'.

And kissed him.

He'd enjoyed teasing her. He'd loved the way her cheeks had turned pink with only the candles and moon bringing light to them. And the way she'd been adamantly trying to deny that she wasn't fazed by the prospect of the physical side of their relationship.

Perhaps if *he* hadn't been as affected by her casual reference to their children some day—the reference that reminded him of *how* those children would get there—he wouldn't have kept pushing. But, because he had, she was now on his lap, making it perfectly clear how she felt.

And those feelings were anything *but* fear.

Someone who was scared would not be kissing him with so much passion, so much heat, that he worried he was no longer breathing. But what did breathing matter when he could taste the fire he'd wondered about earlier? Fire that burned his lips, his mouth, that set his entire body ablaze?

His arms went around her waist, pulling her closer so that he could feel her body against his as their tongues met, duelled. But her position on his lap was too awkward and he broke their contact to lift her dress, drawing one leg over his own so that she straddled him.

She gave him a lazy smile that had the temperature of his body soaring even higher, before dipping her head to return to what they'd been doing. He wasn't entirely sure what was happening—how he had the woman he'd demanded marry him kissing him—but he didn't care. He was much too taken by how she captivated his every sense.

How his eyes, though closed, still saw her sexy smile. How his ears heard her tiny little moans, a stark contrast to the crashing of the waves against the rocks. How she tasted sweet and fiery at the same time, how her smell mingled with the sea, the most intoxicating scent he'd ever been offered in his life.

And then there was the feel of her.

He thought he was in heaven as he ran his hands up the thighs exposed to him now. But the thrill—the indecency— of it told him it was more than likely hell. Tempting him to rip off the dress that kept the softness of her magnificent skin from him. Taunting him with what he could feel—the curve of her waist, the softness of her breasts—because now he knew exactly how they felt in his hands. And how much better they would feel without her dress covering them.

He stood then, holding her with one arm and using the other to clear the table before setting her down on it. He ignored the crash of the plates, utensils and whatever else was on the damn table, and instead focused on how laying her down changed the dynamics between them.

He could deepen their kiss now, and give her just as much as she wanted. And take just as much as *he* wanted. He could break the contact of their mouths to run his lips down the slender column of her neck. His hand settled on her breast as his lips suckled, kissed, *claimed* every piece of skin he could access, but still he wanted more. He ran his hand down her side and up her dress…

And froze when a chilly wave crashed down on them.

There was a stunned silence as they both processed what had just happened, and when he opened his eyes he saw the surprise on Nalini's face. He watched as her eyes widened and closed again, and in that brief second realised it meant they were about to get a repeat performance.

Not that bracing for it helped. The wave was just as chilly, just as surprising. But it spurred him into action and he moved quickly, jumping off the rock before lifting his arms to help Nalini down too. They barely missed the third wave and he took her hand, leading her back up the beach, away from the water.

'Well,' was all he managed as he looked down at himself.

His clothes clung to his body, his shoes completely drenched. He took a moment to appreciate that the unexpectedness of the wave had settled his arousal too, saving him from the potential embarrassment of having to face it now that they were no longer in the throes of passion.

He turned to her and saw that she hadn't fared any better. Though he wouldn't complain. Not when her white dress was now transparent, and plastered to the body he'd got to enjoy only a few minutes ago.

'Well, indeed,' she said finally, and her eyes met his.

Barely a second had passed before they were laughing.

He wasn't sure he would have been able to explain the moment to anyone had they asked. Yet there he was, laughing about being drenched with water during a heated makeout session. And that that make-out session had come after they'd both shared aspects of their lives neither of them had wanted to share before. He was beginning to understand why she'd pushed him away the night before, though why she'd walked away that afternoon was still a mystery. But he was making progress. And that was enough for him.

For now.

'Didn't you check when high tide would be?' she asked, squeezing the water out her curls.

'Yes,' he replied indignantly. 'And that *wasn't* high tide.' His eyes lifted to see storm clouds coming their way. 'I think we're in for one of the island's surprise summer storms,' he said and grabbed her hand just as thunder boomed.

'Shouldn't we clear the—'

She broke off when she looked back, and saw that there was nothing to clear from the rock they'd been on. The ocean had claimed the table and food, and a flash of lightning joined the ominous thunder.

'Come on. We should go before—'

With another boom above them, rain poured down, cutting his words off. Together they ran down the path they'd come from, the candles now extinguished, the rain coming down so hard that there was no smoke giving away that they'd once been lit.

Knowing how far the front of the castle was, Zacchaeus led Nalini down the side of the building, a route he hadn't used since he was a child. He saw their guards ahead of them now and realised—of course—that they would never really have any privacy. He thanked the heavens that he and Nalini had been stopped before they'd given their guards a more exciting show, and was grateful when he saw the door he'd been heading for open in front of them.

A few seconds later, they were inside the castle's kitchen.

It looked nothing like it had when he'd been a child. Though, as his eyes moved through the room, he realised that was largely because it was empty. The only people there were them and their two guards—one from Kirtida and one from Mattan—both of whom he dismissed to get into dry clothing.

'We should probably change into some dry clothes too,' she said, crossing her arms in front of her chest. It blocked his view of her breasts, though, considering the state of her clothing, that was probably for the best.

'Yes,' he replied. 'But we haven't eaten anything yet.'

'What? Oh, yes, of course.'

'You have to eat.'

'I do?'

'Especially because you didn't have dinner last night either.'

'Oh, it's fine. Besides, it's late,' she said, removing one arm quickly to gesture around them. 'There's a reason no one is here.'

'We are.'

'And now you're going to tell me that you have an amazing set of culinary skills?' she asked dryly.

'Actually, yes, I do.'

CHAPTER THIRTEEN

'YOU'RE KIDDING, RIGHT?' Nalini scoffed. 'There's no way you have the abilities it takes to work in a kitchen like this.'

He crossed his arms, drawing her eyes to the muscles she could see clearly through the wet shirt he wore. She swallowed.

'Would you like to make that bet with me, Your Royal Highness?'

'I would certainly like to make that bet with you,' she replied, but right at that moment a chill went through her. 'But does it have to be now? I'm freezing.'

'I can make a fire for us.'

'There's no fireplace in here.'

He smirked. 'Follow me.'

He led her through an archway on one side of the kitchen to the cosiest room she'd ever seen in her life. It was small, with just enough space to fit its two armchairs and a coffee table comfortably. There was a fireplace on the other side of the room—small, too, though she knew it would fill the room with heat. The windows gave her a view of the ocean thrashing against the shore, the rain-drops partially obscuring it.

She felt her eyebrows lift. 'Are you trying to impress me?'

'Yes,' he replied, giving her that lazy smile again. Her stomach tumbled and a faint throb of panic began to

pump through her veins. She ignored it and watched as
he crouched down and in a few quick movements had a
fire crackling.

'This room's been here for as long as I can remember.
I think it must have been a pantry at some point long ago,
but then became a place the kitchen staff could relax in. To
me, it was always just the place I would come to when—'
He broke off abruptly.

'When...?'

'When I needed company,' he said with a smile, but it
held none of the ease of the one he'd given her before. 'The
chef had a particular fondness for me.'

'Had?'

'Yes. He died a few years ago.'

'I'm sorry.'

'Thank you,' he replied softly. 'He was a good man. And
he taught me how to cook. Prepared to eat your words?
Literally?'

She laughed. 'Go ahead, impress me.'

He left the room and Nalini took the chance to survey
the damage the ocean and rain had done. Her dress was
clinging to her body, the material giving everyone who
cared to look a free view of her underwear. She shivered,
but knew it wasn't because of the cold. Rather, it was the
reminder that *Zacchaeus* had cared to look. In fact, he'd
done a lot more than look...

Warmth went through her and she kneeled in front of
the fire, using it as an excuse for the increase in temperature. She didn't want to think about what had happened
between them. About what had *nearly* happened. If she
did, she would be giving into the panic she still felt in her
blood. And in that moment she didn't want to panic. She
didn't want to think about what she should or shouldn't
have done.

So instead she focused on what had come before the kiss.

They'd shared things with one another. Had teased. Flirted. The time she'd spent with Zacchaeus that evening had done a lot to bridge the distance between them. Distance she knew she had caused, too.

It had been a shock to learn that King Jaydon was ill. But the more she thought about it, the more she realised that it shouldn't have been so surprising. She'd heard the whispers, just as she'd told him. Xavier had mentioned it too, when he'd spoken about Zacchaeus. But both of them had brushed the possibility aside. It seemed too far-fetched that the reason for Zacchaeus's behaviour was something so simple. Too easy.

But, after listening to Zacchaeus, she knew it had been anything but easy.

Knowing that the coup wasn't something that he'd wanted had her seeing him in a different light. Or perhaps not, she considered, rubbing her hands together. She hadn't really wanted to believe that he was capable of overthrowing his father. She might have convinced herself that he was, but that was only because *he'd* wanted her to.

It made her wonder what had changed. Why had he decided to tell her the truth now? Why was he showing her that the ruthless, selfish man he'd claimed to be the night she'd arrived on Kirtida wasn't the real Zacchaeus? Did he know that what he'd told her showed her the opposite? That a man who would give up his reputation to make his sick father happy was actually selfless and kind?

'I've brought towels and blankets,' Zacchaeus said, walking back into the room. He'd changed, she saw, and frowned. Even though the long-sleeved top he'd paired with jeans made him look more casual and just as hunky as ever.

'That's not fair.'

'That I brought you towels?'

'That you changed.' She took a towel from him and gestured for him to put the rest on the seat next to him.

'I agree. But the guards brought down these dry clothes and what was I supposed to say? No, thank you?'

'Yes,' she told him. 'Because if you're forcing me to stay wet and miserable down here, the very least you could do is be wet and miserable with me.'

He gave a long-suffering sigh. 'You're right. Which is why I also brought you this.'

He took out a T-shirt and sweatpants from between the top two towels, and she felt a smile creep onto her lips.

'Why couldn't you lead with that?' she asked, taking the clothes from him.

'Because you scrunch your nose up when you're annoyed, and I really like it.'

As though proving his point, he pressed a soft kiss on her nose and left the room again before she could process it. Somewhere in her mind, a voice was shouting at her for the way his action made her feel, but it was so foggy and vague that she ignored it.

She dried off and changed quickly, and realised the clothes she was now drowning in were his. It had her frowning when he came in again, this time with two steaming mugs.

'Are these yours?' she asked, watching him set the drinks on the table.

His eyes ran over her. 'Yes. The guards didn't want to search in your things, so they took whatever they could find from my room. You don't like them?'

'No, no, they're fine,' she said hurriedly, and gave her hair one last pat with the towel before curling in the armchair, throwing a blanket over her and picking up her drink. She moaned as she took the first sip of hot chocolate, and then blushed when she saw the look in Zacchaeus's eyes.

'What brand is this?' she asked, trying to avoid a repeat performance of their make-out session. Even though her body was urging her to do just that. 'I've never tasted anything like this before. It's delicious.'

'You wouldn't have,' he replied. 'I made it from scratch.'

'You're lying.'

'Nope.' He grinned, and she thought he'd never seemed less like a king. 'I told you I had skills.'

'Remind me never to doubt you again.'

Something passed between them after she'd said the words, and it stayed with her even after he'd left to finish making their meal. It was as if she'd been pledging her loyalty to him, she thought. And realised that, essentially, she was doing just that.

Because, despite the fact that she now knew Zacchaeus hadn't wanted to overthrow his father, she had no intention of telling her brother or Leyna. Even though it might help the negotiations for Mattan. Even though it might mean that she wouldn't have to marry him.

The thought sent a shiver down her spine and her fingers tightened around the mug she held with both hands. What was happening to her? Did she *want* to marry Zacchaeus now? All of a sudden? When the hell had that happened? The thought made the panic harder to ignore, and when he returned with two plates she had to fight to keep herself from acting differently than she had before.

'This looks delicious,' she said, taking the plate and fork from him.

'All I could do on short notice, I'm afraid.'

She nodded and dug into the creamy pasta dish. One part of her brain told her it *was* delicious, while the other kept bringing up the thoughts she was trying very hard to ignore.

'What's wrong?' he asked her, and she looked over at him in surprise. His plate was empty, as was hers, and she realised that they'd eaten the entire meal in silence.

'Nothing,' she told him, setting the plate down next to his on the coffee table. 'It was really wonderful.'

'What's wrong, Nalini?' he asked again, his voice soft but urgent, and she found herself answering him before she fully knew that she was.

'Why didn't you come to the State Banquet?'

He'd been waiting for the question since he'd told her the truth about the coup, and yet somehow, he still felt unprepared for it. Again, he wondered whether he should tell her. His heart told him to—and that frightened him more than the voice inside his head telling him not to.

But he'd been led by his head for so long. He wanted to follow his heart for just one night. This night.

He took a breath, felt the tension of what he was about to say stiffen his muscles. 'I wanted to. I was going to. But my father…' He trailed off, leaned forward, but didn't look at her. 'He had a bad night that night, and I needed to stay with him.' Now he did look at her. 'It wasn't a choice.'

'And after? Why didn't you call us? Why did you refuse to see Xavier and Leyna?'

He opened his mouth but no words came out. Tried again, but the same thing happened. It was harder than he'd thought it would be, he realised, rubbing a hand over his face. He'd never spoken about his mother before. He'd never told anyone about her infidelity. Of course, he was sure the staff knew. His mother had gone on way too many 'diplomatic trips' for it to be a secret.

But *he'd* never told anyone before. And though he wanted to tell Nalini and continue building the trust between them, it just wasn't that easy.

'Let me guess,' she said softly. 'It's complicated.'

'It is,' he replied gratefully, but saw the hurt in her eyes. 'I'm not just saying that, Nalini. The situation I'm in—the one *we're* in—is complicated.'

Silence followed his words. He sighed. 'Why is it so important for you to know?'

'Because it's the reason I'm here.' Her voice was still soft, but there was fire in her eyes. 'If you'd come to the Banquet, none of it would have got to this point. Xavier and Leyna wouldn't have got engaged, and neither would we.'

'So that's it.' Disappointment sharpened his words. 'You're asking me because you're still angry about me forcing this marriage.'

'No, that's not it.' She ran her fingers through the front of her hair, and when they couldn't go any further shook out the curls. 'I'm not angry any more. I actually don't think that I ever was angry at you. I understood your political position. I looked at Xavier and Leyna, and knew that both of them would have done the same. *Had*, even.'

She paused and did the same thing with her hair, but from a different angle. 'I came here for political reasons. But those aren't the only reasons I'm staying.' Her hand fell down to her lap and clutched the blanket over her legs. 'You can trust me, Zacchaeus. I want you to trust me.'

She hadn't told him how that related to the other reasons she was staying. But he could connect the dots for himself. There was something…more happening between them. And, because of it, she was asking him to trust her.

He could ask her for the same. And he would, he thought. But, right now, the uncertainty in her eyes told him that she needed him to take the first step.

'My mother isn't on Kirtida.' He said the words in a rush, and braced himself to tell her the rest. 'She left over two months ago, right before I took over the Crown.'

'Why?'

'Because she's been having an affair with the vice-president of Macoa.'

Stunned silence greeted his words, and then she stammered, 'I… I'm not sure what to say.'

'You don't have to say anything. It is what it is.'

'What it is…is terrible. I'm so sorry.'

He nodded, accepted her apology. And waited for her to realise what his words meant. He didn't have to wait very long.

'Wait—Macoa? Is that why—?'

'Yes.' But because it didn't make sense without her having the full story, he took a deep breath and told her. 'The affair started long ago. I don't know exactly when, but I remember hearing my parents fight once. My mother told my father she'd given him an heir—why did he still care about what she did with whom? So I know it started long ago.'

'When did you find out?'

'On my eighth birthday. It hadn't been the first fight I'd witnessed between them, and it wasn't the last. But it was the first time I'd heard about the affair.'

'On your birthday,' she murmured. 'That's terrible.'

He shrugged. 'It didn't really matter. I was never under the illusion that my parents had the best marriage. I'd understood long before then that there was a difference in the way my parents acted when they were around people and when they were alone—or with me.' He paused. 'It didn't affect me too much.'

'I don't think that's true,' she said softly.

'Maybe not,' he allowed, but shrugged again. 'I survived it.'

She nodded. 'What did this have to do with the Banquet?'

'We got word that night that my mother wanted a divorce.' He exhaled unsteadily. 'They were demanding it, and threatened us with economic sanctions if we didn't agree. There was even a threat of more.'

'That's *terrible*. How did the vice-president manage to make his personal business political?'

'He has more power than the president, and the man

knows it. The only reason he's still vice-president is because he wants my mother by his side before he moves up.'

'That's what he told you?'

'He didn't have to. When I heard that she'd left, I spent weeks thinking about it. I'm not one hundred per cent sure, and I might be wrong, but I think he wants to be in power with her. To form some kind of political power couple. I don't know,' he said, shaking his head.

It had seemed so logical in his mind, but now it sounded foolish. Unless he faced the unwelcome fact that his mother and Francisco were genuinely in love and wanted to rule together. But that made his mother sound more human—more sensitive—than she was.

'And then you told your father about it,' she said, realisation dawning on her face.

'No, she contacted my father directly and told him. The shock worsened his already weak heart, and I couldn't attend the Banquet.'

'Why didn't you just come to us and tell us the truth? We would have understood.'

'That we'd made up a coup so that my father didn't seem weak in front of his estranged wife and her lover?' he scoffed. 'You really think they would have understood that?' He shook his head. 'No one knows about my father's illness—not definitively, at least—except the two of us.'

'Not even your mother?' He shook his head. 'How did she not suspect?'

'She didn't care,' he said bitterly, and then told himself to rein it in. 'But she'd left before his symptoms became visible.'

'So you couldn't tell us anything.' She frowned. 'But you knew you had to tell us something eventually.'

'Yes. Which was exactly what I had to figure out in the month that I refused to see them. To talk to them.' His fingers itched for something to do so he didn't have to feel so damn helpless. 'I was lost and I didn't have anyone to talk to. I couldn't talk to my father in the state he was—still is—in. I had to figure it all out on my own.'

'And Xavier and Leyna's marriage gave you the push you needed.'

'I knew I had to ask them to consider adjusting the Protection clause. I was afraid the sanctions would only be the beginning. I still am.'

A long pause followed his words, and he watched as she played with her fingers in her lap. He had no idea what she was thinking. Had no idea whether she'd be on the phone to her brother as soon as they parted ways to tell him the truth.

'Is that why you brought out your fleet? To protect your kingdom?'

'Yes.'

'So you never intended to use it against Mattan and Aidara.'

'No.'

She nodded and bit her lip, turning it white. 'And everything has felt so rushed, so urgent, because you want to make sure your kingdom is protected?'

'And the Isles,' he added. 'My people first, yes, always, but I never wanted to jeopardise the alliance between our kingdoms. When I heard about the economic sanctions I knew it would affect Mattan and Aidara, too. And then I heard about Leyna and Xavier's engagement and I realised that we needed to be strengthened in the same way.'

He paused. 'I'm not saying I didn't take advantage of the situation to get what my kingdom needed, but I want the Alliance of the Three Isles intact. I want us to be just as strong together as we were when my father ruled. And that meant marriage to you. I'm… I'm sorry that you were collateral damage in that.'

Her eyes told him that she accepted his apology, and

he felt relief spread through him. And then she said, 'You don't know when you'll get another threat from Macoa, do you?'

'No. But it could be any time.'

'And you won't ask your father to give your mother a divorce.'

He clenched his jaw. 'I can't, Nalini. If I did, I'd be responsible for killing him.'

'You think she won't go to him again? Directly?'

'I've made sure that won't happen.'

There was a long pause before she spoke again.

'It sounds like you need to speed up the negotiations, Zac,' she said softly. 'Because we're setting a date for our wedding. For next week.'

CHAPTER FOURTEEN

NALINI COULDN'T QUITE believe that she'd made the offer.

She wasn't sure if it was the look on his face or the way he'd trusted her. Or the fact that he'd just confirmed to her that he was a good man—and that he didn't see himself that way.

Perhaps it was because no matter how much she wanted to offer him the same courtesy—to completely trust him with her own secrets—she couldn't bring herself to say them out loud.

'Excuse me?' he said, disbelief clear in his tone.

'You heard me,' she replied mildly, despite the way her chest tightened. 'We'll get married next week.'

'But...how? *Why?*'

'We'll manage it. And because...' She faltered. 'Because it'll help you. Won't it?'

'Yes, but I don't expect you to do this for me.' His eyes were solemn, his voice sincere, and she felt her heart palpitate.

'Fine then, I'm not doing it for you.'

'Liar.'

She lifted her shoulders. 'It's happening, Zac, so you can—'

She was cut off when his lips touched hers—a fast, fierce kiss that told her exactly what her offer had meant to him. Her throat closed when they parted—when she saw the emotion in his eyes—but she smiled.

'I don't expect you to do this at all.'

'I know.'

He nodded and when the emotion whirled inside her she realised it was time to leave.

'We can meet tomorrow to start discussing things, okay?' She uncurled her feet from under her and set them to the ground.

'Sure.'

When she looked at him she saw that his thoughts had distracted him, and she murmured, 'Goodnight,' before she walked back to her room.

She took her shower quickly, and vigorously rubbed her body dry when she got out. As though it would help her to no longer feel as dirty—as guilty—as she did. He hadn't asked her for the details of it—about what she was keeping from him, though she knew he wanted to know. Though she was sure that he'd stopped himself from asking her what that *thing* was that she'd spoken to him about.

And the fact that he'd told her about his father, his mother... Her heart ached just thinking about it. About what that poor little boy had gone through. No wonder he hid his emotions. No wonder he didn't want to open himself up. He'd been hurt—terribly—by the people who were supposed to love him most. His mother through her infidelity and his father by forcing him to become someone he was not.

But now she had to face the fact that perhaps he'd told her about his troubles because he wanted the same honesty from her. And she wanted to tell him, but the story in no way compared to his. It was stupid, she thought now. Petty even. And had nothing to do with whether or not she could trust her gut with him now.

No, a boy who had broken her heart didn't come close to

what he'd been through. It was trivial, she thought again, and ignored the inner voice that told her there was so much more to what had happened to her that night on the beach than just her heart being broken.

It didn't matter, she told herself. She would commit to planning their wedding and take some of the pressure off Zacchaeus. He had enough to worry about.

Her plan might not come close to opening up to him, but it was all that she could give him.

She hoped it would be enough.

Zacchaeus wasn't entirely sure how to feel about the current state of things between him and his future wife.

They were knee-deep into planning their wedding—three days in, four more to go—and she'd been avoiding him. Not physically—they saw each other often, more so since he and Leyna and Xavier had finalised their negotiations.

But the day after she'd told him they would move their wedding up, she'd gone with him to Mattan to tell her family. And whatever that discussion had entailed had her pulling away from him.

Whenever he broached the topic she would make up something about the wedding to talk to him about. She hadn't mentioned anything he'd told her that night again and, since nothing had changed in his negotiations with Leyna and Xavier, she obviously hadn't told her brother about it either.

It had quietened the voice that told him he'd been a fool to tell her about his parents. And now that it was quiet he could feel the relief flooding through him that he'd finally told someone. And not just anyone—Nalini. She had a way about her that made him feel as though he could tell her anything. Finally sharing the secret he'd been carrying alone for years had made him feel free, as if he were no longer pushing against an invisible force whenever he wanted to move forward.

It killed him that the person who'd finally freed him from that was now pulling away from him.

'White or purple?' she asked as he walked into the room that had become the wedding headquarters. He narrowed his eyes at the concoction—it was the only word he could come up with—of flowers she was standing in front of, and tried to figure out what she wanted him to say.

'White?'

She gave a satisfied nod. 'I thought so, too.'

'Then why did you ask?'

'It never hurts to have a second opinion.'

He would have smirked if he hadn't noticed that she immediately walked away from him, putting the table with the flowers between them. When she didn't look up at him again, he felt his jaw clench before he made a split-second decision.

'Out,' he roared, and felt surprise ripple through the people in the room. He knew he would have to do damage control after, since he was acting in exactly the way they expected him to, but told himself it was worth it. He couldn't take another day of this Nalini.

And he sure as hell didn't want to marry this Nalini.

He shook his head at her when she moved around the table as well—as though she were going to leave, too—and waited until they were alone before he spoke.

'What did they tell you?'

'Who?' she replied in a bewildered voice.

'Your mother and grandmother. What did they say when you told them we were moving the wedding up?'

The colour drained from her cheeks, but she straightened her shoulders. 'Nothing worth repeating.'

'But clearly it was important to you because you've

been treating me differently since the moment you left that room with them.'

'I have *not*.'

'Yes, you have,' he growled, and felt his fingers curl into a fist. 'It's like that day at the beach never happened. And since we both know that it did—' he gestured around them at the proof of it '—the very least you can do is tell me why.'

'Nothing's changed, Zacchaeus.'

'So the fact that you're calling me that doesn't mean anything then?'

'That's what I've called you all my life,' she said impatiently. 'I'm going to need time to get used to calling you something else. So, since I'm telling you now that I haven't been pulling away from you, can we call back everyone who's been helping us plan this wedding?'

He didn't answer, and waited as the silence stretched. Waited in the hope that she would give him the honesty he'd given her. Or at least tell him why she couldn't.

'Is this really how you want things to be between us?' he asked her quietly when waiting didn't help.

'Things are fine—'

'No, they're not,' he snapped. 'Do you remember what you told me once, when you first got here? That I wouldn't be alone—that I didn't have to be—if I confided in you? And now that I have, you're telling me that you're not interested in giving me the same courtesy?'

A long silence followed his words, and then he shook his head and turned to walk out.

'I don't know how to confide in you,' she called after him. 'I don't know how to tell you this…this *thing*. It's so small compared to what you went through. How am I supposed to tell you about it when it's so insignificant?'

'But clearly it's not,' he told her, turning back. He wanted to walk to her side—to take her hands in his and squeeze, comfort. But his feet were cemented to the ground and he couldn't find the willpower to move them. 'Whatever you've gone through has affected you so much that you can't tell me about it. Just based on that, it's significant.'

She bit her lip, and then sighed. 'They weren't happy. My grandmother and mother, I mean.'

Though it wasn't what he wanted from her, it was a start. 'I didn't imagine they would be.'

'It's what's best for the kingdom.' Her eyes changed with the words, and he knew it was because that wasn't the only reason. 'And the funny thing is that I think they would have agreed to it if it had been their idea.'

'So they're not unhappy about you marrying me, just that you're marrying…against their wishes?'

'Basically.'

'Surely that's not true.'

'Unfortunately, it is.' She brushed away a curl that had escaped the tie on the top of her head. 'When you live your entire life that way it becomes more believable.'

'And it's why you can't tell me about that *thing*, isn't it?'

'Probably.'

He nodded, and tried to figure out his feelings about it. Could he feel betrayed that she didn't want to tell him? He wasn't sure if he *could*, but he certainly felt that way. Because he hadn't had anyone to trust growing up either. Not about the real stuff, anyway.

His father had been an excellent guide on becoming King. He'd been patient and open about what he'd learnt. But when it came to Michelle, he was the complete opposite. Zacchaeus would never be able to talk to him about how much his mother's disinterest had hurt. He would never be able to ask his father why Michelle had hurt him in that way, or why she'd chosen a random man over her family. The only time Jaydon had truly spoken about what his wife had done was after she'd already left.

And that was because of what she'd left behind.

'It's not easy for me to talk to you either, you know,' he heard himself say. 'But I did. Because I thought that… Well, I didn't want to be alone. But I guess that, despite that, I still am.'

His hurt—his anger—had him walking out of the room without waiting for a reply.

CHAPTER FIFTEEN

'YOU SHOULDN'T HAVE to do this,' Alika said in that sweet way she had. Except today that sweetness was tinged with anger and indignation.

'It doesn't matter,' Nalini said, and smoothed down the front of her dress. 'I *am* doing this. Though I'll admit, it isn't happening the way I'd imagined.'

'Of course not. You should be getting married in your own kingdom to a man you chose for yourself.'

Nalini whirled around. 'You didn't choose your husband for yourself. How is this any different?'

'Oh, you know what I mean,' she said, and waved a hand.

Nalini narrowed her eyes as she watched her sister busy herself with her make-up. She *wasn't* sure what Alika meant. All she knew was that her sister looked more tired than Nalini had ever seen her. And it worried her.

Not only for Alika's sake, but for her own too. Because it was Alika's unhappiness that made her look that way. As if she'd given up hope. And if *Alika* had given up hope, what hope did *Nalini* have?

Especially now that she'd alienated Zacchaeus, who would be her partner after they married.

Not for the first time since that night she'd offered to move their wedding up, she wondered whether she'd made a terrible mistake. Whether she'd let her sympathy after hearing about Zacchaeus's life, about his parents, about what it all must have meant for him growing up, sway her into marrying him when she should have waited. When she should have used what he'd told her as leverage to release her from this marriage.

But then she'd meant it when she'd said that she'd forgiven him for forcing their marriage. She *did* understand his political decision—and, now that she knew the facts, didn't blame him for acting the way he had. But now she knew that she'd hurt him. She knew that pushing him away, not telling him about Josh, had hurt him. And, despite how much that fact hurt *her*, she couldn't bring herself to do anything about it.

And now here they were. On the day they were going to be married. The Protection clause had been finalised, and Zacchaeus had signed the papers reaffirming the alliance that morning. It had been a sign of faith on his side, she knew. He'd been repaying her for keeping what she knew to herself.

Even though he was still angry with her.

A knock on the door kept her from thinking about it again, though it sent an entirely different uneasiness through her stomach. She thought of the night before—of welcoming her family to Kirtida for the rehearsal dinner. And thanked the heavens—again—that they'd opened the dinner to all guests who had arrived at that stage.

If they hadn't, it would have been much *more* awkward than it already was. Zacchaeus's family's absence was the elephant in the room, one they'd blamed on the coup. But the truth was that anyone who saw Zacchaeus's father would know the man was gravely ill. Nalini could confirm that, considering she'd finally been able to meet with him. She'd hidden her shock and had spoken to the man as she would at any other time. Zacchaeus had thanked her for it and, for the first time then, she'd seen the effect his father's illness was having on him.

And then, of course, there was his mother. Who would *definitely* not be attending.

Though there were times that evening that she'd envied Zacchaeus. Her own mother and grandmother had barely looked at her, and hadn't said a word to Zacchaeus. Leyna, Xavier, Alika and her husband, Spencer, had all made an effort, but things were still tense. Xavier was still angry. Alika was sad. And Nalini had felt responsible for it all, unfairly, she knew, and had busied herself by focusing on all her other guests.

It meant her wedding wouldn't be as wonderful as she'd imagined once upon a time. But what did that matter? Hadn't she given up on a fairy tale wedding years ago? Hadn't she given up on the hope, the romance, she'd wanted it to have?

She shut her eyes against the thought that Zacchaeus had woken all those dreams in her again, and forced herself to be in the present. Though she knew it was that thought that had her keeping things strictly work-related between them.

She blew out a breath as she made it from the little cottage on the church's property to the church. Her heart thudded at the prospect of what was about to happen, but slowed when she saw Xavier waiting for her outside.

'There's still time to pull out,' Xavier said as soon as he saw her, much like he had the day she'd decided to marry Zacchaeus. And, just like she had then, she refused.

'I'm not pulling out, Xavier.' But she brushed a kiss on his cheek. 'I know what I'm doing.'

'Do you, though?' he asked, his eyes serious. 'I've seen the way he looks at you. And the way you look at him,' he added when she opened her mouth to protest.

'Oh, that's… I mean, that's nothing. There's nothing,' she said more firmly. 'We've just become friends.'

'With that tension between the two of you?' he replied with raised eyebrows.

'Let's just get on with it, shall we?' she told him, determined not to get cold feet.

'If that's what you want?' he asked one more time, and when she nodded he took her arm and slid it through his. 'You look beautiful, by the way.'

Love warmed her chest. 'And you couldn't start out by saying that?'

'No. That would contravene the brother code. I'm violating it as we speak.'

She laughed and squeezed his arm, thanking him silently for distracting her. And then she squared her shoulders and prepared herself to get married.

The music started playing, and Nalini watched as Alika walked through the church doors as her only bridesmaid. Her heart sped up again, but it didn't keep her from noticing that the hard work she'd put into the details of her wedding had paid off.

A floral arch made entirely of different kinds of white flowers framed the door to the church. She let Xavier lead them as she walked through it, and instead looked at how perfectly they matched the all-white décor in the church.

And kept her eyes on the flowers on either side of the altar instead of the back of the man she was walking down the aisle towards.

But then she remembered she was supposed to look like an excited bride, and put a nervous smile on her face. Not that she had to pretend much about the nerves. Even though their wedding was small compared to other royal weddings—with only guests who could make the short notice present—she still felt anxious. As though each one of them could see straight through her. Through them.

All the while she was studiously avoiding her mother and grandmother's gazes.

She and Xavier reached the front of the church then, and Zacchaeus turned towards her. Her breath caught at the sight of him in his uniform. She'd seen him wearing it countless times before, but somehow, now, her mind decided to notice every aspect of him. Probably because it knew how much she was trying to fight her attraction to him.

So, of course, she suddenly saw how his military jacket fitted him as if it had been designed with his broad shoulders in mind. How those intimidatingly sexy lines of his face seemed to match the tone of the uniform exactly. Serious, powerful, *demanding*. And now all of that was hers—the unwanted thought popped into her mind and she forced it away.

But then came the emotion. She wondered if her own was as clear on her face as what she saw on his now. It had her heart beating even harder, but Zacchaeus gripped her hand tightly as Xavier handed her over, and just before they turned to the priest he whispered, 'I don't think I've seen any woman look more beautiful than you do right now.'

The words made her flush, and she squeezed his hand. Then she pulled back her shoulders and faced the priest, focusing on getting through the ceremony.

She didn't quite feel as if it was happening to her. No, she felt as if she'd floated up above herself and was watching two people who were marrying for convenience say vows that she'd once thought should mean something. It was only when the priest announced that Zacchaeus could kiss his bride that she fell back into herself. Except it didn't feel like falling—more as if a vortex was sucking her back into her body.

She held her breath as she faced him, and then felt the air leave her lungs when she saw the emotion on his face.

She didn't deserve the compassion, the tenderness she saw there. She'd pulled away from him because she'd realised that night they'd spent on the beach had gone too far. They'd gone too far. And that that night had somehow taken the place of the last time she'd been on a beach with a man. That now the beach was a beautiful place for her again, and not a reminder of the mistakes that she'd made.

Except she feared that it was. As she looked into Zacchaeus's eyes—as she felt herself anticipate his kiss—she knew that something had changed between them. She knew that the fact that she'd offered to marry him sooner to protect his kingdom—to give him peace of mind—had come from that. And because he'd somehow eased the pain of what had happened with Josh, that change had been extreme.

She was so scared of it that she'd refused to speak to him other than about the wedding. He'd told her his deepest secrets and that was how she'd responded. It was terrible. But what choice did she have? She was falling—fast—and she didn't know whether she was prepared to hit the ground.

So she didn't know why he was looking at her like that now. Or why he'd lowered his head and kissed her softly, his arms going around her reassuringly, as though he would always comfort and support her.

Or why she'd kissed him back, and felt her arms do the same.

And then the kiss was over and she went back to watching it all happen outside her body.

She wasn't quite sure how she got through it all. But, before she knew it, she was sharing her first dance with her husband.

Husband.

'You did an amazing job at planning this in such a short time,' Zacchaeus said softly.

'*We* did,' she corrected, her eyes moving over the

flowers, the draping, the fairy lights that created quite the scene. Almost like the wedding she'd pictured before she'd convinced herself it was all pointless.

'I'm not entirely sure if that's true, but I'll take it.' He twirled her around and then drew her in closer than the dance required. 'You're unhappy.'

'What? No, I'm not.'

'You mean it doesn't bother you that your grandmother and mother glower at us at every opportunity they get?'

She winced as her gaze swept over the two women, who were doing just that. 'There's nothing I can do about it.'

'But you want to.'

'I suppose. Even though I know it's pointless.' She thought back to that day on the beach, and how terribly they'd treated her when she'd come back. And now, how poorly they were treating her even though she knew she'd done the right thing. 'But I'm learning to get over it.'

'And this all started because of that…that *thing* that happened when you were younger?'

His eyes missed nothing, she thought. 'Yes.'

'But you won't tell me about it because you've decided it's easier that way.'

She kept the space between her eyebrows smooth, though it desperately wanted to crease. 'I'm not sure what you mean.'

'It's done now, Nalini. We're married. What are you going to use as an excuse to pull away from me now?'

The music ended and after they bowed, he walked out of the hall without another look at her. For a moment she stood there, stunned that her new husband had just walked out on her, and then Xavier was there, taking Zacchaeus's place.

It took her a few seconds to realise what had happened, and then she cleared her throat. 'Thanks.'

'You're welcome.'

'Just say it.'

'What?' he asked innocently.

'I know you have something to say. When have you ever not? So, say it.'

He made a non-committal sound deep in his throat, and they danced for a minute before either of them spoke again.

'Come on, Xav,' Nalini said impatiently now.

'What do you think I want to say, Lini?'

'Aren't you going to ask me about why Zacchaeus left?'

'Why did he?'

'I don't know.' But she did, and when he didn't answer her she sighed. 'I upset him.'

'Why?' Now *she* didn't answer *him*. Because what could she say? That she'd hurt him by pulling away from him after he'd trusted her? That when he'd asked her to do the same she'd refused?

It had strained things between them worse than ever before. Worse because now they were hurting each other. Because feelings and trust meant they had more power over each other. And because she knew that she sighed again.

'I need to speak to him.'

Xavier nodded. 'Fine. After the song.' And when the song finished he brushed a kiss on her forehead and looked down earnestly into her face. 'Be careful.'

She smiled. 'Is that your way of giving me your approval?'

'You're married to him now, Lini. There's not much I can do about it.' His tone was serious, but then a light glinted in his eye. 'Besides, Leyna told me to butt out. So...' He shrugged and then grinned at her, and she couldn't help but laugh.

'I think I'm going to like having her as a sister.'

'I think so too.'

She nodded and threw her arms around him. Squeezed. 'I love you.'

'You too. And I'm proud of you.' When she drew back she saw that his eyes shone with sincerity. 'I know I didn't support you about this at first, and that was wrong of me. Because I can see that you've grown, and changed. You're going to be okay, Lini. I know it.'

Her throat thick with emotion from the words she'd longed to hear, Nalini kissed his cheek and went to find her husband.

CHAPTER SIXTEEN

ZACCHAEUS FELT AS IF he were carrying a rock on his shoulders. That was how bad the tension was between him and his new wife.

He closed his eyes at the term—at the emotion the term brought.

Because his *wife* was the reason he felt so damn raw. How did she manage to make him *feel* so much when he was so mad at her? How had the moment he'd seen her in that wedding dress crept so deeply into his heart? And why had he wanted to show her, the moment they'd kissed, that he wouldn't take their vows for granted—that he didn't want her to either?

It didn't bode well for his future. And it had turned him into the surly man everyone already thought that he was. Except now he had no hope of changing their minds when he'd be facing the reason for his mood every day for the rest of his life.

'I don't suppose I should be worried that my husband's run away from me on our wedding day?' a voice said from behind him, but he didn't turn when he answered.

'The wedding was just a farce,' he said in a steely voice. 'It shouldn't matter what your husband has or hasn't done, considering that he's only a husband in name.'

'But that's not true, is it?'

He felt her move in next to him, though she stared out

of the window of the tower room just as he did. Just then he realised why he'd been drawn to that room out of all in the castle. Not only had it given him the privacy he'd craved, but it also reminded him of her. Of how, for the first time, he'd seen himself through her eyes. Of how, for the first time, he'd seen himself as something other than the man—than the king—he thought he was.

He also finally understood why his ancestor had jumped from the window.

Zacchaeus didn't know what else *he* could do to show Nalini she could trust him. That she could confide in him. Did he need to jump, too? Why did he suddenly feel so desperate that that option seemed viable?

'You know there's more between us than a farce.'

'Really?' he asked mildly, ignoring the effect her words had on his heart. 'Because I was under the impression that you were happy with the way things are between us.'

'I'm not.' She walked to the front of him, forcing him to look at her. And, damn it, it was as if she knew exactly what seeing her in that flowing white dress, her curls spiralling around her face underneath her crown, would do to him. 'I've hurt you. How can I be happy about that?'

'You seem happy with it,' he replied in a biting voice. 'You seem fine with keeping me at a distance.'

'Well, I'm not. But, like I told you before, I don't know how to tell you this.'

'If we're going to repeat this—'

'It happened when I was too young to know about the reality of the world,' she interrupted him. 'Of *our* world. And now it feels foolish. *I* feel foolish, and I don't want you to see me that way.'

He didn't move—couldn't. Afraid that if he did, he would break whatever was happening between them.

'When I came here, I realised it was an opportunity for me to start over.' She turned her back to him now, and stepped aside to give him back his view of the sea. 'You didn't know about *that day*—' she said those words bitterly '—and you couldn't judge me for it. You wouldn't think of me as careless. So I didn't want to tell you, and I still don't.' There was a pause. 'But if you need to know, Zacchaeus, then just say the word and I'll tell you.'

'That's not fair,' he said in a low voice. 'If I tell you I want to know, you'll hold it against me for the rest of our marriage.'

'I won't.'

'Really? Because I've seen resentment in a marriage. I've seen one spouse blame another for things that couldn't possibly be their fault. So forgive me if I don't believe you.'

'Maybe I just need to hear you ask,' she said softly.

'Maybe I just need to hear you tell me even though I didn't ask you to. Like when I told you about my parents.' He was angry now, and he knew it came from hurt. From doubt about whether he should have just kept things to himself. About whether telling her had been a terrible mistake. 'You're asking me to trust you, Nalini, and you haven't given me a reason to.'

'I haven't—' she said in disbelief. 'I haven't given you a reason to *trust me*? What about this wedding?' She gestured between them. 'What about the fact that I didn't tell my brother or Leyna about the real reason you needed the alliance's protection? That I put your kingdom ahead of my own so that you could have peace of mind?' Her chest heaved beneath the lace detail of her dress. 'I might not be able to tell you about the day I was lured to the beach by a man I thought loved me, only to be made a fool of, but I did do all the rest. For you. For you to trust me. If that's not enough…'

She shook her head and then he saw the colour fade from her cheeks as she realised what she'd said.

'He hurt you?'

The anger he'd felt earlier was nothing compared to the heat that burned in his veins now.

'No.' She closed her eyes. 'Not in the way you mean.'

He couldn't resist now, and slid an arm around her waist. 'Tell me.'

Her muscles stiffened under his arm, and then he felt them relax. She was doing so deliberately, he realised, and marvelled at her strength.

'I was in love with him,' she started in a whisper. 'The hopeless, stupid kind that can only be felt by a teenager.' She paused. 'I met him at a festival in the castle. He was normal, and didn't have anything to do with high society or royalty. He was such a breath of fresh air.'

She sucked in a breath now and moved out of his embrace to lean her hands against the window pane. 'I told you I'd always been a little rebellious. The undutiful child. I hadn't got myself into any trouble to earn those labels, but my mother didn't need that. I just wasn't as amenable as my brother and sister, and listening to my mother's every word, every desire, for me was so *boring*. So if she told me to run along to my piano lesson, I'd detour to the library first. Or if I had etiquette training, I'd sneak away to practise the piano before. Or to paint,' she said with a smile over her shoulder for him. But it had already faded by the time she faced back to the window.

'Anyway, I met this boy—Josh—and I was so taken by how kind and free and *handsome* he was that I found ways to get him back to the castle. We'd only known each other for a month, but I was convinced that I would marry him. No,' she corrected herself, 'I was convinced that *he* would marry me. He told me he would, promised me that we'd spend our lives together. And then he'd kiss me so softly and sweetly, so what choice did I have but to believe him?'

'But he lied.'

She clenched her jaw. 'He lied. But not before he'd managed to get me to agree to sneak out of the castle with him. I'd refused before, knowing it would be unsafe. But he told me that he wanted to make our relationship more official, and somehow I got it into my mind that he was going to propose.' She gave a harsh bark of laughter. 'How stupid was that? I was seventeen years old and I thought a boy was going to propose to me. I thought I'd actually be able to marry him. A boy I'd met at a festival who had no part in high society or royalty.'

She shook her head again. 'Saying it aloud makes me sound even more stupid than I was.'

'Which was why you didn't want to tell me about it.'

'Yes. And I'm not even done yet.'

She walked away from the window and began pacing the floor. He was helpless to stop her and only watched as she did this to herself. Soon, he told himself. As soon as she was done, as soon as she'd got it all out, he would comfort her. And tell her that nothing she told him made him think of her as a fool.

'So I dressed up. I put on my finest jewels, my prettiest dress. I told myself that this would be the first night of the rest of our lives together. I would finally get the independence, the freedom, I'd always longed for. I'd ignored my grandmother's warnings about Josh—she'd realised what was happening when I began to find more and more reasons for him to come to the castle—and she'd told me that it would never last. That it would never last *and* that he didn't really want me.'

She laughed again, but this time it sounded horribly strangled. 'But I'd trained myself to ignore them. My mother and grandmother were so critical about everything and by then I already knew they saw me as the difficult one. As the problem child,' she added, and gave him a smile that reminded him of his words the first night she'd come to Kirtida. He understood now why she'd reacted the way she had.

'They just didn't want me to be happy, I told myself and snuck out of the castle to meet Josh where he told me to. It was on the beach,' she told him, and stopped pacing. Faced him. 'It was a lovely evening, and he was being as sweet as he always was. And I thought I was on an adventure. It was thrilling and so romantic. Until we started walking down the beach and I saw a group of teenagers around a fire.' She took another shaky breath. 'He assured me that he didn't know them, and that they wouldn't recognise us, but they were both lies. And when we reached them...' She faltered, and he watched as she drew herself up even taller. 'When we got there he left me and watched as the group tore at my clothing and jewels.'

'Nalini,' he whispered, horrified. She didn't back away when he moved forward, gripped her hands. They were like ice in his.

'He laughed at me,' she replied dully. 'They all did. And I could see in his eyes that he'd done all of it because he wanted to impress his friends. Never because he wanted to impress me. Or because he liked me even.'

'*He* was the idiot, not you,' he told her, and pressed a kiss to her forehead.

'He wasn't the one who thought they were in love with someone after a month.' She tried to rustle up a smile, but all he saw was a painful attempt to make something that had hurt her seem like it hadn't.

'What happened?'

'The castle guards found me. Alika had realised I was missing and had told Xavier, who sent the guards out for me.'

'They saved you.'

'Yes.'

'Were you hurt?'

'Bruises, scratches.' She lifted her shoulders and pulled her hands gently from his. 'I think they might have done more—' the words were said in a shaky voice that undermined the nonchalance she was attempting '—but the guards came in time.'

'You must have been terrified,' he murmured.

'And badly shaken,' she said with a nod. 'I was in such shock when they took me home that I barely heard what my mother and grandmother said.'

'Barely?'

'I wish I hadn't heard any of it,' she admitted softly. 'I was so hurt by what this boy I thought I loved—because how could it have been real?—had done but they insisted on saying *I told you so*. My mother hadn't been as in-the-know about it as my grandmother, but it didn't matter. They ripped into me, and made me regret I'd ever taken a chance like that.'

'But it wasn't only that,' he said, knowing they'd merely given Nalini a reason to believe what she'd been telling herself all along.

'Maybe not, but did it really matter? I'd done such a foolish thing. I hadn't only put myself in danger, but the Crown too. I was third in line to the throne—didn't I realise what that meant?' She sighed now. 'But they were right.'

'No, they weren't.'

She smiled. 'You don't even know what I was going to say.'

'Yes, I do.' He shoved his hands into his trouser pockets to stave off the temptation to take her into his arms again. 'You were going to say that they were right to point out that you shouldn't have left the castle. That you shouldn't have fallen for someone below your position. That you should have listened to them. That you should have obeyed.' He paused. 'It was probably very similar to what they told you when you decided to come here. Or when you told them about the wedding.'

She blinked, and then nodded. 'Okay, fine, so you do know. But I thought that they were right. Then. And every day after, I made sure that I didn't ever put myself into that position again. I did what they said, I listened. I wanted to prove that I was responsible.'

'Except with me.'

'I thought they'd eventually see that I *was* being responsible in coming here. In saving our kingdom.' She paused. 'But I think I always knew that they wouldn't.'

'So why did you come?'

'Because I was so unhappy,' she admitted. 'I did everything they wanted me to and I… I lost myself. I mean, I'd lost a part of myself on that beach.' She rolled her eyes. 'The part that believed in love and romance and happiness. I realised that for me, for us—*royalty*—those things weren't a reality. But I used to be excited about things. About painting and music and sometimes even my royal duties. And then…then I wasn't any more. I was just going through the motions of my life without living it. I may not have believed in the things I did before, but I sure as hell didn't want to just go through the motions.'

She hadn't moved from where she was in front of him when she'd pulled her hands from his, and now she laid a hand on his cheek for a brief moment before dropping it. 'You gave me a reason to *live* again. And to be excited about things. Like painting.' She bit her lip and there was hesitation in her eyes when she spoke again. 'I hadn't painted a picture like the one I did for you since that night. A painting with emotion and…and *passion*.'

Moved, he cleared his throat. 'But you painted the picture of the beach? After, I mean.'

Her eyes turned contemplative. 'Yes, you're right. But

that painting wasn't for joy. It was a form of therapy. And a reminder to make better decisions. To be careful.'

He realised then why she'd been so upset when she'd seen it. 'Your grandmother sent it to you because she knew?'

'I never told her, so perhaps she didn't know exactly.' She was angry, he saw, and wondered at the fact that he could read her expressions now. Something turned in his chest. 'But she knew enough. And I knew she wanted to remind me about what happened the last time I made my own decision.'

'Unbelievable.'

'But true,' she replied mildly. 'That's why I was so determined to make things work between us. That's what it was the first day,' she continued. 'I wanted to prove to us both that my decision wasn't a mistake. If it had been—'

'It would prove what she'd been saying all along.'

'And I would go back to doubting myself.'

'Do you?' he asked softly. 'Do you still doubt yourself?'

'I don't know,' she replied in the same tone, but her eyes twinkled when she looked up at him. 'Was this a mistake?'

He smiled, and felt his heart thunder in his chest. 'I don't think so.'

'Neither do I.'

Silence beat between them, before Zacchaeus pulled his hands from his pockets and settled them lightly on her waist. 'You're not a fool. And what you told me… It isn't foolish. You had every right to feel the way you felt about it. And I know why you kept it from me.'

'Th…thank you,' she said in an unsteady voice, and then cleared her throat. 'Thank you for understanding.'

'I would have,' he replied. 'I always would have understood. I wouldn't have judged you. I never will, no matter what you do.'

Her hands moved to his chest, one resting over the heart

that was still thumping. 'I know. You're better than I ever imagined you would be. This was definitely not a mistake.'

His lips curved. 'So you trust me now?'

'Do you trust me?'

'More than anyone else I've ever known,' he whispered, and found that it was true.

It stunned him, but he was too caught in her eyes, in the way he could suddenly read exactly what she wanted to care.

'Me, too.' She licked her lips and the pounding of his heart rippled through his blood, creating a heady ache in his body. 'We should go back,' she told him.

But she moved closer to him.

'They'll miss us,' he replied softly.

His eyes flickered down to her lips that were still moist. 'At the very least they'll wonder where we are.'

Her hands moved from his chest to around his waist.

'And they'll make up reasons about why we didn't return.'

His thumb brushed over her lips.

'It'll cause a scandal.' Her body pressed against his. 'A husband and wife leaving their wedding reception before their guests.'

'A newly married couple.' His hands loosened the buttons at the back of her dress. 'Sneaking off on their wedding night.'

'It's unheard of.'

She pushed his jacket from his shoulders. Started on the buttons of his shirt.

'Absolutely.'

The dress fell to the floor just as she finished opening his shirt, and he swallowed at what it revealed. 'Somehow I don't think I'll care,' he told her hoarsely.

She nodded, her eyes hot, and before she touched her lips to his, whispered, 'Me neither.'

CHAPTER SEVENTEEN

NALINI WOKE UP with the sun shining on her.

It took her a while to realise that she wasn't in the bed that had become familiar to her over the past weeks, but in Zacchaeus's. And some more time to realise why the heat of the sun had woken her.

She was lying on the side of the bed directly opposite the window.

She was also naked.

It didn't take long for the memories to return then, and she felt her body grow hot from embarrassment just as much as it did from remembering what they'd got up to the night before. She was prepared for neither. And didn't have the chance to ponder on either before realising she was alone in the bed, too.

It took longer than anticipated to convince herself that it didn't mean anything. And she had to repeat that to herself as she took her shower. The heat of the water soothed aching muscles, sensitive flesh, and the breath shuddered from her lungs at the reason for them.

She was annoyed that she'd woken up alone. And that annoyance covered her panic at what she'd done, no matter how many times she told herself that she hadn't done anything wrong. Still, the uneasy feeling sheathed her heart, forcing her to acknowledge it with every pump.

It would go away when she saw him, she thought, as she

chose her outfit for the day. There was only the briefest moment of hesitation before she picked out a bright yellow dress that would tell the world she was a happy bride who had been thoroughly ravished on her wedding night.

Well, one of those was true.

She hated that she still had doubts after what she'd shared with Zacchaeus the night before. An intimacy that she couldn't have imagined in her wildest dreams. Not only physically—she laid a hand on her chest as though it would keep her heart from reacting to the thought—but emotionally, too. She'd told him about Josh, about the beach. She'd told him about all her insecurities—had revealed that she doubted herself, her decisions.

It wasn't unusual under those circumstances to want to wake up with the person she'd opened up to. To see his face and know that she hadn't made a mistake. That the love she'd felt between them the night before hadn't only been in her head.

Love.

She'd been ready to leave the room and go down for breakfast before she'd thought that. Before she'd found that it hadn't been a realisation but an acknowledgement. The *realisation* had come the night she'd agreed to bring the wedding forward. And the process of it had started long, long before that night.

She'd been in free fall ever since.

Nalini knew now that part of the reason she hadn't wanted to tell Zacchaeus about Josh was because it would strip away that guard she'd put up to prevent herself from admitting she loved him. She'd used what she'd felt for Josh after one month as an excuse not to acknowledge the more intense feelings she'd felt for Zacchaeus in half that time.

Because somewhere in her mind she'd known that when she told Zacchaeus about Josh, the word, the emotion—*love*—that now came naturally with Zacchaeus would no longer be able to taunt her. And she hadn't been sure whether taunting would be better than knowing.

But she couldn't pretend that she didn't know now. She'd told Zacchaeus the truth, and the tumultuous feelings inside her told her she couldn't ignore the cause any more.

But the part of her that wanted to jump for joy that she loved *her husband* was silenced by the part demanding to know why he'd left her.

Because she'd learnt how intuitive Zacchaeus was the previous night. He knew exactly what to say to make her feel warm, comforted. Feelings she'd rarely—if ever—felt before she'd got to know him. He also knew exactly what to do to make her body feel things she'd never felt before, too…

She took a steadying breath and went down to breakfast.

The first thing she noticed was that Zacchaeus wasn't there. Nor were her mother and grandmother, or Alika, Spencer and the nephew she'd barely seen the night before. The only people who *were* there were Leyna and Xavier. She plastered a smile on her face when they looked over at her, and then felt it fall away as soon as she got a good look at Leyna.

'What's wrong?' She strode to the table. 'Should I call for the royal physician?'

Pale as she was, Leyna offered her a weak smile. 'That's not necessary.'

'But you look awful.'

'Nalini!' Xavier said sharply, but Leyna smiled more broadly now.

'It's fine, Xav. She's probably right.'

'No, she's not,' Xavier replied in a soft voice, shooting Nalini a thunderous look.

'He's right,' Nalini said quickly. 'I made a mistake.'

'No, you didn't,' Leyna said wryly and nibbled on a piece of dry toast. 'But, honestly, it's fine. I really don't have the energy to pretend like I care what anyone thinks about how I look.'

'So you *are* ill.'

Nalini watched as Leyna and Xavier exchanged a look, and quickly realised what it meant. Her eyes widened and a smile—wider than she'd ever thought she would give that morning—spread across her face.

'No,' Xavier said quickly when Nalini opened her mouth. 'Don't say it aloud. Not here.'

Annoyance dampened her excitement. 'The people here are perfectly trustworthy. No one will know you're a *fornicator*.' She whispered the last word, but so salaciously that even Leyna chuckled.

'Now that you're married you think you know everything, don't you,' Xavier said dryly—though was that a flush on his skin?

She smiled, but shook her head. She wasn't going to fall into that trap. 'I'm very happy for you both. How far along?'

'Early enough to have it be a honeymoon baby,' Leyna answered.

'An extremely premature one,' Xavier added, a frown furrowing his brow.

'But your invitations are out,' Nalini offered, hating to see her brother so perturbed. 'You're marrying early autumn. It's only a few more weeks away.'

It had been another reason to rush her own wedding. Not that she'd thought of it when she'd offered to bring the date forward, but it had been a good idea after all. She wouldn't want to overshadow the excitement of the wedding of the century. While hers had been merely a royal society wedding, considering that she was a princess, and her King… Well, her King wasn't entirely liked by the world at the moment.

'I'm sorry if I affected your plans in any way,' she told Leyna.

'You haven't,' came the reply. 'Besides, we're indebted to you. If you hadn't agreed to this, we might not be sitting here together, sharing this meal.'

'We don't know what will happen in the future,' Xavier said darkly. 'Macoa is still a threat.'

'Which we'll deal with if and when the time comes,' Leyna said smoothly, and Nalini felt relief flood through her. Her gaze moved between Leyna and Xavier, and envy took the place of relief, before giving way to guilt.

She shouldn't feel jealous of what Leyna and Xavier had. She should be happy that her brother was finally happy. She thought of all he'd been through—having his heart broken by Leyna when he was barely an adult, and then having to mourn the death of the wife he'd married shortly after. Her brother *deserved* the second chance he'd got with his first love.

So why was she suddenly wishing for a chance at love, too?

Just because she'd discovered she was in love with Zacchaeus didn't suddenly mean she would be unrealistic. That she would *hope*. Because though the weight of the night on the beach with Josh had been lifted somewhat, it didn't mean that she'd gone back to being the Nalini she'd been before.

But that's not entirely true.

She frowned at the inner voice and busied herself with preparing her breakfast so she didn't draw attention to herself. But she didn't think she would be able to eat the croissant she'd placed on her plate. Panic and worry were churning in her stomach, destroying her appetite.

She knew she didn't trust the Nalini she'd been before that night on the beach but... But hadn't she told Zacchaeus just the night before that she'd *wanted* to be the person she'd been before that night? That she wanted her will to live back—that she wanted to be excited, to be *happy* about life again?

The uncertainty of it turned in her mind and she sipped her coffee, hoping the caffeine would offer her mind some clarity. She gave it a few minutes, and sighed in relief when it seemed to work.

Yes, she'd wanted to live life again, but that wouldn't make her naïve. Just because she wanted to be happy, excited, didn't mean she wanted to go back to making mistakes. She just wanted to believe in herself again. To stop trying to change the way her family saw her. To claim back the self-belief and confidence that night—and her grandmother and mother's reaction to it—had robbed her of.

And it had worked somewhat, she thought, remembering Xavier's words to her the night before. Her brother no longer seemed to think of her as the reckless teenager he'd warned to be careful before she'd come to Kirtida. And since she knew her grandmother and mother wouldn't be changing their minds—not when they didn't seem to want to—she told herself that that would be enough.

To prove it, she asked Xavier about her family members' absence.

'Did Mama leave?'

'Early this morning,' Xavier confirmed, apology flashing in his eyes. 'They'll get over it, Lini.'

'Like they got over the whole Josh thing?' Nalini said lightly, and told herself it would take time for the wounds to heal. 'Alika?'

'They left with Mama. I don't think they had a choice, but Alika asked me to tell you they were sorry and that she'd call you later today.'

Nalini nodded, and forced the emotion from her voice. 'And Zacchaeus? Have you seen him this morning?'

'We haven't.' Xavier frowned. 'Did you two not sort

things out last night? When you didn't come back last night we all assumed—'

'No, we're fine,' Nalini interrupted her brother, her face burning. She didn't care what he'd assumed—he was still her brother. And she could live her entire life without knowing that he knew what she'd done on the night of her wedding. 'He must be out for his morning run.'

Nalini had no idea whether that was true, but she wasn't going to admit that her husband had slipped out of bed that morning to avoid her.

You don't know if that's true, the voice in her mind supplied, but she ignored it. 'When are you two leaving?'

'We were supposed to be gone a while ago already, but Leyna wasn't quite feeling up to it.'

'I'm better now,' she piped up, the dry piece of toast half-eaten and the colour back in her face. 'We should probably leave before that changes.'

Nalini saw them off and, as she waved, felt both relieved and anxious about being without them on Kirtida. Relieved because she knew her brother saw too much. When he'd kissed her goodbye, he'd given her a long, hard look that had her blushing and looking away. But he'd only murmured that she should look after herself—Leyna's work once again, Nalini thought.

And now that they were gone, along with all the other guests who'd come for the wedding, she was forced to face the fact that she was alone. The fact that she would have a completely new life on Kirtida. There was no more ignoring it. She was now a queen, and would be for the rest of her life. She'd disrupted her entire world because of it, and now she'd be living the reality of it.

But, in a more immediate sense, Nalini was alone because her husband had abandoned her. She rolled her eyes at the thought, and as she set out to find him, hoped she was just being dramatic.

* * *

'Oh, you're alive,' Nalini greeted him when he walked into the bedroom.

Emotion tumbled through him when he saw her. She was wearing a bright yellow dress, a stark contrast to the darkness of the night clear in the windows behind her chair. The last time he'd seen her, she'd been completely naked, sleeping in his bed. Beguiling, beautiful, and so very tempting.

He'd had to escape as soon as he could.

'I had matters to attend to.'

'Me too,' Nalini replied. 'I had to see off the last of our guests.'

'Only your family remained.'

'They were guests,' she repeated, her voice tight. 'I also had the pleasure of lying to them about where you were.'

'I'll send them a note to apologise.'

She laughed mockingly. 'Yes, do that.' When she stood, her dress fell to her knees, drawing his attention to her legs. Legs that had been wrapped around him the night before...

'And now that I know you weren't in some kind of danger, I'll leave you to write your note.'

She tried to walk past him, but he stopped her by sliding a hand around her waist. 'That's what you thought? That I was in danger?'

'How was I supposed to know?' she snapped. 'You just *left*. I didn't know what to think, and danger was preferable to the other thoughts I had, quite frankly.'

'What did you think?' he asked quietly.

'Well, we got married yesterday and then I told you about the most defining experience of my life and we made love.' He winced at her bluntness. 'So, thinking about you in danger was better than thinking you'd run away from me.'

His arm dropped to his side. 'I wasn't running.'

'Of course not. It's not like you've run away from everything that's forced you out of your comfort zone.'

'What's that supposed to mean?'

'I've just noticed a pattern, Zacchaeus. Like this whole thing with Macoa. Instead of turning to your allies for help, you waited *weeks* before saying anything. And the only reason you did was because they'd forced your hand.'

'You know why—'

'And then there's your parents. Have you ever dealt with the way their actions have affected your life? Or have you just been going along with it, ignoring it day after day, *running*?'

'You don't know what you're talking about,' he growled, and resisted the prickling in his chest at her words.

'Maybe not. But I'm not running.'

'You haven't been running away from what you told me last night?'

Her eyes flashed. 'The second part of your sentence contradicts the first. Try again.'

'Do you want to talk about last night, Nalini?' He stepped closer to her, feeling the anger radiate off him. 'Do you want to talk about how we kissed, how we touched, how I took your—'

'Don't.' The word was said fiercely, sharply, with so much emotion that it shut him up. 'I don't care what's happening with you today, Zacchaeus, but you will *not* take what happened between us last night and turn it into something dirty.'

Hurt—pure and simple—settled on her face. He didn't think he'd ever feel as bad as he did right in that moment. But when she spoke again he realised he was wrong.

'I know it meant something to you. So much that you felt the need to disappear for our entire first day of being married to deal with it.' She paused. 'Unless I'm wrong? Did something happen with your father? Macoa?'

Shame had the words sticking in his throat, and he shook his head. She gave one quick nod.

'Right, so you were running.' There was another pause. 'Goodnight, Zacchaeus.'

She walked out of the room and, though he urged his legs to move, to go after her, they remained where they were. It was a long time before they did move, and then it was to his shower and not after his wife.

Why did he keep thinking of her that way? It was as if a switch had been flicked, and suddenly he couldn't think of her as anything other than his wife. The woman who would rule by his side. Who would bear his children. Who would ensure that he was no longer alone.

He threw off his clothes and put the shower on full pressure, hoping to drown his thoughts. But they stayed with him. Just as they had during the hours he'd spent aimlessly driving around his kingdom, looking for answers he hadn't found until he'd come home and spoken to Nalini.

He'd been running.

He'd been running from the emotion that had nearly choked him when he'd looked down at Nalini in his arms, her face still flushed from their love-making, but so sleepy she could barely keep her eyes open. He'd been running from the tenderness that he'd felt brushing the curls from her face, from pressing a kiss against those soft, full lips. And the complete and utter infatuation he'd felt when she'd given him a sleepy smile and snuggled into him, her heart beating rhythmically, steadily, against his own.

For the first time in his life he hadn't felt alone. And it was that, and the fact that she was his *wife*, and the feelings thrumming through his blood—feelings that had finally caught up with him—that had prompted him to slip out of the room as soon as the sun had come up and drive around the whole of his kingdom.

He'd known it would hurt her. Had hated himself *for*

hurting her. But he knew he would have made it worse if he'd stayed and she'd woken up to him that morning. If she'd looked at him with that warmth in her eyes and that complete and utter trust. No, her anger was better. He could handle that. He could even handle her disappointment. In fact, he welcomed it.

Weren't those *supposed* to be the feelings of a wife, after all?

He let the water run over his head for a few more minutes and then got out of the shower, dressed and poured himself a drink. If he was honest with himself, he knew that that had disintegrated the box he'd hidden his feelings in.

Thinking about his mother. Witnessing her be a wife to his father. And a terrible one at that.

He knew that being honest with himself would send him down a rabbit hole he would struggle to climb out of again. He'd been keeping himself above it for most of the day—running from it, as Nalini said. But now that he'd thought it, he realised it was too late. It was sucking him in, forcing him to think about his parents.

About all the times he'd seen them argue. About how his mother had blamed his father for things that had never been Jaydon's fault. He remembered the countless instances he'd told himself that he'd never want what they had. That he would never want a political marriage.

And now that he had one, what did that mean?

No matter how long, how hard he thought about it, he couldn't come up with an answer. But he knew someone who could help him figure it out. So he set his drink, still full, aside and prepared to have a long, honest conversation with his father.

CHAPTER EIGHTEEN

SHE WANTED TO PAINT. She also wanted to be outside in the garden.

But she didn't want to paint outside and lose the privacy she had indoors. And since her need to be out in the open, away from the confines of the castle—which were beginning to suffocate her—trumped her desire to release her emotions onto a canvas, she opted for a walk in the garden.

Nalini took a deep breath as she made her way through the trees, following along the stream she'd fallen into at their engagement shoot. Where they'd shared their first kiss that same night. Her life had been significantly less complicated then, she thought. And laughed when she realised she'd thought her life complicated *then*.

But she gave herself the benefit of the doubt, and blamed it on inexperience. It was different from how she'd dealt with her mistakes before. When everything with Josh had happened, she'd hated that she'd been so inexperienced. Naïve. Irresponsible.

But now she knew that she deserved more than to think of herself that way. She knew that it was enough to know that she'd changed. And she felt so sure about all of it that she refused to consider what her inexperience had cost her this time around.

Though she could hardly ignore it.

The pain of her broken heart was there in every breath,

in every movement. The panic that she'd got it all wrong was still lingering in her mind. But she didn't want to live like that any more. She'd left Mattan because she wanted to get away from the person she'd become. That person had been unkind to herself. She'd been so terrified of making mistakes—of living up, or down, rather, to the expectations her family had of her—that she didn't trust that she had learnt. That she had grown.

It had taken an entire week to come to that conclusion. And now that she had she finally felt a sense of the freedom she'd so intensely longed for. *And* the independence she'd wanted, considering she'd been relying on herself for the past week since her husband had seemingly disappeared…

And, yes, maybe she had spent the first half of the week weeping about a relationship that had never existed. She wasn't sure how she'd convinced herself that she was in a relationship—personal, not political—with Zacchaeus. Perhaps it had been sleeping together…

But as soon as that thought had occurred to her she'd dismissed it. She'd thought there was something more between them long before their wedding night. That was the very reason she'd slept with him that night after all.

It had panicked her, but then she'd realised that it wasn't the same as with her and Josh. Because *she* wasn't the same. And that was the difference, she'd realised. She could be terrified that she'd made a mistake coming to Kirtida, marrying Zacchaeus. She could be *petrified* that she'd fallen in love with him.

Or she could accept that it had happened and move forward.

There was plenty else to focus on. She was Queen now. She had a new home to explore and relationships, friendships, to develop. She'd rediscovered her love of painting, and would seek solace in that instead of in the arms of her husband. She would be fine, she told herself over the voice in her head telling her it wouldn't be that easy.

It might not be easy but it would be worth it, she thought, and settled at the bank of the stream, pulling her shoes off to dip her feet into the water.

'Careful. We wouldn't want you falling in.'

Her hair stood on end at Zacchaeus's voice, and the zen she'd felt abruptly disappeared as she heard him settle down next to her. Stubbornly, she refused to look at him. Or to acknowledge him at all. She closed her eyes and took another deep breath, willing herself to focus on how the breeze felt a little cooler today. The first sign of autumn coming, she thought.

But no matter how much she wanted to focus on the weather, she couldn't. Because every time she took a breath she smelled that knee-weakening scent of his. It had her opening her eyes, clenching her jaw, before she managed to grind out, 'What do you want?'

'I thought I'd spend the afternoon with my wife.'

'Too little, too late. I have no intention of—'

'You didn't let me finish,' he interrupted her quietly. 'I thought we could talk.'

'I don't want to talk.'

'Why not?'

'Because I don't want to keep feeling this way. After every conversation we have I feel awful, and it takes me so long to right myself again.' She refused to look at him. 'I'm fine with the way things are. With not seeing each other. I'm fine with you running. I just don't want to keep running with you.'

'I'm not running any more.'

That got her attention and when she looked at him she wished she'd kept to her resolve. Because now she couldn't get the image of him with that wounded look out of her mind long enough to find the strength to leave him at the stream.

'What happened?'

'My father…' Zacchaeus's face paled. 'I think I've… I've finally allowed myself to face the fact that he's dying.'

She reached out, squeezed his hand, and then snatched it back. 'I'm sorry.'

He nodded and there was a long pause before he spoke again. 'I don't want him to die.'

'Of course you don't. He's your father.'

'I don't want him to die,' Zacchaeus said again, almost as if he hadn't heard her, 'when I'm so damn angry at him.'

The anger heated his skin so much that Zacchaeus wished he could take off his clothes and let the stream run over him. But he knew that would only give him temporary relief. He'd tried having a cold shower after every single visit with his father, since that first night he'd decided to speak with him.

But Zacchaeus's first reaction that night had been to face the pain. His father was dying, and Nalini had been right about how he'd dealt with it—he hadn't.

He'd ignored the reality of what his father's illness meant, had instead focused on protecting Kirtida. But now that that was no longer such a pressing factor, he couldn't keep ignoring that the man he loved and respected would be leaving him soon.

During that first meeting with his father he'd been overwhelmed with emotion. Zacchaeus hadn't been able to ask the questions he'd needed to. He'd spent his time telling his father about the wedding, about the alliance. He'd basically spent all that time telling his father he didn't have to worry about the future of Kirtida any more. Zacchaeus had stayed the night at his father's side, afraid that that peace of mind would finally be a reason for his father to let go.

But when he'd woken up the next morning, his father had seemed better, stronger than the day before. And Zacchaeus had realised he needed to ask his questions now, before it was too late.

After that conversation, the heat—the *anger*—had begun, and when he'd returned to his room he'd taken an ice-cold shower. But that had only helped to cool his skin and as soon as he'd finished he'd felt the heat all over again.

And so it had gone for the last week. Somehow Zacchaeus had found himself caught between his anger and love for his father. Between not wanting to see Jaydon again and being unable to stop himself from spending hours there. Just because Jaydon was feeling better again didn't mean he was miraculously healed. In fact, the royal physician had warned that it could mean the exact opposite.

Zacchaeus would never be able to forgive himself if he let his anger—or any of the other emotions he was feeling—keep him from his father. Especially during what could be his last days.

But it was hard on Zacchaeus, and he'd spent hours in silence at his father's side some days. Others, he couldn't stop the questions from pouring out of his lips. His father would answer what he could—or what he chose to.

And Zacchaeus had found it all so dark, so overwhelming, until he couldn't take it any more and had to find his source of light.

Even though he hadn't seen her in almost seven full days.

'You're angry at him?' Nalini asked. 'For dying?'

'No.' Then he thought about it, and realised there was truth in that, too. 'Yes, maybe I am.'

'That's normal,' she said soothingly. But she didn't touch him again, even though he saw her curl her fingers into a fist as if she'd wanted to. 'I felt the same way after my father died.'

'Does it ever go away?'

She didn't answer him immediately. 'I think that first burst of anger does. The completely irrational kind. You realise that it isn't their fault—that they didn't intentionally choose to leave.' She paused. 'But… It's still hard at times. You miss them, and it's easier to blame them for their absence than to face the pain of it. I imagine it must be the same with an illness.'

'More, maybe. Because they're not gone yet and now you know…you *know* that they will be and you have to say everything you want to say to them. But you can't. There's no time and you're…you're stuck,' he ended helplessly, unsure of where all those words had come from.

'You don't have to feel bad about it,' she said softly. 'Don't feel bad for your feelings, whatever they are.'

'But I do.'

'Why?'

'Because *they* are bad.'

'You mean…negative?'

He nodded now, unable to put it into words any more.

'That's fine too. I doubt there's a child out there who doesn't have negative feelings towards their parents.'

'Has your mother been…?' He faltered.

Could he ask about how her mother had been since their wedding? He would have known, after all, if he'd been there. If he'd been an actual husband. Guilt added to the heat.

'Oh, she's been…' Nalini shrugged. 'I haven't spoken to her since the wedding. I figured I'd give her some time to adjust to this new reality.'

'I'm sorry.'

'Don't apologise. It's not like it's your fault.' There was a beat of silence and then she giggled. It was a sound he hadn't expected to hear from her that day, but one he'd desperately needed to. 'Actually, all of this *is* kind of your fault.'

And for the first time in a week he felt his lips curve. 'I'm not sure that's entirely fair.'

Her smile faded and she tilted her head. 'Things aren't always fair.'

He realised then that he hadn't been treating *her* very fairly and told himself to swallow his pride. 'I know I'm a part of the reason you're saying that and… Well, I'm sorry.'

'What are you apologising for, Zacchaeus?'

'For…for not being around this last week.'

'That's it?'

He opened his mouth, but realised that the question was a trap. If he said yes, she would surely tell him all the things that he had to be sorry for. If he said no, she would expect him to elaborate and he wouldn't be able to.

His mind raced through the possibilities, and settled on what she'd said when he'd joined her. That is was too late to spend time with her. But wasn't that what he'd just apologised for? There was more, he thought, and remembered that she'd also said she needed to recover from their conversations. What did that mean?

Before he could ask, she shook her head. 'You know what, you don't have to answer that. Your silence has already answered my question.'

'Now *you're* not being fair,' he said. 'Regardless of what answer I'd have given you, it would have been the wrong one. And now you're telling me that *no answer* was wrong too?'

'Why are you here, Zacchaeus?' she asked again. 'And I don't want any of that "wanting to spend time with me" crap.'

'It's not crap. I really wanted to spend time with you.'

'Why?'

'That's a stupid question.'

'Not as stupid as you being unable to answer me.' She waited, and then gave a bark of laughter. 'I can't believe this.' She slipped her wet feet into her shoes and pushed up from the ground, refusing the help he offered her as soon as he'd realised her intention and stood.

'Nalini, come on. I just wanted to spend some time with you. I've been with my father basically every moment since we last spoke. I need some…some reprieve from that.'

'And what would you like me to do to help? Sing a song? Tell a joke?'

He felt the anger ripple again. 'You know that's not what I mean.'

'Well, you can't seem to tell me what you mean, so how am I supposed to know?' She didn't wait for an answer. 'I'm fine with you leaving me to deal with the aftermath of the wedding, to write thank you notes and call to make sure our guests arrived home safely. I'm fine with you disappearing after we *made love* and ignoring the fact that I'm a human being. With feelings. And that I'd have feelings about the fact that *we made love*.' Scarlet streaked across her cheeks. 'But I'm *not* fine with you using me whenever *you* think it's an appropriate time.'

She took a step closer to him and poked him in the chest. 'Because, regardless of what you think, I *am* a human being and I *do* have feelings. I'm not going to accept being treated like this again.'

She stomped off, leaving him speechless. And when his thoughts had finally caught up with his lips, he opened his mouth to tell her that that was absolutely ridiculous. But she was gone.

He ran back to the castle and asked the first person he saw where Nalini was. Though the man didn't know where she'd been heading, Zacchaeus had a fairly good idea. An idea that was confirmed when he reached the tower room and saw her pacing there.

The room had more paintings in it now, and his eyes flew over them before he spoke. There were paintings of the storm on the beach the night of their date, and of the room next to the kitchen where they'd spent that evening. There was a painting of the church they'd been married in, and of the hall where they'd held their reception.

But there were also paintings of him. One that perfectly captured the way he'd felt when he'd seen her on their wedding day, and the way he'd looked at her during their first dance. There was only one of them together—they were in each other's arms, staring intently into each other's eyes. He recognised it as the moment before they'd made love, and when his eyes finally met hers again he realised what she'd been asking him to apologise for.

'I'm so sorry, Nalini.'

'You've already said that.'

'But now I know… I've hurt you and I'm sorry.'

'I've been hurt before,' she said softly, and her expression told him that she meant him to think that it was no big deal. But he knew that it was, and the fact that she was comparing him to the jerk who'd hurt her so long ago confirmed it.

'But I shouldn't have been the one to hurt you.'

'Spouses hurt each other all the time.'

'You're right. But those who want a healthy relationship should apologise. They shouldn't let it build and build until there's nothing left in the marriage except a piece of paper binding it.'

Her expression softened. 'You're right. But you're not talking about us, are you?'

'No, I am,' he disagreed. 'Just as it should be. Us. You and me.' He blew out a breath, felt his shoulders tighten. 'I've been letting my parents get between us from the moment you arrived at Kirtida. I won't let that happen any more.'

CHAPTER NINETEEN

'THOUGH PERHAPS I should thank them,' Zacchaeus continued. 'They *are* the reason you're on Kirtida, after all.'

Nalini let the attempt at lightening the mood float over her and instead focused on the hurt she saw clear in Zacchaeus's eyes. He was trying to pretend that the realisation he'd just come to hadn't affected him. He was trying to shrug it off, to make it seem unimportant.

But she knew him well enough now to recognise when he was pretending. Hadn't she known from the moment she'd arrived on Kirtida that he wasn't the man he was pretending to be?

And suddenly everything changed for her. All the excuses, the front that she would be fine without him. She only had to look around the room at her paintings to realise that she'd only been fooling herself.

She only had to look at the man in front of her to realise that her love for him wouldn't be ignored.

'They hurt you.'

His eyes met hers and she hoped he would see what she wanted to say in her own. That he didn't have to keep up a front any more. That he didn't have to be alone. She was there, and he could trust her with everything whirling around in his mind. He could lean on her—he would always be able to.

'Yes,' he said, seemingly getting her message. 'I only

realised how much the day after our wedding. After you fell asleep in my arms the night before, actually.'

'You were afraid I'd hurt you like they did?'

'I… I couldn't put into words how I felt,' he said a little helplessly. 'All I knew was that I was completely overwhelmed with emotions I couldn't name and so I… I left that morning to try and figure out what they were.'

'Did you?'

'Not then. But when I came back, after I spoke to you…' His lips twisted into a wry smile. 'I *had* been running from everything that I'd been feeling. I knew it, but that didn't keep me from running. But after speaking to you… I figured I'd talk to my father, because I knew some of it came from my mother. From the fact that their marriage was so messed up. And now that I was married—'

'You were scared it would somehow be the same for you.'

'Yes.' He ran a hand over the back of his neck. 'And I think I was afraid that you'd hurt me, too. Because you'd started to mean something to me, and the only other people I'd cared for… They'd betrayed that trust I gave them.'

Her heart filled, but she forced herself to calm down. This wasn't about whether he cared for her. It was about getting him to be okay with the fact that he did.

'How?'

'It's…complicated. And I'm not saying that because I don't want you to know,' he added with a smile—a nod to their previous conversations. 'I'm saying it because… Well, there are so many feelings. I think they both betrayed me by being such terrible parents. As close to my dad as I was growing up, I can see that he wasn't a good father now. He was a fair one, and an excellent mentor, but not a father. And my mother?' He gave a menacing laugh. 'She wasn't a mother at all. I had no relationship with her. Still don't. But I expected her to stay. To be a queen. To be a family.'

His eyes met hers. 'We were a messed-up family, but it was the only one I knew. And her leaving, and all the stuff that happened afterwards, with Macoa? She broke the unspoken rules of our family.'

'Do you have any idea…why she left?'

'No. But I hate that she did, and that she left such a mess. And I hate that my father asked me to go along with his plan—with the coup—because he didn't want *her* to know he was ill. I feel like I'm a pawn. And now that my father can no longer play, he wants me to take over for him.'

Surprise clutched her heart. 'He asked you to do that?'

'Not directly. But what do you think this coup was?' He began to pace. 'And then I had to pull strings to protect the kingdom. The *kingdom*. They were both supposed to protect it, but instead they put their people in danger. All because of their hatred for each other.'

No wonder he was turned inside out, she thought, and let go of all the resentment she felt about the last week. '*You* protected them, though. They're your people now, and you protected them.'

'But what happens if my mother chooses to go ahead with this plan?' His tone was desperate. 'I wish she would just wait. Just until…' He stopped pacing and braced his hands on his knees. She nearly stepped forward, but he straightened again and she waited for the words that had caused him such anguish. 'Just until my father goes,' he continued in a strangled voice.

Seconds passed before either of them spoke.

'You could ask her,' Nalini suggested softly.

'What? Ask the woman who left her family to live with her lover for *compassion*?'

'People are rarely as bad as their actions make them seem,' she replied, and her thoughts turned to her own family. Perhaps it was time she had an honest conversation with her mother and grandmother, she thought, and then brushed it away. 'It's only a suggestion, and if she says yes…'

She let the possibility linger, and saw that he was considering it. But his eyes changed suddenly when he looked at her, and her heart started to thud.

'What?'

'You're amazing.'

'No, I'm just trying to help.'

'I don't deserve your help.'

'You're my husband.'

'And that means something to you, doesn't it?' He was staring at her intensely and she felt her cheeks grow hot.

'I'm not sure what you mean.'

'I mean that this isn't only some political thing for you. You…you actually believe in marriage.'

She laughed softly. 'I didn't want to. I convinced myself that I didn't, in fact. For a very long time.'

'Because of Josh?' She nodded. 'What changed your mind?'

'You.'

He wasn't sure why the answer surprised him so much. Perhaps because there was still a part of him that was tainted by witnessing his parents' marriage.

But something told him that was about to change.

'What about me?' he asked softly, and breached the gap between them.

'Well, you…' He loved the colour of her cheeks—how, when she was feeling uncertain, she pulled at a curl. 'You…you showed me that I could trust you.'

'No, I didn't.' And it shamed him. 'I probably showed you the opposite when I left you in bed that morning.'

'You're not perfect,' she allowed with a small smile. 'But I understand now. You were scared.'

'You didn't have to understand. You could have been resentful. Angry.'

As he said the words, he thought *he* was beginning to understand what had happened with his parents. His father had told him that their political relationship had turned into love, but that feeling had gone away soon after they'd got married. By the time Zacchaeus had been born, their relationship had been broken.

It hadn't been anything specific, Jaydon had told him, but numerous small things. Resentment had been conceived, anger born, and soon they were living separate lives.

But, throughout it all, Zacchaeus had realised one thing. His father still loved his mother. But his pride, his stubbornness, his hurt, had kept him from telling her that. And now her actions pierced more sharply than Jaydon would ever understand.

He would not inherit his father's foolishness.

'I've *been* angry. *And* resentful,' Nalini answered him. 'But that gave me a life I didn't want. It had me trying to prove to my family that I was someone I already was instead of trusting that *I* knew it. So I forgive you, Zacchaeus.'

'Just like that?'

'No,' she replied, just as he'd hoped she would. 'I'd like to ask you not to shut me out again. I know that you're used to being alone, but—'

'It's not that,' he interrupted. 'Or not only that. I was… scared.'

'Of what?'

'My feelings for you.' He walked towards her, stopping only a few centimetres away. 'I've seen the kind of marriage my parents had. It was a political one, just like this, and it was terrible.'

She frowned. 'You were afraid the same thing would happen to you?'

'Yes.' He leaned his forehead against hers for a moment and then drew back. 'But it won't be terrible, will it?'

'Not if we treat each other with respect. If we talk about things, and don't shut each other out.'

'I agree. But I'm not sure this marriage is strictly political any more.'

Her tongue slid over her lips and his heart began to race. If he remembered correctly, that very thing had got them into trouble the first time...

'I don't think so, no,' she whispered, and when she looked up he saw everything he needed to in her eyes.

'We've been fighting it.'

'*You've* been fighting it,' she said with a smile and wrapped her arms around his waist, resting her head on his chest. 'I've just been trying to figure out how to get it through your stubborn skull.'

'Is that any way to talk to your husband?' he said softly, his own arms drawing her in, squeezing.

'Depends. Am I talking to him as man or king?'

He chuckled. 'They're still the same. Except, I think, they're both a little better for loving you, my queen.'

She lifted her head, her eyes shining. 'Loving?'

'Did you think I spent our wedding night with you for the sake of an heir?' he teased, and grew sober when a blush stained her cheeks. 'You did? Nalini, that's my fault. I'm sorry.'

'The thought crossed my mind. But only because I didn't want to consider that you loved me...' She trailed off and bit her lip.

He smiled. 'You don't have to be ashamed to say it. I *do* love you. And I hope you'll let me make up for the way I behaved last week.'

'Was that ever *not* an option?' she asked with a half-smile. She brushed her thumb across his cheek, and then over his lips, before laying her own there. 'I love you, too,' she whispered when she pulled back. 'And I trust you. I never thought either would be possible again.'

He tightened his arms around her. 'I still hate that you had to go through that.'

'It brought me here, to you, didn't it?' She tilted her head. 'If you have to thank your parents, then I guess I have to thank Josh—my mother, my grandmother—all of them, too.'

'Because they're the reason we're together.'

She nodded. 'But *we're* the reason we'll stay together.'

'For ever,' he promised, and kissed her again.

EPILOGUE

'AND?' NALINI ASKED as soon as Zacchaeus emerged from his library. But she didn't have to hear his answer to know what it would be. The grim, stressed lines across his forehead had eased, and the smile on his face wasn't forced.

But still she let him answer so that she could hear his success out loud. 'She agreed. My mother won't push for the divorce, and there'll be no more threats from Macoa.'

She flew into his arms and laughed when he spun her around and planted a kiss on her lips.

'Everything's going to be okay.'

'Everything's going to be okay,' she repeated, and welcomed her own relief.

She knew that for Zacchaeus, this was about more than just his mother agreeing to his suggestion. It was about speaking to his mother at all, andasking her for something. She was surprised Michelle had agreed but, just as she'd told him, Nalini believed that people were rarely as bad as they seemed.

It was also about giving his father the chance to die with dignity. About protecting his kingdom and now, she knew, protecting Mattan too.

'I can't believe it's going to be okay, that it's all over.' She gave him the time he needed to comprehend it. 'Now we can finally enjoy being married.'

'Have you not been enjoying our marriage?' she asked.

'Because I could have *sworn* you were incredibly happy last night when—'

'Ha,' he said, nuzzling her neck. 'You've become quite the comedian, haven't you?'

'Actually, I think I've always been one. You just haven't really appreciated me.'

She laughed when the nuzzle turned into a nip.

'Now I get to spend the rest of my life appreciating you. Aren't I lucky?' he said wryly, but gave her a smile that told her he thought he was. 'Do you think we should tell Leyna and Xavier? They could still stop their marriage if they wanted to.'

'Why would they want to do that?'

'Because they were forced to marry because of me.'

'You do know that they've been in love for ever?'

'I… Yes.'

'And didn't you take the credit for bringing them together?'

He grimaced. 'It was a power move. I didn't really mean it.'

She grinned. 'Yes, well, I'm sure they're grateful. Now.'

Zacchaeus tilted his head. 'So I'm kind of responsible for the happiness of the entire Isles?'

'I wouldn't go that far, mister.' She poked him in the stomach. 'I can think of at least two people who you've made very *unhappy*.'

He sobered. 'Did either your mother or grandmother take your call today?'

'No, but I know they will eventually.' She'd told herself there was nothing she could do about them not wanting to speak to her. And she reminded herself that it wouldn't last for ever. As misguided as they were, her grandmother and mother loved her. And some day they would see what she'd done for her kingdom and change their minds about who they thought she was. 'Besides, if they don't want to speak over the phone, I'll just pitch on the island. It's not like they can refuse to see me—'

She broke off when Zacchaeus picked her up and threw her over his shoulder. Pretty much like a sack of potatoes.

'Hey!'

'I know that was a jab at me.'

'No! I completely forgot you refused to see Xavier and Leyna when they tried to contact you about the alliance after you became King.'

'Really?' he asked sarcastically. 'You seem to remember the details of it quite clearly now.'

'My memory is better when I'm upside down.' He laughed, and she tapped his butt. 'Put me down.'

He immediately set her on her feet, and she frowned. 'I thought I was going to have to fight for that.'

'I was being silly anyway.' He kissed her nose. 'Come on, let's take a walk on the beach.'

She took the hand he offered and happily let him guide her to the beach. She loved this new life. She'd only been living it fully for two days, but she loved it. She loved the banter with her new husband, and how much easier he'd been to live with—how laid-back he'd become. Because she knew he was finally allowing himself the freedom, the happiness, he hadn't thought would be his.

And, yes, perhaps it was also because she was doing the same. That finally she didn't feel careless—or like a failure—because this decision had worked out. And because she knew that even if it hadn't she still would have been okay.

Waking up next to her incredibly sexy husband every day was an added benefit.

'Last time we tried this it failed horribly,' Zacchaeus said, interrupting her thoughts. She only realised then that they'd stopped a short distance from the rock they'd had their date on a while ago.

'I'm not sure *failed* is the right word.'

'Maybe not,' he replied with a smile. 'But I still thought it would be nice to try it again.'

'A little different now during the daytime,' she said softly, and let him lift her when they reached the rock. The table was set beautifully, with delicious food almost spilling over their plates and their glasses filled with champagne.

'It won't be daytime for long,' he told her. 'Sunset's coming up, and this pretty much gives you the best view of it on the island.'

'And we won't get wet?' she teased.

'We'll leave before it even becomes a possibility,' he replied, and reached into a bag she hadn't seen next to his seat. He pulled out a small square that was wrapped, and when she took it from him she felt the hollow middle that told her it was a canvas.

'What is this?'

'Open it.'

She tore the wrapping open with shaky fingers, and saw a collage of words that had been printed onto it.

'I'm not a painter,' he told her, and she heard the nerves in his voice. 'There would be no chance of me ever being able to create anything as beautiful as the portrait you made of me. But…' He took a breath. 'But I thought that I could still show you what I thought of you. I had all the words I could think of that best described you printed on it.'

Her eyes moved over the words. She knew that she wouldn't be able to read them all then, but she saw enough of them to feel the tears in her eyes. *Strong. Kind. Independent. Sweet.* And then there were the ones that he'd made up. *Kicks-you-in-the-butt-when-you-need-it. Best-kisser. Purest-heart-in-the-world.*

She bit her lip and looked up at him, and saw the anxiety in his eyes before he even asked, 'Do you like it?'

'I love it,' she whispered, and leaned over to kiss him.

'You don't have to say that,' he told her when she settled back again.

She looked at the words again, felt her heart fill as she saw new ones. 'I'm not just saying it. I love it. You know how…' Her voice wobbled and she rolled her eyes with a smile. 'You know I've never really heard any of this before.'

'That's why I wanted to do it,' he said softly. 'I just wanted you to have something that showed you how I see you. Just like your painting did for me.'

'I'm so lucky,' she said, setting the canvas on her lap. She reached for his hand and threaded her fingers through his.

'No, I'm the lucky one. You've changed me.' His hand tightened around hers. 'You've given me the courage to be myself. To trust. To love.'

'You've done exactly the same for me. And you've given me the push I needed to believe in myself. To trust that I know who I am, and to believe that that's all that matters.'

'We're a pretty amazing couple, aren't we?'

She laughed. 'Yes, I'd say that we are.'

She sighed in contentment and settled back to watch the sun set with her husband.

* * * * *

A SOLDIER IN
CONARD COUNTY

RACHEL LEE

To all the men and women
who have made sacrifices the rest
of us can't begin to comprehend.
May you find comfort.

Prologue

Followed by a smaller car, the hearse backed up behind Watkins Funeral Home on Poplar Street in Conard City, Wyoming. The old Victorian-style mansion looked fresh in every detail, although buildings around it appeared a little shabby.

As the hearse stopped, the driver climbed out of the following car. Wearing the ASU blue army uniform— dark blue coat and lighter blue slacks with a gold stripe running up the side of them—he stood staring at the nondescript white double doors bearing the discreetly lettered sign Arrivals. His many ribbons gleamed on his chest, and his uniform sported the insignia of the special forces and paratrooper. His upper arm patch ranked him as a sergeant first class; five golden hash marks on the lower sleeve recorded at least fifteen years of service. A brass nameplate identified him as "York." He stood tall and straight, every line of him like a fresh crease.

Then he settled his green beret on his head, squaring it exactly from long experience. The driver exited the hearse and went to knock on the door. Sgt. York had brought home the body of his best buddy, Al Baker, and he intended to ensure that everything was done right.

The funeral director was waiting. Gil York watched as the flag-draped coffin was rolled indoors on a table, then followed when it was moved to a viewing room and placed on a blue-skirted catafalque. There would be no open coffin. If anyone in the family wanted to see, Gil would prevent it. Some things should not be seen.

"I'll notify the family he's here," the funeral director said in a quiet voice.

Sgt. Gil York nodded. "You arranged the honor guard?"

"We have a group of vets in the area who do the honors," the director said.

"The bugler?"

"Sgt. Baker's cousin wants to play 'Taps,'" the director said. "She teaches music at the high school."

From gray eyes that resembled the hard Western mountains, Gil looked at him. "It'll be difficult. It's tough even when it's not your own family."

The director nodded. "I warned her. She insists."

* * *

An hour later, the viewing room began to slowly fill with quiet, sad life. Sgt. York, now wearing white gloves, stood at the foot of the coffin, still at attention, his beret tucked under his arm, surrounded by the flowers the funeral director had arranged. Quiet voices murmured, as if afraid of disturbing the dead.

Gil stared straight ahead, but he wasn't really seeing the room or the people. Instead he was seeing the years he had known Al Baker, filled with dangerous, tense, funny and good memories. His brother-in-arms. His friend through it all.

The flowers reached through his memories, sickeningly sweet. Al wouldn't have liked them. He'd have understood the need for people to send them, but he still wouldn't have liked them.

What he would have liked was the battlefield cross: the empty boots, the nose-down M-16, his green beret resting on the butt. His buddies had planted one for him in the Middle East at their base camp, and Gil had constructed one here, with a variation: he'd covered the rifle butt not with a helmet but with Al's green beret, a symbol they had worked so hard to win and of which they had both been very proud.

One more day, Al, he thought. *Just one more day and you'll be at rest.* No more traveling, no more being shunted all over the world. Peace at last, the peace they had both believed they'd been fighting for all along. Not the right kind of peace, but peace anyway. Gil wasn't sure if there was a heaven. He'd seen too much of hell in his life, but if there was a heaven, he was certain Al was standing post already, free of fear and threats.

His eyes closed for a moment, and Al seemed to stand before him in full dress uniform. Straight and squared away and…smiling.

Godspeed.

The murmuring voices suddenly fell silent. Instantly alert, he turned his head a little and saw a man and woman walking toward the coffin. The woman wore black and leaned heavily on the man's arm.

Al's parents. He recognized them from photos. At once he pivoted so he faced the room and the approaching couple. Al's mother made no attempt to conceal the tears that rolled down her face. His father looked grim, and his jaw worked as he clung to self-control.

The couple approached the flag-covered coffin, and Betsy Baker reached out a hand to touch it. "I want to see him."

Gil tensed, wondering if he would have to warn her off.

The funeral director hurried over and took her hand gently, sparing Gil the necessity. "Please, Betsy."

"I want to see him," she repeated brokenly.

Gil nearly stepped forward. The funeral director spoke first. "No. You don't."

Then Betsy startled Gil. She turned her head, and her brown eyes, so like Al's, locked with his. "You're Gil, aren't you?"

"Yes, ma'am."

"I can't see him?"

Gil broke his rigid posture and went to the woman's side, taking her hand from the funeral director. "Mrs. Baker, Al wouldn't want you to see him now. He'd be very grateful if you didn't. Trust me."

"Sgt. York is right," said Mr. Baker, speaking for the first time. "He's right, Betsy."

The woman squeezed her eyes closed and more huge tears rolled down her face. "All right," she whispered. "All right." Then her voice strengthened. "There's a supper afterward, Gil. Please come. I'm sure Al would like that."

"Yes, ma'am."

Then he resumed his post, rigid as steel, all the barriers back in place. Little could touch him there, and there he remained. Service tomorrow at two. Interment at three. Then back to base.

He'd done this before. He wanted never to do it again.

At graveside the next day, Miriam Baker, Al's younger cousin, stood nervously by the riflemen who were part of the honor guard. She knew most of the guard because they lived in the county, and they'd let her know exactly what to expect and when she was to play her trumpet. They'd bucked her up, too, assuring her she'd do just fine. She wasn't nearly as certain as she pretended to be. Al's loss had carved a hole in her heart that kept tightening her chest at unexpected moments. If that happened while she played "Taps"...

Another car arrived, one she didn't recognize. It stopped in an area away from the gravesite. Then, unfolding from it, was a tall man in army blue, with white gloves on his hands and a green beret that he immediately put on his head. For a moment, he stood surveying the scene: six uniformed pallbearers waiting beside the gravel road. The three riflemen near her.

Gil York. It had to be, even though he hadn't come to the supper last night.

All of a sudden she felt seriously inadequate. The wind whipped her navy-blue concert gown around her lower legs as if trying to pick her up and sweep her away. Only the familiar weight of the trumpet in her hand pinned her to the ground.

Gil York was Al's best friend. Everyone had known in advance that he was bringing Al home. He was also the NCOIC, according to Wade Kendrick and the other vets who had gathered around her extended family in the days since the news arrived. Noncommissioned officer in charge. He would be making sure the entire honor guard did a clean and perfect job.

And then there was her. She could feel his gaze fixate on her. He exchanged salutes with the pallbearers as he passed them, said something that caused them to relax for a moment.

Suddenly, he was standing in front of her, looking as if he'd been carved from granite and put in that dressy uniform. "Ms. Baker," he said. "I'm Gil York."

"I know," she answered, her mouth suddenly dry. "I'm supposed to stand thirty to fifty yards away, right?" Cling to the orders for the day, try not to think too hard about her loss. Everyone's loss.

"That's not as much my concern, ma'am, as you are."

"Me?" Her voice cracked. She was not ordinarily a mouse, but since word had been delivered that Al had been killed, a lot of things seemed to have turned topsy-turvy.

"'Taps' is very difficult to play, Ms. Baker. And I don't mean musically. This is going to be very difficult for you emotionally. If you have any doubt about your ability, let me know. I have the authorized digital recording with me."

Her back stiffened a bit. "It's something I can do for Al. I want to do it. I'll cry later."

Their eyes locked, hers as blue as the summer sky, his as gray as rain-wet slate.

"Very well," he said after a few stretched-out seconds. "If you change your mind, just let me know." Then he turned to the riflemen, who told him they'd already picked out the location for them and for Miri.

Sgt. York approved, saluted and started to pivot away. Suddenly he turned back. "Commander Hardin?"

Seth Hardin, decked out in dark navy blue, smiled faintly. "It's been a while, Sergeant."

"Yes, it has." He nodded, then pivoted and marched away.

There was steel in the man's spine, Miriam thought. She wondered if he ever walked normally, or if he was forever marching, executing tight corners and sharp about-faces.

Not today. Certainly not today.

She and the riflemen backed up to the small knoll Seth Hardin had chosen for them. Thirty to fifty yards from the gravesite for them and the bugler. Apparently, everything was measured out with these formalities.

She only wished she had a real bugle, but the trumpet was acceptable. At least she was sure she could play it.

Events began to blur. The hearse arrived. Family and friends crowded into the chairs that had been set up at the gravesite. The grave itself was covered by the machinery that would lower Al into his resting place later. For now, everything was hidden beneath a blanket of artificial turf, shockingly green against the duller, dry countryside.

Then she heard commands being barked. The moment had come. Six men in uniforms of various services eased the coffin from the back of the hearse and carried her cousin with measured steps to the grave.

Miri's throat tightened until she felt as if a wire garrote wrapped it. She drew slow breaths, calming herself. Weeping could come later. She had a service to perform for Al.

The minister spoke a few words, led them in a prayer. Then Sgt. York turned toward the distant riflemen and saluted. Even though she stood ten yards from them, Miri could hear the snap as they brought their rifles up and aimed them to the sky.

A command was spoken and three rifle volleys rang out, one after the other. Then, with a snap, the rifles returned to a position that crossed the men's chests.

She glanced toward York and saw him waiting at attention. Her turn. She lifted the trumpet and began playing the sorrowful notes for Al. A hush seemed to come over the entire world. She didn't notice that tears ran down her cheeks. Had no way to tell that no eyes were dry as the lonesome call carried over the countryside.

She made it all the way through. Tears nearly blinded her as the pallbearers stepped forward, folding the flag with perfect precision before handing it to Sgt. York. He pivoted sharply and walked to stand directly before Al's parents. With the flag at waist height he bent forward and spoke, his determined voice carrying on the stirring breeze.

"On behalf of the president of the United States, the United States Army and a grateful nation, please accept this flag as a symbol of our appreciation for your loved one's honorable and faithful service."

Mrs. Baker took the flag and held it to her chest, her sobs becoming audible.

Then the entire honor guard withdrew, leaving the family to its private time of grief.

Something made Miri run, her trumpet case banging against her leg. She didn't run away, but rather straight to Sgt. York, who was about to climb into his car.

"Sergeant!" she called. Her voice sounded disturbingly loud, but she didn't care. He'd been Al's friend. These moments were for him, too.

He paused, then pivoted to face her. Still the stern-faced soldier. "Yes, ma'am?" he asked quietly when she reached him.

"You can't just go. Please at least let us know how to contact you. Al's stories…well, we feel like you're part of the family, too."

He hesitated a moment. "Do you have a pad and pen? There's very little I can fit into a dress uniform without looking sloppy."

"I imagine." She was in a luckier position. Her trumpet case contained the paper and pen. He scribbled down an email address. Nothing more. It was enough. "Thank you. Thank you for everything."

"No need. Al deserved a whole lot more." Then he opened the car door and removed a paper-wrapped parcel, the size of a large book. "Give this to Al's mother and father, please. I had a bunch of photos I thought they'd like. I was going to mail it but… You did well, Ms. Baker."

Then he climbed in the car and, like the rest of the honor guard, disappeared from sight.

Miri stood holding the wrapped package, sorrow and loss emptying her heart. She missed Al like the devil. But she suspected Gil York missed him even more.

Chapter One

Miri Baker waited nervously. Gil York was arriving sometime this evening. Yes, they'd kept up a casual email correspondence since Al's funeral last year, but then he'd dropped out of sight for over two months.

When he resurfaced he'd told her he'd been wounded and that, after rehab, he'd be going home to his family in Michigan.

She wondered what had happened there, because out of the blue, just a week ago, he'd asked if the family would mind a visit from him. After clearing it with Al's parents, she assured him they'd love it, and his response had been brief. "See you Friday evening."

In the few messages they'd traded since he told her he'd been wounded, there had been a lot of blanks, missing lines, little information. She had no idea what to expect, or why he'd leave his family and come here.

She had a casserole ready to go, since his arrival time was up in the air. She had some lesson planning to do, but it could wait. She paced her small house and hoped that everything would be all right.

She had no idea how badly wounded Gil had been. What was he going to say when he learned that Al's family was throwing a big barbecue for him tomorrow? A barbecue in January because of a brief thaw. He wouldn't be expecting that. What if he didn't want to go?

"Simple enough," Betsy, Al's mother, had said as she gave her phone a workout. "We'll have the barbecue anyway. Everyone will have a good time." Especially since no one thought of holding barbecues at this time of year, thaw or no thaw. In a pinch, the barn would do for shelter.

It was nearly a year since the funeral, and when Miri thought over the simple, short emails she and Gil had exchanged, she felt that now he was even more a stranger than he had been when Al had shared stories about him.

"Reserved" might be an understatement when describing Gil York. From the little she had seen of him at the funeral, she would now describe him as distant. Maybe even closed off. She had a feeling that during their brief meeting she'd had her first close encounter with what she'd heard called the "thousand-yard stare."

She'd talked about it with Edie Hardin, a former

combat search and rescue pilot who now worked for
the county's emergency medical services as a helicopter pilot. The woman had a son who had frequent
play dates with Miri's next-door neighbor's son, and
Edie and Miri had developed a friendship over time.

"I know what you mean," Edie had answered. "I've
seen it plenty of times." She had missed the funeral because she was on duty that day, but her husband, Seth,
a former SEAL, had been part of the honor guard.

"I see it in Seth sometimes," Edie had continued.
"What these guys do? Especially special forces like
Seth and Gil...so much, for so long. It's like a brain
shock, or an emotional shock. It haunts them, Miri.
Anyway, don't worry about it. Gil seems to have a
handle on it, from what you said."

Handle on it? Truth be told she was surprised he'd
continued their irregular email conversation. Little
said on his side, while she tried to pass along interesting tidbits about life around here. She kept expecting
him to just not answer.

Then for two months he hadn't. It had been a shock
to *her* to learn he'd been wounded and that he was on
indefinite medical leave. An even bigger shock when
he'd written that he'd like to visit, if that was all right.

Of course it was all right. He'd been Al's best friend
for years. By extension he was family. But what about
his own family, where he'd been headed when he first
told her he was wounded?

As the sun slipped behind the mountains and the
afternoon began to darken into twilight, she decided

she was getting entirely too anxious about Gil's visit. He was probably just taking the opportunity to do a little traveling while he was on leave. He undoubtedly knew people from all over the country and was catching up. Considering that Al had been one of his best buddies, he probably wondered how the Baker family was getting along.

Losing Al still hurt. Grief, she was discovering, never really lessened; it just came less often. Like ocean waves, rolling over her occasionally, sometimes softer, sometimes hammering. Talking with his parents, she'd found they were experiencing the same thing, only much more painfully. Their only child? Indescribable.

The folded flag took pride of place beside Al's official portrait on the Bakers' mantel over the fireplace. Around it were all the presentation cases holding Al's medals, and a white votive candle that was never allowed to go out. Miri had offered recently to get all the medals mounted and framed—an expensive proposition, to her surprise—but they hadn't decided yet.

The Baker family continued to move forward with life, because that was what the living had to do, but Miri couldn't escape the feeling that part of Betsy, and maybe Jack, as well, had been frozen in time, at the moment they'd learned of Al's death.

Jack was still running the ranch; his grief didn't diminish realities. Yet some light in him was gone.

Maybe that was what was going on with Gil. Some light had been extinguished. Well, how would it be possible to spend sixteen or more years fighting for your country on dangerous and covert missions, without a bit of your internal light going out?

Then she realized why she was so on edge, and it had little to do with Gil personally. It had to do with the concern that his visit was going to freshen a grief they all, particularly Al's parents, had been gradually learning to live with.

Outside, the January thaw had thinned the snow to almost nothing. Icicles were beginning to drop from the eaves, tiny spears for the most part, probably a good size for leprechauns.

The day faded rapidly toward early night. Miri hated waiting, but she couldn't seem to do anything else just then. Finally, after what seemed like forever, a dark-colored car pulled up out front. A few minutes later she recognized the unmistakable figure of Gil York.

He looked different out of uniform, wearing a black parka, and as he came around the front of the car, she realized everything about him had changed.

The ramrod-straight posture and confident movement she associated with him were gone. He walked a bit gingerly, using a cane. He wore laced-up desert boots and camouflage pants beneath the parka, an odd assortment of pieces, and she wondered if the camo was simply comfortable, preferred over jeans or regular slacks.

He caught sight of her as she opened the door and gave a small wave. She noticed how deliberate his pace remained and the caution with which he navigated the sidewalk and the porch steps.

"It's good to see you again, Gil," she said when he reached the porch. She noted that sweat had beaded on his forehead, and it wasn't an especially warm day, thaw or not. That walk must have been difficult.

"Come inside. I've got coffee if you want, and a casserole that's just waiting to be popped in the oven."

At last the rigid lines of his face cracked a bit, serving up a faint smile. "Thank you, Miri. Hard to believe that I sat through that long drive and I'm already looking for another seat."

"You've been wounded," she replied, stating the obvious. "It must take time to come back." She opened the door wider and motioned him inside. Her house was small, the foyer about big enough for four people, with the living room on one side and the kitchen on the other. At least the kitchen was big enough to eat in. Two bedrooms and a bath at the back. Cozy. Easy to make crowded.

Gil was a large enough man that he was making her house feel even smaller. She guided him straight to the kitchen and pulled out a chair for him at the battered wooden table, which doubled as food prep space when she needed it. While he removed his parka, revealing a loden-green chamois shirt, she asked, "Coffee?"

"Please. Black."

She placed a large mug in front of him, then slipped the casserole into the oven, which she had preheated more than an hour ago. That freed her to join him at the table.

"I was surprised when you said you wanted to visit," she remarked. "Everyone's glad you are, we just didn't expect it. Was the trip rough?"

Again the faintest of smiles. "It's a long way from Michigan by car. Some really great scenery, though. Mostly, it was peaceful."

There was something important in the way he said that, but she felt she shouldn't ask, not yet. He had an aura that made her feel getting personal might not be wise. That he didn't easily allow it, if he did at all.

"How are Al's parents?" he asked.

"One day at a time. Jack's still running the ranch, although I think his heart has gone out of it. He planned to turn it over to Al when he left the army. Now it's just something he needs to do. He's muttered a couple of times that maybe he can find a Japanese buyer."

Gil arched one dark brow. "Japanese?"

"Oh, that goes back a couple of decades at least. The Japanese were buying up cattle ranches in Montana, then having locals run them, so they could export the beef to Japan. I guess it was pricey there."

"It's pricey everywhere now."

"Not that the ranchers are seeing most of that."

He nodded. "I didn't think so. Al used to talk about the ranch on occasion. Stories from when he was a kid, mostly, but he always had something to share when he came back from leave. And he was always pushing me to join him when we retired."

"Did you want to?"

His eyes were like flint, showing only the faintest of expressions. "What do I know about ranching?"

That finally caused her to smile. "What did you know about special ops when you started?"

"Touché." At last a real smile from him. So his expressions could change from distant to less distant, to even pleasant. He lifted his mug at last and drank deeply of the coffee. "Great joe," he told her.

"Thanks. Listen, I've got a spare bedroom in the back, if you don't mind that it has my home office in one corner. I can guarantee, though, that it's nicer than the motel. And tomorrow Betsy and Jack are looking forward to seeing you." She hesitated. "They're throwing a barbecue for you."

"A barbecue?" He raised one brow. "It's January."

"And there's a thaw. Everyone's looking forward to an early taste of spring. Anyway, you're not obligated to come, but if you do you'll get to meet some of Al's old friends."

He didn't answer and she really didn't expect him to. He'd asked if it would be all right to come for a brief visit, not to be swamped.

After a few minutes, realizing that even their email exchanges hadn't really made them more than acquaintances, she spoke again. "You can bring your stuff in whenever you're ready. Dinner will be in about an hour. And you can think about just what you want out of this visit. In the meantime, after that drive, maybe you need a nap?"

His gaze had grown distant, but it snapped back to her as she spoke. It was a penetrating look, and she didn't doubt that she had his full attention.

"I'm sorry," he said. "Yes, I'm tired. Yes, I'm still recovering. But the thing that wore me out most was my own family."

She drew a breath. His *own* family? Oh, Lord, and she'd just suggested a big barbecue with Al's friends and family. Gil was probably already wishing he hadn't stopped by. "What happened?" she asked, before she could stop herself.

"For years now they've been demanding I get out of the military. My being wounded only strengthened it. They always feared I was going to come home in a body bag, and this time I came close. My dad's a Vietnam vet, and he's been pushing the hardest."

"Oh." She'd heard the same insistence from Betsy and Jack when Al came home. "Jack used to ask Al, 'How many years, son? You've done your duty.'"

Gil nodded slightly. "Part of me understands. I've buried a lot of good men. I've seen a lot of terrible things. But this is who I am."

It sounded like a line drawn in the sand. Being a soldier was his identity. How did you strip that away? She would find it hard to give up being a music teacher. Sometimes she wondered how jobs could become so overwhelmingly important to a sense of self. Wondering didn't make it change.

"I'm not sure you'll get much of that here," she said. "But I can't guarantee you won't get any. Al's parents are excited about seeing you because Al mentioned you so often they feel like you're family. So, no promises."

Again a faint smile. "I know how to leave. Obviously. But let's talk about you. I know you teach music. I know you love it because you told me such great stories when you emailed. But what about the rest? Does Miri Baker have a life apart from school?"

She narrowed her eyes at him. "Does Sergeant Gil York have a life apart from the Green Berets?" Then she laughed. "Of course I have a life. Friends. Community service projects. Sometimes I help Jack and Betsy at the ranch. There are times when they need some extra hands."

"And your parents? Al never mentioned them. At least not that I can recall."

She closed her eyes. Even after seven years she didn't like to think about it. "My dad had an accident with some farm machinery. Mom found him... It was gruesome. Anyway, she died of a sudden heart attack before the EMTs arrived. I'm glad she didn't have to hang around, but I resent it, too." That was blunt enough, she thought.

"So you were left to deal with it alone?"

"Hardly," she said a touch drily. "You're forgetting the rest of the Baker clan. Aunt Betsy and Uncle Jack were there for me, as were a couple of more distant cousins. Then there are the people around here. Unless you deliberately push them away, quite a few will try to be helpful however they can."

He didn't answer immediately. He looked so very

different from when he'd come for the funeral. Then he'd been rigid, sturdy, in control. Now he looked weary, new lines creased his strong features and his eyes weren't quite as flinty. She wondered if he was in much pain, but didn't ask. They were still virtual strangers, with little enough intimacy of any kind. It was like meeting someone new, their past contact irrelevant. For some reason she hadn't expected that.

He rose from the table, moving as if he was stiff and uncomfortable, and the change once again shocked her. He poured himself more coffee, then returned to his seat. He'd managed without the cane, however.

"I stiffen up when I sit too long," he remarked. "I didn't use to do that. Al talked about you a lot."

The switch in topics caught her by surprise. She'd begun to hope he was going to say something about himself, but now went back to Al.

"I miss him," she said. "Even though he was home only a few weeks a year, I still miss him."

"I think he missed you, too. We were sitting behind some rocks one cold night keeping watch, and he told me about how you used to build roads together in the dirt at the ranch. And how you always wanted mountains, so you'd find some rocks, but you were very critical about them. Some were too rounded. Others didn't look like the mountains you can see from here."

She smiled at the memory. "I drove him crazy with my mountains. He had a toy grader and was making roads fast, to run the little cars and trucks on, but I was wandering around trying to make mountains. Then my folks got me a couple of plastic horses and they were too big. I hate to tell you how many times they turned into monsters that messed with the tiny cars."

Gil's face relaxed into a smile. "I can imagine it."

Her thoughts drifted backward in time, and she found herself remembering the happiness almost wistfully. "We tried to build a tree fort but we really didn't have the skills, so we'd climb up into the trees and pretend to be hiding from unspecified bad guys. One time we happened to find a stray steer. Well, that ended our imaginary game. We had to take it home. For which we got a piece of cake, so after that instead of hiding from imaginary bad guys, we became trackers hunting for rustled cattle."

His smile widened. "He didn't tell me you two had hunted rustlers."

"Only in our minds. Kids have wonderful imaginations. So what did you do?"

"I lived in town, so most of our games were pretty tame. Except when we got into trouble, of course. And being kids, we did from time to time. Mrs. Green was pretty angry when we trampled her rhubarb bed."

"I can imagine."

"Oh, it came back. We weren't trying to do any damage, though. Just carelessness. I haven't been home a lot during my career, but it seems like kids don't run around the neighborhood as much as they used to. Yards have become more private."

"And with two parents working, a lot of kids are probably in after-school programs and day care."

"True." He sipped some more coffee.

"When did you start thinking about joining the army?" she asked. "Or did you imagine a series of different possibilities?"

"I don't remember if I thought about anything else seriously. I probably toyed with a lot of ideas, the way kids do. Then September 11 happened. That was it."

"Pretty much the same thing happened with Al. That set his course."

"Yup." Gil nodded slowly. "It set a lot of courses. I trained with a whole bunch of people who'd made the same decision for the same reason. The changing of a nation."

She turned that around in her mind. "Watershed?" she asked tentatively.

"In a lot of ways." But he clearly intended to say no more about it. "And you? Music teacher?"

"Always. Put any musical instrument in my hand and I wanted to play it. I was lucky, because Mom and Dad encouraged me even though it was expensive. Rented instruments and band fees. Then I got a scholarship to the music program at university."

"You must be very talented."

"Talented enough to teach. Nothing wrong with that. I never did dream of orchestras or bands." She smiled. "Small dreams."

"Big dreams," he corrected. "Teaching is a big dream."

As she watched, she could see fatigue pulling him down. His eyelids were growing heavy and caffeine wasn't doing a bit to help. "Why don't you take a nap," she suggested. "I'll wake you for dinner, but you looked wiped."

He didn't argue, merely gave her a wan smile and let her show him the bedroom in back. His limp, she noticed, had grown even more pronounced than when he came into the house. Tired and hurting. She hoped he'd sleep.

Gil didn't sleep. He pulled off his boots, then stretched out carefully on the colorful quilt that covered the twin bed on one side of the room. As Miri had advised him, her home office occupied one corner. An older computer occupied most of the desk, but there was a side table stacked high with papers, and leaning against it was a backpack that looked to be full. Several instrument cases lined the wall on the far side.

He still wasn't sure exactly what had drawn him here, unless it was memories of Al. He *had* needed to get away from his family, all of whom were pushing him to take medical retirement. He didn't feel right about that. He might be confined to a desk after this—hell, probably would—but he still had buddies in the unit, and even from a desk he could look out for them. He owed them something, just as he owed something to all the friends he'd lost over the years.

His family had trouble understanding that. Even his dad, who was a Vietnam vet. Of course, he had taken only one tour in that war before his enlistment finished, so maybe he couldn't understand, either. A deep bond grew between men in special forces, no matter the branch they served in. They were used more often on dangerous and covert missions, often so far removed from command that they might as well have been totally alone. They depended on each other for everything.

And they wound up owing each other everything. Didn't mean they all liked each other, but they were brothers, the bond deeper than most families.

How could he possibly explain that?

So…he'd finally gotten tired of the pressure. His mind was made up. He'd made his choice the day he entered training for special ops, and a wounding, even his second one, couldn't change that commitment.

But the real problem was that he and his family were no longer on the same page. They couldn't be. His folks had no real understanding of where he'd been and what he'd done, and he wasn't going to try to illuminate them. They had no need to know, and the telling wasn't the same as the doing, anyway. He was part of a different world, and sometimes he felt as if they were speaking different languages.

It was a kind of isolation that only being with others who'd been in special ops could break. They had become his family, his only real family now. How the hell could he explain that to his parents?

He couldn't. So he'd put up with their fussing and pressure as long as he could. They wanted to take care of him, they worried about him and they couldn't just accept who he was. Not their fault, but in the end he didn't feel the comfort they wanted him to feel.

Al had been a good reason to move on. Gil told his folks he wanted to come see Al's family, to see how they were doing, to share stories about Al they'd probably like to hear. That was one decision that hadn't received an argument. Maybe because his parents were as tired of trying to break down his walls as he was at having them battered.

He wasn't accustomed to the kind of weariness that had become part of his life since he got caught in a bomb blast in the mountains of Afghanistan. Yeah, he'd gotten tired from lack of sleep in the past, but this was different. Fatigue had become a constant companion, so he let his eyes close.

And behind his eyelids all he could see was Miriam Baker and her honeyed hair in its cute braid. If she meant to look businesslike, she wasn't succeeding.

A thought slipped past his guard: *sexy woman.* Al probably wouldn't want him to notice. Then Gil could no longer hold sleep at bay.

Miri used the time while Gil napped to call her aunt and uncle. Betsy answered.

"He's here," Miriam said. "He looks awful, Betsy. Worn-out, pale, and he's got a bad limp. I don't know if he's up to the barbecue tomorrow. He hasn't said."

"If he comes," Betsy said firmly, "all he needs to do is sit in one of the Adirondack chairs and hold court. Looks like it'll be warm enough to be outdoors, but we're opening the barn so folks can get out of the wind if they need to. He'll be cozy in there."

"And if he doesn't want to come?"

"Then we'll come visit him when he feels more like it."

Miri paused, thinking, and for the first time it struck her that Betsy had used news of Gil's arrival to create a huge distraction for herself. Throwing together a large barbecue on a week's notice was no easy task, and it probably didn't leave much time for anything else...such as grieving. This barbecue wasn't for Gil.

She felt a little better then. She wouldn't have to try to pressure Gil in some way if he didn't want to go, and considering how worn he looked, he probably wouldn't. But Betsy would have achieved what she needed, a week when she was busy from dawn to dusk planning something happy.

Life on a ranch in the winter could often be isolated. Too cold to go out; the roads sometimes too bad to even go grocery shopping. This January thaw was delivering more than warm temperatures. Miri almost smiled into the phone.

"I asked him to stay in my spare room," she told her aunt. "He hasn't answered. He might prefer to go to the motel."

"Well, he's probably slept in a lot of worse places."

"By far," Miri agreed, chuckling. Both of them remembered some of Al's stories about sitting in the mouth of a cave, no fire, no warm food, colder than something unmentionable, until he was off watch and could lie down on cold rock. Yeah, Gil had slept in far worse places than the La-Z-Rest Motel, which was at least clean and heated.

"So," she asked her aunt, "are you ready for tomorrow? Do I need to bring anything beyond a ton of potato salad and two dozen burger buns?"

Betsy's tone grew humorous. "Considering that everyone is insisting on bringing something, we'll probably have more food than anyone can eat. It's been a struggle to ensure we don't just get forty pies."

Miri laughed. "That's about right. So you marshaled everyone into shape?"

"Better believe it. Plus extra gas grills and the manly chefs to cook on them."

Another giggle escaped Miri. "Manly chefs?"

"You don't suppose any woman in this county has let her husband know that she could grill a burger or dog as well as he can? It's a guy thing."

Miri pressed her lips together, stifling more laughter. She needed to take care not to wake Gil. But her aunt was funny.

"I've decided," Betsy said, "that manning charcoal and gas grills has become the substitute for hunting the food for the tribe."

"Oh, that's not fair," Miri insisted. "Most of the men around here go hunting."

"Sure. And most aren't all that successful. Once the masses of armed men hit the woods and mountains, wise animals pick up stakes and move away."

Miri was delighted to hear her aunt's sense of

humor surfacing again. Not since word of Al's death had Betsy achieved more than a glimmer of humor. Now she was bubbling over with it. Miri could have blessed Gil for deciding to visit. And she began to suspect it wasn't just arranging this barbecue that had lifted Betsy's spirits.

Maybe, Miri thought after they said goodbye, it had helped in some way to know that Al's best friend hadn't forgotten him. A reassurance of some kind? Or a connection that hadn't been lost?

Miri guessed she'd never figure out exactly what was going on with Betsy, but somehow she'd needed this visit from Gil.

And maybe Gil had needed it just as much. He certainly needn't have come all the way out here to people he'd never met until a funeral, people he'd barely met before he left.

All she knew was that she herself hadn't wanted to lose touch with Al's friend, even though they were strangers.

Connections, she thought. Connections for them all through a mutual loved one. In that context everything made sense.

Gil didn't sleep long. Years on dangerous missions had taught him to sleep like a cat, and his wounding had only made it more obvious. Fatigued though he was, pain broke through even the deepest sleep.

The fatigue wasn't sleepiness, anyway. The docs had warned him it was going to last awhile, because of how much healing he needed to do. His body was going to sap his energy in order to put him back together. Mostly. Some parts of him would never be the same.

Even back here, through a closed bedroom door, he could smell the aroma of whatever casserole Miri was cooking. Courtesy required him to get up and not keep her waiting for her own dinner.

But the first minutes upon awakening tested him, even though physical discomfort was no stranger. What was it some road cyclist had said? *You need to love pain to do this.* That applied to the kind of work Gil did, as well, although loving pain had little to do with it. You didn't have to be masochistic, you just had to not care.

But somehow he cared during the first couple minutes upon awakening. Maybe because the pain served no real purpose except to make it difficult to move.

Difficult or not, he forced himself to sit up and put his stockinged feet on the floor. He sucked air through his teeth and closed his eyes as angry waves washed through him, as stiffness and discomfort hampered him. He'd been wounded once before. It was part of the job. But this useless response afterward annoyed him. Hampering his movements did no good, not for his body, not for anything.

Because he needed to move. How many times had he been reminded not to let scar tissue tighten up? Hell.

He shoved himself to his feet and grabbed the cane he'd hooked over the back of the office chair. Time to march forth. Time to ease stiffness into a beast he could control, rather than the other way around.

His first few steps were uncertain as he tested his legs' response to walking. Okay. Slow but okay. They screamed at him, but it was a familiar scream now. The burn scars, the skin grafts, they all had an opinion about this. His shattered hip functioned, but not happily. His back didn't think he should stand upright.

Hah. He'd show them.

He opened the door and made his way down the short hallway. The bathroom was on his right, he noticed, marking the terrain. He'd had too little to drink during his drive today. He should remedy that soon.

The kitchen would have been easy to find even if he hadn't already visited it. Delicious aromas would have drawn him with his eyes blindfolded.

Miri sat at the big kitchen table, a stack of papers in front of her. She looked up with a smile. "I thought you'd sleep longer."

"I never sleep long," he answered. "Dinner smells amazing."

"My famous chicken-and-rice casserole. Have a seat. Do you want something to drink?"

"I need to move a bit. But a huge honking glass of water would be wonderful."

She rose at once. "Ice?"

That startled something approaching a laugh from him, and he watched her smile and raise her eyebrows. "Ice is funny?"

"Only if you ever spent months wishing your cave

would warm up. Just water, please. I didn't drink enough on the drive."

"Why not?"

"Because I wanted to avoid getting out of the car for anything other than gas."

He watched her face grow shadowed, then she went to a cupboard and pulled out a tall glass. "You're really hurting badly?"

"It'll pass." His mantra. He wouldn't admit any more than that, anyway.

As he stood there leaning on his cane, she passed him a full glass of delicious water. He drained it unceremoniously, and she refilled it for him immediately. He sucked half of it down, then placed the glass on the table. "Thanks. Mind if I stretch a bit by walking around the house?"

"Be my guest. Dinner's still fifteen minutes away. Longer if you need. Casseroles keep."

Nice lady, he thought as he began to explore the parameters of her house and his ability to move through it. Small place. Some would call it cozy. She'd certainly dressed it up in pleasant colors. Feminine, in shades of lavender and pale blue, with silky-looking curtains and upholstered chairs and a love seat in similar colors. Her kitchen was a contrast in soft yellows. He hadn't really noticed what she'd done with the guest room–office. He imagined she must have taken years to do all this, given a teacher's salary.

But contrasts were striking him. Everywhere he'd gone, he'd seen how people had tried to create some kind of beauty even when they had few resources. A home like this would look like a palace to many.

Then he remembered Nepal, a country full of rocky mountains, dangerous trails, sparse vegetation and racing rivers. The countryside itself was a thing of beauty, but then you went inside a home or teahouse, and the brilliant colors could take your breath away. Wherever possible, every inch of wall had been covered with bright paintings and cloths, a buttress against the granite and glaciers outside. A statement. A psychological expression: this is home. Beauty created by some of the most welcoming people he'd ever met.

He'd found it much the same when he'd slipped across the border into Tibet to collect intelligence, although the Chinese takeover had managed to wipe out some of the brightness, mainly on the faces of the Tibetans. They still wanted their country back.

Drawing himself out of memory, assisted by fresh pain, he tried to minimize his limp as he returned to the kitchen. Limping only made everything else hurt, too. Damned if he did, damned if he didn't. The saga of life.

Miri was serving up her casserole on large plates. "Hungry?" she asked. "I imagine you didn't eat much if you weren't stopping for water."

"I'm starving," he admitted. "Thanks for asking me to dinner."

She raised a brow and lifted one corner of her mouth. "Do you think I was going to let you arrive after a trip like that and not ply you with food? Seems unneighborly."

Again he felt his face trying to thaw. He didn't want to let it. Showing emotion could be weakening. When he was leading men he could joke, he could get angry, but he couldn't go much beyond showing them he'd do everything in his power to get them back alive.

He also admitted it was a form of self-protection. If you didn't feel it, it couldn't hurt you. Straightforward enough.

But now he was among people who had a whole different metric for dealing with life. Only look at Al's cousin, her readiness to welcome him into her home, her offering him dinner, a place to stay.

It wasn't unusual. He'd met that kind of courtesy the world over, unless people were terrified. There was no reason to be terrified here in Conard County, Wyoming. He felt a vain wish that he could have sprinkled that kind of safety around the whole world. Instead, all he'd ever been able to do was chip away at threats… and sometimes make them worse.

He eased into the chair and balanced his cane against the wall.

"So," she said, "I invited you to stay here." A heaping plate of chicken and rice appeared in front of him. "Say you will, because I'm going to feel just awful if you go to the motel."

He looked up as she brought her own plate to the table, then set the casserole dish nearby in case either of them wanted more. "Why would you feel awful?"

"Because you're Al's friend. Because my office-slash-bedroom is marginally better than the motel. I can guarantee you no bedbugs, not that the motel gets them for lack of sanitation. Some of the people passing through…"

A jug of water joined the casserole dish, and at last she quit buzzing and sat across from him.

He arched a brow. "You think I've never met a bedbug?"

Her expression turned into a mixture of amusement and disgust. "I suppose you have."

"Of course, that doesn't mean I like sharing my bed with them. But we have to get impervious to a lot of things."

"I'd guess so," she said after a moment. "Are you saying I'm squeamish?"

He liked the way humor suddenly lit her blue eyes. "No. You're a product of where you live. Most bugs probably stay outside."

"I have a rule," she answered as she picked up a fork. "If a critter is outside I'm happy to leave it alone. If it comes inside, I'll kill it."

"Seems like a sensible arrangement."

"I love nature," she said, almost laughing. "Outdoors, where it belongs. Please, start eating. If you don't like it, let me know."

"Is it hot?"

"Very."

"Great. That's all I ask."

Meals in the hospital had usually been lukewarm

by the time they reached him. He'd developed a strong loathing for oatmeal that would have made a great wallpaper paste. The mess hall was better but, since army cooks had been replaced by private contractors, not what he remembered from the past. As for when he was in the field…

"One of the best meals I can remember eating," he said as memory awoke, "was in a teahouse in Nepal."

She looked up from her plate. "Nepal? What were you doing there?"

"Passing through. I can't tell you any more than that. But they plied us with hot soup full of fresh vegetables, and roasted yak meat and yak milk. And an amazing amount of hot tea. Those people had next to nothing, Miri, but they treated us like kings."

"They sound very welcoming."

He almost smiled. "I'll never forget them. Strangers in a strange land, and we were met with smiles, generosity and genuine welcome." He looked down and scooped up more casserole. "I've noticed in my travels that the most generous people are often those who have the least. By no standard measure would you think the Nepalese were wealthy. But they were wealthy in soul and spirit."

He emptied his plate in short order and Miri pushed the casserole dish toward him. "I'm not counting on leftovers. Eat, Gil."

He was happy to oblige. Hot meals were still a treat.

"From what Al used to talk about, I guess you've seen a whole lot of the world."

He raised his gaze, feeling himself grow steely again. Some matters were not to be discussed with civilians. "Not from a tourist perspective," he said, closing the subject. A subject he'd opened himself, talking about Nepal. But it needed to be closed.

She nodded slowly, her blue eyes sweeping over his face. "Stay here tonight," she said finally. "You can decide about the barbecue tomorrow."

He was content to leave it there.

Chapter Two

Morning arrived, still dark, but already promising a beautiful day. Miri made pancakes and eggs for breakfast. The tall stack of cakes disappeared fast, with much appreciation from Gil.

"Do you cook?" she asked eventually, making idle conversation over coffee before she cleared the table.

"Over an open fire I'm passable. A can of paraffin even better." He shook his head a little. "When we could, anyway. At base camp we often took turns cooking for each other, but my efforts weren't especially appreciated."

She smiled. "So you got out of it?"

"Often as not. Whatever the knack is, I missed it."

She rose, took the plates to the counter and looked

at the thermometer outside her window. Sunshine had begun to spill over the eastern mountains, brightening the morning.

"It's going to be a beautiful day," she remarked. "The forecast said we're going to reach the upper sixties, and we're already at sixty-one. A great day for a midwinter barbecue."

She waited, wondering if he'd respond to the open invitation about the barbecue, but he said nothing. He sipped coffee, his gaze faraway, and she admitted at last that this guy wasn't about to share much of himself. Safe little tidbits here and there, but no more. Or maybe, despite the passage of time, he was still somewhere else, perhaps the place he'd been wounded. She couldn't imagine the difficulty he must experience transitioning between worlds. Maybe it was never easy. Perhaps it was harder under these circumstances.

She spoke, daring herself to ask. "Does your body feel like a stranger to you?"

One brow lifted. "How did you guess?"

"Well, it just crossed my mind. You're used to being in top physical form. That's gone now, at least for a while. You must be frustrated."

"Not exactly the word I'd choose, but it'll do. Let me help as much as I can with the dishes. I need to be moving."

"Betsy said you could settle in and hold court today if you come." Miri waited, nearly holding her breath.

"I'll go," he said after a minute, then pushed his chair back. "But I doubt I'll hold court. Not my style."

He managed to wash all the dishes and put them in the drain rack without any assistance from her. She had to admit to enjoying watching a man scrub her dishes while she sipped a second cup of coffee.

He was a good-looking man, too. Not as ramrod straight and stiff as at the funeral, which had been kind of intimidating. This version of Gil looked a whole lot more relaxed and approachable. Even if it was discomfort causing it.

When at last he dried his hands and returned to the table, she noticed the fine sheen of sweat on his forehead. "You did too much," she said instantly.

"I did very little, and it'll do me no good to sit on my duff and stiffen up. Don't worry about me. I won't push my limits too far. This isn't some kind of contest."

Firmly but kindly put in her place. The man didn't want anyone worrying about him. Okay then. She could manage that. She couldn't even feel slightly offended. This was a spark of the man she'd seen at the funeral. She was glad to know he was still in there. Living around here, it was possible to get to know veterans who had a lot of trouble returning. She supposed it was unlikely that Gil wouldn't have any problems as a result of his wounding and time at war, but she hoped they were minimal.

"You must still be missing Al," he remarked.

"Yes. You?"

"Damn near every day. You know, even when

you're in the midst of the most dangerous situations imaginable, you don't believe the bad stuff's going to happen to *you*."

"How could you?" she asked. "You'd be paralyzed."

"Maybe. What I do know is that we don't think about it until it's shoved into our faces, like when Al was killed, and then we have to shove it back into a lockbox. Anyway, he had plans. I was supposed to come here with him and help with the family ranch. I guess I told you that."

Gil was rambling a little, she thought, but no more than most people in casual conversation. At least he was talking.

"Al," he said again. "Damn. Ever the optimist. He could find a reason to be happy about cold beans on a subzero night."

That was Al. That was definitely the Al she remembered. "I take it you're not as much of an optimist?"

"Maybe I was, too much, anyway. Doesn't matter. Here we are." He gave her a faint, almost apologetic smile.

"Are you going back to duty?" she dared to ask.

"Yes."

There was a firmness to the way he said the word that again suggested a line had been drawn in the sand. "Do you have any idea when?"

"Not yet. Probably as soon as they feel I'm well enough to play desk jockey for an eight- or twelve-hour day."

"So…you won't be going back into the field?"

"No." A single uncompromising word. A warning to back off.

She could have sighed, except she knew she had no right to be asking many questions. He'd wanted to come out here for some reason…and she suspected it wasn't just to tell the family amusing stories about Al. All she'd done was offer him a bed and a few meals. He didn't owe her anything, certainly not answers to questions he might consider to be prying.

Apparently, he must have caught something in her expression. Much as she schooled herself to keep a straight face when necessary, because her young students picked up on even the subtlest of clues, she must have just failed. He spoke.

"Sorry to be so abrupt."

"It's okay," she said swiftly. "You're not feeling well…"

"Feeling unwell has nothing to do with it. Months of arguing with my family does. I'm not retiring, much as they may want me to, and if I can get back into shape for the field I will."

Now she wondered if getting away from his family had been his primary reason for traveling this way. "Families are harder to handle than combat missions?"

He astonished her by cracking an unexpected laugh. "Are you suggesting I turned tail?"

"I don't believe I said that."

For the first time she saw a spark of something in

those flinty eyes. Heat? Humor? She couldn't read it. "No, you didn't. What time is this barbecue and what can I do to help?"

Because night fell so early in the winter, the barbecue had been planned for midday. By noon, Miri had two huge containers of potato salad in the back of her sport SUV, along with four paper bags full of hamburger buns. There'd be leftovers, but she was sure they wouldn't go to waste.

She hesitated, wondering if she should tell Gil to follow her or invite him to ride with her. If he had his own vehicle he could leave whenever he wanted. She stood there, feeling the delightfully warm air blowing over her neck and into the open front of her jacket.

Gil addressed the question first. Apparently he wasn't shy about organizational matters. "Want me to follow you or ride with you?"

"Will you want the freedom to take off? Because once I get there, I'm going to be there for at least a couple of hours."

"I think that I can manage a couple of hours," he said wryly.

"Then hop in."

The ride out to the Baker ranch required nearly an hour of slogging over bumpy roads. Pavement had begun to buckle as usual when water had seeped into cracks and then froze. Gravel roads hadn't been graded in a while. Miri concentrated on driving and left Gil with his own thoughts. She figured if he wanted conversation he knew how to start one.

It was nice to have her window cracked open during the drive. The ground hadn't really started to thaw, and all the growing things were still locked into their winter naps. But the air was fresh and after a few months of mostly enjoying it for only a few minutes, Miri was glad to indulge more than she'd been able to the last few days.

The Bakers had set up a sign pointing to an elevated area of paddock for parking. Dead grasses were thick, and if the ground started melting it should drain fast enough to ensure no one got stuck in mud. A lot of cars had already arrived, and as Miri parked she got a sudden whiff of barbecue grills heating up and the unmistakable scent of smoking meat.

Betsy had pulled out all the stops. Miri guessed nearly forty people had already arrived. Folding tables groaned under offerings, and a stack of paper plates on one of the tables was held down by a snow globe paperweight. A perfect touch.

Gil helped her carry one container of potato salad, leaning heavily on his cane as he did so. He didn't appear steady on uneven ground yet. Miri grabbed the other, plus the bags of burger buns, and they made their way over to the only empty table left.

Betsy didn't let them get far. Wearing a light jacket, she swooped in, smiling. "I'm so glad you decided to come, Gil. Al always said he was going to bring you out here. I'm just sorry you couldn't get here sooner."

As soon as they had deposited their offerings on the table, Betsy gave Gil a tight hug. He seemed a bit uncomfortable and awkwardly patted her shoulder.

Miri cataloged that for future consideration. Walled off. Totally walled off.

Betsy took Gil with her, introducing him around. Miri smiled faintly and bent her attention toward getting the potato salad ready to serve and putting her buns with others.

Then she wandered over to join her uncle Jack, whose smoker was emitting delicious aromas. "Did you start smoking yesterday?" she asked him.

"How else do you barbecue? You doing all right with Al's friend?"

"Gil's a pleasant guy. Restrained."

"Shut down, most like," Jack answered. "I could see it in Al. Do you remember? It was like every time he came home he'd left another piece of himself behind."

Those weren't the memories of her cousin that Miri was trying to cherish, but she felt her stomach tighten as she acknowledged the truth of what Jack had said. War had been cutting away pieces of Al for years.

Or causing him to lock them away. "Jack? Why do they keep on doing it?"

"What do I look like? A shrink?" He lifted the lid on the huge smoker and began basting the ribs. "Almost done." He said nothing for a few minutes. "I can only answer for Al. He felt a real sense of duty. A need to serve. And, to be brutally honest, maybe a little adrenaline addiction. Anyway, I think Al was always testing himself for some reason. I don't know what his measuring stick was, but he seemed to me to be using one. But all that's my guess, Miri, and it may not apply to Gil at all."

Finished basting that side, he turned the meat with tongs and basted some more. Then he closed the smoker lid. "Not much longer. That's almost to the point of falling off the bone." He stepped back, hanging his tongs on a rack at the end of the smoker, and looked around. "Seems like almost everyone's here. And Gil has found himself a place."

Miri turned to look, too. An interesting place, she thought. The old sheriff, Nate Tate, was sitting in the group, a man who had served in the special forces in Vietnam, followed by thirty years as sheriff here. He'd been retired for nearly a decade now and didn't look a day older. But it wasn't just Nate Tate who made the group interesting. Gil had been found by a phalanx of vets, among them Seth Hardin and a few others who had served in special forces. Even Jess MacGregor, who'd been a combat medic, had joined them.

Edie Hardin, who had her own experiences of combat, had gravitated with her and Seth's child to a group of women. Billy Joe Yuma, formerly a medevac pilot in Vietnam and now director of the county's emergency services, had not joined the group around Gil.

Miri studied the group dynamics and wondered what was going on. The meeting of some kind of elite club, no outsiders welcome? Or something else.

Jack spoke. "Go join 'em."

"I don't belong."

"Exactly." Jack gave her a little nudge. "This is a barbecue to make Betsy happy, not to create a support group."

He had a point. Miri took a couple steps in the direction of the knot of men, then hesitated. There might be a good reason for that huddle. She also suspected there were stories about Al that would never be repeated to Betsy, but that Gil could share with these men of similar backgrounds. Maybe that was cathartic for a man who said very little. Except that he didn't appear to be sharing much. The others were talking, and occasionally a bark of laughter would punctuate the otherwise quiet conversation.

There were other clusters, as well. Nearly sixty people. They'd hardly congregate into one large crowd. Miri had been to lots of large gatherings as a teacher, and crowd breakout was common. Conversation became easier.

Jack was right, however. This barbecue, while ostensibly to welcome Gil back, was really about giving Betsy some happiness again. Not since the funeral had she joined in any social events, but now she had organized one in an amazingly brief span of time. And everyone she had called had evidently arrived to support her and Jack.

Gil was only a small part of it, as Al's best friend.

Betsy had decided to rejoin life. For that alone, Miri would feel eternally grateful to Gil. He'd provided the push she needed, the excuse.

So what did Jack expect her to do? Go break up that huddle of men? She didn't think Betsy would want that, especially since she'd said Gil could just find a comfortable chair and hold court—or not come at all if he didn't want to.

Gil was the excuse. Betsy was the one smiling for the first time in ages, having a bit of a hen party around the folding tables that held enough food for an army. Three other men were working grills with hamburgers, hot dogs and bratwursts.

They were going to need another sixty people to eat all this, Miri thought with amusement. She hoped everyone took home leftovers.

Some folks were eating, some still working on longnecks. Miri decided to go join Betsy and her coterie.

She was welcomed warmly by the women, most of whom she'd known all her life, and returned a tight hug from Betsy. She looked into her aunt's eyes and saw their warm brown depths cloudless for the first time in ages.

"Isn't this fun?" Betsy asked. "And all the more special because we can do it in the middle of winter."

"It *is* awesome," Miri replied. "Thaw or not, I wouldn't have thought of it."

Betsy smiled. "I'm glad I did." She leaned in a bit. "We have to carry on, Miri. You know that. But this is the first time since…then that I've actually felt like doing it." She turned and looked toward Gil and the group of vets. "Most of them were Al's friends, you know. At least when he was home. I'm glad they're talking to Gil."

"You don't want to?"

Betsy looked at her once more. "Later, if you're still around. In a couple of hours the temperature will start dropping again as we head into night, and I think nearly everyone will have left. But Jack was talking about building a fire in the fire pit if you and Gil want to hang around for a little while. Meantime, it looks like Jack is pulling those ribs off the smoker. Want to help?"

Miri helped Betsy carry large platters over to the smoker and Jack began piling half racks of beef ribs on them.

"The aroma," Miri said, closing her eyes and inhaling. "Jack, it smells like heaven."

"So go dig in." Jack winked as she opened her eyes. "I heard the potato salad you brought is great. Same for the coleslaw Betsy made."

It didn't take long for the ribs to disappear onto plastic plates. Ceremony was abandoned as people used their fingers to eat meat that was falling off the bone. Someone had brought Gil a plate laden with meat and potato salad, and he was soon eating with the group around him.

Miri was going to let it go, but it occurred to her that those guys had Gil walled off. Maybe there was a reason for it, but it was possible that others at the gathering might want a few words with him. It wasn't as if nobody knew who he was, or his relationship with Al. Betsy had made sure of that.

So she wandered that way with her ribs and coleslaw, and instead of being cut out, she was welcomed, immediately given a chair while one of the men went to find another.

"You guys having fun?"

"At a barbecue?" Seth Hardin asked. "You better believe it." He cocked his head toward the right. "See my dad? He's practically holding court over there."

"People love him, Seth. They always have."

"Well, not always," Seth replied with a crooked grin. "He says he raised hell in his youth. Anyway, at least Edie could come and bring the youngster with us. I suppose I ought to take my share of responsibility here or Edie will never eat." He nodded toward Gil. "You take care, man. See you before you leave, I hope."

Then Seth beelined toward his father, the old sheriff Nate Tate, and his wife and baby.

Breaking into the exclusive circle had an interesting effect. Some of the vets remained. Others left to go join their wives. Soon other women took the emptied seats and the whole context changed. Conversation began to revolve around local events, and different people took turns clueing Gil in, trying to make him feel a part of the community. He smiled faintly, nodded as he listened and ate, and said very little.

When Betsy joined them, conversation turned to Al and some of his youthful escapades. Laughter accompanied the memories, and Miri took genuine pleasure in watching Betsy laugh. As often as she had played with Al as a young child, she hadn't realized what a scamp he was at times.

"One of the cats climbed up into a tree one time," Betsy recalled. "Now I ask you, how many cat skeletons have you seen in a tree? They tend to find a way to get down as long as there isn't a coyote or something holding them up there. Anyway, Al, all of five years old, was scared the cat would never get down, and it was one he was particularly fond of."

Miri nodded, smiling as she recalled Al with the barn cats. Betsy and Jack got most of them neutered, but kept some so they could breed. Barn cats served a lot of useful purposes out here. Anyway, Al had loved those cats, but there was one in particular, a black cat with a half-white face that he'd almost turned into a house cat.

"It was Benji who went up the tree, right?" she asked.

Betsy smiled at her. "Yup. Anyway, despite me telling him that Benji could find his way down when he was ready, as soon as I wasn't watching Al climbed that tree to get him. The next thing I knew, Al was stuck in the tree with a contented cat sitting on his lap, and no way down."

Laughter passed through the group.

"A tree wouldn't have stopped him once he grew up," Gil remarked.

Everyone fell momentarily silent, then Betsy eased a moment that shouldn't have turned awkward at all. "I have no doubt of that. But at the time I quite enjoyed standing at the bottom of that tree and asking him how much help he'd be now that he was stuck, too."

"Ouch," Maxie Walters said. "Did he get mad at you?"

"No, he just said he'd figure it out. Then Benji jumped down, completely unharmed, and Al was stuck up there by his lonesome. The thing was, without the cat he found it a whole lot easier to get himself down. I had to give him credit for that. He said he'd figure it out, and he did."

"He was like that," Gil remarked. "Always." Then he fell silent again, growing pensive.

He looked so weary, Miri realized suddenly. He evidently wasn't as close to being healed as he'd tried to pretend. It wasn't just the stoicism that she'd seen at the funeral. He looked exhausted.

A lot of the guests were beginning to say their goodbyes, coming to speak to Betsy and thank her. Betsy left their group and began to urge people to take leftovers with them, most especially if they'd brought it in the first place.

Miri heard her aunt's voice on the cooling air. "Please. Where will I put it? No one wants all this to spoil."

"It might freeze tonight," someone joked, but containers of food began to vanish from the tables. Disposable tablecloths and plates quickly disappeared into the ranch's huge trash bin.

"We'll leave soon," Miri assured Gil. "I just want to help with the cleanup. Are you warm enough?"

"I'm fine. Let me know if I can help."

Right now he didn't look capable. She wondered if his ability to recognize his own fatigue had been dulled during all the years of active duty. It wouldn't be surprising. "Sure thing."

She went to help roll up the last of the disposable tablecloths and to fold the tables and carry them into the barn. Jack helped her with an extra-long one. "Gil doesn't look good," he remarked.

"Tired, I think. He mentioned that the docs told him it would take a while to get his energy back. Something about most of it going to healing him right now."

"How badly was he hurt?"

"I honestly don't know. He's not the kind of person who makes you feel that prying would be welcome."

"No," Jack agreed as they leaned the table against the growing stack in the barn. "He also strikes me as the kind of man who must be chafing because right now he can't help. I was thinking."

Miri paused and looked at him.

"Even if he wasn't worn-out, I suspect he wouldn't be too keen to sit around a campfire tonight. Sure, it's a treat for the rest of us, but we haven't spent maybe hundreds of cold nights huddling around one to keep warm."

"I didn't think of that," Miri admitted.

"Just occurred to me. And if I make the offer, he'll

probably feel he has to accept it. Another time. Just get the man home so he can warm up and rest."

She looked over and saw that Gil had risen and was making his way carefully over to Betsy, the uneven ground giving him a bit of trouble. She wondered why he was even out of the hospital. Right now she had the impression he should be in convalescent care. What the hell had happened to him?

"Go get him, Miri. Just drive your car up there and pick him up." Jack was firm. "We'll come by your place to visit him after church tomorrow if he hasn't already moved on."

She turned toward Jack and gave him a huge hug.

"What's that for?"

"You have plenty of reason right now to be hard or bitter. You're not. I admire you."

The light was dimming, but she thought she saw him color a bit.

Then she followed orders, trotting over to her SUV and pulling it up close to Gil and Betsy. It *was* getting colder again. Maybe the thaw was almost over.

She climbed out, feeling the nip afresh, and rounded her vehicle to join Betsy and Gil. "We need to get you home," she said bluntly.

Betsy laughed. "I was just telling Gil the same thing. Dear man, you look worn to the bone. If it's all right, Jack and I will stop by after church in the morning." As Gil nodded, Betsy turned to Miri. "Is that okay by you? I'll pick up some sweet rolls at the bakery like I used to do for Al. Jack will love me forever. He's not allowed to have them anymore, but I think we can make an exception this once."

Leaning very heavily on his cane, Gil said good-bye and eased his way into the SUV. Miri closed the door behind him as soon as he'd pulled his cane inside, waved across the yard to her uncle and gave Betsy a tight hug. "If you need help out here tomorrow, let me know."

Betsy shook her head. "Not much left. Our neighbors did a great job. Now you get that young man home."

Gil had started to feel chilled to the bone, and exhaustion had been annoying him for at least the last hour. He hated his weakness, even though it was temporary, but he'd been taking orders for enough years that following them was automatic. Rest, the doctors said, so he rested. Mostly. Leaving his family behind and driving halfway across the country probably wasn't what they meant by rest.

Nor was this barbecue, not that anyone had given him a chance to do much except sit in a comfortable chair and mostly listen to the conversation. Nobody had seemed to expect him to speak at any length, which was good. What did he have to talk about, anyway?

"I hope you didn't leave early on my account," he said to Miri, feeling a twinge of guilt.

"Absolutely not. Betsy and Jack were thinking about building a fire to sit around tonight, but they were reconsidering. Most of the extended family had already left, too. The air feels like the thaw is almost over."

"It does," he agreed almost absently. Night had begun to settle over the land, early as always at these latitudes this time of year. The hours at the barbecue had showed him a bit of why Al had been so proud of his home. People were friendly, he'd always had food on his plate and a beer in his hand, without even asking. Middle-aged angels swooped by every now and then to replace whatever plate he was holding. Often as not, one of the men who'd gathered with him had brought him another longneck.

They hadn't questioned him, either. No one had wanted to know about his wounds or how they'd happened. Of course, all of them had been in combat and they probably didn't need exact details. But there'd been the lack of pressure of any kind. They'd simply included him in their group and chatted about nearly everything under the sun, mostly things that were happening locally, making him feel welcome and leaving him unpressured.

A pleasant change from the visit with his family in Lansing. It wasn't that he didn't love them, because he did. It wasn't that they didn't love him, he was sure of that. It was that they wanted a different version of Gil York, and after seventeen years in uniform he wasn't about to give it to them. That didn't keep them from pressing him, though. They wanted change. They wanted him home.

And he wasn't at all sure he was anywhere near

ready to go home and stay. Besides, Lansing no longer felt like home. It felt more like a place he visited every year for a week or two. It didn't even qualify as a vacation unless he rented a car and headed for Lake Michigan or the Upper Peninsula.

Years and distance had put a gulf between him and his family, such that he'd felt more comfortable among a group of strangers today. Maybe because they understood where he was coming from.

He suddenly became aware of the silence in the SUV as they made their way back to Miri's house. Silences didn't usually trouble him, but this one did. He was being discourteous.

"Al's friends and family all seem like great people."

"Most of them are," Miri agreed.

A quiet chuckle escaped him. "Only most?"

"There are problematic people everywhere." She laughed. "Some can be enjoyed as characters. Others need to be watched out for. But by and large, I agree with you. Jack and Betsy are great people. So are most of their family. They raised Al, didn't they? And they attract the same kind of people as friends."

Small talk just wasn't his thing. Ordinarily not a problem, but it felt like one right now. He'd spent so much time involved in operations and their executions with a bunch of guys who had a lot of shared experiences to talk about, whether humorously or seriously. Miri was making him aware of a lack in himself. She'd been welcoming, sharing her house with him, feeding him, taking him to the barbecue… Sitting here is stony silence almost seemed like an insult.

"Was it getting colder, or was that just me? I mean, I know the day was fading, I'd expect the temperature to drop, but it was beginning to feel bitter."

"It's dropping," she agreed. "I think our midwinter thaw is over. Anyway, we'll get you warmed up and then you can decide how much is the weather and how much your own fatigue. You can burn an awful lot of energy trying to stay warm." Then she laughed. "I guess you know that. I'll check the weather report when we get home."

When they reached Conard City, he paid attention to the place for the first time. He'd been so tired when he drove in yesterday, he hadn't cared. But now as they drove down the winter-bare streets, he saw compact charm left over from an earlier time. There wasn't much to jar a visitor into remembering time had moved on, apparently leaving this town in its wake.

He tried to focus, but didn't quite make it. He was in a lit-up town again, but the drive home had been a struggle. They'd been far enough out that there'd been no lights to interfere with the star-studded sky.

And for a minute or two, just briefly, he'd been cast back to Afghanistan. He'd managed to cling to the present, but a sour, troubled feeling remained. As did some unaccustomed anxiety.

"Is there some well-lit place where we can get coffee or something?" he asked abruptly. He knew what he needed.

"Sure." Miri didn't even question him. He wondered if she could begin to guess what a relief that was after being at home with his family. He'd been constantly questioned. Understandable, but not comfortable.

"Do you want a bar or a diner?" she asked.

"Diner." He'd been plied with delicious food for hours, but now he was hungry. Really hungry. He'd also been served enough beer that he wasn't sure how many weeks it would be before he wanted to see another. A friendly group, good company, and now somehow he felt as if he'd been through the wringer.

Before he went home with Miri, he needed to be sure he'd silenced the demons that had been awakened by a very dark Wyoming night.

They'd merely whispered to him, but he wanted them firmly shoved down into their pit before they grew louder and possibly disturbed Al's cousin, who'd been so kind to him.

She pulled into a space in front of The City Diner near the center of town. Through the windows he could see a chunky woman at work wiping tables, and only a few other people.

Plenty of space. He needed it.

"Maude's diner," Miri said cheerfully. "Everyone calls it that because Maude has owned it as long as anyone remembers, and she's quite a character. She's even been known to pick your meal for you. I would label her as graceless but not mean. As far as I know, anyway."

He felt miserably stiff as he climbed out of the vehicle and walked into the diner. A lot of things hurt because of his injuries, but other parts seemed to be screaming because of the cold, or maybe years of abusing his body. At this point he couldn't tell anymore. When you let things rest, they had time to stiffen up. Problem was, right now he had to let himself rest, moving only as much as necessary to keep scar tissue loose. He'd failed at that one today.

Inside, the diner was warm. Patched leatherette covered stools, chairs, and benches in the booths. His hip made dealing with a booth problematic, but he chose one anyway, because it would put his back to a wall. The need didn't always trouble him, but tonight it did. Maybe because the drive through the darkness had stirred up some of his PTSD. Sometimes there was just no avoiding it.

He soon saw what Miri had meant about Maude, but she didn't trouble him in the least as she slammed cups on the table along with menus. The coffee was poured quickly, hot and aromatic. It might drive the day's cobwebs away for a bit.

Holding the mug in both his hands, he raised it to his lips and drew a deep breath of the aroma. "Perfect."

"Are you hungry, too?"

"Considering how much food I ate today—all of it delicious, by the way—I probably shouldn't be. I might want a tank topper, anyway."

"Then I suggest Maude's pie, whichever kind she has. She's famous for it."

He managed a faint smile. "It's been a while since I ate pie."

He rested his elbows on the table, holding the hot cup of coffee right in front of his face, watching as tendrils of steam wafted upward, seeing Miri through it. Beautiful woman. Kindly woman. Today he'd had the sense that a lot of people at the barbecue were welcoming him on Al's behalf. A tight-knit community. And the vets who had dominated the group that had gathered around him…

He closed his eyes briefly, feeling it all over again. And he had felt it—men he didn't know, brothers-in-arms, and the brotherhood had come through. They'd surrounded him, trying to make the situation easier for him, as if they understood.

Well, of course they understood. They'd all walked in his shoes and knew that a crowd of strangers could be uncomfortable, at least for a while. The safety net gone, out there all alone, and in many places that had been a threat. It was hard to ease past all that, hence him sitting here with his back to a wall.

He opened his eyes in time to see a large wedge of pie slammed down in front of him. "Dutch apple," said the woman, her tone almost challenging. "What about you, girl?"

"One scoop of vanilla ice cream."

Maude arched a brow. "Reckon you ain't heard it's a cold night."

Miri laughed. "Got me there, Maude. But it sounds good, anyway."

Maude stomped away and Gil looked down at the pie in front of him. "It's warm," he remarked, the scents rising up to join with the coffee he still held. Very warm. He couldn't remember the last time he'd had warm pie.

"A special favor for you," Miri remarked, smiling. Maude returned with her ice cream in a metal dish, then marched away, disappearing into the bowels of the diner behind the counter somewhere.

The last two people in the place got up, threw some bills on the table and headed for the door, nodding as they walked past.

Suddenly the world shook itself back into place, and Gil was able to sip his coffee and dig into the pie. "You were right," he said, after he swallowed the first mouthful. "Best pie ever."

"Be sure to tell Maude." Miri scooped a small amount of ice cream onto the tip of her teaspoon, but paused before she ate it. "What happened, Gil? I could feel something change when we were driving back."

He made it a rule never to open up about most of his experiences to civilians. Yes, something had changed on the drive back, but he wondered what he could recount that wouldn't upset Miri. He'd lived a violent life in service to his country, but he could see no damn good reason to let that violence touch someone like this woman. Yet he sensed he might annoy her, or upset her, if he just shut her out. She was asking sincerely and deserved some kind of answer.

"I don't talk much about my service," he said finally.

"Al never did, either. But after he began to go on missions, when he came home he was different. It was like he knew he was coming from another planet that we couldn't even begin to understand."

"That nailed it," Gil admitted. "Miri, it's a simple fact that I know what I'm capable of in a way most people never will. And it's not something I want to dump all over anyone like you. Someone who's never been there."

She nodded. "I get that. Honestly. Al was frank about it, too. But it seems so sad, like he could never come home again. Like you can't."

Truer than she knew, he thought. But she needed some kind of answer. She'd evidently felt his demons trying to escape during the drive back. He owed her *something*, given the hospitality she had offered so freely.

"It's dark out there at night," he finally said. "You don't find that kind of darkness in a lot of places these days. But you find it in Afghanistan and other places in the Middle East. Jolting down a road in the dark… I guess it stirred some memory or other."

"Does the darkness bother you?"

"Depends." He shrugged one shoulder. "It can be a friend or an enemy. Driving down back roads could be dangerous, though. Sometimes they provided a perfect opportunity for ambush. And headlights didn't always catch the IEDs."

Improvised explosive devices. She knew the term from the news, from Al and from how Al had died. A cold little shiver ran down her spine.

"I vastly preferred to be on foot," Gil added truthfully, then said no more. There was no need to say more. She had her answer, a truthful one even if it was abbreviated. On foot, especially, the darkness was his friend.

But he'd hovered close enough to memory's precipice. Now that he'd told her what had happened, he wanted to change the subject. They were sitting here in a brightly lt diner over coffee and pie. No reason not to enjoy it. "Do you like teaching music?"

"I love it," she said with a smile, a tiny spot of ice cream in the corner of her lips. As if she sensed it, she pulled a fresh paper napkin from the dispenser and dabbed her mouth. Too bad, he thought. He'd have liked to lick it away. And she would have justifiably objected. He enjoyed some internal amusement at his own expense. Here he was, too tired most of the time to do more than sit or pace, with a mangled body, and his genitals wanted to rise to the occasion. Miri was having an unusually strong impact on him. If he'd been capable of carrying out his desires, he'd have been smart to move to the motel.

But he was no threat to her, he assured himself. Al's cousin. A deep bond he still honored, and that extended to respecting Al's family.

Chapter Three

Miri watched him turn his attention to his pie, realizing that the man who had brought Al home really was as reserved and distant as he had seemed that day. He hadn't been controlling his emotions in order to carry out his duty to Al. No. This guy never unleashed any real feeling if he could avoid it. Was he that worried or uncomfortable with his emotions? Did he live behind walls on purpose or by conditioning? She guessed she would never know. Sergeant Gil York had no intention of exposing himself.

"I always loved music," she said, to cover her rather brief response to his question. "I was lucky in that I could play almost any instrument I picked up. Not well enough to claim a position with a band or orchestra or anything, like I said." Then she laughed quietly at herself. "Maybe because I never focused on *one* instrument. Anyway, I was lucky to be good enough to teach it. Although when you have to learn your art as a craft, it makes a difference."

That caught his attention. "How so?"

She tilted her head. "Well, it's one thing to just play from the heart with joy. It's another to break all that down into theory and methods and so on. Teaching makes me be more conscious of the process. Sometimes it can be hard to shake off, enough to just play without ever thinking about it."

He nodded slowly.

"We have a writer in this county, Amanda Laird. She once told me that her writing gets messed up for weeks if people start talking about *how* to do it. She doesn't even like to go to the schools to talk to English classes. And she's death on the idea of themes."

"Meaning?"

Miri flashed another smile. "She says she hates being asked what the theme of her book is. She doesn't consciously plan one, and she gets the biggest kick out of the way her readers participate in the creation by coming away with different reactions and interpretations. So I'm a music teacher and that keeps me out of the clouds, because I have to pass along important basics. What I hope is that my students, after we get past the basics, can use their music to fly again."

One corner of his mouth lifted. "I like that phrasing. I hope they fly again, too."

She dared to ask a question that might turn him once again into granite. "Do you ever get to fly?"

"Only on a troop transport or a helicopter." Then he resumed eating his pie, leaving her feeling like he'd just frozen the conversation.

Then she considered what Gil did for a living. She doubted he could afford to let his head wander in the clouds at all. Ever. His dreams had become a harsh reality, and now there was no room for dreams anymore.

Al had given her the same feeling on his visits. A realist at all times. He hadn't even seemed to want to talk about memories of their childhood, although he occasionally made an effort. *Effort* being the operative word, she thought now.

"Do you guys never think about the future?" she demanded finally.

"Of course. We have to plan ahead."

And that probably said it all. This far and no further. Not five years down the road, but a few weeks down the road. A very narrow telescope for life.

Yet how else could they survive?

She stifled a sigh, spooned the last bit of melting ice cream from her bowl and sipped coffee that was growing cold. That caught her attention immediately. Maude never let coffee get cold.

She looked around and saw that Maude was nowhere in sight. As uneasiness struck her, she said to Gil, "I'll be back in a moment."

Then she ventured into the dragon's lair of the kitchen that served the diner. There she found Maude on the floor, breathing too rapidly, sweat beading her brow. Miri called out instantly. "Gil!"

"Yo?"

"Call 9-1-1 now!"

"I'll be okay," Maude groused, in a voice that was way too weak.

"Sure you will, Maude. But you need someone to look at you. Something's wrong."

But she knew what was wrong as Maude lifted a hand and rubbed the center of her chest.

"Never felt it coming," Maude whispered.

"Women often don't. Just take it easy for now. Soon the medics will be here and you can yell at them."

"Call Mavis. Number by the sink. She's gotta close up."

"Relax. I'll get Mavis. She'll take care of everything. Half the folks in town will probably help take care of everything. You just take it easy until a doc says you're fine."

The call to Mavis was unexpectedly easy. As taciturn as her mother, she said she'd come right away. No histrionics.

Then Miri sat on a recently mopped, still-damp floor and took Maude's hand, watching intently for a change, ready to crawl out of her skin as she waited.

Gil had limped to the doorway and was talking into his cell phone. "Maude at the diner. Yes. She's gray, sweaty and lying on the floor. Still breathing. Conscious."

"Dammit," Maude whispered.

"I agree," Miri answered. She gave Maude's hand a small squeeze. "Hang on. You'll be around to grouse at another generation of customers."

"I'll wait by the front door to wave them through," Gil said. Miri was glad he didn't add that every second counted.

Because it did, and this county wouldn't be the same without the irascible Maude.

It took only six minutes for the paramedics to arrive. Mavis, a younger clone of her mother, wasn't far behind. She took over the task of reassuring Maude, while the medics started an IV and took vitals, talking with someone at the hospital over the radio.

"What can I do to help?" Miri asked as the medics finally wheeled Maude out.

Mavis looked almost lost. She shook herself. "Nothin'," she said. "Mom had most of it done. I just need to take care of the register and lock everything up. Then I can go to the hospital."

"Okay."

"Guess I should put the Closed sign up. Whatever, ain't likely to be serving breakfast by six."

"No." Miri studied Mavis, seeing the near panic in the woman's eyes and the confusion as she tried to absorb everything and make plans. All she wanted to do was follow her mother to the hospital.

"You're sure I can't close up for you?" Miri offered.

Mavis shook her head. "You run on home. I'll do it, won't take long…"

Then she walked to the front door to watch the ambulance pull away, before returning to the back of the diner. "You run home," she said again.

Miri couldn't mistake that Mavis wanted to do this by herself. Maybe needed to do it, just so she'd be busy.

Miri grabbed a receipt book and scribbled her number on it. "You need anything at all, let me know. I mean it."

"Thanks." Mavis looked at the pad, but hardly seemed to see it.

Then there was nothing to do but go home with Gil.

When they arrived at Miri's house, she was surprised to see how early it still was. Well, of course, they'd left the Baker ranch as it started to get dark and cold, which was early at this time of year. Then the long drive into town, stopping at Maude's apparently just after dinner hour, judging by how empty the place was.

So Miri shouldn't have been surprised when she looked at the clock for the first time since morning and realized it was just past eight. Maude would have expected to be open until ten tonight, and to reopen at six in the morning.

Miri didn't know how the woman kept such hours, even now that she had the help of her daughter. But maybe she'd just seen the effects of having no life except work.

She shucked her jacket and flopped on one edge of the couch, leaving it to Gil to decide what he would do. She was disturbed again, but for a very different reason. Now she was thinking about Maude.

"I'm sorry about your friend," Gil said. He'd doffed his parka and now settled with evident caution into the rocking chair.

"She's not my friend. I'm not sure she's anyone's friend, but she sure as heck is an icon in this county."

Gil shifted his weight onto his other side, as if he couldn't quite get comfortable.

"If that chair's not good for you, there's room over here."

He shook his head. "I'm fine. And I'd venture to say Maude must have had a friend at one time. She has a daughter."

Miri couldn't help laughing. "True. And she has two daughters, actually. A few years back, the other one was here for a few months helping at the diner, then she took off. I've no idea where. But there was always a possibility that Maude simply cloned herself."

It was his turn to smile. "Having met Mavis, I'd agree that's a possibility."

Miri closed her eyes a moment, remembering. "Do you think she had a heart attack?"

"I'm not a doctor, but that would be my first guess. It could probably be other things, though."

"If she eats what's on her menu, it's probably the heart. But what a delicious menu. Her steak sandwiches are famous. You need to try one."

Then she heard her own words, implying he'd be around long enough to do that. Hell, she thought sadly, he was probably already on some kind of internal countdown clock, getting ready to move on. Staying in one place for long didn't seem like a quality that being in the Green Berets would nurture.

"Al got antsy when he was home for more than a week or two," she remarked, even though it would sound like a total tangent to him. "He'd help his dad with everything, including livestock, and do a lot of visiting, but even so I could tell he wanted to get back to work. You must be miserable."

"I wouldn't say that." Gil paused as if choosing his words. "After a while the unit becomes your family. Then we have certain ways of doing things that feel orderly to us for the most part. It becomes comfortable. Being away from it is like…"

"Being a stranger in a strange land?"

"Sort of like that, yes. But that doesn't mean I'm miserable. I've traveled through so many cultures in my career that the worst I could say is that this is just another one. We become chameleons. As for Al…" He shrugged slightly. "It's harder to come back to a familiar place."

"Is that what you felt at home in Michigan?"

"Not exactly. My parents moved to Lansing about ten years ago, from Traverse City. It wasn't my childhood home I went back to. I just went back to the same complaints and pressures."

"I guess they aren't getting the message."

"Apparently not." He passed a hand over his face, as if wiping something away. "They'll get their wish soon enough, one way or another. Either I'll be judged unfit to continue on duty, or I'll retire at twenty. Not long now. But I'm not going back to Lansing."

"You don't like it?"

"I'm too old to go back to living near my parents. I can't be their kid again."

"Ah." She thought she got it. Evidently they still wanted him to be the child they remembered, not the man he'd become, and hadn't adapted to his being grown-up. She guessed he hadn't been around long enough for them to get used to the changes. She'd seen it from time to time, when grown children had some difficulty carving out a different relationship with their parents. She would have thought it would be easier for someone who was away as much as Gil.

For that matter, coffee and pie hadn't made Gil look any less weary.

"Gil, you don't have to stay up on my account. If you're tired, go to bed. I'm used to being on my own most evenings."

He nodded, but didn't move for a minute or so. "Thanks for your hospitality," he said at last, then pushed himself to his feet, reaching for his cane. "I'll see you in the morning."

She watched him limp from the room and listened to his uneven gait as he walked down the hall. The man who had marched so firmly and confidently when he'd been here for Al's funeral now walked unevenly and with much less confidence.

God, apart from his injuries and the pain he appeared to still suffer, the changes must be hard to live with. She hoped they were temporary.

She'd forgotten to get her laptop and lesson plans from the bedroom, so she flipped on the TV to some program she hardly watched. Maude. Gil.

A lot to worry about for one day. But she was having a serious problem dealing with finding Maude on the floor like that. The woman had seemed indestructible, as if she'd always be a part of this place. Nothing would be quite the same around here without her. Mavis, though she was a lot like her mother, really wasn't the same.

Swinging around, Miri put her feet up on the couch and leaned back against the padded arm. She felt tired, too. Drained.

She hoped tomorrow would be better. Then she drifted off to sleep.

It was still dark in the morning when she woke. Gil evidently wasn't stirring yet, so she made her way to her own room, took a shower and changed into fresh clothes, a sweater and slacks. In the kitchen she flipped on the radio at a low volume to listen to the weather. Not that she really needed it. The heat was blasting in the house, and there was a chilly draft near the window over the sink. The winter cold had returned overnight. Silently, which seemed strange, but it had come.

She would have expected some wind, she thought as she waited for the coffee and made herself some whole grain toast. A little bluster. Almost as soon as she thought it, she heard the window glass rattle quietly. There it was. Satisfied that her weather sense hadn't flown the coop, Miri stood staring out at the still-dark world while she nibbled her toast, wondering how soon she could call and find out how Maude was doing.

A lot of people would be in for a shock today. Never in the history of the diner had it been closed in the morning. There'd be no coffee, no toast, no scrambled eggs and ham, nothing for the regulars, mostly retired, who camped out there every day, and nothing for the church crowd that occasionally stopped in with their families. The diner wasn't that big, but on Sunday mornings it could groan with all the people.

None of that this morning. Mavis would be tied up at the hospital, most likely, and there was no one else to keep up the flow. Miri hoped Mavis had remembered to call the dishwasher, Maude's only regular employee these days, and tell him he wouldn't be needed.

And all of this was pointless mental buzz, she thought as she took her half-eaten toast and coffee to the table. The diner wasn't her problem. She was concerned about Maude, naturally, but the rest of it... not her concern.

What concerned her was the man sleeping in her office-slash-bedroom, who'd looked almost hollow-eyed last night. As if he were running on his last reserves. She hoped he stayed a few days to catch up with himself before he took to the road again.

But it wasn't just that. Uncomfortable as it made her

feel, she squarely faced the fact that she was attracted to Gil, had been since the funeral and still was even in his beat-up state. She'd been shoving it aside as totally inappropriate and most likely a waste of energy, but the fact remained that she felt seriously drawn to him.

Like she needed that.

At last the weather report emerged from the radio. Not surprisingly, the thaw was indeed over. What she hadn't expected was to hear that the temperature was going to plunge precipitously throughout the morning, reaching below zero around noon. And more snow. While the percentages were far from definite, they faced the possibility of a blizzard later, too.

Great. Well, if Gil had any ideas about hitting the road today, he was going to be disappointed. With sufficient wind, two inches of snow could become a blizzard around here, creating a nearly total white-out. Sensible people would hunker at home, starting this afternoon.

The phone rang and she snatched it quickly. There was an extension in her office that could easily wake Gil.

"Hey, kiddo," said one of her fellow teachers, Ashley Granger McLaren. "Looks like the weather is mad at us again."

"Or decided to return to normal," Miri answered drily. "So what's up?"

"I heard something on the grapevine about Maude. What's going on?"

"I don't know, exactly. She collapsed at the diner

and had to be taken out by ambulance. She was still conscious, though. Beyond that I don't know a thing."

"Well, that's going to upset some applecarts around here. I can think of at least a dozen or more men who are going to *hate* missing their morning at Maude's. Now they'll actually have to stay home with their wives."

Miri laughed. "I hadn't thought of it that way."

"That's because you almost never go over there in the morning before school. I do. I hear it all when I'm buying my coffee. You never heard a bunch of guys with more complaints about everything."

"They're all retired, aren't they? What else are they going to do?"

"Beats me. Well, let me know if you hear anything about Maude."

"Will do." As Miri pivoted to hang up the phone, she saw Gil standing in the doorway of the kitchen. Today he'd donned a sweatshirt with loose slacks. She wondered if restrictive clothing bothered him, because not even for the barbecue had he worn jeans. "Come on in," she said. "*Mi casa es su casa* and all that. How are you this morning?"

"Stiff but fine. Well rested, certainly."

That was debatable, she thought as she took in the dark circles under his eyes. "Grab a seat if you feel like sitting. Coffee?"

"Please."

She went to pour him a mug, speaking over her shoulder as she did so. "I was just debating whether to make breakfast sausage or bacon to go with eggs. Any preference?"

"Either one classifies as manna from heaven."

Smiling, she brought him his coffee. "Come on, they must serve that in the mess hall or whatever they call it these days."

"The hospital didn't believe in fats, and by the time meals reached me they were less than lukewarm. Besides, when I wasn't on base, I was usually dining on prepackaged meals that astronauts wouldn't have envied." He smiled faintly. "On my list of luxuries are hot showers and hot food."

"Well, you're welcome to both here." Reaching into the fridge, she pulled out a roll of breakfast sausage and began to make it into patties. "I haven't heard anything about Maude yet, and I doubt the hospital would tell me a thing if I called. So I guess I have to wait."

"Wouldn't Mavis call you?"

Miri shrugged. "Who knows? She must have much more important things on her mind right now."

"Very likely, unless her mother's been given a clean bill of health."

As soon as she finished cooking the sausage and eggs, Miri put a platter on the table and told him to help himself. He allowed he'd like a few slices of toast, so she made them the easy way, bringing her four-slice toaster to the table and working from there. She didn't much care for cold scrambled eggs herself.

Gil took over making the toast and buttering it for the two of them.

"Do you have someplace of your own to live?" she asked, watching his dexterity with the toast. "Or do you live in barracks or whatever they call it now?"

"I share an apartment with three other men. Most of the time some of us are away, so it never feels crowded. But yeah, I had my own place, sort of. Just didn't make financial sense to get an apartment to live by myself."

"I can see that. Like when I was in college. Three of us shared an apartment. Unfortunately, it didn't always work well."

"But they move on, don't they? Roommates, I mean. A frequent flux."

As he ate, energy seemed to be returning to him, and along with it the attraction she felt. Somehow she needed to get that this was dangerous. Not that she believed he'd be abusive or anything, but Gil was a man used to being on the go, who probably wanted to return to where his unit was stationed, and who might even manage to get himself back into good enough shape that they'd consider putting him in the field again.

Fifteen-plus years of experience had to be invaluable, and she had no idea of the extent of his injuries.

"You know," she remarked, "I always thought it was odd that Al never once had a serious relationship. When we were kids he seemed like the kind of guy who'd eventually want a family."

"Maybe he did. Women certainly fluttered around the guys. But when you have to pack up and go on a moment's notice so often...well, I think that ruined a lot of budding relationships. Which is not to say none of us married and had kids. Just that many of us never encountered that most amazing confluence, a woman who could live with our jobs that we could also want to marry."

Miri smiled faintly. "I don't think that's easy for anyone to find, really. Maybe you guys were just more cautious."

"Meaning?"

"Look at the divorce statistics in the first year of marriage. Seems like most people fly by the seat of their pants."

She was glad to hear him laugh. Maybe the guy was loosening up a bit.

But she doubted he would loosen up much, if ever.

With the kitchen cleaned up and the day growing grayer by the moment, Miri glanced out and saw the trees beginning to toss, bearing their message of a weather change.

"I hope you can stand being cooped up for a while," she said to Gil as she took their coffee into the living room. "Weather's changing, with snow this afternoon and the possibility of a blizzard."

"I thought it was getting colder. Do you think Al's family will still drop in?"

"Probably. There's time for that."

"Good."

Today he skipped the rocking chair for the more upright gooseneck chair. He propped his cane on the arm, the curved handle hooked over it.

"I guess you didn't get to talk with them much yesterday. And they're the whole reason you came out here."

He nodded. "I got to thinking they hadn't seen him in a while before he was killed, and that they might want to know more about how he was, what he was doing…within the limits of operational security, of course. I know I'd have a lot of questions if I hadn't been with him."

"That's thoughtful of you."

"Not really. I think it's what Al would want me to do. The fog of war extends far beyond the battlefield, to the families, who seldom get the straight dope. And I wanted to see you, too, of course."

She blinked. She hadn't expected that. "Whatever for, other than that Al was my cousin?"

Gil shook his head a little. "You stayed with me, Miri. You became part of my memories of Al. And there's another thing."

"Yes?" Her heart sped up a bit as she wondered what was coming.

"I needed to see you differently from the funeral. You were glued in my mind's eye, a young woman so alone, grieving, and playing 'Taps' so bravely. A sad image. So thanks for some more cheerful ones."

Over the months since Al's funeral, Miri's grief had settled down. It never went away, and could still come in waves, but acceptance had arrived. Now, all of a sudden, she felt her eyes prickle with tears she hadn't shed in a while. Forever, she thought. She'd miss Al forever, but in her mind and heart her memories of him would now always be wrapped in the sad strains of "Taps."

"I'm sorry," Gil said swiftly. "I didn't want to make you sad all over again."

She shook her head. "I've never stopped being sad."

"Sorry," he said again. Then he rose and limped out of the living room. She expected him to go down the hall to the bedroom, but instead she heard him grab his jacket and leave through the front door.

He was going to freeze out there, she thought almost absently. Then she let the tears come. Tears for Al. Tears for his best friend. God, life could be so cruel.

Outside, hip notwithstanding, Gil did his best to march along the sidewalk. The wind had grown cutting as a knife, but he was used to it and worse from his time in some cold mountainous countries. He tried to keep his pace even and firm, but his damaged hip still wasn't ready to give him all the mobility he wanted. Of course, the best way to deal with any of this was to push through the pain.

Use it. Loosen up that scar tissue and make damaged joints do their work until he had enough muscle built up to accommodate a full range of motion. At least that was the hope. The docs gave him fifty-fifty at best.

Fifty-fifty was good enough. Gill had faced far worse odds.

He was also beginning to wonder what he was

doing here. Sure, he'd felt he might be able to answer some questions for Al's family. Maybe share a few of the funnier stories they might not have heard. He'd certainly felt it was like an homage.

But there was something else: Miri. He'd never been able to forget her from that day of the funeral. Never been able to forget the way she had stood tall and straight, playing "Taps" for her beloved cousin. That woman had amazing strength.

But over the months they had corresponded, he realized something else was happening. He wanted to see Miri again. Wanted a chance to get to know her. And before his wounding he'd even entertained a few sexual thought about her, although out of respect for Al he hadn't let them go too far. It wasn't that Al hadn't had his share of flings when the opportunity presented, but family was a whole different ballpark.

Miri was a strikingly attractive woman although she didn't seem aware of it. She had a great smile, almost always ready, and a kind demeanor. He imagined that the kids in her music classes thought highly of her.

His mouth twisted a little as he rounded a corner and felt the slash of wind mixed with ice against his cheek. Reaching back, he pulled up his hood. Miri didn't need a personal reference from him, although that seemed to be what he was trying to build. Why?

Pointless exercise. He wouldn't be here long. He had some other people he intended to visit, men and women who'd been wounded and retired for disability, or had just left when their terms of service were completed. People from the history of his own seventeen years in uniform, many of them the kind of friends you could make only when facing danger again and again together.

So today he'd visit with Al's family, then once this snow blew through he'd hit the road again.

And that meant he didn't need to figure out anything about Miri. He might feel attracted to her, but that wouldn't matter. It couldn't matter. He simply would not allow anyone to get that close to him. Not anymore. Al had closed that chapter of his life by dying. It didn't pay to care.

Gil came across a park bench and decided to sit for a few minutes. A pretty park, he thought, despite having been browned completely by winter except for a few evergreens around the edges. It wasn't large, and held only a few playground items. He thought he remembered seeing an even bigger one on his way into town.

Small town, more than one park. Nice. He heard approaching footsteps and looked up to see a face he recognized from yesterday, Nate Tate. The man people had referred to as the old sheriff.

For a retired guy, he didn't look all that old. "Sergeant," Tate said, taking a seat at the other end of the bench. "Getting old has certain requirements, probably not so different from you. Gotta keep in shape somehow, although it's a long way from the old days."

Gil smiled faintly. "Just call me Gil, Sheriff."

"Nate. Ain't the sheriff anymore, but I feel sorry

for Gage Dalton, who is. I retired more than a decade ago and they still call him the new sheriff."

Gil's smile widened a hair. "I'm not surprised."

"Things change slowly around here. Except the weather, which seems to be changing fast today." Nate chuckled. "Good of you to come back to visit with Al Baker's family. I'm sorry I didn't get more of a chance to visit with you yesterday, but it seemed like our younger vets had you pretty well in hand."

"They did." He wondered if Nate was just being neighborly or if he had a larger point to this.

"Vietnam," Nate said. "Multiple tours with the Army Special Forces. I hear you all are branching out wider these days."

"Sometimes," Gil answered cautiously.

"Didn't figure you were going to give me any details." Tate shook his head a bit. "That old French saying 'the more things change the more they stay the same' probably fits. I crossed a lot of borders I prolly shouldn't've crossed, but I had my orders. Anyway, I'm not trying to give you the third degree. You ought to come over sometime. I think you'd enjoy getting to know Seth and Edie better, as well as my daughter, Wendy, and her hubby, Yuma. He was a medevac pilot in Nam. And that Edie's a pistol. She used to fly combat search and rescue. And I guess you know that Seth was a SEAL."

"He mentioned it."

"Well, hang around for a while. You'll find plenty of others in these parts with your kind of background.

And now I need to finish my walk before my wife wonders what happened to me. Take it easy, hear?"

Gil watched Nate Tate stride away, recognizing the easy step of a man who'd walked many miles and knew to keep his knees soft and ready for sudden changes in the terrain. Apparently some things never went away.

Gil rose, too, and started back to Miri's house. He'd heard church bells and decided it wouldn't be long before the Bakers arrived. He didn't want to be rude, although now that he faced the conversation he had no idea what he could tell those people. Their son had shown great courage and had died honorably in the service of his country.

That was the long and short of it. The stuff in between? Most of it no longer mattered or couldn't be shared. A life came down to a single sentence. He supposed a guy was lucky if he got that much.

It occurred to him as he walked the last block to Miri's house that this town was almost trying to wrap itself around him, to welcome him. An odd sensation, but he was having it, quite a contrast to the many towns he'd walked through with the certainty that death might be hiding behind any door.

There was absolutely no reason for this town to give a fig about him one way or the other, good or bad. Maybe he was the one looking for something and projecting it onto the people he'd met. Sure, they'd all been nice, but so what. Common courtesy, was all.

Inside, he doffed his jacket, grateful for the warmth

of the house. Miri popped her head out of the kitchen, asking, "Hot drink?"

"Whatever you've got. It's getting really cold out there."

"I wondered if you'd notice," she said lightly. "Local weather has us down in the single digits now, with more to come. Some reports of sleet."

"I'll second that report," he said as he limped his way to the kitchen. "Felt it sting me on the face once while I was out. Ran into your old sheriff, too."

"Nate? He walks every morning, but usually there's a stop at the diner along the way. I still haven't heard about Maude, by the way."

Gil pulled out a chair at the table. "Surely there's some way to find out?"

"It'll get on the grapevine pretty soon. All it needs is for Mavis to tell one person. Oh, and I'm sorry, but Betsy and Jack won't be coming this morning, after all. Jack was worrying about the weather, and I can't say I blame him. It's a long drive back to the ranch, and just about impossible if there's a whiteout. The wind's already strong—I guess I don't need to tell you that," she said with a little laugh. "Anyway, once snow starts to fall it won't be long."

"I've been in a lot of weather like that. Better safe than sorry." True as that was, he wondered again if he should have come here. Maybe he was rocking a boat and the Bakers were trying to avoid it. Maybe it wasn't just the weather. "Miri?"

"Uh-huh?" She placed a teakettle on the stove and lit the burner.

"Did I make a mistake coming here?"

That seemed to surprise her. She turned from the stove to frown faintly at him. "Why would you think that? Because Jack and Betsy decided they needed to get home before the weather got too bad?"

"Not really."

"I hope not. I haven't seen Betsy this animated since she got the news about Al. She had a truly great week with planning the barbecue. It eased my heart to see how excited and happy she got. So why should you think coming here was a mistake?"

"Because I'm not sure what I'm doing. I thought I'd come and share stories of Al with them, but there isn't a whole lot I can or should share, and there's probably a lot they wouldn't want to hear."

"Then how about you just let them ask questions whenever we get together. There are probably a lot of things they want to know, and I'd bet most of them are very small."

He regarded her steadily. "Small how?"

She shrugged a little. "I'm not a parent, but I some-how don't think I'd want to hear much about my son's war adventures. I'd want to know the little things, like did he often go hungry, did he suffer from the cold… things like that. His comfort. Whether he seemed content with what he was doing. Basically, the one thing he might never talk about with me—did he have re-grets?"

Gil stood abruptly. From time to time he had serious problems being indoors. He felt confined, nearly trapped. "I'm going to step out onto the porch. I won't be long."

"Do you still want that hot drink?" she asked.

"Please," he said over his shoulder, and repeated, "I won't be long."

Because the pain was crawling up and down his side again, burrowing like an auger into his hip. His spine raised a bit of a ruckus, too, reminding him it wasn't perfectly straight anymore, and oh, by the way, did he have *any* idea how much everything else hurt from his continual limping?

Yeah, he knew, and willed his screaming body to silence.

Miri stood chewing her lip while the teakettle behind her began to whistle. Something was going on with Gil, although to be fair she really didn't know him that well. He seemed reserved even now, although she'd wondered if that tower of granite at the funeral had been a man trying to contain a whole lot of pain.

But there was still some of that about him. He hadn't opened up in any really significant way. Maybe self-control of his inner workings was necessary to his survival. Maybe living in a steel tower was a necessity. How would she know?

But watching him now, hearing him wonder if he should have even come to see her family…that seemed somehow sad. And it wasn't because *he* didn't want to talk about Al, as near as she could tell, but because he was concerned he might cause others pain.

Somehow he'd seemed to need to come out here, and now that he was here, he was having second thoughts. Why?

Aw, heck, she didn't know, and had no way to know what was going on inside that steel box.

She turned down the kettle enough to keep it hot without boiling, and opened her pantry to root around inside. Since her aunt and uncle weren't coming by with the promised rolls from the bakery, she had to figure out something for lunch. Since Gil had been out walking in the cold, preferably something warm and filling.

Just about the time she settled on grilled cheese sandwiches with tomato soup, a childhood favorite turned into a comfort food on cold days, the phone rang.

She reached for it, expecting to hear the voice of one of her friends. She almost didn't recognize Mavis, who had never called her before.

"Mom's gonna be okay," Mavis said.

"What happened? Are you all right?"

"I'm fine," she said almost irritably. "It was a heart attack. Not real bad, the doc says, because she got help quick. Thanks."

"I'm just glad I found her. So what's next?"

"She'll be coming home tomorrow, supposed to take a few days off and start a lot of medicines. She don't like that idea, but too bad. Anyway, she wants me to open the diner this afternoon in spite of the weather. Might do short hours until she gets back on her feet."

"I'm sure that's wise. And everyone's going to be so happy to hear that Maude is all right."

"I know I am." Without another word, Mavis disconnected.

Miri took the receiver from her ear and stared at it until she heard the dial tone. Shaking her head, she hung it up on the wall base. Those two women were something else. She supposed she ought to be glad Mavis thought to call her. And it was good news, too.

Wondering if Gil was going to stay outside long enough to turn into an ice sculpture, she opened the fridge and pulled out Havarti cheese for the sandwiches. That cheese was a bit of an extravagance, but sometimes she refused to cut corners. The market had sliced it for her, making it ready to go on sandwiches.

Then she pulled a couple cans of tomato soup out of the cupboard.

This might turn into a very long day.

Gil hadn't pulled on his jacket. Standing outside in nothing but a sweatshirt and camo pants was a fierce punishment as the wind and temperature became more dangerous. It was also stupid.

Like it or not, he'd have to go inside soon, but for now the threat of freezing at least quieted the rest of his body's complaints. Somewhat, anyway.

It had struck him, when Miri had told him that the Bakers wouldn't be able to come over because of the weather, that he really had no idea why he'd come here. Sure, his parents drove him nuts with their constant pressure on him to leave the army. They should have gotten the obvious by now: he wasn't going to quit. He wasn't a quitter. Period. He felt he still had more to offer, although that was up in the air, given his physical state.

But all that aside, he'd come here ostensibly to talk to Al's family about his friend. But what could Gil really share? A few possibly amusing stories. Probably very little that would ease their loss one iota. But he hadn't thought that through clearly, a fact that troubled him.

He wasn't a man given to self-reflection, probably a good thing considering what he did. But now he was reflecting. It had begun just a little after he'd started to recover from his wounds, but he'd pretty much suppressed it. Why? Because it was uncomfortable? What the hell about his life was comfortable?

He sighed and watched the cloud of his breath blow away. His ears were beginning to feel pinched. Time to go in.

The cold had stiffened his hip. He should have kept moving, pacing the porch maybe. Leaning heavily on his cane, he started to take a step toward the door when he was struck by a moment of piercing self-understanding.

He needed more. Al's death had awakened that need in him. Life was too damn short, and his army career might not be enough for him anymore. He wasn't going to quit, no way, but maybe it was time to admit that something was lacking.

Maybe he'd come here to check that out. Unlike him, Al had often mentioned thoughts for the future, had looked forward to returning to work on the family ranch. Gil had never allowed himself to look beyond his eventual retirement. Instead he'd listen to Al spin an occasional dream and tell him he'd make Gil part of it. Not that Gil had ever been sure he wanted to go that way, but maybe Al had been viewing the future for both of them.

Then Gil had had a near-death experience. That might be all that had him unsettled. He could have been killed, and his body had been wrecked. He didn't want to leave the army, but now he had to face what it meant when eventually he'd have to, now or later. He had too much time on his hands to ignore it any longer.

He muttered a curse under his breath and opened the door. Not only had his body been messed up. His brain felt as if it had been put in a blender.

Chapter Four

A couple hours after a truly satisfying lunch, Gil sat in the living room alone. Miri had excused herself to do some work for school. Teachers, she had told him lightly, didn't really get time off.

"What about summer?" he'd asked.

"We get about a month off, from the time we finish closing up our classrooms until the meetings for next year begin. Everything from refresher training to organizing and planning. It's not what most people see from the outside. I work every evening on planning and homework, and fit in at least a few hours every weekend. You should see me in early August, when we start band camp three weeks before classes. I'm running constantly."

Things he had never thought about. Things he'd never had a reason to think about. There was probably a whole lot of that, given the structured, mission-oriented life he'd chosen.

If he were to be honest, perhaps that constant focus he'd developed had been a sort of protection. It wasn't as if he *never* had time to look outside his box. He just hadn't. Didn't.

He stared out the front windows at a world that was steadily going nuts. Just yesterday it had felt like spring. Now the fierce wind was beginning to blow snow around. Snow that hadn't existed twenty-four hours ago.

Much as he suddenly wanted to get in his car and leave, he understood two things: he couldn't drive safely in the approaching weather, and he couldn't leave himself behind. He had become uncomfortable baggage in his own life.

Then there was Miri. He didn't want to be rude to her. She'd opened her house to him, welcoming him almost as family because of Al. Unfortunately, one reason he wanted to leave was because of the sexual heat she awakened in him. It had been a while, but now he was experiencing a virtual storm of hunger inside himself. Even if she felt the same, casual sex would be a lousy way to repay her hospitality.

So far she'd exhibited none of the desire to attract a man that he was used to. No makeup, not that she needed any, hair in that long braid rather than carefully coiffed and clothes that steamed his brain when they clearly weren't intended to: jeans far from skin-tight, loose sweatshirts or flannel shirts, and either socks or boots on her feet.

Everything about her was laid-back and casual. But then, maybe that had something to do with living in this small Western town. He couldn't imagine who would have to dress up around here. Maybe the ranches had been dictating local styles forever.

Then his thoughts flashed back to the funeral, to Miri standing there in a long, dark blue dress, and appearing so small to him, even when she approached to speak to him.

She'd had the strength it took to play "Taps" for her cousin, so he figured her for a very strong woman. "Taps" had a way of bringing people to helpless tears, especially at a funeral for someone they loved. Yet she had stood tall and proud, and not a single note had wavered.

Kudos to her. He'd admired her then, and he admired her now. For example, the quick way she'd responded to Maude. He'd seen the older woman go to the back of the diner and it had never occurred to him there was something wrong. Then suddenly Miri had sprung into action and found Maude in trouble.

Because, according to Miri's explanation later, the coffee was never allowed to cool down at Maude's diner. So Al's cousin was observant and astute. She didn't just brush it aside. She went to see what was going on.

A caring woman, from everything he'd seen, caring and strong. And maybe the nicest thing about her was that she seemed happy with her life.

The phone rang, and she must have answered it in her tiny office space in the corner of the bedroom he was using.

Sitting there, thinking it was time to move again before he began to freeze up, Gil wondered what it would be like to grow up in one town, to know so many people, to have friends you'd known all the way back to childhood.

He couldn't imagine it. His home was his unit. And unfortunately, too many people he had known were gone, some for good. If he had any roots, they were planted squarely in the army…and that was temporary. Never at any point had he viewed it as permanent, simply because every single mission raised a possibility that he wouldn't come back, or would come back as he had this time.

And while he hoped they'd keep him on, even if it meant taking a desk job, he knew damn well that when his convalescence was over they might give him a medical discharge.

Hardly surprising that he was beginning to think about matters he'd held at bay for a long time. He might need to carve out a very different future.

Al's pipe dreams of them working the ranch together had merely been a time-filler for Gil. Something to think about, but something he'd never planned to follow through on. Now it appeared that it might be time to find a plan for himself.

"Hey."

He looked up from his rather gloomy thoughts to see Miri hovering in the doorway. She was smiling.

"Need anything?"

"I'm pretty much okay, except that I'd like to take another walk."

"I don't think that's going to happen right now." She waved toward the window and he realized that while he'd been wandering unfamiliar paths inside his own head, trying to take charge of them, the world outside had disappeared in white. He could barely make out the shape of the house just across the street.

"It looks like a snow globe," he remarked.

"Worse." She entered the room and perched on the edge of the rocker. "We're only supposed to get a few inches, but with the wind blowing this way it might wind up looking like ten feet. You must have seen plenty in Afghanistan and other such places."

He nodded slowly. "Sure. Up in the mountains it wasn't unheard of to get several feet overnight. Of course, that could happen a lot of places when you get into the mountains. I don't need to tell you that."

"Nope. Last I looked, we had some mountains around us," she teased. "But we're in what's called their rain shadow. The dumping usually occurs at higher elevations before it reaches us. Usually. Not always."

He glanced out the windows again. It looked wicked and this had barely started. "But it'll clear out by to-morrow?"

"Maybe not. That phone call I just got was from one of my friends, telling me we're going to have a conference call with school admin this evening. Depending on how it looks, we may cancel school."

"Why decide so early?"

"Because around here, school buses have a very long way to go to reach all the kids. Just as importantly, the plows may not be able to get to many places early enough."

"I hadn't thought about that." But remembering the drive out to the Baker ranch, he figured a school bus would take even longer. "I don't recall Al saying anything about it, not that it's the kind of thing to come up in conversation."

"I doubt it would."

He sensed her studying him in a way that didn't quite go with the casual, pointless conversation they were having. Of course, he wasn't used to this kind of conversation unless it happened over a few beers in a bar with some of his friends. Then they'd get casual, often with humor that might shock outsiders. But inside that circle, humor blew off steam, and it was often black humor.

Then Miri astonished him by asking, "Do you ever let your hair down?"

His gaze jumped to her face. She was serious. "What do you mean?"

"At the funeral, I likened you to granite poured into a uniform. I don't think I've ever seen anyone express so little emotion. I didn't know if that was the real you, or if you were under tight control because of the circumstances. But now you've been here since Friday and I still feel like you're granite. Oh, you've smiled and even laughed from time to time, but it doesn't go deep, does it."

She wasn't really asking, and he felt no real need to explain anything to her. He was what he was, mostly because life had happened to him the way it happened to everyone. You did what you needed to get by... within reason.

But the image she had painted of him caught his attention. Granite? He wasn't sure he liked that. He wondered if he should apologize, although for exactly what, he wasn't certain. But she forestalled him.

"Al was a little like that when he came home, too. There were parts of him well beyond reach. It felt kind of strange to me, because I'd known him so well when we were children. I figured it had to do with experiences none of the rest of us could ever share. But you know what I wondered?"

"What?"

"How many of those parts of him had been left behind on his missions, not just buried but gone for good. Or whether they were still there but had changed."

"My knowledge of Al is limited to the years we served together, Miri. I wouldn't venture to guess how much they changed him." Especially since he'd been going through changes of his own at the same time, and probably pretty much at the same rate, he had no way to measure any of it.

But he wondered what she was hoping to discover. More than one person he'd known in spec ops had noted that when they went home they felt like aliens. No secret in that. Most combat vets probably felt the same way. They'd seen things and done things nobody who hadn't been there could truly comprehend. Best to shut your damn mouth and do your utmost to pretend you'd left all that behind.

"It changes us," he finally said, even though she'd already figured that out. "We don't quite mesh with the rest of the world anymore. Inevitable."

"So you shut down?"

He definitely didn't like this line of questioning. Shut down? He didn't think so. But he was extremely careful about how he spent his emotions. Too big an investment could cost heavily.

Nevertheless, her words struck him even as he argued internally with them. Nothing had been the same since he'd regained consciousness and faced the degree of his injuries, the dawning realization that no amount of recovery would be able to put him back in the field, no matter how hard he tried.

Perhaps the changes had begun even earlier with Al's death, when he'd just put more cement in the chinks in his armor—a temporary patch, it had begun to seem.

But the fact remained that he'd been dealing at some level with the realization that nothing was going to be the same. No amount of denial was going to alter that.

As he looked at Miri, her face so earnest and concerned, he felt obliged to admit something to himself. "I tried to be granite. I guess that made me less than a whole person."

Just saying it caused his mind to teeter on the edge of something deeper and darker. How much of himself had he amputated to do his job? And what would those parts think of him if he brought them back? Being stone had been useful. Being human might give him a whole new set of problems.

Dropping back into civilian life caused a lot of difficulty for many vets. It was never seamless, and sometimes it got crazy and painful. Gil didn't want to be one of them, but he had to admit that as long as he had the job the demons didn't rise very often. No room for them.

That was changing. He'd been fighting it, but he knew that sooner or later he was going to lose. Sooner or later he'd have to find a way to deal with all he'd done and experienced. There was no shame, but there was understanding that he was no longer like people who'd never walked the paths he'd walked.

"It's daunting," he said, though he hadn't meant to. This woman didn't need to hear any of this, nor was he sure he wanted to share it. Outside, even though the light had dimmed a bit with the waning afternoon, he saw the whirling, blinding snow and figured that was probably pretty much what was going on inside him. Or would be going on when he dropped the protective barriers and gave up the denial.

"What's daunting?" she prodded gently when he didn't speak for a while.

"The idea of being a civilian again."

She rose, then surprised him by sitting beside him on the sofa. She surprised him even more by reaching out to lay her hand on his arm. He'd been avoiding human touch for a long time now. It had the potential to slide past his defenses. His skin tightened beneath her hand, tensing at her touch even through his shirtsleeve.

"Why is that daunting?"

"Because the person I've become doesn't fit. Because I've got things locked away I don't want to risk letting escape. Because like everyone else who's ever gone to war, the only place I fit anymore is with others like me."

Rising, slipping away from her touch because it awakened him in ways he couldn't afford, he started to pace. He had to keep moving, keep stretching the scar tissue. After a few turns around the tiny living room, he bent and tried to touch his toes. Better than a couple weeks ago. Looser. But his hip shrieked fit to kill.

"What exactly happened to you?"

The bluntness of Miri's question shouldn't have surprised him. She'd already struck him as a woman who saw the world clearly and had no particular desire to be shielded from its ugly realities. Maybe because she hadn't been exposed to many of them…but then he remembered the story of what had happened to her parents. Ugly realities and she were not strangers.

"I was shot." She didn't need any more details.

"And?"

And she was going to demand them, anyway. He didn't like to talk about it, but even as he considered telling her that, he heard the rudeness in the words he'd speak. She knew what had happened to her cousin. Why not share the latest edition of what happens when you go on a covert mission?

"And?" he repeated. "We were covertly infiltrating a country where we weren't welcome, and we were ambushed. I suppose I shouldn't be alive. I took five bullets and some of the blast from a grenade."

"So you pretty much got chewed up." Her voice didn't waver.

"Sort of. Bullets smashed my hip, injured my spine and managed to miss major arteries. The grenade got me with flash burns and some shrapnel. So here I am."

He hoped she didn't ask more. The edited version was quite enough.

More than enough, it seemed, because walls in his mind were shredding, turning from concrete to flaps of paper blowing in the wind. The memories were not only insistent, they forced their way in, filling his mind's eye with horror and his heart with fury. He was tipping over an edge, and he struggled to catch himself but he couldn't.

In an instant he was back in the place where Al had died. Except Al hadn't died there. They had carried him out after they cleared the threat, carried him and his severed leg and arm for miles to where a rescue chopper could dart in and take him. It had taken the chopper long enough. Long enough for Al to die. Toward the end they might have overdosed him on morphine. Gil couldn't be sure, but Al was in so much agony, begging them to kill him.

The family didn't need to know that, but he couldn't forget it. Would never forget how he had failed his best friend.

But then he slipped again, this time into the place where he had nearly met his own end. Memories of the bullets striking, feeling like a sledgehammer, the explosion and concussion and...

Things began to become muddled and mixed up, turning into a stew of many places, many fights, many losses. They usually got out with everyone alive, but not every time. There were the wounds, the screams, the gore, the memory of people, innocent people, getting caught in a crossfire, memories of the enemy... All of it swirled around inside him, riveting him, taunting him, filling him with anger and pain and grief and hatred and...

He fell into the abyss.

Miri saw Gil freeze and stand as stiff as a statue. Soon, a look on his face, especially his eyes, told her he was no longer with her. He was seeing something only he could see, and it didn't appear pleasant.

A flashback? She didn't know, but wondered. She had some familiarity with them because of her friends but was in no position to say with any surety where Gil's thoughts had gone...or why.

She also didn't know what to do, if anything. Should she try to draw him back to the present or leave him alone?

Leave him alone, she decided. Any sound she made, any movement, could strike him as a threat if his mind had carried him back to war. Better to feel helpless, much as she hated it, than trigger something they both might regret.

Most especially she didn't want to cause him any regret. "Just leave him alone" was a mantra used by some of her friends. It would pass.

So eventually this would pass. Sooner or later, Gil would break free of the prison and return. She just had to be patient and wait.

But she *was* feeling an urgent need to answer the call of nature. She studied where he was standing and where she sat, and tried to envision a trajectory that wouldn't startle him.

Then she heard him expel a huge sigh. After a moment, he moved a bit, as if stiff, and his gaze trailed toward her. "Was I gone long?"

"Not really." A surprisingly short time, considering what she'd heard from her friends. "Five minutes? It must have seemed longer to you. Anyway, if I could run to the bathroom?"

He seemed a little surprised, then frowned darkly. "I'm sorry."

"No need." She rose, trying to appear happy. "Hey, everybody has some problems, right?"

"I don't do this."

She didn't ask what he meant, mainly because she didn't want to stir a pot that might still be simmering. "No worries. I'll be right back and we can talk as much or as little as you want."

Once in her bathroom, Miri was astonished by how much tension had filled her. Hardly surprising considering what an intense man Gil was even when he was trying to be pleasant. There was always an undercurrent to him, a sense that he could spring at any moment. Like a panther or leopard, sunning itself in a tree one second and then grabbing some prey in its jaws the next.

Like a cat, she thought as she leaned against the sink after washing her hands. She'd read that cats never really went to sleep the way people did, that their ears never turned off and they could wake in an instant at a worrisome sound.

Well, in some way Gil was like that. Did he ever really relax? Could he if he wanted to?

Aw, heck, what did it matter? He'd be buzzing out of here as soon as he could.

The main thing was that he was probably feeling pretty uncomfortable right now. He'd said he didn't do that. She could only guess that he meant he didn't flash back to the war. But whatever it was, it had left him exposed for several minutes, and he could be perceiving it as a failure on his part.

So she needed to get back out there and normalize things again, so he didn't get the impression she was trying to avoid him. He didn't deserve that.

Still, the breather had been good. She smiled faintly at her reflection and then marched back to the living room, only to find him staring out at blowing snow, his hands clasped behind his back. Despite having the heat on, she felt a chill snaking through the house. One of these days she was going to have to figure where her weatherizing needed some work.

"I'm thinking about a cup of tea," she said. "You want some?"

He turned a bit, exposing the side of his face. "No, thank you. I'm fine."

It had been a while since lunch, and soon she would need to provide some kind of meal, but Miri found herself drawing a complete blank. Cooking was not at all her favorite thing, though on her own she was quite capable of scrounging up a halfway decent meal from her fridge or pantry.

But now she had someone else to think about. Distracted, aware that Gil was apparently going to share not one thing about what had just happened, she headed for the kitchen. Didn't she have several cans of New England clam chowder? Especially tasty when she threw in some bacon bits, a staple in her refrigerator. They could make anything taste better, from salad to soup to scrambled eggs.

Rearranging cans in the cupboard, she found the clam chowder she remembered, and an unopened bag of oyster crackers. A footstep alerted her and she glanced over her shoulder. Gil had joined her.

"You okay with clam chowder?" she asked. "From a can."

"Haven't had that in ages, and I like it. What can I do?"

"Not much." She smiled. "Canned soup is hard to turn into a group cooking affair." She paused. "Are you all right, Gil?"

"I'm fine," he said immediately. "But I guess I owe you an explanation."

She shook her head as she lifted down three cans of the soup, hoping he would be hungry. "You don't have to explain anything to me. Not a thing."

He took the cans from her hands and placed them on the counter while she brought out the oyster crackers.

"My dad especially loved these crackers with soup," she remarked. "He was a fan of almost every kind of cracker, but these were a treat. I don't know the difference other than shape, but the habit stuck with me."

"I haven't had them in years."

"Well, you can rediscover them this evening. I suspect they didn't get soggy in the soup as fast as a regular soda cracker, because to me they don't taste any different."

"I'll let you know."

When everything was on the counter and she'd closed the pantry, he touched her forearm lightly. "I *do* owe you an explanation, unless you just don't want to hear it. But talking might help me understand what I just did."

At that she gave him her undivided attention. Miri was eager to listen. She felt seriously attracted to him, and that frightened her, because he was a great big unknown.

"I'm listening." Such a lame answer to what she suspected had been a difficult offer for him to make. He'd already pretty much said he didn't talk about anything except to other vets. He felt alienated, different.

Well, he'd been living in a different world from folks like her. Coming back had to make him feel like the odd man out.

She waved him to the table as her teakettle began to whistle. One green tea bag in her mug, boiling water, then she turned the kettle off. Sitting facing him seemed like a safer place than kitty-corner to him. If she grew any more attracted to Gil, she'd be daydreaming about him, wasting her time and setting herself up for a fall. Man, even now he looked scrumptious, but as near as she could tell there was no part of himself that he was prepared to give anyone.

She tamped down her female awareness of him and forced herself to wait patiently. Ordinarily she wasn't short on patience, but Gil had some unusual effects on her. She very much wanted to hear what he might say, and the longer he hesitated the less likely he was to speak.

"I've never had one before," he said slowly, "but I think I had a flashback."

That struck her. "Never?"

His expression grew slightly wry, surprising her. This was a grim subject, she would have thought.

"Never," he repeated. "Not in any real sense. Memories, yes, but not the kind that make me feel I'm right in the middle of it all again. I think I've been too busy. Just about the time something might have begun bubbling up, I was off my leave and back on duty."

"Where flashbacks don't intrude?"

"I can't speak for everyone. For me, no. It was like if I stayed on the rails, I couldn't divert. I diverted today."

When he fell silent in thought, she dared to speak again. "That must be...unsettling, to put it mildly."

"Very," he said bluntly. "I don't like my mind playing tricks on me. It's the best weapon in my arsenal."

She felt her mouth trying to fall open and quickly looked down, lifting her tea bag in and out of the hot water. She liked it strong. "I, um, never thought of my brain as a weapon."

"Of course not. You've never had to. But consider my position. What soldier could function without a brain? A zombie?"

The way he said it drew a small laugh from her. She believed he did so intentionally. Trying to get over rough ground as lightly as possible? "Okay, I get it. It just wasn't a comparison I'm used to drawing."

He nodded. "Anyway..." A sigh escaped him. "That came out of nowhere and I don't like it. Who would? All of a sudden I was back in some of the worst times I've had, reliving them. It's one thing to remember. It's another to relive."

"Absolutely!"

"Maybe I will have some tea. Green tea?"

She nodded. He rose before she could, added some water to the kettle and placed it on the burner. "You wouldn't believe how many places in the world I've drunk green tea. Or some really black tea. Anyway, no point going there, because I can't tell you."

Those last few words seemed to be tied up with a frown that appeared on his face. "I can't really tell you anything," he said after a minute. "I'll just have some tea with you and we'll forget this."

She didn't like the withdrawal. Maybe he couldn't talk about his missions, or even the countries involved, but he could surely share his feelings about it.

"You know, Gil, you not only reminded me of granite when we first met, but now you're reminding me of a bottle of champagne that's been shaken and the top is about to pop."

He lifted his brow at that, and there was not only a change in his expression, but a change in his posture. Not so straight and square, leaning more heavily on his cane... Shrinking? No, not that. Maybe weary, and not just physically.

The teakettle whistled and he ignored it for a few seconds, then seemed to shake himself. "Tea bags?"

"Just sit. I'll get it all. How do you like your tea?"

"Straight. Listen, I'm not helpless."

"I don't think you are. But I'm fussy about people rummaging in my cupboards. Space is limited, so everything has a place."

Another attempt to divert the conversation? she wondered as she pulled out a small canister with green tea bags, plus a mug, and put everything in front of him as he eased into his chair again.

He was soon dipping his own tea bag. "Part of what happened was that I went back to the day Al was killed."

She sucked in a sharp breath. For some reason she hadn't expected that, or to hear it so bluntly. Not with the way he'd been edging around it.

"And to the day I got wounded this last time," he added. "But when it comes to reliving experiences, I'd choose to relive my own wounding a thousand times instead of Al's."

Now she was on unfamiliar ground. She didn't want to sound trite, but what he'd just shared certainly deserved an acknowledgment. "That says a lot," she said carefully. "It must have been horrific."

His jaw worked and his gaze didn't meet hers. He didn't want to talk about it. That was fine by her. She'd learned all she needed to know when they'd been advised not to have an open coffin. Her imagination was already too good.

He dropped his tea bag onto the saucer she'd earlier placed on the table, beside hers. Then he lifted the mug and drank deeply. Evidently his tongue didn't scald easily.

He blew out a long breath. "I've had too much time on my hands," he said, as if that explained it all.

"Too much time for my mind to wander into places it shouldn't go."

She chewed her lip for a moment. "Isn't it going to have to go there eventually?"

"Probably. But I won't complain if it waits a few decades."

He looked at her then, and she was astonished to see a half smile on his face, reflected in his eyes. Talk about a fast mood change.

"I'm not always gloomy and rigid," he said. "I've been known to have a good time and crack a few jokes."

She tilted her head, thinking he was a puzzle. This felt like a non sequitur. "I believe you," she murmured.

"No, you probably don't. No reason you should. When you met me, I had a certain role to perform for my friend and for the army. Now I come here and all you see is someone who's been wounded and isn't even sure he's ready to pick up any thread of life."

That grabbed her attention. "You're just tired," she suggested. "You've been through a lot and you're probably awfully tired most of the time. Wouldn't that be normal?"

"You don't have to make excuses for me," he replied, his smile fading. "I'm not good company. The worst part is that I don't especially care if I am. I came here with some lamebrained notion, thinking I could share a few stories with Al's family that they might enjoy knowing, but I haven't managed it yet. And the main reason I haven't managed it is because all I can damn well think about is him dying!"

Chapter Five

Gil strode out of the kitchen, if you could call it striding while he was leaning on a cane. His hip felt as if fiery pokers were digging into it and that at any moment it might just suddenly give way.

He was glad that Miri didn't follow him, though. He was venturing too near to some things. Flashbacks to those awful hours when Al had been hit, when they'd gathered him up and raced over rugged, defiant terrain to reach the landing zone and the helicopter that might save his life. Six men, using everything training and God had given them to keep up a punishing pace.

But they'd been too late.

Until the day *he* died, Gil was never, ever going to forget Al's screams, his demands and pleas that they just kill him, his prayers that God would take him now. Al had never reached the painless place of shock. He'd never lost consciousness. He'd suffered every damn second.

Until the very end, when he was gone before the chopper set down. Morphine? Maybe. They'd done the best first aid they could, but his wounds were severe, severe enough to have killed him. Maybe the horror was that he'd hung on so long. But then, Gil hadn't seen a whole lot of clean kills in combat. Nope.

He could still hear the sounds, smell the odors, feel the effort, the fear, the bullets blowing out the muzzle of his rifle. He was there again, but without losing his place in time and space. He could still see Miri's living room around him, could hear her stirring in the kitchen. The sound of the wind blowing crystals of snow against the glass reached him. Not a flashback, but a powerful memory.

The memories he could handle. They were never far away. But slipping his cogs and falling into the past? No thanks. Wherever his future might lead him, flashbacks would only complicate everything. Especially if there weren't obvious triggers he could avoid.

He walked over to the wide window that overlooked the street and saw no mercy in the blowing blizzard. Hard to believe that just yesterday afternoon he'd been sitting in the Bakers' ranch yard enjoying the warm sun and a barbecue. Meeting a number of people with backgrounds like his. A welcoming group on a beautiful day.

Now he was looking at winter reclaiming the world, as if it realized it should never have let go. Yesterday had been out of sync, and probably all the sweeter for that.

Out of sync. He rolled the words around in his head, because if there was one thing he'd figured out a long time ago, it was that he was out of sync with the world he was supposed to return to eventually. But now, after being wounded, he felt more out of step than he ever had.

Ah, hell, no point thinking about it. He wasn't a brooder by nature, although since getting out of the hospital and basic rehab, he'd been inclining that way. Probably because he didn't know if the army would take him back in any capacity, let alone special forces. He told himself he could do plenty for his unit without going into the field. There was lots to do, planning missions, setting up schedules... Yeah, he could do a lot of things while leaning on a cane. He could even supervise training.

The question he wasn't prepared to answer was what would he do with himself if they insisted on medical retirement. He couldn't imagine that he owned any skills other than what he'd been doing for nearly eighteen years.

Crap, was he about to become an outdated-model car?

He passed his hand over his face and told himself to cut it out. Of course being wounded had left him pondering a lot of things, everything from mortality to a future.

Remembering Al...well, that didn't help, either. No, Gil never wanted to forget his best buddy, but that loss was so recent and fresh that when combined with the mess of his own body, he was plumbing depths better left to philosophers.

He'd had sixteen years under his belt when he buried Al. Now he was past seventeen and less than a year away from another hash mark for his sleeve. What had he thought? That those hash marks would keep coming indefinitely?

At some point there had to be a reckoning. A time when everything would change. Maybe he hadn't wanted to think about that at eighteen, but now he was thirty-five going on thirty-six, and somewhere in all that time shouldn't he have spent a minute thinking about what he'd do when he mustered out?

Or maybe he'd just believed he wouldn't survive it.

Well, didn't that make him the butt of his own joke.

He started pacing to loosen up, steering his thoughts into happier lanes. He could think about Miri, for example. The more he saw of her, the better he liked her. And the more he wanted to hold her close and explore her subtle curves until he knew them by heart.

It might make him uncomfortable, but that was okay. It was the first time he'd felt a spark of sexual interest since Al's death. At least that part of him was coming back to life.

She was pretty, attractive, sexy as hell when she

moved, even if he suspected she had no idea how she drew a man's thoughts. But he had sensed something else. If he wanted anything to do with Miri, he was going to have to open up more. As long as he kept his distance and tried to remain essentially a stranger, he wasn't going to be her type.

Although did that really matter? She had a life, and he couldn't look at long term when he felt as if he'd been run through a jet engine and come out the other side in a heap of pieces. Everything was screwed up now. Everything. His body, his head, his identity, his future...

Yeah, that guy wasn't going to make it with Miri Baker. She deserved better than that. She deserved not to be hurt.

After a few toe touches and some other stretching, he turned back to the window, watching the world don a new white cloak. It seemed to be in a hurry, as hard as the snow was blowing. Miri's porch railing was drifted over now, and he suspected her front steps were buried, too, though he couldn't see that far through the white cloud.

A true whiteout. He suddenly remembered sitting in the mouth of a cave watching a storm just like this. The whiteout was so great they'd dared to build a small fire farther back inside. Along with the sting of ice that occasionally struck his face when the wind eddied a bit, he'd smelled hot coffee, rations heating. And he'd heard the voices of his buddies.

They were a small group that time, meant to infiltrate without drawing attention. Covered in rags that wouldn't fool anyone for long, up close. One look at their boots would give them away. People in these parts would kill for boots like that, and to see three men wearing them all at the same time? Might as well have worn their uniforms.

But they'd worked hard at staying out of sight, at avoiding villages and shepherds with their flocks. In short, they'd practiced complete stealth.

As he remembered that moment, Gil also remembered why they were there. In and out. Randy was the sniper. Al was his spotter, doing all the complex calculations necessary for the shot.

And neither of them really liked his job. They'd been picked, given an opportunity to bug out if they didn't want to do it. Of course they'd wanted to, before they actually went. How cool was it to be a sniper?

Well, they'd found out. Gil shook his head. He'd been the baggage assigned to watch over them and see that they both got out, if he had to carry them on his shoulders.

They had a job. They did it. And that's as much as they wanted to think about it. Enough that they were necessary.

A lot of his life had been like that, he thought now. Doing what was necessary, leaving as little room as possible to think about it.

Gil heard Miri move almost silently behind him. His senses were still acute.

"Looks like we still have a storm," she remarked.

"Soup's simmering on low heat, so whenever you get hungry we'll eat."

"Thanks. I was just looking outside and remembering a time I sat in a cave watching a storm like this." He turned from the window and summoned a smile. "It's a whole lot more comfortable here."

"I should hope so!" she said with mock indignation.

He offered up a laugh, a sacrifice on the altar of a normalcy he no longer knew. Well, he suddenly thought, this was getting gloomy and maudlin. He had a whole lifetime to sort through his past, and he didn't need to do it this weekend.

He glanced toward the window again. "When is this supposed to be over?"

"During the night. The wind might keep up another day or so, making it impossible to tell that the storm has passed, but…it'll ease, too. I imagine school will be closed tomorrow, though. The radio keeps saying the temperature is falling steadily. We're about fifteen below zero right now, with worse to come, so even if everything clears up and the plows get through, the parameters change."

"How so?"

"Too cold for the kids. What if no one can drive them? What if a bus breaks down? Better safe than sorry."

He got it. And glanced again at the window. "The weather changed fast." As if he hadn't seen it happen before, often to the complete contradiction of the forecast. Life-threatening emergencies could come out of sudden changes like that.

She spoke after a moment or two. "If you're through looking out at the storm, I'd like to close the thermal curtains. The heater is going to be working overtime tonight."

Miri drew heavy-looking damask drapes in navy blue to block out the whirlwind. Almost at once Gil thought he could feel the room grow warmer. A figment of his imagination because he could no longer tell what was going on outside?

He didn't usually fall prey to such fancies, but nothing was usual anymore.

"Gil?"

"Yeah?" He made himself turn toward her, surprisingly difficult when he knew exactly which rut his thoughts were about to fall into. Then she startled him into a whole different rut.

"Are you having survivor guilt over Al?"

He froze. "What makes you think that?"

"I don't know. Something about what you said before you left the kitchen. It wouldn't be surprising, given how close the two of you were."

He felt himself icing over. Some things just weren't meant to be displayed, and that was one of them. All the mixed-up feelings he had about Al's death... What gave her the right to even ask? Because she was Al's cousin?

But then an ugly self-defensiveness surged in him

and snaked past his guard, issuing words he would wish unspoken. "Don't you? Over your parents?"

Her face seemed to shrink. All the energy seeped from her body. "Of course," she said quietly.

He'd attacked and he'd hurt her. He'd thrust a caring question back in her face and awoke feelings that still speared her. That she was probably still dealing with. What was his excuse?

Without a word, he reached for her and, against all his usual rules, tugged her into a tight hug, loosening his hold a bit only when he felt her arms lift and close around his waist.

Then, with his face buried in her sweet-smelling hair, he spoke. Murmured, really. Getting enough air to force the words out had become strangely difficult. His chest ached as if wrapped in a steel belt. Nameless emotions clogged his throat.

"I have lots of survivor guilt," he mumbled. "Al wasn't my only loss. As I rose in rank I took on more responsibility. Every loss fell on my head."

Her arms tightened around his waist, offering silent comfort. At least she didn't offer any trite phrases. His feelings weren't negotiable and couldn't be swept away by anyone else. It was one of the reasons he preferred not to think too closely. This was something he had to live with. Nobody could make it go away.

Nor should it go away. He needed to remember his ghosts, because every one of them counted. They should never be forgotten, not their names, not their faces.

Their sacrifices deserved at least that much. Al was one of many in that respect. Some Gil hadn't known well at all, but they'd still been comrades. And they all remained indelibly imprinted within him.

Only now, holding Miri so close, did his soul recognize how much he had been yearning for human touch. Human comfort. A weakness? Maybe. But he needed it more than he could ever recall. Miri leaned into him, her cheek on his shoulder, her arms snug around his waist, and her very presence in his arms seemed to remind him that he was a human being like any other, and that he was entitled to the good things, not just the bad.

For years now, humor and happiness had been fleeting, as if they had been stolen from more important ventures. He could go to a bar when they were between missions, yuk it up with the others, have a few too many beers and call it fun.

This was different, and this had been missing for a very long time. This went far beyond fun, reaching places within him that had done without sunlight for a very long time.

A woman's embrace. So simple. So profound.

But it was nothing he was entitled to, as his hip hastened to remind him. Shards of steel and glass seemed to penetrate it, and he suspected if he moved wrong his leg would give way. Without even realizing it, when he had reached for Miri, he'd dropped his cane, so if he wasn't careful he'd fall himself. *Damn cane*, he thought, tightening his hold on Miri simply because he didn't want to let go of this precious time. Infinitely precious.

But the pain was intensifying because he wasn't moving, because he'd been standing for so long in one position. There was no way to prevent it from winning. When he needed it, his willpower could be steely, but when it came to his damn hip no amount of willpower could keep it from hurting.

"Miri…" Her name came out a whisper. He loosened his hold a bit.

"Lean on me," she said gently. "Just grab my shoulder. I'll get your cane."

"Are you a mind reader?"

"A people reader," she retorted. "I could feel a tremor. Get yourself balanced."

So he gripped her shoulder and took all his weight on his other leg, which of course was no longer perfect, but for the moment…

Miri bent slowly, as if to give him time to adjust, then as she straightened he felt the head of his cane press into his hand. When she was upright and he was stable, she stepped back, tilting her head and eyeing him. "Why don't you get a walker?"

"Because if I'd had one, I wouldn't have been able to hug you."

He watched the color flare in her cheeks, enjoying it, then the play of a smile around the corners of her mouth. He wondered if her lips were as soft as they appeared. "Good point," she said. "Ready to eat?"

She handled it so easily, avoiding any awkwardness

that might have arisen from his spell of weakness. A remarkable woman. An amazing woman. "Sure," he said, realizing that he *had* grown hungry. "Just give me a few minutes to work out my stiffness."

She pursed her lips. "Are you supposed to get any more physical therapy?"

"Eventually. They want some more healing first and I'm looking at another surgery down the road."

"Well, I guess I can see that," she said. "I'm sure some things can be taxed only so far." She turned. "I'll go set out the soup and crackers."

He watched her walk away and felt a huge heap of loneliness in her wake. Dang. He *never* felt lonely.

Miri didn't know quite how to take what had just happened. The man of granite had reached out to her, obviously seeking some comfort, but how much comfort could she offer? He spoke of survivor guilt about others, as well as Al. And he probably had more problems than that. She couldn't think of a darn thing that could help him.

Who was she, anyway? A music teacher. Training as a teacher and a musician didn't exactly offer a lot of psychological insight. Or any methodology that she'd have felt safe applying to another human being with a major problem. Mostly she was trained to know when she should get a student to the school psychologist.

Good as far as it went. Not good enough to help Gil in any meaningful way. If he even wanted help.

She poured the soup into her grandmother's tureen,

covered it and set it on the table beside the ladle. She skipped the matching soup plates, because it was a cold day and even indoors with the temperature set at an energy-saving sixty-eight degrees, the soup would cool fast enough in deep bowls. Right then she was reaching for warmth.

And Gil. She realized she wanted him to open up to her, and she supposed his revelation would qualify as momentous for him, but for her it was only a tiny peek. Maybe the only peek she'd get into the soul of a totally self-sufficient man.

But as she put out napkins and a bowl of oyster crackers, she wondered if she really wanted to get inside that man's head. Al had considered it important not to talk about where he'd been or what he'd done. When he came home, she'd had the sense that he was wearing a mask the whole time, trying to be the Al everyone remembered, concealing the Al he'd become.

Why should it be any different for Gil? Maybe it really just was as simple as knowing that someone who had never gone where they had could ever begin to understand in any meaningful way. She suspected that much was true.

How much isolation could a person live with? Or flip the question around: How much did she really want to know about what isolated him? Words could skim the surface. Hollywood could romanticize it or glorify it. But the gut understanding?

She shook her head at herself and tried to move past the minutes when they'd held each other. It could never be more than that, a moment of tenuous connection. She would never fully understand where'd he'd been, and maybe he'd never be able to fully come home.

But she knew what had really disturbed her: how she had felt surrounded by Gil's arms. She'd occasionally had boyfriends who hugged her, but nothing had ever felt to her like being in Gil's arms. Everything else in the world had simply vanished. For those few minutes, nothing else had existed beyond her and Gil, wrapped together, while deep inside she had felt herself melting.

Softening. The sensation was amazing. Every bit of tension had fled her body, leaving her warm and soft and in another world. She'd like to feel that again.

It was at that instant that she realized she was undergoing an emotional earthquake. She'd never dreamed that a simple invitation to her cousin's best friend, asking him to stay with her while he was in town, could turn her upside down. Sudden fear gripped her. Fear of herself. What crazy thing was she getting into here? She'd never been a wildly impulsive person, but had chosen to live her life in the calm waters at the edge of life's seas.

Yes, she'd met tragedy. Everyone did. What had happened to her parents had been especially gruesome. Al's death had carved a hole in her. But otherwise she was inclined to be levelheaded and sensible. Unlike some of her friends and acquaintances, she felt no desire to stir life up with drama, either major or minor.

Real drama came along often enough to convince her she didn't need to manufacture any.

Indeed, she avoided it. The loss of Al was still recent enough to sting. To make her ache with the hole he'd left behind. But she could accept that easier than she'd accepted the loss of her parents, probably because Al had been away so much of the time. Little in her life acted as a reminder that a part was missing.

That would all be different for Gil. Al had been a big part of his life for many years now, always there, a part of most everything they ever had to do. Now for Gil there'd be a big hole. And from what he'd said, there was more than one.

She suspected that his wounding had given him too much time to count his dead. That just added an extra agony to everything else he was dealing with. Too much time to think.

At last she heard him coming. She wondered if the cold was affecting him, because his step seemed heavier somehow.

Then he came through the door, nodded at her and eased into the chair he usually used. Miri didn't say anything. While silences in social settings sometimes made her feel chatty, she wasn't inclined to say much right now.

She served him piping hot soup, then offered him the bowl of crackers. When they were both served, she picked up her spoon, raised it to her lips, then paused. This didn't feel right at all.

"Gil?"

He lifted his head. He hadn't started eating. "Yeah?"

"Are you okay?"

One corner of his mouth curved. "Always."

"That's not what I mean and you know it. If I'm getting too personal, just tell me to shut up."

He picked up his spoon, but instead of dipping it in the chowder, he turned it slowly in his hand, as if watching the play of light. Outside, the banshees of winter began to keen, an eerie howling that always disturbed Miri no matter how many times she heard it. Lonely and haunting, occasionally even threatening. It was just the wind, but she invariably had to remind herself of that.

"Are *you* okay?" he asked, turning the question back on her.

"As okay as I can be," she retorted. "Having lost my cousin, having lost my parents... What's the point, Gil? We all suffer losses."

"Exactly," he said as he dipped his spoon at last.

She had no idea if she'd just been shut down or not. She decided to be pushy, a quality she ordinarily avoided but was well aware that she owned. "You have an extraordinary number of them, though."

"Depends on who you're talking to."

God, the guy could be like a lockbox. "I'm talking to you," she finally said bluntly. She scooped more soup into her mouth and felt it scald her tongue. Idiot.

"What are you trying to get at, Miri? Just come out and say it."

"There's more bothering you than pain."

His face darkened, and for a second or two she thought he was going to leave the table and his meal. Not that it was much of a meal.

Then he released a long sigh, like air seeping out of a balloon. "Yeah, I've got a lot of things on my mind. Sorry. I've got to go back for physical therapy and more surgery in a month. Nobody's making any promises. For all I know, this may be the best I get. But I'm also wondering if I'll even have a job after this is over. I'm staring at a big blank where once I had a road to follow. I'm trying not to worry about it too much unless I have to, but it's still hanging out there. I only know how to be one thing, Miri. A soldier. A Green Beret. It's more than a job, it's a damn identity."

Whoa, she thought. She'd gotten her answer and it was huge. His *identity*? But then she wondered why that hadn't occurred to her before. If she lost her teaching job, which was so much a part of her, she didn't know exactly how she'd handle it. But she had an advantage: a townful of people she knew, tons of friends, and every one of them saw her as essential Miri Baker, no matter what she did for a living.

It was different for Gil. Why wouldn't it be? His job was overwhelming, consuming, dangerous…and from what she gathered it didn't leave much room for anything else. It was an entire lifestyle.

She lifted another spoonful of the rich, thick soup to her mouth, but spoke before she ate it. "Have you been trying to think of what else you might want to do?"

"Never had to. Al was always so certain I'd come

back to the ranch with him, and while I didn't think that was the way to go for me, it left the whole question in the distant future. Now the future's here. Take me out of uniform and I don't know who the hell I am."

He shook his head and resumed eating. Taking the conversation as closed, she, too, started sipping her soup again. Well, sipping and chewing. This brand of canned soup didn't short either the potatoes or the clams.

He consumed his entire bowl and she suggested he help himself to more. She wasn't surprised when he filled up again and put a handful of crackers on top. As a big man, a powerful man even now, his appetite seemed natural.

But after eating for a couple more minutes, he spoke again. "I keep telling myself they'll find a place for me. Maybe they will. It won't be in the field, that's for sure, but there's plenty else I can do. Then I wonder if I want to be stuck behind a desk to hand out advice, schedules and discipline. Because that's probably what I'd wind up doing."

"You're a man of action," she suggested.

"Well, I've always been in the action. That much is true. Anyway, in my present condition I'm not much good for anything physical. I'm sure it'll get better with time—"

"But not necessarily less painful," she interrupted.

"No," he said shortly. "No. But I can live with pain. I've been ignoring pain for years. Right now I can't even trust my hip to hold me, but they're going to fix that on the next go-round. That's the hope, anyway."

He insisted on helping with the cleanup despite leaning very heavily on his cane. She didn't protest, understanding the need to help. He wanted more coffee, so she made them half a pot and brought mugs into the living room.

Even with the heavy insulating curtains drawn, she didn't need to look to know the wind was still keening. If she checked her email, she was sure she'd find that school was closed tomorrow. It didn't happen often, but then this kind of weather didn't happen often.

Of course, they didn't often hold a barbecue in January, either. Amused by the contrast between yesterday and today, she sipped her coffee and let Gil enjoy the silence. This situation had to be a bit difficult for him. He didn't know her, yet he was staying with her, and Al didn't provide enough of a bridge between them. Gil might have been more comfortable at the La-Z-Rest Motel, which would at least have given him privacy and the freedom to do as he chose.

Well, she reminded herself, if he needed privacy, he could have gone to the bedroom he was using. She wouldn't have trespassed there short of a house fire, not when he was in there.

He was clearly lost in thought, and from the few things he'd mentioned, she suspected he was wrestling with the idea of an entire life change. Not really a unique situation, but unique to him. It was seldom helpful to remember that others had walked this path.

Each person who walked it had to whack their own trail through the undergrowth.

"I never married," Gil said suddenly.

"Meaning?"

"Just that. Never found time, never made time, never met the right person...who the hell knows."

"Maybe you could do that now." What else could she say?

"Sure. A friend once told me that it was stupid to get married if you weren't already happy with yourself. Right now...well, I hardly recognize myself."

She turned on the sofa, putting her coffee down and facing where he sat on the other end. "You recognize yourself, Sergeant. You're still Gil York. Moving on to a new phase doesn't change that. You learned how to be a Green Beret. It's like we said earlier. If you can learn that, you can learn whatever else you need to know. It may be wrenching for a while, but you can do it." She tilted her head. "From the stories I heard from Al, getting that beret in the first place was pretty wrenching."

Gil closed his eyes for a few seconds before they sprang open, as intense a gray as she'd ever seen them. "You're right. I sound like a whiny baby."

"I didn't say that."

"You didn't have to. Listen to me. Crap, a self-pity party."

"Well, when you're in constant pain and every-thing's up in the air..."

"That's exactly the time not to indulge." He shook

his head as if to escape an annoying mosquito. "I'm beginning to discover that perhaps I'm not best left alone with my thoughts for too long. I'm used to being busy all the time, making plans for the next step. Not contemplating my navel."

She couldn't help it; a small laugh escaped her. "I wouldn't call it that, Gil. You've got a lot of things to sort out. You're trying to make plans for an unfamiliar future. That's hardly contemplating your navel."

"It is when I don't have any parameters. How can I plan when I still don't know how this will all turn out?"

"Contingency planning."

He gave her a cockeyed smile. "All the answers?"

At once she felt embarrassed. She was treating him flippantly and he didn't deserve that. "Sorry," she said. "I just feel so helpless. Talk away. I'll keep my mouth shut."

"I don't want that." Then he caused her to catch her breath by sliding down the couch until he was right beside her. He slipped his arm around her shoulders, and, despite her surprise, it seemed the most natural thing in the world to lean into him and finally let her head come to rest on his shoulder.

"Holding you is nice," he said quietly. "You quiet the rat race in my head. Does that sound awful?"

How could it? she wondered, when she'd been amazed at the way he had caused her to melt, as if everything else went away and she was in a warm, soft, safe space. If she could offer him any part of that, she would, gladly.

"If that sounds like I'm using you…"

"Man, don't you ever stop? Do you ever just go with the flow?" Turning and tilting her head a bit, she pressed a quick kiss on his lips.

"What the…" He sounded surprised.

"You're analyzing constantly," she told him. "This isn't a mission. Let it go. *Let go.* Just relax and hold me, and I hope you're enjoying it as much as I am."

Because she was. That wonderful melting filled her again, leaving her soft and very, very content. Maybe even happy.

"You are?" he murmured.

"I am. More than I've ever enjoyed a hug." God, had she ever been this blunt with a man before? But this guy was so bound up behind his walls and drawbridges she wondered if she'd need a sledgehammer to get through.

But then she remembered Al and the distance she'd sensed in him during his visits. Not exactly alone, but alone among family. These guys had been deeply changed by their training and experience. Where did they find comfort now? Real comfort?

Her thoughts were slipping away in response to a growing anticipation and anxiety. She was close, so close to him, and his strength drew her like a bee to nectar. He even smelled good, still carrying the scents from the storm outside and his earlier shower, but beneath that the aroma of male.

Everything inside her became focused on one trembling hope, that he'd take this hug further, that he'd draw her closer and begin to explore her with his hands and mouth.

Her breasts began to ache with a hardening need to be touched. An electric excitement passed through her straight to her center, until it was all she could do to hold still.

Her body was making demands of its own, and she was almost afraid to move for fear of rupturing the moment, canceling the growing, hopeful anticipation of his touch. Drawing a breath became difficult, as if all the air had left the room.

Maybe she moved. Maybe he did. She wasn't certain, but suddenly she was closer, and his mouth had sealed over hers, depriving her of the last of her breath.

Reaching up, she forked her fingers into his short hair, pulling his head closer, for an even deeper kiss. His hands, one after another, settled on her back, rubbing up and down, and impatience began to grow. She wanted those hands elsewhere, on her breasts, between her thighs. A primitive drumbeat ran through her blood, drawing her forward into the unknown.

He released her mouth and she gasped for air, throwing her head back, baring her throat. At last, at last his hand moved to her front, finding her breast, covering it, squeezing gently, and in that moment she hated every layer of fabric she was wearing. She wanted skin on skin, everywhere. Just as she was about to pull herself around, to straddle his lap, he began to pull back.

His mouth left hers. His hand dropped from her breast. No!

"Gil?" She could barely summon a whisper.

"Too soon."

Too soon? Who put a timetable on these things? Anger began to seep into the hole left by desire. She wanted to rail, she felt cheated…and she realized she had no right to feel those things.

Eyes closed, releasing a long breath, she twisted away from him until she slumped against the back of the couch. She had no right to demand he take this further. After all, wasn't she one of the people who taught kids at school that no meant no? Men could say no, too.

Eventually she settled down, letting the fever pitch of emotions slip away. Letting sanity return.

"I'm sorry," he said gruffly.

"You didn't do anything wrong." Truth. *Men can say no, too.*

"You're very attractive," he said. "I've been wanting to do that since I got here."

Which didn't answer anything at all. In fact, it sounded like an attempt to patch up her ego, and maybe that wasn't fair. But nothing about this was fair. An attraction existed. He'd made the moves once she was in his arms. And his entire reluctance might stem from his own sense of being a leaf in the wind just now. Perhaps even some misguided loyalty to Al.

The problem was, if he didn't explain why he'd

pulled back, she'd be left guessing. It wasn't right for her to demand he explain himself. Would she want someone to do that to her if she changed her mind midstream? Heck no. And they hadn't even gotten to midstream.

The wind chose that moment to strengthen, sounding desolate as it rattled windows and made the house creak. Winters here could be long and cold, but this kind of savagery was rare.

Finally, she decided she had to do something. She couldn't just sit here like rejection personified. Not good for either of them. "Want some more coffee? Or maybe I could rustle up a dessert."

"More coffee sounds great right now."

Yeah, it probably did. They'd hardly touched the two mugs she'd brought out here. Maybe there'd be enough left in the pot for him. She didn't want any.

He started to rise, but she pressed his arm. "I'll get it. You pace or stretch or whatever you need."

She needed the escape suddenly. She wanted to be in a separate room, where she could be in control of when she next saw him, not waiting here for his return.

She needed to make more coffee. There was so little in the pot it smelled slightly burned. Clattering loudly to let Gil know what she was doing, Miri sought her center, trying to regain her balance.

The man would be moving on in a few days. She needed to find a way to get through this unscathed.

Chapter Six

Miri went to bed rather early, Gil thought. Eight thirty? He must have worn her out with his pity party today. Or offended her by pulling back before exploration could turn into lovemaking.

He couldn't blame her for wanting to escape. He was about as much fun to be around these days as a compost heap.

Anyway, she'd been kind enough to invite him to stay with her rather than at the motel—he'd heard plenty about that place from Al, who'd sworn Gil would stay with the Bakers when he came to visit— and having a houseguest could be wearing. When this weather cleared, he needed to find some way to show his appreciation.

And all those thoughts, every one of them, were dancing around the immediate issue, the immediate reason she'd probably retreated. He might not let many people inside, but that didn't mean he couldn't read them.

He'd seen the emotions flicker across her face, the disappointment, the short-lived rise of anger, then withdrawal. But there wasn't any possible way to tell her that he just didn't want to hurt her. Not Al's cousin. Not Miri.

Because if he'd tried to tell her that, he was certain she would have argued, and he could easily imagine some of it. She was an adult, capable of making her own decisions. True. She could handle it. And maybe she could. But he didn't want to find out the hard way that she couldn't. At least now she'd have to give it some thought, rather than giving in to an impulse.

An impulse he wished they could have shared. He enjoyed women, and not just sexually. He'd had a few relationships over the years, but none of them had been able to make it over the hump of his sudden disappearances...or they hadn't really suited him as time went by. Regardless, stable relationships outside his unit seemed fungible. He wasn't at all sure he was capable of nurturing one long term.

Maybe there was something wrong with him. There certainly was now. Looking ahead at a big blank, with the only red-letter days being his next surgeries, he'd be wise not to get involved.

On the other hand, Miri called to him as no one

ever had. He was still trying to figure that out. Was it because she was like Al in some way? No, she didn't remind him of Al at all. She was very much her own person.

Gil had only to close his eyes and remember her playing "Taps" at the funeral to know how strong and determined she was. Few family members could have achieved that without breaking up. It had required steady breathing, steady hands, no choking… He'd honestly thought she might not be able to do it, and that he'd be pulling out the prerecorded CD and the battery-operated player.

A special dispensation had been made to use a recording of "Taps." There simply weren't enough people in uniform, whether reservist or active, to play it at all the funerals. A military person was entitled to that honor, but not only were they dealing with the fresh casualties like Al, but they had veterans from past wars, all the way back to the Second World War, and there were many, many of them.

But Miri had insisted on doing the honors, and other vets from around here had joined in to give him full honors, from the rifle salute to carrying the coffin. Gil had been surprised, but then wondered what he had expected. Naturally, people who'd known Al would step up.

The wind was knocking at the windows again. Curious, he flipped the small flat-screen TV on and hunted for a weather station. Soon he learned that this storm wasn't likely to blow out before midday tomorrow. Warnings of deadly cold and wind chills ran along the foot of the screen and popped frequently out of the reporter's mouth. The guy was totally intent on his mission to communicate.

Gil turned the volume down, leaving the TV as a distraction, but his thoughts refused to be distracted. Instead of returning to war, however, they returned to past girlfriends. LeeAnn, for example. He'd been seriously thinking about proposing to her until the day he'd found out that she was a sham.

Well, maybe that was unfair, but she'd put a bright face on a whole lot until the day he was stuffing his duffel once again and she flat-out told him she'd had enough of his disappearing act, enough of not knowing where he was going or for how long, or even where he'd been. She was tired of living with fear, most of all. She wanted a man who'd be home every night, not taking off on forty-eight hours' notice for undisclosed locations. Not one she could never be sure would come home in one piece.

Well, he could sure understand that. He was just glad they hadn't tied the knot and maybe had a kid before she realized she couldn't stand it.

One of his buddies hadn't been very sympathetic. "You need to find yourself an army brat," he'd said. "Someone with realistic expectations."

Maybe so, but Gil had never clicked with one, not for long, anyway. He saw some of the other guys making it just fine in marriages, and after he'd blown a few relationships, he came down to one ultimate conclusion. The problem wasn't the women, the problem was *him*.

He hadn't been exactly certain what he was doing wrong, but he hadn't given it a lot of thought, either. His job was always first on his mind, and everything else seemed a distant second.

Until Miri had described him as resembling granite poured into a uniform.

When she'd spoken those words, he'd immediately put them aside. It was good he'd struck her that way. Serving as the noncommissioned officer in charge of Al's funeral had been one of his most painful responsibilities. He'd needed to be granite, because he had to ensure that everything was properly carried out. His last service for his best friend.

But now he wondered. Was he like that all the time? To some extent, he supposed he was. He'd parked himself inside some very high walls to keep the pain and ugliness out. He simply couldn't afford to let things get to him. Period. It would have interfered with his duty, his responsibilities to his men. He had to stay cool as much as possible. In fact, the only time he didn't was when he could justifiably become enraged. That could be useful.

But if he'd truly become what Miri saw, or if that was all that others saw in him, he could understand why women decamped, or made his life miserable enough that he marched away.

So, he was granite. Maybe even deadened inside for self-protection. Except that lately, without the demands of duty to divert him and keep him in line, he was discovering some painful truths.

The first one was that he evidently felt he was in imminent danger all the time. Other than men in his unit, he must feel that no one had his back. That he was out here alone and at risk. He wasn't inclined to trust anyone.

That by itself was bad. He was home now, as reasonably safe as anyone else walking the streets. Safer than he'd ever been in most of the places he'd gone.

But those walls stood between him and the rest of life. A life he hadn't had much time for until now. Did he want to continue this way?

He could remember Al so clearly, talking frequently on long, isolated nights about the future he envisioned for himself when he retired and returned to the family ranch. It wouldn't have been an easy life, but if Al had wanted easy he'd never have volunteered for special forces. And yet the ranch offered promises that couldn't be kept anywhere else: open spaces and plenty of animals to tend. Even horses.

Al had had a special fondness for horses, and some skill with them, as he'd proved more than once during dangerous missions in the middle of nowhere. He'd sometimes found abandoned horses, usually half out of their minds with terror because of whatever had happened in the area. The men couldn't know what had passed, but the horses had made it clear that fright had been stamped in their hearts.

And Al had soothed them and brought them along

and then mounted them. Once he was sure they'd settled, the guys would take turns riding them, when it was safe. A perk, Al called it.

It was more than a perk. Those horses had pleased them all. Then there had been the goats, wandering wild... Well, Al had gathered them up, taught the men how to herd them and had made them lifelong friends in the next town they approached simply by giving the goats away.

Al should have lived.

The corollary to that was that Gil should have died. He was convinced that he didn't have as much to offer, not by a long shot, as Al had. But it was Al who was gone.

Gil supposed a shrink would have had a field day with that. Survivor guilt to the max.

But when a man who believed he had no future thought of a man who had been looking forward to one, how else was he supposed to feel?

He wasn't sure exactly when he realized he was no longer alone. He'd been standing in the middle of the room, generally facing the TV, trying to avoid sitting because of how fast he could stiffen, when he felt eyes on him.

Turning, he found Miri standing at the entrance to the room. She was covered by a thick, dark blue robe that zipped up the front, with matching slippers on her dainty feet.

"Can't sleep?" he asked. Lame question. She was

standing in front of him nearly an hour after she'd excused herself to go to bed.

"No," she answered. Her tone wasn't sharp, and she didn't sound annoyed. Just maybe a bit lost.

She shook her head a little. "I need some tea. You?"

"Sure." He followed her into the kitchen.

She put the kettle on the flame on her stove, shoved her hands into the slit pockets of her robe and leaned back against the edge of the counter. "Warm milk," she said, evidently following her own train of thought. But she didn't move or explain herself.

Then she said forlornly, "I can't stop thinking about Al. I thought the worst was over finally, but now the grief is back almost as fresh as ever. It hurts!" She pulled a hand out of her pocket and wiped her eyes on her sleeve.

Gil stood there feeling supremely useless. What was he supposed to do? What comfort could he offer? Eventually he murmured, "Me, too." A useless but true statement. "Maybe I'm making it harder on you. Tomorrow—"

"Oh, stop," she begged. "You're not causing this. It's just happening. Are you going to tell me it doesn't happen to you, too?"

He couldn't. It had been happening to him this very evening, with the feeling that he should be in the ground, not Al. "I can't."

"I thought not." Her voice wobbled and then she crossed the small distance between them, walking straight into his embrace. He still was leaning on his cane, and right now he didn't dare let go of it. He wrapped his free arm around her, trying to tell her she was welcome. He wasn't at all sure how else to say it.

Her arms closed around his waist, clearly clinging. "Why?" she asked brokenly. "Why?"

"No comforting answers. There aren't any. You want to know the worst part?"

"What?"

"It's all random. Every damn bit of it. Wrong place, wrong time. Your number's up. However you want to phrase it. And that holds for civilians, too. God knows, plenty of them wind up casualties. I won't even talk about kids who get cancer. Random."

She rested against him, her arms tight around him. After a few minutes he could feel that his shirt was growing damp. She must be weeping, but she didn't make a sound.

Damn it all to hell! He wished he could dry those tears, but he believed she was entitled to shed every single one of them. Al's death had ripped a huge hole in her life, too. A man in his prime had been yanked away from everyone who cared about him.

War did that. Life did that. Crossing a street could do that. Part of what he found so awful about it all was that there was never a good *reason*. Argue all you wanted that Al had chosen a dangerous life, but that didn't change the essential thing: his death had still been random. He alone of the unit had been killed. The worst that had happened to anyone else was a bullet graze.

Or take himself. Gil had survived injuries that should have killed him. Why? There were no answers.

So he held a weeping woman and accepted that there wasn't a thing he could do to make her feel better. Maybe he'd even made it worse by coming here and stirring things up. Al was buried and he wasn't. Why should anyone feel good about that?

The teakettle began to whistle. Miri had reached the point of drooping against Gil, the wave of grief having left her weak. She had to summon what was left of her energy to ease back, mumbling, "Sorry," as she went to start making the tea.

"Just sit down," Gil said almost abruptly. "I think I can make the tea for us."

She didn't argue, instead sagging into her usual kitchen chair, resting her elbows on the table and putting her face in her hands. As the flood of grief began to ebb, she realized she wasn't being fair to Gil. She'd lost a cousin, but he'd lost his best friend. Worse, he'd been there when it happened. She didn't want to imagine the horrors that stalked his dreams.

She listened to him open the cupboard, heard the can strike the table gently, followed by the duller sound of two mugs and saucers. Forcing herself to lift her head, she reached for a napkin from the basket she kept on the far end of the table and began to wipe her face. The tears were drying rapidly, leaving her skin feeling sticky and ready to crack.

Soon they were each making a mug of green tea,

both very focused on the simple action of dunking a bag and then allowing the leaves to steep. Banal. Ordinary stuff. Making a cup of tea.

After the wrenching emotions that had just washed through her, it seemed almost ridiculous, yet contradictorily soothing.

"What about you, Gil?" she asked quietly. "You've said little about your injuries."

"Little enough to say. Shot five times. Bullet near my spine still remains. My hip and pelvis shattered. They're putting it all back together a little at a time, waiting for each new step to heal. I'm short a spleen, but they saved everything else. One more surgery, maybe. I hope that's all. Each one feels like starting from ground zero again."

Her heart squeezed. "The bullet near your spine?"

"They're hemming and hawing about whether they want to try to remove it. Basically, if it stays put, they'll probably leave it alone. If not, they've got to take the chance and yank it."

"Chance?" She didn't like the sound of that. Not one bit. "You could be paralyzed? Is that what you mean?"

"Yeah. That's what I mean. It's a chance. That random thing again. I could be perfectly lucky."

"Seems like you could use some luck." She realized she hadn't given a whole lot of consideration to what he must be facing or experiencing. She knew he'd been wounded, that he was in pain, that he needed to stretch scar tissue, but…he could still become paralyzed? It was like the wounding that would never end.

The thought appalled her. He'd been wounded worse than she imagined, and it had taken her this long to ask about it.

"What else?" she asked, determined to face it all.

"Nothing but scars from being wounded, from burns. I have to work at keeping it all loose, but I told you that."

Burns, too. Her stomach felt as if it were on a fast elevator to the subbasement. He shouldn't be suffering from survivor's guilt. He should be suffering from survivor's envy.

"Hey, I'm pretty much in one piece," he said. "It might look a bit like a puzzle, but everything necessary is still there."

"Will you ever be out of pain?"

"I'm not counting on it." He dropped his tea bag onto the saucer and tasted the brew. "You have to tell me where you get this. I've always liked green tea better than black and this one is really great."

"It's my vice," she admitted. "Special ordered from a place on the West Coast."

"Can you put me in touch?"

"Easily. They're on the web." More banality. It was almost as if they were using it like a rope to pull themselves out of the pit they'd dived into. Talk about the easy things, because the alternative was…what? Hell? Most likely.

"Gil?"

He lifted his head, gray eyes almost flinty, but she didn't feel that was directed at her. "Yeah?"

"Do you have *any* idea about what you might want to do if you can't go back to active duty? Simple things?"

"Like what?" he asked almost sharply. "Making paper dolls? Whittling with my KA-BAR?"

She dropped her gaze instantly as her heart began to tap nervously. What had made her ask such a question? She'd already gathered that he wasn't looking down the road of the future. Not yet. He still faced a whole lot before he would really know what he'd be capable of. "I'm sorry. I must be tired, not thinking clearly."

His voice gentled a bit. "No, I'm sorry. It was a reasonable question. So far, no answers. I guess being caught twixt and tween is trying my temper. I can't be sure I won't be cleared for some kind of duty. If I'm not, that's a whole other can of worms. I don't really feel I can plan yet."

"It hasn't been that long yet, anyway," she said quietly. "My world is so different. I can look ahead and see myself teaching until I retire. I can't imagine not being able to do that." Cautiously, she glanced at him again and found one corner of his mouth tipped upward.

"I hear you," he answered. "I used to see it all laid out ahead of me, too. Funny how plans go awry."

There was a good point in what he said. She nodded. "I guess we all tend to think that everything will go on the way it always has. Then something happens."

"Exactly. Something happens. But we get by because we assume we can predict. Guess not."

"Guess not," she agreed. Al had planned a future at his family's ranch, probably had thought he'd settle down with someone local and raise the next generation of Bakers. Gil hadn't looked that far ahead. As for her…maybe she was living in a fantasy world. Miriam Baker, music teacher, surrounded by a tight-knit group of friends and family. Heck, she'd even stopped dreaming of the white wedding that had seemed so important to her back in high school. She rather liked her life now. If something came along to change it all… well, she wasn't so sure she'd be any quicker than Gil at figuring out a different future.

"Random," she said, repeating the word he'd used a little while ago. "It's all so random, but we keep on making plans. Why?"

"Maybe because we like the illusion of control."

She stared at him. "Illusion? Isn't that an odd choice of word for a guy like you? So much must depend on planning."

"We plan, all right. But there's a saying I really like that kind of encapsulates it. 'Every battle happens in the dark, in the rain, at the corner of four map sections.'"

Map sections? It took her a minute to imagine piecing a big map together and the corners of those four sections meeting…and being difficult to read. Maybe not even a perfect match. "Wow," she said.

"So you plan, and to some extent you're still walking blind." He shrugged one shoulder. "Life is a bunch of contingencies, and no plan survives first contact."

"Why plan, then?"

"Because some of it will always come in useful."
His smile widened a bit. "Is it driving you crazy that
I'm at loose ends?"

"I'm not so sure you are," she admitted frankly.
"We all have to roll with the punches. Like when my
dad died. Nobody planned that. Nobody planned my
mother following him so soon, either."

Gil's smile faded. "I'm really sorry, Miri. That must
have been a terrible time for you."

"It was. It was hell. After Dad was killed, the entire family pitched in to save the crops, but then...
well, anyway."

"Did you sell the farm?"

"It was always Baker property. Al probably would
have worked it along with a cousin or two until he took
over the entire operation."

Gil finished his tea. "So the Bakers have a lot of
property?"

"Enough. My dad raised the fodder and the herd
was fair-sized. So the family made it through even
when times got tough, which happens frequently
enough on a ranch."

"And what about you? You aren't a part of the family ranch?"

She almost smiled. "Peripherally. The land has
never been split up. In a good year, I may receive a
small share of proceeds, but I don't count on it. I'm
not doing the work. I don't actually deserve anything,
and it was more than enough that my dad was able

to send me to college. That's a better start than most people receive."

"You're doing well enough for yourself."

"Exactly." She tilted her head a bit. "You know how you said Al always wanted you to become a part of the operation and you weren't especially interested? That's how I am. If I wanted a part in it, they'd make a place for me. Just like Al would have for you. I just know it isn't my cup of tea. I grew up as part of it, and all I could think about was music. I got what I wanted and that makes me very lucky."

"The family seems close-knit."

"We are. Not many would have made it for over a hundred years without splitting the land or having some squabbles over it. They never did. *We* never did. Which is not to say everyone's perfect."

His smile had returned and she was relieved to see it. Her breakdown had been normal, but she couldn't help being a little embarrassed by it. Al was gone, he'd left a big hole in a lot of hearts, but this man was here and now, and he had some pretty big problems of his own.

Imagine having to live with a bullet near your spine, uncertain if you might become paralyzed. Or having your hip shattered badly enough that one operation couldn't put it all back together. It was mind-boggling.

Gil watched the expressions flit across her face. He liked that he could detect the brief changes in her mood as she thought about matters she didn't mention.

He didn't need to know what exact pathways she followed; it was enough to know how she felt about them.

Then, surprising himself, he rose from the table, grabbed his cane and held out a hand to her. "Come sit with me in the living room. Chairs with hard seats are a kind of torture these days."

"Oh! I didn't know. I should have gotten you a pillow." She looked horrified and he couldn't smother a grin.

"How were you supposed to know? Besides, you have a very comfortable couch in the next room. Coming?"

She smiled, an unclouded expression he was glad to see, and took his hand.

Hers felt so small inside his. Delicate. Fragile. Yet those hands of hers must be powerful, too, to play musical instruments. A different kind of strength.

Once in the living room, he sat at the far end of the couch, up against the arm. It gave him some back support, but also gave her the choice of how close to sit. But he didn't immediately let go of her hand, making it clear he didn't want her to draw away.

She didn't even hesitate before she sat right beside him.

"It felt so good when you hugged me," he said frankly. And it was feeling good again. He didn't know how to describe the sensation, except that she softened against him, almost as if she wanted to melt into him, become part of him. He'd never experienced that with anyone before.

He cleared his throat, deciding that this was one time just holding it all in might be the wrong thing to do. If he were reading her body language correctly... And if he wasn't, he might as well know now, because a part of his body was stiffening and beginning to throb, narrowing the focus of his world to the woman beside him.

Such a rare feeling, this hunger, this hovering on the edge of anticipation and uncertainty. The years hadn't jaded him one bit. This woman was precious, and what he wanted from her equally so.

He cleared his throat again and said bluntly, "I want you."

He felt a slight tension in her.

"I realize..." He tried to continue. Realized what? That he'd only really met her two days ago. That all she knew about him she'd heard through Al, and Gil couldn't imagine what that might be. Not even all their Skyping since Al's funeral had been intimate enough to say he knew her.

But he wanted her. And he was startled when she said, "Don't. Just hush and hold me and..."

That was all the invitation he needed. He started to twist his screaming body so he could embrace her, but she took him by surprise. As soon as she drew her hand from his, she reared up and swung her leg over him, tucking her knee into the narrow space between him and the sofa arm. Straddling him. Inviting him.

Her robe rode up, baring her thighs, creating a warm, dark cave between them. Her womanly scents filled his nostrils, enticing him, and when his gaze lifted from that dark, aromatic crevice, it fixed on the zipper that would completely undo her robe.

Not yet, some hazy thought said. *Savor. Take it easy. Slowly...*

But God, it had been so long for him his body didn't want to wait. It wanted to pillage, plunder, take her for a wild ride she'd never forget.

Her hands settled on his shoulders, and his heavy-lidded gaze rose higher, taking in her face, the way her head was tipped back, her eyes were closed. Her breathing had become rapid, and he could see the rapid pulse beat in her throat. She had given herself over completely.

That amount of trust made his throat tighten in a totally unusual way. It also warned him to be careful. Extremely careful. Not only was she Al's cousin, but she had made herself so vulnerable that Gil ached.

All the self-control he'd been cultivating for years proved to be a sham. He knew he shouldn't do this, but he couldn't stop himself. Miriam Baker was a siren, and he couldn't resist the promise she held out right now.

A long, shaky breath escaped him as he gave in. Reaching up, he pulled down the zipper, ignoring the enticements below. The slider on the teeth sounded loud suddenly, ratcheted up his desire.

He'd hardly dared hope she'd be naked under the robe, but she was. As he pulled the fabric open wider, he saw the globes of her breasts hanging before him like delicious fruit ready for his touch. He slipped his hands inside the fabric and found her slender waist, slowly sliding them upward, feeling every curve and hollow, his mouth going dry with anticipation. At last he reached the underside of those globes and lifted her breasts in his hands, squeezing them, drawing a low moan from her. His thumbs found her nipples and stroked them almost instantly into hardness.

Then his view was blocked as he lowered her head and pressed her mouth to his. He gave her entry, and her tongue darted inside his mouth, tasting of tea, and began to drive him nuts by rubbing against his tongue and brushing lightly against the insides of his cheeks.

His body arched upward instinctively, but he stopped it almost immediately, fearing a swelling of pain in addition to the turgidity of his member, which already ached enough that he wondered if he could wait until Miri was with him.

But as he caressed her nipples and returned her kisses, he felt her begin to rock against him. It was going to be over before they knew it.

He pulled his mouth away, drawing deep gasps of air. "Miri...too fast."

"Hush. We can do this again."

He was eager to accept that plan. Very eager.

"Besides," she whispered in his ear as she began to rock against him again, "I want you completely naked."

Well, that wasn't going to happen right now. No escaping it. His mind whirled with sensations. He throbbed and now it was more than his loins. His entire body was one big drumbeat of passion.

Sliding a hand downward, he found that dark cave between her thighs, that aromatic place he hadn't yet explored. As his fingers touched her, he found her damp, but barely had time to register that as a cry escaped her and she pressed herself so hard against him that his hand was caught between her and his rod.

She might as well have poured gasoline on a fire. He felt surrounded by her, trapped by her, and it fueled his desire into a raging conflagration that threatened to burn him into a cinder.

Helplessly in thrall to the needs they shared, they rocked together like a boat on stormy seas until... until...

He heard her cry out, felt her body stiffen against him. Then he let go, feeling as if he turned himself inside out as he jetted his way to completion.

Chapter Seven

Miri felt as if she'd taken a ride in the center of a whirlwind. Collapsed on Gil, she couldn't move, didn't seem able to quiet her heart enough to fully catch her breath.

His arms closed around her back, holding her close, and time passed before she commanded her thoughts enough to wonder about him. "Did I make you hurt?" She hadn't even thought of that as she'd acted like a wildcat in heat.

"You hurt me so good," he murmured. His fingers tangled in her hair and tipped her head so he could kiss her.

Oh, heavens, was she about to lose her mind again? Cave in to the cravings he awoke in her? Surely it was too soon. At any moment reality would come crashing back in and she'd wonder if she was crazy. Because she'd never acted like this before in her life and she wanted to do it again. Soon.

But he stirred beneath her eventually, and, reluctantly, she tried to sit up. He needed to help her. When had every muscle in her body become spaghetti?

"Join me in a shower?" he asked.

She looked into those stormy gray eyes and drew a sharp breath at how soft they looked now. Like flannel rather than flint or granite. If she could help him to look like that all the time…

"It's a small stall," she said, her voice cracking.

"I think we can manage nicely."

They'd hardly be able to squeeze a sheet of paper between them, but that didn't seem so bad. Smiling at the thought, she slid off his lap, again with his assistance, and managed to get stable on her own two feet. She didn't care that her robe still hung open where it had been unzipped.

What she wanted was to see him naked. She'd been denied that so far, and her insides quickened at the thought. He might be wounded, but she was sure he'd be magnificent anyway. Perfection had never appealed to her.

She walked down the hall and turned into her bedroom to use the bath there. Better than trying to stand in the tub in the other room. Even with the mat she'd put down, it always seemed too slippery. In her shower at least, there'd be walls to lean on if necessary.

She reached in, turning the water on to a moderately hot temperature, then closed the door. As she turned she watched Gil enter the bedroom. He looked around, nodding to himself, then moved to the foot of her bed.

He faced her, a crooked smile on his mouth. "Are you ready?"

"Ready for what?"

He shook his head a bit. "Not pretty. But for my lady's pleasure…"

He dropped his cane on the bed and reached for the buttons of his shirt. She ached to help him with that because it would allow her to touch his skin, but as she took a little step his way, he shook his head.

He needed to do this, she understood. Help would have diminished him right now. Okay. She got it. She shrugged her robe off, letting it fall to the floor.

He shrugged off his shirt and tossed it on the bed. His chest was broad, powerfully muscled despite everything he'd been through. Holding her breath, clenching her hands, she made herself wait even as her very core began to grow heavy and throb again.

His arms looked as if he could lift a grown man in each one. She wondered if he always worked out to that degree or if this was some kind of compensation. But then she caught sight of scars in his side and across his abdomen. She bit her lip, holding back any sound of dismay.

He reached for the button on the loose camo pants he seemed to favor, and they slid off him as if they'd long since become too big.

She bit her lip harder as she saw that his legs were nowhere near as heavily muscled as his upper body. They weren't twigs by any means. Nicely shaped...

Oh, Lord, those were burn scars running down one side of his leg. She could almost see the shadow of flames licking up from below. My God, what had happened to him?

He sat on the bed, working on his boots, finally kicking them aside, followed by his socks. Then he stood again and reached for the waistband of his boxers with his thumbs.

"I need to warn you," he said gruffly. "Lots of scars, not all from surgery."

He'd already showed her enough to rip her heart out, but she managed a nod and waited for the rest of it.

His briefs hit the floor, but she barely saw it. He hadn't been kidding. His hip looked like the creation of a mad doctor. Scars. The scars of an awful lot of stitches. No longer smooth. Flesh was gone, and probably muscle, as well.

She couldn't stand back any longer. Closing the distance between them, she reached out with one hand and began to run her palm over him, from the scars in his side, and down to his hip.

"So much pain," she murmured. "Oh, Gil..."

He stood stiffly, letting her continue her inspection, as if he needed something settled right then.

She wasn't in the least repulsed, if that was what he feared. Instead she felt a kind of awe. This man had survived so much, would survive more. She wasn't sure if she'd have been able to endure what he had… and still did.

She found every scar with her hands, pockmarks she thought must be bullet holes, the sharper lines of surgery, the burn scars down the side of his leg…all of it. And as she went, she dropped kisses on them.

Finally, he said through teeth that sounded as if they were gritted, "Shower."

She straightened, catching sight of his renewed erection, and despite everything she laughed.

"Vixen," he said, a grin reframing his mouth from hard lines to soft ones. Lighting his whole face in a way she hadn't seen before. He still had the capacity for laughter, and that delighted her.

The shower stall was tight, but not too tight. It certainly wasn't too tight for him to lather her in every place he could reach. He spent some extra time on her breasts and between her legs, until she was panting.

Finally, she grabbed the bar of soap from him. "My turn."

He even turned so she could get his back. Nothing hidden. Not one damn thing. Then she pulled down the showerhead on its long hose and began rinsing him. She had no idea how long the hot water would last and she didn't think either of them would enjoy a blast of icy water.

"Oh, I like this," he said, taking the sprayer from her and beginning to rinse her. "I can imagine all kinds of trouble I could get into."

The water was just beginning to cool by the time

they stepped out onto the mat. Miri grabbed a stack of towels from the small linen closet and learned that friction could be amazingly delightful, too.

Then, dried at last, he gathered her close and held her.

"You're wonderful," he murmured. "Perfect. Beautiful. Kind. Amazing."

She wanted to answer his extravagant praise in kind, but he swallowed her words with a kiss, making her melt all over again. He was so sweet, and right now he smelled of soap, and the heat from the shower still radiated off him, filling her senses.

Abruptly, reality returned.

"I need my cane." His voice had suddenly grown tight, and he released her.

Before she could offer to get it, he'd propped himself with his hand on the wall and took the two steps to grab the cane. He carried a towel with him as he limped into the bedroom and laid it on the bed to sit on.

The air felt chillier than usual after he released her. Without a word, she went to her closet and pulled out another robe, this one of thick, green terry cloth. Wrapping it around her and cinching the belt, she went to sit beside him.

His eyes were closed, his jaw clenched. She wondered if she should even touch him. "Are you cold?"

He gave a little shake of his head, and she fell silent, waiting for him to deal with the pain that must have suddenly overwhelmed him. She hoped she hadn't caused it.

A couple minutes later he opened his eyes. "I must have moved wrong. That came out of nowhere."

She hadn't realized how stiffly he'd been sitting until she felt him beginning to relax beside her. "That must have been a doozy."

Another one of his patented half smiles. "Yeah. Sorry. Not very romantic."

She pursed her lips and pretended to ponder. "I don't seem to remember asking for romance or that you be romantic. Not that I have anything against it. I'm just pretty sure I didn't ask for it, so don't apologize." Then she grew serious. "Anything I can do to help?"

"Afraid not. It's easing back to normal levels. I'll be fine in a minute."

Then, like a voice out of the depths, her stomach growled loudly. She clapped her hand to her mouth, unsure whether to giggle or apologize.

Gil laughed. "I think we need to feed you something."

She dropped her hand, allowing her smile to show. "I don't usually do that. I'd have a classroom full of hilarity if I ever did. Are you hungry, too?"

"In my line of work, you quickly learn to never turn down a meal or snack." He pushed himself gingerly to his feet. "Shall we go explore?"

She knew what kind of exploring she'd have *liked* to do just then, but figured it would have to wait. Besides, another stomach growl like that would ruin a mood instantly.

She rose, too, and waited, but he waved her on. "I'll be along in a second."

Reluctant to leave him behind—what in the world was going on with her? She was going only twenty feet—she walked to the kitchen and started sorting through cupboards and the refrigerator. Apparently soup and crackers hadn't been enough for either of them. They needed something more substantial, but, honestly, she wasn't used to shopping for more than herself, and even looking forward to this visit she'd assumed she'd just be able to run to the store if she needed anything more.

Enter one inconvenient blizzard. Well, she thought with a secret smile, maybe not so inconvenient. She glanced at the clock on the microwave and realized it was just past eleven. Hardly late, but too late for cooking a real meal. Not that she had many recipes up her sleeve.

She gave a sigh. Life alone, devotion to teaching, not preparing herself in any way, thinking it was great to spend time with her friends, at most getting together with a few other people to do small concerts for church charity...well, she was amazingly incompetent at small things. Most people who lived alone could cook, couldn't they? But at some point she'd decided she hated to do it, and her diet had become simplified and easy. Boxes and cans stared at her, and in her freezer a package of cubed ham for adding to eggs or...

Hmm. She eyed a box of red beans and rice. She

could add some of the ham to that and make it in about twenty-five minutes in her rice cooker.

Because making her life easy had involved lots of handy little appliances, like a rice cooker, and an egg cooker that always delivered perfect eggs even if she became absentminded over her schoolwork. Automated cooking. Yeah, that was her style.

She heard the uneven steps approaching and readied a smile. Gil came through the door wearing a black T-shirt, a fresh pair of dark boxers, and black socks on his feet.

"Are you warm enough?" she asked, genuinely concerned.

He laughed. "I have more clothes if I want to put them on. And when I look at you, I get hot, anyway."

She felt her cheeks flush. They'd been intimate, but she didn't know if she was ready to be so open about it. Gil evidently didn't have any such qualms. He was grinning at her, a totally cloudless expression, and appeared to be enjoying her blush.

"Um...I'm trying to decide what to make for us. Is it too late for you to want a heavy meal?"

"Three squares got left in my distant past. Like I said, I can eat at any time. My stomach lost all faith in the clock a long time ago."

"Okay then. Unless you don't like red beans and rice..."

"Say no more. That's a favorite of mine."

"Well, it won't be restaurant fancy. Straight out of a box with some ham added."

He leaned on his cane and crossed the few steps between them to touch her arm. "Stop apologizing. I've eaten more freeze-dried meals out of boxes and vacuum packs, and cooked over a small paraffin flame, than you can possibly imagine. I've also been at forward operating bases where we took turns doing the cooking with whatever we had, and I can tell you I didn't run into too many French chefs. Whatever you make will be delicious, okay?"

She nodded and felt her blush deepen a little. What was with her? She didn't usually care about such things. She wasn't much of a cook. So what? Was she falling into a stereotype because she was interested in a man? God help her if that was the case. No Donna Reed in this house.

Not that Gil seemed to expect one.

Letting go of her apprehensions, all of which seemed to be pointless, she pulled the rice cooker out of the lower cabinet. A few minutes later, she had added the rice and water, and cubed ham to make a double batch. If Gil was hungry he'd get enough. If not, it reheated well.

She flicked the switch that turned on the rice cooker, then asked if he wanted something to drink.

"Water. I'd really like some water. Where do I get a glass?"

She pointed and let him get it for himself while she poured herself ginger ale. Sitting at the table, she watched him down two full glasses of water from the tap before he brought another glassful to the table with him.

"Man, you were thirsty," she remarked.

"Guess so." He fell silent, staring at the rice cooker, which had just started to billow steam.

She sat with both hands wrapped around her glass, beginning to feel nervous. Was he regretting their lovemaking? Wondering how to extricate himself just as soon as the storm was over? Oh, man, she hoped he didn't think he'd just made a disastrous mistake.

Because for her it hadn't been a mistake at all. No way. Even if he left tomorrow, she would never regret the experience they'd shared.

Closing her eyes, she tried to cement every moment in her mind, etching it so that she'd never forget that this man had showed her pleasures she'd never dreamed of. How or why, she didn't know. It wasn't as if she'd never had sex before, although not very often. But Gil…he'd touched her in places that felt as if they'd never been touched before. Took her to heights she'd never reached. No, she wasn't ever going to regret this.

Then an errant thought crossed her mind, and suddenly Al was there with her, saying, "Told you so."

She caught her breath as she remembered. All the times he'd talked to her about Gil. How many times he said she should to fly out to visit him when he was stateside so he could introduce the two of them.

How she'd laughed, told him not to be silly, and that if Gil wanted to meet the family he could come to Conard County.

The time his crazy grin had vanished and he'd said, "I was talking about you, not the family."

She'd let it pass, but then there were other times he'd said, "You've got to meet Gil. I think you'd get along like a house on fire."

"Sure," she'd answered, and then forgotten about it. But now she remembered all those times, so many over the years.

I told you so. She heard him as clearly as if he stood beside her.

"Oh, Al," she whispered almost inaudibly. He'd been right. She and Gil got on well. But his point had been what? Why did she feel Al was laughing at her right then?

At that moment she remembered another time, when he'd practically twisted her arm to fly back with him when he returned to his station. "You'll like him, Miri. A whole lot."

"What are you? A matchmaker?" she'd demanded, starting to feel pressured and annoyed.

"No," he'd answered frankly. "I just want nature to have a chance to take its course."

That had been his last visit. She'd shoved all that far from her mind from the instant she'd learned that Gil was bringing Al home. Whatever the point behind Al's teasing all those years, it no longer mattered. And she'd believed that she'd never see Gil as anything but the man who had accompanied her cousin's remains home for the last time. A link too painful to be anything else.

Apparently not. Al had tried to tell her. Exactly what, she couldn't know, but he'd been right about her liking Gil. She liked him a whole lot. And right now a little more than that.

"Miri?"

She opened her eyes reluctantly.

Gil eyed her with concern. "Are you okay?" he asked.

"I'm fine. I just remembered something." And now she remembered the few video calls and all the emails she had exchanged so casually with Gil since the funeral. It had seemed light, friendly, not terribly important except that she had wanted to keep in touch with Al's best friend.

But had it been more? She'd learned a little about him. He'd probably learned a lot more about her. Look at them now. There was no way she could think this was light and casual even if she never saw him again. He'd never struck her as a man to do things lightly or casually, and, as she had discovered tonight, she wasn't able to do it, either.

But that was okay, she assured herself. At least she'd have this fantastic memory.

The rice cooker clicked, startling her. It had moved from steaming to spending the next ten or fifteen minutes getting rid of excess water.

Gil still watched her. His attention wasn't unnerving or too intense, however. She rather got the feeling that he enjoyed looking at her more than looking at the walls. That wasn't hard to believe and it wasn't even particularly flattering. A snort of laughter escaped her.

"What's so funny?"

She smiled. "The way you were looking at me. I figured I was easier on the eyes than the walls, but that wasn't especially flattering. I mean, look at the comparison."

A chuckle escaped him, but he shook his head and reached across the table for her hand. "The *Mona Lisa* wouldn't hold my attention as much as you do."

Her heart skipped, but she stuck out her tongue, anyway. "I don't think she's an especially beautiful woman. Wasn't she a self-portrait of Leonardo as a woman?"

"I don't know about that." But his smile was widening. "Okay then, refuse my compliments. I think you're gorgeous, no comparison."

"Now you're over the top." Rising, she got some bowls from the cupboard and soup spoons from the drawer. "Another few minutes. I wish I had some andouille sausage instead of the ham for this, though."

"The ham will be great. I'd eat it without any meat at all." He reached for the bowls and took them from her hands, setting them on the table. "Tell me about teaching music."

"What about it?"

"Well, I gather you love music or you wouldn't teach it. How is it you can survive all the out-of-tune and missed notes of little kids?"

She laughed. "They're learning. And when you

watch them try so hard to get it right, how can you not love it? They also learn incredibly fast. Playing an instrument has an advantage over a lot of other things they try to learn, too. Music gives them instant feedback. They hear when they hit the wrong note and want to correct it. Tone deafness is extremely rare. Most kids are capable of pitch matching, and they're good at it. Many just need a little training."

"The patience of a saint?"

"Not really. I teach all the grades and work with the band and choir."

"Busy, huh?"

"Very. I have aides to help, but not a lot of free time during the school week, or on weekends when there are home games or competitions. But anyway, back to the learning music thing. I had one young woman in tenth grade who got up with her guitar and sang in a talent contest. Gil, she sounded like an angel, and I asked her why she'd never joined the choir. Her answer? 'I can't sing.'"

"Couldn't she hear herself?"

"It wasn't that. When I could get her for a couple of minutes of conversation, it turned out that she'd been hearing all her life that she couldn't carry a tune. I asked her what she thought had happened to change that."

"And?"

"She said she got a guitar and taught herself to play. In the process of doing that, she gained all the mastery of her voice that had been missing before. And she wound up sounding like an angel."

He nodded slowly. "I never thought of singing as being something that could be learned. But I don't sing much."

"This girl was amazing. She could pick out melodies on the piano or guitar without music, and when it came to listening, she had perfect pitch. But *pitch matching*… That had to be learned. Syncing her voice with the notes she could hear in her head, or around her. She got to be pretty good at it, and she was by no means the exception. Given that learning is part of the process of music, because not everyone is a Mozart, I enjoy what I do even more. I watch kids blossom."

A smile seemed to dance around the corners of his eyes, crinkling them attractively. "I like your passion." Then he winked. "*All* of it."

Pleasure rippled through her. She'd have liked to pursue that right now, but she'd promised something to eat, it was ready now and her stomach again offered a plea, quieter this time.

Time to put red beans and rice into the bowls.

Then maybe later… Ah, yes. She hoped there'd be a later.

The pain in Gil's hip eased enough that he enjoyed the supper she'd made and enjoyed helping her clean up. Then he wanted to enjoy something more.

Carefully, he caught her hand and turned her toward

him. He heard her catch her breath, then saw her face reflecting the same eager hope he felt.

After slipping his arm around her shoulder, he limped with her down the hallway to her bedroom, anticipating the pleasure to come. The passion. Because she elicited a strong, deep passion in him, one that drove away common sense and resistance and reason.

He wanted Miri. Beginning and end of it. If there were to be any regrets, they'd just have to come later.

The only light in her bedroom was a small bedside lamp. It had been burning the first time they had come in here, and she'd never turned it off.

For just a moment, he took in the room, really saw it for the first time, and noted that it was bare of girlie frills. Instead it seemed to reflect her straightforward approach to life. Her strength. The bedspread, rumpled from when she had tried to sleep earlier, was a deep blue plaid that matched some scatter rugs. The furniture looked older, probably from her childhood home. The dresser, plain wood, showed numerous dings. A hand-crocheted doily topped it. A chair in the corner was straight-backed and undecorated. Even the curtains were sensible, matching the spread, looking thick with insulation. No pictures on the walls...

Here, at least, she lived like a monk. The rest of her house showed more personality, maybe because she had her friends come over, but back here—her bedroom and her office, which he was using—she'd wasted no money or real time on either one.

But none of that really mattered. The thoughts

skittered quickly through his mind and were just as quickly dismissed as he dropped his cane and reached for the belt of her robe.

Miri was all that mattered. He felt like a kid about to open a present on Christmas morning...a time and place so far away that he was surprised he could recollect the feeling.

But that was what this woman did to him. As easy as it was to slip her robe off and let it fall to the floor, he still swallowed hard, his heart hammering with renewed excitement. Had he ever wanted anything this much?

She was exquisitely formed, at least to his perception. Gently sloping shoulders, a pulse beating in the hollow of her throat like an invitation. Full but not large breasts, enough to fill his hands with their smooth weight. Narrow waist, but not too narrow. A tummy that wasn't perfectly flat, a sign of her womanliness. Then lower to legs that were strong, and knees... When had he ever noticed a woman's knees before? Dancers would have died for these.

He reached out at last, listening to her rapid, shallow breaths as he traced her loveliness from her throat to her hips, and to the secret place between them.

At last she whispered raggedly, "Gil..."

He lifted his hands to lightly touch her engorged pink nipples, and smiled as he saw a shudder of delight pass through her.

But it seemed that his exploration had gone on too long for her. She reached out, gripping the hem of his

T-shirt and pulling it upward. He raised his arms, aiding her until she pulled it off and tossed it aside.

Then she reached for his boxers, his last claim to modesty, because he knew exactly how engorged he was. Almost out of his mind with desire. As she pulled them down, they caught on his flesh, then fell to his ankles.

She took his breath away by wrapping her hand around his erection and squeezing gently, then stroking lightly.

"So smooth," she whispered. "So big…"

Had she just said that? Fireworks went off in his head as he mumbled, "You keep that up and we'll be done so fast."

A quiet little giggle escaped her, one that conveyed satisfaction and delight. She liked her control over him, and truth be known, he didn't mind it one bit.

Then, hesitantly, she touched the collection of scars and dips in his hip. He held his breath, afraid she would find it repugnant despite her earlier response. He was such a mess now…

But she proved that her earlier actions has been honest as she once again bent to scatter kisses on that severely punished flesh.

The last of his self-control fled. Whatever damage his body had taken, he hadn't lost much of his strength.

Bending, ignoring the screech from his hip, he scooped the woman up and managed to keep his footing as he carried her around to the side of the bed and lowered her to the messy comforter. Then he straightened, hoping the industrial-sized pain that drilled him didn't show on his face.

He pulled the comforter from beneath her, mindful that the room was a bit chilly, and drew it up over her. He hated covering that beauty, but he didn't want her to grow cold and distracted. Although at that moment, she didn't look as if anything could distract her.

He rounded the bed, gritting his teeth, refusing to use his cane at this juncture. It would have poked into this incredible moment like an arrow from the past. No reminders, not unless he couldn't avoid them.

He was a little less than graceful getting into the bed, rolling onto his uninjured side. An instant later all the rest ceased to matter because Miri turned onto her side and reached for him.

Flesh met flesh, igniting an instant conflagration. Skin on skin, the most precious and wonderful sensation in the world. Two bodies coming together to join in a single mission of oneness.

His hands roamed her, soon to be followed by his mouth. She wasn't shy, either, her hands searching and touching, and then her mouth found one of his small nipples and he jerked from the unaccustomed sensation.

Oh, man, him too? he wondered. How had he ever missed this?

The pulsing in his body deepened until it reached every cell inside him. He felt her writhing as if she were with him. Musky scents filled the room, adding to the exquisite minutes.

He cupped her rump to draw her closer. Then he ran his hand down the cleft between her cheeks, and it was like setting off a flare.

Suddenly he was on his back and she straddled him, wide open, his for the taking. She rubbed against him, back and forth, and her eyes opened narrowly, looking down at him, as a smile danced around the edges of her mouth. A wide-open invitation.

Miri felt almost as if she were outside of herself as strong sensations pounded through her blood. Want and need had become the same thing, driving her, pushing her, demanding. Her very center grew so heavy and achy that it cried out for a strong firm touch. Yet his hands kept dancing away, teasing her until she felt she would go out of her mind. She buzzed with sensation, feeling as if she had never been this awake in her entire life.

One moment of sanity touched her. Earlier, before they showered, she'd watched him toss a couple familiar square packets on her night table. She reached for one desperately now, which brought her flat down on his chest.

Oh, it felt so good, so *good* to feel his power beneath her, the heat of his skin, the unmistakable movement of his pelvis, trying to claim her. Surely she didn't need to… Her head aswim, she might have let the moment go.

Except that Gil wouldn't let her. He breathed heavily, his eyes almost closed, but he pushed her up and back just enough. When he opened the packet, she snatched it from him and reserved for herself the pleasure of slipping the protection on him, watching his erection dance at the touches, enjoying the way his entire body jerked.

She couldn't wait any longer. Not one minute. Swept away on a tide of tingling, aching, pounding need, she lifted herself a little and he entered her.

It had been so long that she gasped as she felt her soft tissues stretch, but an instant later it felt so good to be filled by him. As if she'd been yearning for this forever.

Need. Was there anything else?

She felt herself carried upward on a tsunami of irresistible force, turning pleasure into pain and then back to pleasure again. She approached the culmination, half terrified, half desperate, because she knew this time it would be so powerful it hurt.

She could never have imagined such a thing, but as she teetered precariously on the tip of the peak, she feared the fall to come. Then she tumbled, crying out in both pain and delight, feeling as if the sensation rocketed through her entire body like a powerful explosion.

Pinwheels whirled inside her as she collapsed, breathless and replete, as minor explosions of delight still rocked her.

Then Gil joined her, with one mighty thrust that

seemed to claim her all the way to her soul. He froze, rigid, then slowly, with a moan and shudder, relaxed.

Then his arms surrounded her and she drifted away into a new universe.

Chapter Eight

They lay together on their backs under a heap of covers, hands entwined. Bodies had long since cooled off; breathing had resumed a normal rhythm.

But that did nothing to erase the magic, Miri thought. She felt as if she had touched the stars and taken a flight to the farthest reaches of reality. She didn't want anything to interfere, to shatter her charmed state of bliss and wonder.

It couldn't last, but she could cling to it for every possible moment. She wanted this night never to end, though she knew it must.

Beneath her hands, granite had become malleable, but no less powerful. He'd bent until they were one, and made a comfortable place for her in his arms. He'd shared himself in the most intimate way imaginable, yet she felt as if a part of him was unreachable. That part had been there from the moment she'd met him, and Miri suspected it would be there until the end of his days.

But she'd come to accept it. It was as irrevocably part of him as the gray color of his eyes. It no longer made her curious or uncomfortable.

Everyone, she thought mistily, had private places within themselves, including her. Places that needn't be shared or couldn't be shared. In her case it was the death of her parents. The grief that had seared her and clawed at her, then had been put away into some sub-basement of her heart.

She sighed, realizing the treasured moments were beginning to slip away much as she tried to cling. Whether they'd ever be able to recover that magic she didn't know. Nor did she know if she'd ever have the chance.

"You okay?" Gil asked, hearing her sigh.

"I think I'm landing. I really don't want to."

"Me, neither." His hand squeezed hers.

Silence returned, except for the sound of the hostile wind outside. In here, next to Gil, she had found sanctuary from the storms, however brief.

Something was happening deep inside her, but she wasn't sure what. She'd dated like any woman her age; she'd even had longer a relationship that had approached the stage of living together. But she'd never,

ever, felt like this, and she feared this was going to leave with Gil.

He'd been here only a couple days. How could she have reached this point so fast? She smothered another sigh so as not to disturb him, and decided there were just no answers for something.

It wasn't as if he'd been a total stranger when he arrived. Al had spoken of him frequently. They'd been exchanging brief emails since the funeral. And then he'd come here and revealed he was nowhere near the stony man he'd appeared to be at the funeral.

A man like any other, carrying a boatload of pain and probably a whole lot of bad memories he couldn't share but had to live with. Yet he still remained caring and even kind, with her, anyway.

And a helluva lover.

A giggle escaped her then, and she rolled over, laying her hand on his powerful chest.

"What?" he asked.

"I was just thinking that you're a helluva lover."

A snort of laughter escaped him. "Wait till my hip gets fixed. I have tricks I haven't showed you."

She liked the sound of that and rested her head on his shoulder, liking the feel of his skin, of his warmth, and the sound of his beating heart. She tried not to take his words as a promise of any kind of future. He'd go back, get fixed up as much as they could, and then he'd have the rest of his life to deal with. Maybe he'd keep his career, maybe he'd have to find something else, but she didn't see how she could be any part of that.

Small-town schoolteacher, with roots as deep around here as any. Wanderlust had never captivated her.

Stop thinking of these things, she advised herself. *Just enjoy the now however long it lasts.*

He covered her hand on his chest with his much bigger one, and she could feel how hard his palms were, hardened from tough use. Not a musician's hands, or a teacher's.

"Do you rock climb?" she asked.

"I can when necessary."

She bet he could do a lot of things when it was necessary. "I thought about it, but got talked out of it. I need my hands for my music. Of course, I need other parts of me, as well."

Another quiet laugh escaped him. "Very nice parts, I might point out. I'd hate for you to lose any of them."

She smiled against his shoulder. "Would you ever rock climb for fun?"

"Conquering El Capitan isn't necessary to prove my manhood."

That caught her attention. An interesting way to put it. Had he left all those things behind? But what would he have left to prove, given all that he must have done? A man without insecurities, at least about his masculinity. She liked that. Some men got past all that, but she had often sensed that in the right situation many guys still thought they needed to prove how tough they were.

How nice to be free of that, although she probably didn't want to know the price he'd paid to get there.

"What else have you avoided because of your music?"

"Not much, I don't think. It's just that at an early age my tutor impressed on me how important it was to take care of my hands. Since then a handful of people have reminded me."

"They're very nice hands," he remarked, stroking the back of the one that rested on his chest. His fingertips caressed her lightly, sending delighted shivers through her all over again. "They charm me when they touch me."

His thoughts ran so close to her earlier ones that she was a bit surprised. Had they developed some kind of psychic link?

"You're gonna hate me," he said, humor in his tone.

"Why?" Her heart skipped an uncomfortable beat.

"I'm hungry again."

She had to laugh. "I think I am, too." Reluctantly, she eased away from him. "Want to eat in bed?"

"Not really. I've got better plans for this bed, and crumbs could be a problem."

He hated to pull on any clothes, but the house felt full of chilly, snaking drafts. It must be cold enough outside to set up a differential, because this place didn't appear to be leaking like a sieve. Frankly, getting dressed was a pain these days, so he settled on shorts, boxers and a heavy flannel shirt that had been buried in his suitcase. Then he followed her to the kitchen.

She was wearing her terry cloth robe again, appearing cuddly, and looking through cabinets and her freezer.

"I'm eating everything, aren't I?" he asked.

"Not really. I just didn't know what you'd like to eat, and it didn't occur to me that I wouldn't be able to get to the store."

"Toast will do, if you have bread. Or peanut butter sandwiches."

She didn't answer immediately. He settled on a chair, propping his cane against the wall, and watched her lean back a little from her open fridge while she chewed her lower lip.

He had to fight not to just scoop her into his lap and get them both into some more trouble, but he was the guy who'd opened his yap about being hungry. Which was kind of ridiculous because he'd gone hungry for long periods. That particular gnawing in his stomach was just background.

Or had been until after the hospital. Maybe his body just kept demanding fuel for repairs. He guessed that wouldn't be surprising. Whatever, his appetite had mushroomed.

"When the weather clears tomorrow, I'll go out and buy something. I guess I've been eating you out of house and home."

"Hardly," she answered, glancing over her shoulder. "So you're not leaving as soon as the weather clears?"

"Not unless I get an invitation to."

She smiled before returning her attention to the contents of her refrigerator. "You won't get it from me."

Somehow he hadn't thought he would, although he seriously needed to think about what he was doing here. He didn't want to hurt this woman. He knew he was going to have to leave, for surgery, for rehab, maybe to return to the service. If he had a future, he didn't think it was here, although she made it very tempting. But no way was he going to depend on a woman, so he had to make himself independent.

He just didn't want to hurt her in the process.

But maybe it was already too late. He didn't think of himself as extraordinarily stupid, but maybe he had been this weekend. Where had his self-control gone? He'd depended on it his entire adult life.

Poof. Not cool.

She pulled a loaf of bread out of the freezer and tossed it on the counter. "For tomorrow," she said.

"It doesn't sound much calmer out there."

"No, it doesn't. I was sure it would be dying out tonight." The microwave clock said it was two in the morning. Already. This night was passing too fast, but emotionally, it felt like a lifetime. He'd experienced so much, felt so much in these hours with Miri. The only thing he could compare it to was the intensity of combat, and he didn't want to do that. He'd just enjoyed the most beautiful hours of his life. No comparisons there.

She closed the fridge. "If you can hang on a little while, I can make some muffins. Box mix."

"I don't want you going to so much trouble at this hour—"

She shook her head, silencing him. "I'm hungry, too, and nobody sleeps well hungry."

"We're going to sleep?" He loved the way she cracked up at that. He'd like to make her laugh like that all the time, but didn't seem the type of guy to cause much of that kind of laughter. Too sober and serious, at least until he had a few beers in him? Maybe.

God knew he laughed enough with his buddies when they were home and could hit a bar or have a barbecue in someone's yard. Knitted together in a way few would ever understand.

But since Al's death...well, he'd stopped laughing as much. Yeah, he'd lost men he cared about before, but Al had been unique. They'd gone through so much together over the years, shared so much experience, good and bad. He'd heard plenty of troops say they didn't bother to get to know the new guys because they wouldn't last long. Well, he and Al had never had that option. They'd been welded in training. While people had naturally come and gone over the years, he and Al had remained.

He suspected Al wouldn't like knowing he found it hard to laugh anymore. His friend wouldn't appreciate that at all.

Lost in memories, Gil was surprised when he realized that Miri was already popping a pan of muffins into the oven. Well, she'd said it would be easy, but it was impolite of him to have drifted away and left her alone while she did it.

But she didn't seem to mind. She came to the table and sat with her chin in her hand, looking drowsy. "Twenty minutes."

"Are you sure you don't just want to go to bed? I can take the muffins out of the oven, and you look ready to doze off."

"I'm feeling really good," she said, a sleepy smile on her face. "So relaxed. I don't want to snooze it away."

In the end, however, as soon as the muffins came out of the oven, without eating any, they went straight to bed. Sleep demanded its due, so curled together, they let it take them.

Morning came well before the sun, with an insistent ringing of Miri's phone. She lifted it off the cradle beside her bed, and without even opening her eyes, listened to the recorded message telling her that school was closed for the day.

Big surprise.

Gil, who had managed to roll onto his uninjured side and wrap an arm around her waist, mumbled, "It's too early, Teach."

"No kidding." She placed the receiver back into the cradle and, glancing at the clock, saw that it wasn't quite six yet. The sun wouldn't be up for a while, and since she had nowhere to go, she had no special desire to get up.

She sighed, loving the way Gil held her, enjoying his strength and warmth. Then, between one instant and the next, she fell into a sound sleep.

When she woke again, the sun still hadn't risen, but habit made her feel as if she were late. She was usually out her door and on her way to school at this time of year, when the sky was just beginning to lighten. She loved the experience of watching the day begin, then as spring drew closer, watching the sun rise earlier and earlier until it beat her to school.

She started to stir and heard Gil say, "Must you?"

"I must." The relaxation that had earlier filled her was beginning to transmute to anxiety. The storm would be over soon. Gil would be talking about moving on. Somehow, some way, she needed to put this night into a box for admiring but not touching.

She had to admit she felt weird as she rose, pulled on her robe and headed to the bathroom for her morning ablutions. Washing her face, brushing her teeth, debating whether the house was still too chilly to try to take another shower—these were ordinary things that didn't feel at all ordinary this morning.

She tossed Gil a smile as she emerged from the bathroom. He was sitting up against pillows, looking sharp-eyed now, watching her.

"I'll make some coffee." She headed down the hall to the kitchen, trying to pretend it was like any other morning in her life, making coffee, having a muffin for breakfast.

But it was not at all like any other night in her life,

and she knew it. She felt it all the way to her bones. Her world had been rocked and she didn't know if it would ever be able to settle into its familiar paths again.

Get over it, she told herself sternly. Sheesh, she'd been with the man for only three days. Everything before that had been secondhand from Al, or unrevealing from their emails. Gil couldn't have possibly made himself indelible so quickly, and she couldn't possibly be foolish enough at her age to turn all sappy over what was surely a one-night stand.

She had herself pretty well convinced by the time she heard Gil's uneven steps in the hallway. She'd be fine and could let him go.

The coffee started brewing, and she drew back the café curtain over the sink. "Oh, man," she said.

"What?" Gil asked from just behind her.

"There are two cars in my driveway. I know the sun isn't going to rise for a few more minutes, but right now all I can see are pink snowdrifts when the wind stops blowing."

She felt him come up behind her, instantly causing her every sense to grow sharp. She could smell him, a delightful scent of man mixed with lovemaking. She could feel his heat radiating from his body when he was still a short distance away. The sound of his uneven steps had become totally familiar, and now she couldn't imagine not hearing them.

She tried to pay attention to the cars, because they really were a sight. Then Gil, with the simple act of slipping an arm around her waist and leaning into her back, dropping a kiss on her neck, blew all resolutions to smithereens.

Then, as if nothing had happened, he said, "That's a lot of shoveling. I don't know how much I can help."

"You don't need to. There's a youngster down the street who likes to make a little pocket money by shoveling for me. If school weren't closed today, he'd probably have been here about the time I was getting the call."

The wind, though far less threatening than yesterday, still hadn't calmed completely. Zephyrs blew gently, but were strong enough to make the snow scatter like glitter in the brightening red light of dawn. Some larger flakes continued falling, but nothing like yesterday's whirlwind. The storm had nearly reached its end.

She felt him lean to one side before he spoke. "The roads look about the same. Buried. I thought I heard a plow in the wee hours."

"You might have. The wind defeats all comers. The snow we get here is usually pretty dry, and it blows and drifts forever. As bad as it was, if they were plowing it was for the sake of emergency vehicles."

She heard the hiss from the coffeepot, indicating it had finished. "Want some coffee and a muffin?"

"I'd like to stand right here like this with you forever, but I guess that's not possible."

She closed her eyes as his arm slipped away, feeling the loss of his touch as if skin were being ripped away. No, it wasn't possible. None of it was possible and she'd better wrap her head and heart around that. He'd never spoken a word to suggest that this hadn't been just a little friendly sex on a cold and miserable night when they both were probably feeling a bit lonely.

He got the mugs and small plates for the muffins. She brought the pot and the food to the table. As smoothly as if they'd been doing this for years.

But then there was no escaping it. Two people, virtual strangers, had just passed the most amazing night, as if a wedge had been cut out of time and set aside for their enjoyment, but then time flowed on as if it had never happened.

But it *had* happened and she wondered how she was going to deal with it all when he left. She wouldn't be able to slice out the memories.

He finished two muffins and was on his second cup of coffee when he at first said something innocuous. "Box mix or not, those were great blueberry muffins."

She crooked up one corner of her mouth. "You're just spoiled by military rations."

That drew a snort of laughter from him, but then his face sobered. "I didn't want to hurt you."

"What makes you think you have?" she retorted as her heart climbed into her throat. He was already regretting last night. She had a feeling it would be easier for her if he just walked out the door later today or tomorrow morning with a "See ya" rather than a discussion of the night past.

"I'm not fond of one-night stands or the women who are, and I'm pretty certain you're not one of them."

Something set her back up. She wasn't characteristically truculent, but she felt annoyance leap to the surface. "How would you know?" she demanded sharply. For as little as it was worth, she had the pleasure of seeing him taken aback. She hadn't thought that was in his repertoire of reactions. Granite man.

After nearly a minute, he replied. At first his tone was almost sarcastic, but quickly tapered into near gentleness. "Yeah, how would I know? I don't know you at all, really. Except you don't have that freaking hardened edge to you. You come at experience with a freshness I happen to like. Hell, I more than like it. You've reminded me the world can still hold beauty and innocence."

She caught her breath at that, stunned into silence. Did he really mean that?

"But I have to go," he said. "I've got one more family to visit, then I need to get back for my rehab and upcoming surgery."

At that her heart and stomach both began to sink, as if there was no bottom to the hole.

"Miri, I meant it when I said I don't want to hurt you. If Al were around, he'd kill me. So while I'm gone, I want you to think. We'll correspond—I might even get better at it now that I know you—and you can decide if you want me to come back this way."

She eyed him uncertainly. "You would need to decide, too."

He smiled. "I pretty much have. But I'd hate myself

if I didn't give you time to make up your mind without my persuasions."

She was going to miss his persuasions, but she knew deep within that he was absolutely right.

The blueberry muffin tasted like sawdust despite having been made with blueberries from the can, all nice and juicy, but she knew she needed to eat. Life must go on. She'd learned that the hard way. Her own mother, grief-stricken as she was, had forced food on her after her dad's death.

Just remember, Miri warned herself, he'd only said he'd come back this way. That meant next to nothing except friendship. She'd be foolish to count on anything more. And maybe he didn't mean anything at all. Maybe it was just a sop to her feelings, when all he wanted was to get away from here. From her. Making a semigraceful exit.

But then she found herself wondering just exactly what she wanted. Surely she didn't think she was in love already? She knew that this was hurting, a new kind of anguish. But why?

At last she stabilized her teetering emotions and managed a tight smile. "Still hungry? There are plenty more."

"No, thanks. They were great."

Then the anger began to bubble in place of the pain of impending loss. Yeah, and she'd been great last night, and she was a great woman with a lot to look forward to, and she couldn't possibly want to pursue a relationship with a broken-down soldier who couldn't even envision a future for himself.

Hell, she thought, rising with the plates, she could write his farewell speech for him. But she wondered how much of this had to do with Al. Did Gil feel he was betraying Al? Her thoughts were bouncing all over, while her heart ached, and anger tried to drive back the ache.

"Your timing stinks," she told him frankly, putting the plates and forks on the counter with a clatter. "We just had a great night together and you dump me before we finish breakfast?"

"Dump you?" He sounded startled.

"This is a kiss-off. For all I've had little experience, I can tell when I'm being told to get lost. Is this about Al?"

His voice came out a near growl. "Why would this be about Al?"

"Why wouldn't it be? You only came here because of him. You've spent more time here than you intended because of the storm. And here I was, the country girl who turned out to be easy pickings. Want me to write your farewell speech? Because I can."

"Miri…"

"Oh, shut up. You've said enough. Let the little lady down easy. Tell her you'll be back after you take care of important stuff. Tell her that she needs to think about it. Think about *what*, for Pete's sake? You haven't even been able to choke that out."

She turned to glare at him. "I don't have anything

to think about. There's nothing. We had some fun last night. That's it. It's done. No more."

She considered storming out, but then stayed as she was, feet planted, because she refused to act like a child. His expression had gone blank, like at the funeral, revealing nothing. The man of granite once more.

An eternity seemed to pass before he spoke again, his voice quiet and modulated. "While it may be true that I tried to stay in line because of Al, because I didn't want to take advantage of you, pretty soon nothing was about Al anymore. You crossed that chasm as if it wasn't there."

"Whee," she said, almost under her breath.

His flinty gray eyes met hers, holding her gaze and making her somehow unable to look away.

"Come off it," he said. "I trespassed. I'm willing to take any repercussions. What I don't want is to compound my sins here. There are so many things you don't know about me, and I don't just mean the things I'll never talk about. There are a whole lot of things I don't know about you. You just showed me you have a temper. That's something I didn't know about you. I like it, but, regardless, I didn't know, and there are probably a million more things I don't know. Most of them need years to discover, but right now we're still practically strangers."

She folded her arms, her eyes burning with tears she refused to shed, but anger kept her afloat. "Then why do I already feel like you're part of my life?"

He closed his eyes briefly. "For all you know, I could be a monster."

"True. But I doubt you'd have made it all these years in Uncle Sam's Army if you were. Nor would Al have liked you very much. You come with a sterling character reference. My cousin."

Gil swore softly and stood, grabbing his cane to lean on. "I'm trying to prevent a disaster here."

"Then when Lewis comes, I'll have him clear your car and your way out of here, and you can go. I don't want to be anyone's disaster."

As she spoke, the unmistakable roar of a plow sounded in the distance. It seemed to be heading this way.

"See?" she said. "You'll be able to escape soon."

Then, still angry and hurt, she tried to brush past him, but he snagged her with one arm, tight enough so that she couldn't twist away. In the next instant he'd sat down and pulled her onto his lap.

"Cut it out," he said softly.

She pushed on his shoulder with one hand. "Cut what out? Let me go."

"No." Just that one brief syllable.

"No?" She couldn't believe this. One minute he was telling her he was dumping her and the next she was imprisoned on his lap.

She pushed at him until she realized it was futile. All she could do was sit stiffly where she was. "What do you want?"

"For you to listen," he said bluntly. "You're an incredibly smart and talented person, so I'm sure if your feelings weren't getting in the way you'd realize that this is not a kiss-off and that I'm a lousy communicator when it comes to stuff like this. I can take a rebel-held cave, but I do a lousy job of talking about anything but strategy and tactics. So here I am, trying to run this like a military operation and everything is coming out sideways, and you can't read through the fog. I'm sorry."

She allowed herself to relax a hair. Besides, her outburst was beginning to embarrass her. She didn't usually act like that. In fact, it was rare. Man, had he gotten under her skin in a way almost no one did.

"I'm going to try again. We've been acquainted, mostly by email and through Al's stories, for a long time. But we only started to get to know each in real life on Friday. Today is Monday. That's not a very long time, Miri."

She hated to admit he was right. Last night had opened parts of her heart that she was quite sure had never opened before. Could that be illusion? Maybe.

He raised his hand and ran his fingers through her now-loose hair. A traitorous shiver ran through her.

"Last night was incredible," he continued. "No woman's ever made me feel as you have. It's important. I'll cherish it always. But is that firm ground on which to build? You know I'm already a bit messed up about my future. Do you want me to drag you into my mess just because of one fantastic night? Do you?"

She wanted so badly to say yes, but then she didn't

know exactly what he was talking about. Future friendship? Occasional flings? Something permanent? Oh, she hardly dared hope for that even though she yearned for it.

"The thing is," he continued, "I've never gone on a mission without meticulous planning."

"Which you said always blows up." Her voice was a little hoarse.

"True. But you need to know your goals and have some idea how to achieve them. So. Can I be blunt?"

"I thought you were."

He gave her a gentle squeeze. "I've been dancing around some things. Maybe I need to stop dancing. I think I love you, Miri. But I can't promise that after only three days. For the first time in my life you have me thinking about permanence, even though I try to avoid it. That's huge. And because it's so huge, we both need time. For all either of us knows, when I've been gone for a week you might be glad I'm not here. Let the intensity wane just a bit."

"So what do you want?" Her heart was racing again. It had started when he said he thought he loved her, then sped up even more when he mentioned permanence. Even so, she felt the niggle of uncertainty. He was right; they were still virtually strangers.

"Some time is all. I'll finish my surgery and rehab, we'll burn up the phone lines or video conference every night when possible, and we'll see. We'll see a whole lot better when you know if I'm asking you to pin yourself to a man who's going to be living halfway across the country because of his job, or if he can see his way to living here with a wonderful music teacher."

So he *was* talking forever. As in marriage. That *was* a huge decision, and she was keenly aware that it shouldn't be made in a rush. And as he'd just reminded her, there was so much uncertainty still to be resolved. The tight band around her chest began to ease a little. Not hopeless. It wasn't hopeless.

Then he caught her chin in his hand and tipped her face so that he could kiss her deeply and passionately, until she clung to him, nearly breathless.

When he lifted his head, she opened her eyes to see his face.

"Dammit, woman," he said, "I'm asking for a long engagement."

That word settled it and made everything crystal clear for her. Anger and pain fell away before a burst of joy. *Engagement.*

"Yes," she whispered. "Oh, yes."

His smile was amazing, so bright and free of shadows. He nuzzled her lips with his.

"The campaign," he said, "begins now."

She could hardly wait.

Epilogue

Miri realized that she had lost the attention of her marching band. They still stood on the grassy field in front of her, beneath a cloudless sky in a soft, warm breeze that ruffled their tees and shorts, but they certainly weren't looking at her. They looked past her toward the school parking lot.

She turned to see what had their attention before calling them to order. Her heart lodged in her throat.

Gil York, in full dress uniform, looking as he had at Al's funeral, was watching from the edge of the field. She gaped at the sight.

"Don't mind me," he called. "Just a spectator."

Giggles ran through the band, letting her know that not all of them quite believed that. Why not? At the moment she hardly cared. A glance at her watch told her they had twenty minutes left before parents would arrive to pick up their kids.

But Gil's presence had diverted her, just as it had her students. She hadn't expected him, although lately they'd been talking more and more about him coming to visit, about a long-term future together.

But without warning? She tried to key in on where they were in the process of learning their marching patterns and where she wanted to go from here.

The band's formation had started to get a little sloppy. Girls were whispering to each other and eyeing Gil as if he were a cake.

The beginning of the school year was always hardest. These students hadn't even started their classroom semester. They showed up for these camps because it was a requirement for those who wanted to be in the marching band.

"Dress right," she called out. "Straighten out those ranks."

Before long, they'd feel the entire performance. Their steps would come naturally and they wouldn't have to keep checking one another to make sure they were in the right place. But first they had to get all this correct more than once, and they were just beginning. By the first football game, they'd be impressive.

So she walked them through another ten minutes of evolutions, then had to follow everyone into the band room. Instruments needed to be put away in their cages or packed up to go home for practice, and she had to make sure that the last band member's parent had arrived to take him or her home.

It felt like everything had slowed down to sludge. Her mind was silently ordering her students to hurry it up, even though they were having their usual relaxed gab sessions as they put everything away. All she wanted to do was see Gil.

She could hardly maintain her usual composure. Impatience was swamping her, but at last the final student walked out the door. Just as she picked up a few items from the floor and prepared to turn out the lights, she heard Gil.

"Miri."

She turned slowly, a piece of crumpled paper in her hand. "Tell me it's not another funeral," she said, indicating his uniform. God, he looked good in it. Her mouth was growing dry and she reached for a bottle of water on the corner of her desk, making herself swallow, making herself wait.

"It's not a funeral. And look, no cane." He held out his arms.

Her throat tightened. He'd come to tell her he was going back on active duty, and then she'd have to decide whether to follow him or stay here or… "That's truly great news," she said honestly, even though his unannounced visit was raising unpleasant specters in her mind.

"Stop catastrophizing," he said. He closed the distance between them and drew her into his arms. "I've waited so long for this," he whispered. "So long."

Every other thing in the world flew from her mind as they kissed, as she nearly tried to burrow into his strength.

"I love you," he said, lifting his head. "I truly love you, and I don't care what I have to do, we're going to make this work. Unless you don't—"

"Oh, I do," she said swiftly, without any lingering doubt. Her heart felt as if he'd just filled it with helium and it was rising into the sky. "I love you, Gil. I love you, love you, love you, and I've missed you so much every single minute of every day."

He smiled down into her eyes. "I have choices, Miri, and some of them involve staying here in Conard County. We can discuss that later. What I want to know is will you marry this broken soldier and make him the happiest man on earth?"

Her heart sang. "Yes. Absolutely."

"Kids, too?" he asked.

"Kids, too." Then she leaned into him, letting him surround her with his power and strength.

She thought of Al, suspected he'd wanted to encourage this and decided he must be feeling smug right then.

But an instant later she forgot everything else except the man who held her and had just promised her the best of all possible futures.

* * * * *

MILLS & BOON

Coming next month

BABY SURPRISE FOR THE
SPANISH BILLIONAIRE
Jessica Gilmore

'Don't you think it's fun to be just a little spontaneous every now and then?' Leo continued, his voice still low, still mesmerising.

No, Anna's mind said firmly, but her mouth didn't get the memo. 'What do you have in mind?'

His mouth curved triumphantly and Anna's breath caught, her mind running with infinite possibilities, her pulse hammering, so loud she could hardly hear him for the rush of blood in her ears.

'Nothing too scary,' he said, his words far more reassuring than his tone. 'What do you say to a well-earned and unscheduled break?'

'We're having a break.'

'A proper break. Let's take out the *La Reina Pirata*—' his voice caressed his boat's name lovingly '—and see where we end up. An afternoon, an evening, out on the waves. What do you say?'

Anna reached for her notebook, as if it were a shield against his siren's song. 'There's too much to do . . .'

'I'm ahead of schedule.'

'We can't just head out with no destination!'

'This coastline is perfectly safe if you know what

you're doing.' He grinned wolfishly. 'I know exactly what I'm doing.'

Anna's stomach lurched even as her whole body tingled. She didn't doubt it. 'I . . .' She couldn't, she shouldn't, she had responsibilities, remember? Lists, more lists, and spreadsheets and budgets, all needing attention.

But Rosa would. Without a backwards glance. She wouldn't even bring a toothbrush.

Remember what happened last time you decided to act like Rosa, her conscience admonished her, but Anna didn't want to remember. Besides, this was different. She wasn't trying to impress anyone; she wasn't ridiculously besotted, she was just an overworked, overtired young woman who wanted to feel, to be, her age for a short while.

'Okay, then,' she said, rising to her feet, enjoying the surprise flaring in Leo di Marquez's far too dark, far too melting eyes. 'Let's go.'

Continue reading
**BABY SURPRISE FOR THE
SPANISH BILLIONAIRE**
Jessica Gilmore

Available next month
www.millsandboon.co.uk

LET'S TALK
Romance

For exclusive extracts, competitions
and special offers, find us online:

f facebook.com/millsandboon

⊙ @millsandboonuk

🐦 @millsandboon

Or get in touch on 0844 844 1351*

For all the latest titles coming soon, visit
millsandboon.co.uk/nextmonth

Want even more
ROMANCE?

Join our bookclub today!

'Mills & Boon books, the perfect way to escape for an hour or so.'

Miss W. Dyer

'Excellent service, promptly delivered and very good subscription choices.'

Miss A. Pearson

'You get fantastic special offer and the chance to get books before they hit the shops'

Mrs V Hall

**Visit millsandbook.co.uk/Bookclub
and save on brand new books.**

MILLS & BOON